Please Find Me:
A Love Story for Today and Tomorrow
by John Harasimo

© Copyright 2016 John Harasimo

ISBN 978-1-63393-325-5

Published by

ROMAN SOUL BOOKS

in association with

Please Find Me

A LOVE STORY FOR TODAY AND TOMORROW

JOHN HARASIMO

ROMAN SOUL BOOKS

A 'Thank You' to my readers

I wrote this book as a form of entertainment for the mind. My sole purpose was to elicit a smile at least once during your reading of it. If you *do* smile, then I have succeeded!

The story told here is just that, a STORY. It was not intended to influence anyone's personal beliefs, or to introduce my own to my readers. These are just settings for a tale that I hope you find interesting, and make the book hard to put down.

I truly hope that you find value from your purchase of this book.

Thank you,

John Harasimo

Chapter 1

DEATH GRIP

HIS EYES FLEW open as his head was thrown backwards. He struggled to focus as his head was violently slammed forward until his chin hit his chest. The impact was so hard that his neck popped and brought immediate tears to his eyes. Although he didn't hear himself moan, he was certain that he had.

Waking from a sound sleep, his mind had trouble processing everything being passed from his eyes to his brain. Both hands frantically searched for the armrests and latched on the moment they were found. It was a feeble attempt to steady himself from being thrown around in his seat. Thank God for that seat belt! The plane was bumping up and down as if it were on a bad railroad track. He remembered closing his eyes just after the plane had left the runway. How long had he been out? What the HELL was going on?

Finally, the hectic scene in the cabin fell into focus. Several overhead storage compartments had sprung open, and their tightly packed contents were tumbling onto the heads of those seated beneath them. He watched helplessly as a rather large computer bag escaped its confinement and slammed into an elderly woman's head. She immediately crumpled and went totally limp in her seat. Her left arm hung into the aisle over the armrest, and it was now flapping lifelessly with every new jerk the plane made.

Above all the noise, he heard a pop before the little overhead doors all fell open at once and the oxygen masks were deployed for people to use. They dangled in front of each row of seats and began swaying with every roll the plane took. They looked like a swarm of orange-bodied jellyfish being tossed around in a violent surf. If he hadn't been so scared, he would probably have gotten seasick from their swaying back and forth. He watched as hand after hand made a shaky grab for the moving targets. Nearly everyone required two or more stabs upward before being rewarded with the lifesaving air.

The lady seated beside him made a hasty grab for one several times but came up empty. He turned to look at her. It was obvious that she had given up on getting one and had closed her eyes. Both of her hands were turning red from the tight grip she had on her fastened seatbelt. Without knowing why, he reached up and snagged one. Then he hit her shoulder fairly hard with his elbow to get her to open her eyes. As her eyes focused on him, he pulled it right in front of her face and yelled "TAKE IT!"

He waited for a moment, wondering why she didn't reach for it. He shook it right in front of her face and again yelled "TAKE IT!" She still made no motion towards the mask. Her eyes darted from the mask to his face, and back to the mask. The size of her wide-open eyes convinced him that she was too scared to let go of her seat belt. As much as he didn't want to take his other hand off his own armrest, he let go and used both hands to start putting the mask's strap over her head. The moment the mask touched her face, she finally grabbed at it with one hand and pressed it hard against her cheeks. He continued to pull the strap the rest of the way over her head and then tugged the end of it until it was tight. Only then had he struggled to get a mask for himself and secure it around his head as well.

As the air started to flow into his lungs, he knew he had waited too long. A massive migraine headache was pounding in his head due to the lack of oxygen. He again surveyed the cabin and noticed that there were many people who were obviously unconscious from the lack of oxygen. Their heads were rolling left and right on their seat backs. The unused masks were swaying above their heads and keeping perfect time with the rolling of the plane. He thought that perhaps they had the better deal. If this plane were crashing, they would go more peacefully than those who were breathing and wide awake.

At this moment he became very calm inside. Everything became quiet to him, and things appeared to be happening in slow motion. How odd this all seemed. His mind cleared, and in that instant, he accepted that he was about to die. So what? As fast as they were going to hit the ground, it would all be over in less than a second. There couldn't possibly be any pain associated with this type of exit from the world. Of course, he didn't want to die! But at least this would be very quick.

His life hadn't been all that great anyway. He was always alone. He lived alone and worked from home. How pathetic was that? He liked people, but had never learned how to deal with others on a personal level. He always wanted to have friends. At least one best friend would have been enough for him. But he had none. Not even the one. He almost chuckled at the thought that it would be weeks before anyone even realized he was gone.

He found himself looking out the window at the clouds. If it weren't for the window jumping around in his view, the sky would have looked very peaceful. It was quite the opposite from the scene inside the cabin. This was when it dawned on him that the screaming had totally stopped. Those without masks were unconscious while those with them were busy breathing rapidly. He thought that he heard the occasional sound of muffled crying, but he wasn't sure.

His senses told him that the plane was practically in a vertical dive straight down. That was when the body of a flight attendant looked as though it was simply floating by on its way to the rear of the plane. As it passed his seat, her head rolled so that her face was looking right at him. Her eyes were open but not blinking. There was a big gash in her forehead that disappeared into her hair and blood had run down the side of her unconscious face. As the body disappeared from his view, he recalled how the astronauts trained for weightlessness in large jet planes that were intentionally taken into steep dives. He wondered if that was what was at work here in this plane's cabin as well. So this was what weightlessness felt like? Of course, the astronauts enjoyed their experience a little more than the people on this plane.

Then the view outside the window broke free of the clouds. He could see the tops of snow-covered mountains. There seemed to be a valley between the high peaks. Was that a lake? No, it was a group of low, dark clouds that covered a hidden valley from exposed peak to exposed peak. He found himself really being morbid now, and wondered if they would hit a peak or disappear into the clouds over that valley instead. His preference was for a peak. At least they would have sunlight until the end.

He watched the earth zoom closer and fill more of the window's view with each passing second. That is when he felt it. There was something soft and warm on his hand. What the hell was that? He turned his gaze to his right hand as it held tightly to the armrest. What? Whose hand was that? It was hers.

His eyes followed her arm upwards until he was looking the woman straight in the eye. She had taken her mask off and was smiling at him. Her eyes were red from crying, but she was smiling, and at him.

She leaned towards him as he took his mask off. She very clearly said, "Thank you. Do you mind if I hold your hand?"

It was the first time in his entire life that he actually felt he had the nerve to talk to a girl. He released his grip on the armrest and rolled his hand over. Her small hand fell into his palm, and he gently closed his hand on hers. To his utter amazement, she then put her other hand on top of those two hands and forced her cheek against his shoulder. Both of their heads were being pushed back against the headrest, as the plane continued to accelerate in its downward search for the earth. He couldn't believe that only here, in the last few moments of his life, did he get to experience holding a girl's hand. Perhaps "girl" wasn't the right word, but that's what it felt like to him. To have her head touching his shoulder! Well, that was the pinnacle of his contentment, even as his ride carried him to meet his death. Odd, but he found himself smiling and feeling more fulfilled than at any other point in his 32 years.

He had an urge to take one last look out the window, but didn't. What was about to happen just didn't matter anymore at all. He knew he wanted her face to be the last thing he saw in this life. So he tilted his head downward and towards her. His movement caused her to look up at him and smile. It was then that he did what he had always longed to do. Talk to a girl.

"It is an honor to hold your hand."

• • •

There was a man standing behind the air traffic controller who had been assigned to the ill-fated plane. Max had one hand on the shoulder of the controller who had been in contact with the plane's crew when they declared an emergency by yelling, 'MayDay, MayDay, MayDay' over the radio. The young man was sitting with his head down and eyes closed. One of his legs was still bouncing up and down rapidly, just as it had during the entire four-minute ordeal. Yes, four minutes was all the time it had taken from the crew's report of the explosion in the plane's tail baggage compartment until their radar signature fell off the screen.

The plane had accelerated to over 600 miles an hour as it fell from its original 40,000 foot altitude. They never had a chance. The explosion had torn away an extremely large section of the plane's tail and with it, most of the vital flight control surfaces. The pilots had fought to keep it level, but the stress on the remaining tail structure was just too great. When the rest of the tail section tore away, the loss of all control caused the plane to roll over on its belly and go nose down into a vertical trajectory. There was nothing that anyone could have done to save them.

Max was the senior controller who had come to oversee the activity once the emergency had been declared. He called out, "I need to reassign four flights, and I mean NOW! Bob, you take wide 312 and Heavy 241. Cindy, you got both Seattle's 336 and 229. I need acknowledgements, people. Do you have them?"

Two voices sang out, "312 and 241, got em!" and then "336 and 229 are on me!"

Again, Max called out. "Anyone free? I need somebody to take Billy here outside."

Another controller who was returning from a break came running over and started helping the visibly shaken younger controller to his feet.

"I got ya, Billy. Come on, son. Let's go outside. That's it. It's over. Come on." He slowly walked the young man out of the control area.

Max was finally free to do some tasks that needed to happen immediately. He knew there was absolutely NO WAY that anyone had survived that crash, but there were FAA rules that dictated timely notifications in instances such as this. After a flurry of phone calls, he approached the floor supervisor.

"Tom. Here is where we are. I made the official 'Plane Down' notifications already. Our emergency management center is on it. I spoke to Richard in Search and Rescue just now. He had me on the line while he was talking to a local search post, and they're mobilizing right now."

"Thanks, Max. You okay?"

"Yeah." He paused for a minute to look towards the door that Billy had exited. "You know. I'm worried about Billy. We need to get a counselor with him soon. I don't want to lose him like we did Paul."

"Already made the call, Max. I asked for Linda, if at all possible."

"Thanks, Tom. She's good. I like her. I just hope Billy pulls through this. Did you see how hard he was shaking? Damn. He's such a nice guy, but so young and innocent."

"So, Max. What do we know about where it went down?"

"Well, like I said, I was on the line and heard what the local rescue chief was saying. Seems they had the plane on their radar as well and watched her come in. Said it looked like they went into a box canyon in the Rockies called Cantor Basin. Doesn't sound good at all. The only access to the canyon is through a southern pass. The northern end is the boxed end, and not accessible at all. Just the one way in and out of there."

"What, no roads in the valley?"

"Yes, one logging road winds its way straight up the center. The problem is the height and density of the trees. From the road, you wouldn't see a crash site, even if it was only 50 yards away from you. They'll have to carry out an air search to pinpoint the location. Just no other way to do it. They also said the canyon walls are extremely steep and still covered with snow. The valley floor should be all melted, but it's a virtual carpet of tall trees. Tom, it gets even worse."

"What do you mean?"

"Well, the guy said that the valley itself is covered by thick low clouds and will probably be that way for at least another day or two. That storm front is kinda stuck over it, so the clouds aren't going anywhere until the sun burns its way through."

Tom was looking around and letting out some heavy sighs of his own. He looked down at his feet and began shaking his head before asking. "They say how low the ceiling was in the valley?"

"Yeah. Not good either. They said this time of the year, the clouds hover 50 feet or less above the treetops in the basin. In some places, the treetops are actually in the clouds."

Tom looked Max in the eye. "They'll never get choppers in there under those conditions. The crosswinds in there would be absolutely horrible. Look, Max. You and I both know that nobody survived that crash."

"I know, Tom. The guy on the phone said the same thing. He even added that the temperature on the valley floor is in the mid-40s during the day, but falls to the low teens after dark. At best, that means 10 more hours of very cold darkness down there. Even if some of the passengers did survive, they'll die of hypothermia before any rescuers can get to them. The whole damn scenario just sucks."

There was the sound of a metal door closing at the other end of the control room. A very attractive brunette slowly walked up behind Tom and nudged him in the back. Before he could turn to see who it is, Max said "Don't look now, but it's the shrink, Linda."

She wrinkled her nose at Max before she replied, "Nice to see you too!"

Tom looked over his shoulder and asked with surprise, "Linda? How'd you get here so quick?"

"I was in the parking lot talking to Suzie. The call came in, so I just walked on up. So, how many?"

Tom raked his lower lip against the back of his upper teeth before answering. "The manifest says 137, crew and all. Thank God it wasn't full. But 137 is still too many."

"So, where's Billy?"

Max pointed to the back door. "I had Bob take him out there. He's in bad shape. I hope you can help him."

She walked between the two men and headed for the back door. "I'll do my best. But you know as well as I do. It is up to him to deal with it. I can only try to talk him through it. We'll see." She made her way to the door, opened it and disappeared before it closed behind her.

The two men stood there staring at the closed door, listening to all the activities in the control room. Tom finally spoke before he turned to walk away. "Well, it's out of our hands now. The boys in Search and Rescue have it."

• • •

A lone car approached the administration offices of a remote airfield located 40 miles from the south entrance of Cantor Basin. The driver parked in the last available front row spot and killed his engine. The door opened and a tall man in his early 50s emerged, carrying a large briefcase. He held his overcoat closed with one hand as he rushed through the cold and into the warm building. Once inside the main door, he was immediately approached by a very husky older gentleman with a large unlit cigar sticking out of his mouth. He stuck his hand out to greet the newcomer.

"Good evening, Sir. I'm Samuel Stanford, head of operations for the field. You are?"

"I'm Chris Mathews. They assigned me as the IIC for this one. Glad to meet you."

"So you're the Investigator In Charge? I'm sorry to say, but you're going to have your hands full on this one. The terrain up there is absolutely terrible in good weather, and you can tell this ain't good weather."

"I hear you. That's all I've been thinking about since I got the call three hours ago. Where can I set up shop?"

"Oh, yeah. I set up an empty office for you already. It's right down that hall. Only one with a light on and the door is open. Make yourself at home. You want some coffee, Chris?"

"Yes, I do! Just let me put this stuff down and I'll walk along with you. I need to warm up a bit so my teeth will stop chattering. I don't want you guys to think I have a speech problem."

They both laughed and he turned to walk to the only open office down the hall. After dropping off his coat and briefcase, he stood in the door looking around the office. He finally said out loud, "Well, better get used to it. It's going to be home for the next several months."

With a hot cup of coffee in his hands, he took several sips before he started asking questions.

"So, Sam. Oh, is it okay for me to call you Sam?"

"Yes, but most around here just call me SS. It's up to you. I'll answer to most anything."

"Well then, Sam feels right to me. So, is anyone else here yet?"

"The guy from the NTSB will be here in six hours and the plane manufacturer's rep about the same time."

"What about the engine manufacturer's rep?"

"No idea. Haven't gotten any calls here yet. Oh, by the way. I have two large empty hangars at the other end of the field for you if you want them."

"How big? You think we'll need 'em both?"

"Don't worry about it. You take the one you want, and you can have the other one later if you need it."

"I spoke to the FBI coordinator on the way up here. I talked him into holding off on sending anyone until I get a feel for what we are really looking at."

"FBI? " Sam asked with a very quizzical look. "Why the FBI?"

"The initial call out from the pilot was that there had been a major explosion in the tail baggage compartment. So, explosion equals possible bomb, so the FBI is interested. I need to prove or disprove this part quickly. Those guys can really be pains in the ass! I don't want them here, unless it was one."

"I see. I just can't believe it would be a bomb. You think?"

"Well, there are some pressurized canisters for the hydraulics close to that area of the plane, but we won't know until we get in and look at the wreckage. Do some swabs on the metal from that area. If the tests don't show traces of explosives, then the FBI will have no reason to be here. It would just make my job a hell of a lot easier too."

"Well Chris, this is my first one of these, so I don't know what I'm doing here. We mainly handle search and rescues of lost hikers and climbers who thought they were in better shape than they really were. That sort of thing. So, you just tell me what you need, and I'll get it for you or make it happen."

"Thanks, Sam. I'll be taking you up on that. Promise! Hey, you say I'm the first one here? This is good, because I'll have some time to get settled before the real show starts."

"Well, you're the first of the investigators."

"What do you mean? Who else is here already?"

"Well, actually they've been here and have already gone out."

"Who has?"

"Oh, sorry. There was a chopper crew dispatched from the local Army Reserve Center. They landed here about an hour ago and refueled before heading off to Cantor Basin."

"They *what*? In this weather? What are they, CRAZY? That's all we need. I don't want another set of victims up there. Didn't you try to stop them?"

"Hey, I'm with you. I tried to talk 'em out of it. Believe me! But the pilot had a good point."

"What good point?"

"Well, his chopper is equipped with current combat avionics. Seems he also has some advanced tactical thermal sensing device of some kind. Said he could hover in the clouds and scan for hot spots over the entire valley floor. Hell, he said he could pick up rabbits running around on the ground. He said a crash site should be super easy to find. He said he wanted to get up there before the wreckage started to cool off. Once it's the same temperature as its surroundings, he won't be able to detect it."

"That would be great if he could pinpoint the site for us. Otherwise, it's going to be like looking for a needle in a haystack! So, you know this guy? Hope he is as good as he thinks he is. The winds in that valley are going to be extremely treacherous."

"It's the first time I've met him. Heard about him though. His second stick has flown in these mountains for years. His name is Willy Jackson. I've always known he was good. But, he told me that this new guy is something else. Seems he was a hot shot of some sort over there in Iraq and Afghanistan. Mountains, bad weather and night flights, seems to be nothing to this new guy. He supported ground troops and when they called, he went. No matter what! At least that's what Willy told me on the side. Right after I tried talking them out of going, of course."

"Well, I hate to be crude. But you and I both know that there aren't any survivors up there. I just hate the thought that these two could die for nothing."

"Me too. But there wasn't any stopping them. Like I said, they landed, refueled and took off. Only on the ground for about 40 minutes. And most of it was spent with me trying to talk them out of it."

The two men walked over to the big glass windows that looked out towards the mountains. They held their oversized coffee cups with both hands, staring as if they could see something in all that darkness.

"So Sam, when do you think they'll be in the valley?"

"Already there, I reckon. I'll bet he's been flying on cockpit instruments for at least the last 15 minutes. No need for them to be looking out the windows. That guy must have nerves of steel. I couldn't do it!"

"Sam, I'd like to listen in on his radio traffic if you don't mind."

"You bet! Come on. Let's go to the tower. I'm curious myself."

• • •

"Tower. This is Rescue One. You copy?"

"Copy, Rescue One.""

"We just cleared the southern pass into the valley. We are beginning our descent. Will advise on 15-minute intervals. Going to be kinda busy up here, guys. Copy."

"Rescue one, we copy that. Keep focused boys, and sing out if you need us. Over."

Turning his head slightly, the pilot said, "So Willy, you ever been in this canyon before?"

"Yep, lots of times. But on the ground!"

"Well, since you know this place. How about looking out and telling me where we are. I don't seem to recognize anything."

"What? Look out at what. This is like flying in smoke. You sure you know what you're doing?"

Willy was leaning his head up as close as he could to his door window. There was nothing visible outside the glass except a dull white. It was tinted with a little red every second or two, as the blinking light on the copter's belly flashed.

"Ah, stop your worrying. Come to think of it. I need you to be really quiet, so I can listen."

Willy turned his head back to look at the pilot. "Listen for what?"

"The sound of the trees saying, 'OH SHIT! Is that a chopper?'" He began laughing.

Willy started shaking his head. "I can't believe they let you fly. I REALLY can't believe I'm up here with you!"

"Ah, this is fun. Look, let me show you how this works." He hit a button on the console and a screen right below it came to life. "Now you see that line there. It is signal back from the canyon wall. If I rotate a little, see that, we can see the wall very easily."

Willy sounded truly amazed. "That's so damn cool."

"Yeah, it is. But the problem isn't the canyon walls. It's going to be the very tops of the trees. You see. They are moving with the rotor wash, and too small to kick back enough signal to detect 'em. We are blind to the treetops my friend, and they'll bring us down in a heartbeat if we aren't careful. I'm just going to kick a little forward stick, and we'll move up the valley slowly. But I do need you to keep your eyes sharp, Willy. We're flying level, but the valley floor could be rising, which means the tree tops could be getting closer and that could end poorly."

"The valley floor does actually rise as we move north, so you need to adjust for it. I'd say about a five-degree up angle till we hit the center of the valley, and then it climbs more like 20 or so degrees all the way up to the north wall."

"Got it. I'm going up a little more, no need to push it."

Willy noticed something on the thermal imaging screen. "We have movement on the scope!"

"It's a critter. Too small to be a human, and it's zig-zagging. Yep, critter. I think we'll just stop here and rotate the thermal scanner in a 360-degree turn."

The pilot was holding the craft in a perfect hover and both men's eyes were glued to the little screen on the dash. Willy finally said, "Nothing. Move forward a little."

The chopper methodically moved up the center of the canyon. It would stop to scan 360 degrees before moving up a little more.

The pilot said, "Well Mr. Willy, we are running out of canyon here. That north wall is, oh, I'd say about three quarters of a mile or less, dead ahead. I'll bet we'll start picking up some cross winds soon. All that wind rushing up the valley is going to cause a lot of chop hitting that north wall. I hope we find it soon, or we're going to be buffeted around very badly, my friend."

"Yeah, I know it's a comin'! Oh, wait, STOP! You see that!"

"I do. Yes, I do. Hello!"

"You think that's it?"

"No I don't, Willy. It's a fire all right, but too small for what we're looking for. Let me swing that way and see if there's more."

"How do you read this thing? Can you tell how big it is?"

"I'd guess the size of a compact car or smaller. I have a hunch that the main site is close though. Let's go up a little more and get a better down angle on things." He moved the craft only 10 yards higher and began rotating the scope. "Wow. There she is! Damn, heat everywhere!"

Willy said, "I have the coordinates. What now?"

The pilot replied, "We'll have to take her up higher to contact the tower. Then we'll come back down and poke around a bit before we head back."

After climbing high enough for the radio signal to clear the walls of the southern pass, the pilot called in.

"Tower, Rescue One. Copy."

"Copy Rescue One."

"We found what appears to be the main crash site. Huge debris field and lots of heat signatures below. Have coordinates as follows."

After the exact location of the wreckage was given, the tower replied, "Copy the location. Good work, boys! Now get your asses out of there and come on back."

"That'll be a negative on the return. We have fuel, so going to poke around the edges of the site, see if we see any movement."

"Rescue one, there's nothing more you can do up there. Get out of there. Now!"

"Like I said Tower, have fuel and going to look a bit. Maybe 30 more minutes on location and then we're out of here."

The pilot had already dropped below the canyon walls again, so they didn't hear Sam order them back.

"Damn it! They're already back down below the wall."

Chris said, "Hey, he's regular military. He's not going to listen to us. I can't believe they found it. Damn, that guy is good. But you should still chew his ass when he gets back."

Sam smiled. "Guys like that get chewed on all the time. He'll just stand there with a blank face and wait for me to pause. Then he'll say 'Is that all? Can I go now?' or something like that."

They both laughed a little before Chris added, "This is a good break, though. But it won't change the outcome here. There just can't be any survivors up there. He's wasting his time and just adding to the possibility of another set of casualties."

· · ·

The pilot started talking to Willy. "I want to go out over the center of the site, but we'll need to go up a little more to keep all that hot air from killing our lift."

Willy responded, "Good idea. You mind if I operate the thermal this time?"

"Actually, I'm thinking you're going to have to do it. Got my hands full at the moment. Lots of turbulence here. Hard to hold her. Shit!"

"Take her up, TAKE HER UP!" Willy was yelling.

The pilot had already reacted, but still joked at his copilot, "Gee, why didn't I think of that?" Once the buffeting calmed down, he added, "High enough for you there, buddy?"

Willy just said, "You're one crazy MOTHER! Damn it. But, HEY! Did you see that on the screen right in the middle? It was only there for a second, then gone."

"Willy, I was a little preoccupied at that moment. What did you see there, buddy?"

"Well. I'm not sure, but it almost looked like blurred shapes of two people. But it couldn't have been people standing there."

"Why not?"

"Well, they appeared to be standing right in the middle of the fire. No, I must have just been seeing things. Hey! You going back?"

"Yes! If you thought you saw somebody's shape, we need to find out for sure. Willy, I'm right over the center of the crash site again. You'll have to look quick, I'm having a hard time holding her over all this fire. But, hey! Make sure. Real sure. I don't want to miss somebody if they are alive down there."

"I'm panning now. Nothing yet. Hold her steady. Almost done. Just another second. Take her up!"

The pilot pulled the chopper up quickly and moved away from the center of the fires.

"So?"

"Nothing. Sorry. It's just odd how they were there for a second, then gone. At least, I thought I saw something. But the colors on that little screen, probably just messed with my mind."

"Hey. Don't give it another thought. I once swore that I saw a horse run across that screen. Of course, I had just flown three back-to-back jumps to support some Marines. The colors on that screen can play tricks on your eyes. Forget it."

Willy noticed that the craft was drifting to the right. "Now what the hell are you doing?"

"I told you. I want to poke around the edges of the site. It must be less than 30 degrees down there. If anyone is alive, they'll be close to the edges of the site and trying to keep warm. Like sitting by a campfire. Get it?"

Willy nodded as he began to understand that there was some reason to this pilot's madness. "That's smart. Makes perfect sense, but what made you think of that?"

"Oh, long story. We were on a night mission in Afghanistan, way back in the mountains. Supporting a small ground force on a hit and run sort of thing. There were two of us flying cover. Riley took a hit from a shoulder-fired ground to air missile. He never had a chance to react. They were on a ridge and hit us, just as we came over it. Anyway, he went down. I slid behind a ridge and waited a few minutes. Then I eased up over the ridge just enough to see a lot of body signatures and guess what they were doing?"

"They were sitting around the crash?"

"Well, they were standing, but you get the idea. Must have been about 20 of them just standing around for the heat. They thought I had skedaddled I guess. It was winter time there, and the grunts on the ground were freezing their asses off."

"So you hit 'em?"

"You're DAMN straight I HIT 'EM! I'd flown with that guy for over a year. I dumped several bursts of a few hundred rounds each from the mini cannon. They never saw me coming! I hung around for a few more minutes, but there was no way he survived. His ship blew apart in midair before it had gone down. But I wanted to make sure. Then, just as I turned to go back to cover that ground unit, I picked up the heat signature of one of their truck engines. They had tried to hide 'em behind some huge boulders. It turned out there were three trucks, and they had several guards too. So, another small burst from the mini, and they were toast. Then I went ahead and hit the middle truck with a missile. The damn thing must have been loaded with ammo, because it blew and took both of the other two with it. Then I logged the coordinates for recovery and went back to guard the grunts."

"So, why you up here now?"

"My unit rotated out. I was going to re-up, but I got a job offer from a guy I used to fly with. It was too good to pass up and my wife was on my ass to get out. So I did. I told her I'd be happy if I could at least roll into a reserve unit and still get to log hours."

"But why up here?"

"Wife is from a small town just outside of Denver. She has family all up in here. It was a good fit. It worked out really well. Hey, the winds are kicking up more. I need you to focus on that scope. I'm going to move around the edge of the site a little quicker. "

Willy started moving his head in a jerky motion, back and forth. "Hey! What's that noise?"

The pilot calmly said, "Well, if you look down from your window, I'll bet you'll see some movement. Got to be treetops. I knew they'd be out here on the edge. The site doesn't have any trees standing, for obvious reasons. But as we get out along the edge like I wanted to . . . "

Willy jumped in. "Trees! Yep, I see 'em. SOOOO?"

The pilot again calmly said, "So, what?"

"PULL UP, numb nuts! Damn it."

"You know Willy. I'm beginning to think that you don't like to have fun anymore. How old did you say you were?" Then he started to laugh.

"Old enough to know better than to bust the tops of trees with my skids!"

"If you insist, buddy." After completely traveling around the entire outer edge of the crash site, he added, "Well Mr. Willy, it's

time to go home. I don't see any movement at all down there."
He pulled the craft to a higher altitude and swung the tail around
to head back down the valley towards the airfield. "Rescue one
to tower. Copy."

"Copy Rescue one."

"We're headed back. ETA 20 minutes."

"Find anything?"

"That's a negative, tower. No movement detected."

"Come on home, boys. We were worried about you. Good
job. We got fuel and hot coffee for you when you land. Good job
again. Over."

"Roger on the coffee."

"Rescue one, be advised that Sam may be looking to bite
your head off on return. But you didn't hear it from me!"

"Roger on the ass kickin'. Out."

• • •

Chris was getting his desk laid out the way he wanted it when
Sam came scooting into his office.

"Just thought you'd like to know. They just touched down
and the gas crew will have them come up here. I figured you'd
want to chat with 'em before they flew back to their base."

"Thanks, Sam. You care to sit in? I could use an extra pair
of ears on this."

"Yeah. Be glad to. Those pilots are going to want some hot
coffee. You need some?"

"Yes, I do. Let's greet them and we can all go back there
together."

Sam held his coffee mug in his hand and waited while Chris
dug through his brief case for his special cup. "Ah, there it is." He
then poured the last of his coffee from the Styrofoam cup into
his real cup, and the two men headed towards the front door. It
opened just as they walked up. In stepped two men dressed in
Army flight suits.

Sam stepped forward with his hand out to the pilot.

"Captain. Glad to have you back, sir." Then he turned to his
friend Willy and shook his hand as well. "Willy. Glad you both
are back. It must be a real bugger up there."

Willy smiled. "Sam, I have to admit that was the hairiest ride

I've had in quite a while." Then he pointed to the captain. "I just want you both to know, he's the best pilot I've ever flown with, but he's a damn maniac at heart!"

They all had a little laugh before the captain looked at Sam. "I understand you wanted to talk to me, sir?"

Sam glanced at Chris before looking at the captain. "Consider your ass chewed. I'm just glad you both are back." Then he pointed towards Chris. "Gentlemen. This is Chris Mathews, the IIC. He's the Investigator In Charge from the FAA. He wants to talk with you before you head back to your base."

"Call me Chris." He had stepped forward and extended his hand towards the captain. "You both look like you could use some hot coffee. Let's get you both warmed up first. Then I'd like a few minutes of your time to chat about what you found up there."

"Coffee sounds really good right about now, sir."

The captain smiled as he motioned for the two older men to lead the way. They all talked about the weather and temperature as they made their way back to the break room. With a round of coffee for the group, they wandered into Chris's temporary office.

"Gentlemen. Please, have a seat." After each is seated, he continued. "I just want to start off by saying that must have been some top-notch flying you did there, captain. I'm very impressed that you found the crash site so quickly. Very impressed."

"Thank you. But the bird is why we found it. That ship has some powerful technology on her. So, what do you want to know?"

"Well, first off, the obvious. I'm sure with your background, captain, you've seen crash sites before. What do you think?"

The captain turned his head and looked at the blank wall for just a second before he answered.

"Well, I'm sure you already know what I'm going to say. The short of it. There are NO good outcomes in that valley. Not possible."

"So, how big would you guess the debris field is?"

"I'd say, roughly 100 yards by 200, maybe less. It looks like they came down almost vertical. The biggest thing you're going to find in one piece is the wheel assemblies and the engines. It must have exploded on impact. It's a real mess. I hate to think what it's going to look like in the daylight." He was shaking his head as he looked Chris directly in the eye.

Sam asked, "What about the fires. Big, small, what?"

"Nothing to be concerned about. There were trees still burning, but they'll be out in a few hours. Their tanks must have been full, lots of fire on the ground." He turned and looked at Willy.

Willy took it as a request to comment, "It was the eeriest thing I ever saw. It just looked like a sea of fire right in the center of the site. It had scattered smaller fires all around. But just odd how everything was on fire right in the middle."

Sam commented, "Your coordinates put it almost to the north wall. The terrain up there is just going to add time to our trek."

The captain asked, "So, what else can we help you with?"

Chris responded, "That's all I needed, Captain. I know you're both anxious to get going. I want to thank you again for what you've done here tonight." He stood then stepped towards the captain to extend his hand yet again.

They shook hands while the other two were already in the hall and headed towards the front door. Once there, Sam shook Willy's hand again.

Willy said in a low tone, "That guy's the best damn pilot I've ever seen. So calm, so confident, reacts without emotions. He's a very cool customer. I'm going to learn a lot from this guy."

Chris and the captain came walking up. The captain shook Sam's hand and said, "Well, sir. We're going to get out of your hair. But, I just want you to give us a call if you find you can't move men down on the ground. I have some ideas about how I could do it. Just give us a call. I don't envy either one of you during the next few weeks or months. I would never want your jobs. No way."

Chris opened the door and held it open.

"Have a safe flight, gentlemen."

Chapter 2

DREAM MIST

ED'S EYES SLOWLY opened, one at a time. He was looking up at clouds that were so low he felt he could reach out and touch them. Where was he? He lay there as he looked up, and was fascinated by a light that illuminated the bottom of the clouds. It was mystical as it danced across the rounded shapes of the clouds. Then he heard the crackling of a fire. Raising his head up just a few inches, he now saw the wreckage of the plane as it burned only a few yards from where he lay.

Then his mind began replaying all the frantic memories of the chaos that took place in the plane's cabin. The horror of what he saw. It was a movie that he wished he could stop, but the pictures flashed faster and faster. Just as he feared he would be sick, a woman's face appeared and all was calm.

He no longer saw the low hanging clouds above him. His head was once again on the ground, and all he saw was a mental rendering of her face. He started to relive every one of the last few seconds before the crash. He smiled again at the remembrance of her holding his hand. His grin widened as he recalled that she had put her cheek on his shoulder. Wow, what a GREAT feeling that had been. His thoughts were of these things that he had wanted his entire life.

Most of the lonely nights in his apartment had ended the same way. He watched a movie or played his online video games until the early hours of the morning. Then, with TV and computer turned off, he would sit alone in the dark. Minutes and sometimes hours would pass as he thought of the girl he hoped to meet one day. One that he would feel comfortable talking to. A girl that would actually like him. One that would WANT to be with him. Yes, a special lady who would knock down all the emotional walls he'd surrounded himself with over the years. If only he could find her. Oh, how he longed to find her. Only then, would he finally he able to live.

LIVE? Wait a minute! He sat up rapidly and began to survey his surroundings. There was wreckage everywhere. How was that metal burning? He didn't understand it, but it was all on fire. As he slowly turned his head from side to side, he acquired a panoramic view of utter destruction. Were those trees at the edge of the darkness? He squinted to see them. They were trees, and every other one was on fire. The flames were burning at different heights along the trunk of each one.

HOLY SHIT! I'm alive! How? He sat there shaking his head as he blindly stared straight ahead. *WHO CARES HOW! I'm ALIVE!* Then he saw his legs stretched out in front of him. *Well, there are my feet. That's a good thing! I can't believe I'm ALIVE! Look at all this mess around me. How the HELL did I survive?* As his spirit began to swell with great amounts of joy, he tried to get up so he could dance around! His attempt to rise was stopped by a weight on his right hand. His first thought was, 'Damn. I'll bet it's stuck under something.' It was only then that he finally looked down and saw HER.

She was lying there and still had a death grip on his hand. He quickly looked from her head to her toes and thought, 'Great! She's all in one piece too! No blood anywhere!' Then his high level of JOY plummeted as he strained to see if she was breathing. *OH GOD, NO! She's not breathing.* He didn't feel any warmth from her hand. His mind was reeling from emotions that suddenly raged inside him. He couldn't believe this was happening! Not when he had FINALLY met a girl that he could actually talk to. He DID talk to her. *OH, PLEASE NO!*

With tears forming in his eyes, he lay back down and rolled

over towards her. Though he was afraid to know the truth, he slowly moved a shaky hand towards her face. He hesitated, thinking he would die if she were dead.

Just as he was about to touch her, movement to the left of them caught his attention. With his hand frozen near her face, he turned his head to see what was moving.

OH MY GOD! It's a man and woman. They were walking towards him. No, wait, they were walking past? They didn't even look his way. He thought to himself, 'Why do they appear so fuzzy? I must have hit my head on something, and it's affecting my vision.' He shook his head as if that would clear up his sight. It didn't. He couldn't believe they were just going to walk past without saying anything at all. So he spoke. "Hey! You two okay? Hellooooooo! Mister? Hey, lady! Where you going?"

They both walked right past him and never looked at him at all. He stayed focused on them until they disappeared into the wall of darkness that guarded the treeline. He could barely see their outlines in the darkness under the trees. What were they doing? They seemed to be just standing there. Then, as his eyes became adapted to looking into that darkness, he noticed more movement. I'll be damned, he thought. There are more people out there.

As he moved his eyes to the left, he noticed even more. Why were they all just standing in groups out there in the dark? Were they all in shock or something? Then it dawned on him. Maybe they wanted to get away from the wreckage in case something else blew up. That could be it. Might be a good idea, now that he thought about it.

While he lay there wondering what the people were doing, there was another movement that grabbed his attention. His hand moved. She's moving! Oh, how he wanted to put his face close to hers and ask if she was all right. He decided that could go badly, if she opened her eyes and thought he was trying to kiss her while she was out. No, that would not be good. So he lay his head down again to insure that his eyes would be the first thing she saw.

Her eyelids were quivering ever so often, and she finally wrinkled her eyebrows a little before she spoke.

"Who you yelling at? Why do I feel so, so, odd?" Then she opened her eyes and saw him. "Oh, it's you again. What happened?

I feel funny. Was that you yelling?"

He was so happy that she was talking! She was looking at him, talking to him. He saw her eyes scanning his face. Was she expecting him to say something? Oh no! Those old feelings of insecurity came crashing in on him and he started to pull away. He couldn't do this. It's not an emergency any more. She's going to realize she didn't need him anymore. But just as he was starting to slip back into the shell that he'd lived in for his entire life, she smiled.

"Did I tell you 'thank you' for holding my hand? I was so afraid. I thought for sure we were going to, uh, wait a minute." She sat up quickly and so did he. She was doing exactly what he had done when he first became aware of what had happened.

"We CRASHED! Oh my GOD, we CRASHED!"

She was panting and quickly looking from side to side. Then her free hand started slapping at the air, as if she were trying to cool herself off by fanning her face. She was still looking at the mess before them when she began speaking very rapidly.

"We made it? Look at this mess. How's this possible?" Looking at her arms, then her feet and legs, she said what he had said. "I'm all in one piece! I just can't believe it. I'm ALIVE!"

She was overcome with joy and started to stand so she could dance around, but stopped the moment her hand felt the weight of his. Then, to his amazement, she quickly fell flat on the ground and covered her face with her free hand while never letting go of his hand.

"Are there dead bodies out there? I don't think I can handle seeing bodies. I'll throw up."

She had just gone from elation to shaking out of fear. He knew he should say something. Try to console her or something. But he's not sure again. Looking at her shaking on the ground caused him to overcome his shyness. He reluctantly said, "I haven't seen any bodies. It's ok. I haven't seen any dead people."

"Really?" she asked, as she split her fingers apart and looked at him through the crack.

"You're absolutely sure? I'm warning you. I'll do it. I'll throw up for sure. I know I will."

Again he tried to console her. "I haven't seen anything to be scared of here. The worst is over. You made it!"

"You mean, 'WE' made it!" She had dropped her hand from her face and was again smiling at him.

This forced a small smile from him as they both lay facing each other. Did she just say 'WE'? She said 'WE'! Forget surviving this awful plane crash. This girl is smiling at him and referred to them as 'WE'. He couldn't believe this was happening. A real girl, a real conversation and she was smiling at him! He told himself not to get too cocky, or he'd blow it. One stupid word or look, and she'd stop talking to him. It always happened like that. Maybe he shouldn't talk anymore.

"So, the cat got your tongue?" she asked with a sheepish grin on her face.

"No."

"Well then, talk to me. What do we do now? Do you think that anyone else made it?"

"Well, it looks like a lot of other people made it just like we did."

"They did? Where are they?"

Once more, she sat up quickly. But she immediately covered her face again with her free hand. She tilted her covered face downwards and peeked at him from under her hand.

"You sure there are no bodies? Promise?"

"I haven't stood up yet and looked around. Let me do that first. You just keep your face covered until I tell ya."

He was tugging at his hand, trying to free it from her grasp, so he could stand up. What was she doing? She had tightened her grip more. She almost sounded desperate as she asked, "Hey! What are you doing?"

"Well, if you let go of me for a minute, I'll get up and look around for ya."

"Oh, no! I don't want you letting go of my hand. Can't you just look around right by us while you are sitting here?"

"Well, yes, but I've already done that. I can't see very clearly or very far through this mist."

She was now childishly trying to look around by peeking out underneath the bottom of her hand. He said, "You know. You aren't going to see more than two feet around us like that."

"Well, it's enough for me to see what you mean about the mist. It kinda looks like a misty dream. Isn't it very odd how we can have all this fire and it still be misty-looking out here?"

He rubbed his face with his free hand before he replied, "Yeah, a really bad dream." His heart sunk the moment he said it. He KNEW he'd say something stupid. She just let go of his hand and pushed it away fairly hard. He couldn't believe he screwed this up already. Damn it!

She didn't see that he had his head down when she asked, "So? You going to stand up or what? But don't you dare take one step away from me. I mean it. NOT ONE STEP!"

Hey, she's not mad. Wow, she didn't want him going anywhere. So, he hopped up and actually stepped so close to her that his jeans were touching her arm. He couldn't believe it when she leaned onto his leg, just to make sure he was there. He thought to himself how he could barely feel her against his leg. Well, she was scared and just wanted to know she was not alone. It's not like she was hugging his leg. Yeah, that had to be it. She just wanted to feel his presence next to her, so she would know she was not alone. For whatever her reason was, it didn't matter. His smile was back and he was staring down at the top of her head when she spoke again.

"So? What do you see? Anything? Please talk to me."

Hearing her voice snapped his head into motion. He started doing what he was supposed to be doing, looking around. He decided to talk as he looked.

"Well, I don't see anything but burning metal objects. It's amazing that there aren't any bigger pieces of the plane than this. Maybe there is another area that has the main body of the plane."

"Yeah, yeah, yeah, but are there any bodies? You see ANYTHING that looks like one? Or, God forbid, a part of, of, well . . . you know."

"I don't see anything. I guess I can see about 30 or 40 feet all around us. Nothing! Come on, open your eyes."

He extended his hand to her as she revealed her face. "You can get up. Really? I don't see anything scary here."

She took his hand, and he was immediately transformed by a feeling of euphoria at the realization that he was helping a girl up. He's changing. He could feel it. Should he dare to think that she could like him? He decided not to push it. It's probably better to take it slow. He'll let her make the moves. That way, he'll know for sure what she's thinking. Or will he?

She was standing up beside him now. He started to tell her not to squeeze his hand so tightly, but he didn't. He liked holding her hand, and nothing was going to stop him from doing so every chance he got.

"So where are all those people you said survived like us? I don't see anybody." She was talking while looking all around.

He raised his hand and pointed out into the trees. "There. See them? There looks like, oh, maybe four or five of them right there. See 'em?"

She was straining to see anything in the darkness around the trees. Finally, she did see something.

"Yes. Oh, there they are! What are they doing? Why are they out there?"

"Well that's the question all righty. Let's go ask 'em." He started to lead her that way, but his arm was stopped as if it were handcuffed to a rock. He looked at her, "What? I thought you wanted to know what they are doing out there. Come on, let's go see."

She was looking out into the trees. She stepped right up against him and grabbed the top of his arm with her other hand. "I'm not so sure that I want to go out there."

"Why not? It's the only way to find out what they're doing. Come on." He nudged her a little with his shoulder. But she wasn't having any of it. She was NOT moving.

"Maybe you should just holler out at them. Let's just stand here in the light and you can yell at them." She turned her head upwards and looked into his face, "Go on. Yell at them."

"I'll do it, but it won't work. I tried talking to that man and woman that went by earlier. They never even looked at me. I even yelled at them. Nothing."

"Oh, that's right. I remember you yelling right before I opened my eyes." She was now looking out into the dark again. "You sure they heard you?"

"Well, you heard me. How could they not hear me?"

"Where did they come from? You said they just walked past us. From where?"

Her eyes followed his hand as he pointed towards the other side of the wreckage. She was looking at the path he said they had walked towards them. "That can't be right. Look, that ground is all on fire. How's that work? Wait a minute. You say they WALKED past us from there? Were they on fire? They couldn't have walked through all those flames."

He was looking at the flames and wondering why he hadn't noticed that before. But they had walked from there. They passed just a foot away from where he and she were lying. He was making gestures with his free hand. He dragged his finger through the air, along the path the man and woman had walked. Then he pulled that finger up to his mouth and tapped it on his lips, as if his mind was replaying what he'd seen.

"You know. I can't explain it, but they walked right across there. I was lying on the ground, facing you, here. They walked right by us, there. I know that is what happened." He rubbed his face with his free hand and then shrugged his shoulders. "That's what happened. I'm telling you, that is what happened."

"Well, was there anything strange about them? Besides them walking through fire and not wanting to talk to anyone?"

"Well, not really. They just looked straight ahead. Like we weren't here. Like they didn't see us for some reason." He stopped, and his face showed that he was replaying something else in his mind.

She noticed this. "Hey, what are you thinking about so hard? Talk to me." She tugged on his hand and arm at the same time.

He was shaking his head and started to say something, but stopped. "Well, uh, nah, it sounds crazy."

"What sounds crazy? What? Come on, talk to me. What is it?"

He had wrinkled his eyebrows and was again looking along the path they had walked. "Well, the more I think about it, the more I remember thinking that they looked, well, fuzzy."

"Fuzzy? What do you mean fuzzy?"

"I don't know how to explain it. They weren't really well-defined. Like the edges of them was, uh, not clear. I don't know. This is just too weird."

She was now looking along the path those two would have walked. She was constructing her own mental image of what he might have seen. Then her eyes grew large as it dawned on her what they must have been. She began to quiz him very slowly and deliberately.

"When you say fuzzy, could you mean that you saw through them?"

"What? Are you, nuts or something? Don't tell me you think I saw ghosts. That's nuts! There are no such things as ghosts." He looked at her as she was staring at the burning ground the man and woman would have crossed.

As they stood looking around, the sound of a loud whoosh startled them. It preceded the reflection of a large flash of pure white light from behind them. It's the type of sound you hear when the air rushes out of a car as you slam the door in summer time. It seemed to have come from the trees where those people were all standing around. They both spun around to look into the trees. Their eyes were straining to find those shapes of the people they had just seen there. Where were they? There must have been 10 or 20 of them just a moment ago. Where did they go? What the hell was happening out there?

As they frantically searched the shadows in the trees for more shapes, he finally saw some other people just a few yards farther to the right of where they had been looking. "Look, there." He pointed for her to look. "There are some. Is that some little kids with them? I remember seeing a group of families up front on the plane. They each had several kids with them. I wonder if that's them?"

She was looking and nodding her head in agreement. "Yes, there. I see them. There are, one, two, looks like five kids and six, no, seven adults. Please tell me that's what you see too?"

He counted to himself. "Yes. That's right. But where did the others go and what was that big flash of light?"

Then it happened again. While they were both looking at the families standing in the trees, there was a blinding white flash of light and that eerie sound again. They were both temporarily blinded by that bright flash. Their heads shook and eyes blinked. They heard that eerie sound happen several more times in rapid succession. Though they still couldn't see again yet, they both felt certain that a very bright flash of white light had accompanied each of those eerie sounds. Each new sound seemed to come from a different place.

His eyes weren't focused yet, but he spoke anyway. "What the hell. Man, that was bright. You see that?"

"Yes, but I can't see anything but white spots before my eyes now. You?"

Their eyes slowly adjusted again to the darkness. They once again were searching that area of the trees where the families had been standing right before that flash.

She said, "I, uh, I don't see them anymore. Do you?"

"Nope. I can't see any of them. What is going on? Where'd they all go?"

He turned his gaze to her and said, "You look that way, and I'll look this way. Let's see if there are any others out there around us. I know there were lots of them earlier."

They both turned slowly as their eyes scanned the darkness underneath the treeline. Once they had both gone full circle, they were again facing each other.

He was scratching his head and looking this way, then that. "I just don't get it. This is kinda weird. There one minute, then a flash of light, and then they're gone. What is happening out there?"

Again she stepped right beside him, took his hand and ran her other hand between his arm and his chest. "Well. I just have one question."

He was still looking around. There was a questioning expression on his face as he asked, "And what's that?"

"You still want to go out there and see what they were doing?"

His head snapped around so he could look down into her face, "Well, that's a big NO! I think you had the right idea all along. Let's just stay here in the fire light until the sun comes out. I don't think we need to be poking around in the dark out there."

"So, why aren't you willing to go out there now? Don't tell me you're afraid you might run into some . . . ", and she paused to smirk at him, "GHOSTS!"

He exchanged a stare with her. Then he looked into the dark one last time before saying, "There are no such things as ghosts. You can't really expect me to believe in ghosts. Not really?"

"Well, if not ghosts, what do you think is going on out there?"

"I, uh, who knows. We'll find out in the morning."

She was obviously still in a playful mood as she spoke.

"So, what do you want to do until daylight? We can sit here and hope the fires don't go out before morning."

He was still looking around. "Yeah, that sounds good. Besides, it has to be cold out here since we're in the mountains like this. It just has to be cold. Odd, I don't feel cold. You?"

Her smile had faded. "You know, I don't feel cold at all. Maybe it's because of these fires all around us. Yeah, that's got to be it." She started trying to pull him back down to the ground. "Let's just sit here and talk. OK?"

Though he allowed her to pull him back to a seated position, he wasn't so sure about the talking part. He didn't do well when talking to girls. Up to now, he'd been doing pretty good, but here is where he usually freezes up or starts saying stupid stuff that drives them away.

Then he remembered. He was going to let her do all the talking and lead the conversation. Yeah, that's it. He'll just talk about whatever she starts talking about. That's the ticket! Again, he was filled with euphoria as she locked her arm in his and pulled herself close to him. Man, he was happy.

"So, what's your name big fella? You have a name, don't you?"

"Of course I have a name, silly."

"So, are you going to share it?"

He was starting to tense up a little. But seeing that she was acting a little playful, he found himself relaxing. In fact, he had NEVER been so relaxed talking to a girl. She's, well. She's different. She's friendly. He liked her.

"Oh, sorry. My name is Ed. Well. I mean. My name is Edward McGowen. But everyone calls me Ed."

"Ok, Ed. I'm Martha Tildon. I'm very glad to meet you. I know I've already thanked you, but I just want to say it again. I'm really glad that I had you to go through this with me. I'd have been a basket case without you here. I don't get . . . " She stopped without finishing her thought.

He wondered if she was like him. "Out much? You don't get out much? Is that what you started to say?"

He felt her grip loosen on his arm right before she said, "Uh, yeah. I just stay home a lot. Me and my kitty cat, Boots. He's so funny."

Wow, she's just like him. He needed to know more. "Why don't you get out much?"

He felt her loosen her grip even more. "Well, uh, oh, I might as well tell you. You're going to figure it out sooner or later."

Now she had completely let go of his arm and hand. She was starting to scoot away as she said, "I'm not like you. I'm, well, different."

"What do you mean, different?"

"Well, look at me. I don't get out because, well, because I look like this."

He squinted at her as he continued.

"Look like what? I'm afraid you've lost me here. What are you talking about? What's wrong with the way you look? And what do you mean you're not like me? What am I like?"

"Well, I'm not all that pretty. There, I've said it. Happy now?"

"What? What makes you think you aren't pretty?"

"That's easy. No guy ever looks at me. You didn't look at me while I was coming up the aisle on the plane, or even when I was sitting down beside you. That's what I mean. I'm, I'm just not pretty enough for a guy to look at. I don't know what I've been thinking here. You seemed so nice, and you held my hand. I thought maybe, just maybe . . . oh, forget it."

She swung her feet around so that her back was now towards him, wrapped her arms around her raised knees, and hung her head.

He was looking at her back and thinking to himself. 'Wow! She's just like me! But, she *is* pretty. I should tell her. Yeah, I will, no, wait. I'm going to mess this up. What do I do?' Then he surprised himself and mustered enough courage to admit an earlier transgression.

"But I did look at you."

"Oh, yeah, right. Maybe for two seconds, then nothing. Right?"

"Well, actually. Uh, I looked at you several times. I just didn't want you to know."

She raised her head but kept her back to him. "You did. When? Why?"

Oh, no. Here it is. It's time to be personal, understanding, all those things that he's not. Oh, this was not good. He's going to blow it for sure.

"Well, I looked at you once, no twice, as you were coming down the aisle. Then, I looked at you a lot when you were busy putting your stuff in the overhead compartment before you sat down."

She twisted at the waist and let her knees fall over together on the ground. With her eyes on him, she said, "You did? But why?"

Oh, no. She's put him on the spot here. What's he going to say? Well, can he tell her the truth? Oh no. That would be bad, or would it. He decided to go for broke.

"Why? Well, at first because I was hoping you'd be the one that had the seat next to me. Then when it was you, and you were busy looking up, I was, well, you know . . . "

She began to smile. It appeared that she was getting in a playful mood again, as she had been earlier.

"No, I don't know. So tell me. Why?"

"Well, this isn't fair. You know why."

"No, I don't. So tell me?"

"I, I, well, I'm a guy. I was . . . You know . . . checking you out. Get it? Now, that you've embarrassed me, you happy?"

She turned back around and slowly scooted a little closer to him. He could see that she had that smile again. He liked her smile.

"You were? Really? Are you making this up?"

"What? No! Look. So I was, you know, looking."

She had now scooted right up against him again and slipped her hand back into his. "You were looking at me. Ah ha! Just being a guy! Is that all you guys think about? BOOBS? Really!"

He's embarrassed now. "No! Well, maybe. I'm not talking anymore. That's it."

She giggled and leaned her head out a little, so she could see his face before asking, "So, uh, what did you think?"

Well, if he was ever going to blush, it was now. Thank God it's dark out here. She'll never know how much she is getting to him.

"Ah, you're blushing. Aren't you?"

He panicked. How could she possibly see that?

"No. Don't be silly. Why would I do that?"

"Because you just admitted you were looking at my boobs! That's why." She sat up a little straighter and glanced down at her chest. "Hey, you never answered me."

"About what, now?"

"So, if you checked out my boobs, what did you think?"

"Are you kidding me? Hey, you're enjoying this, aren't you." He pointed at her with his free hand.

"Enjoying what?" She tried to look innocent.

"You know what. You're embarrassing the crap out of me here, and I think you are enjoying it! Aren't you?"

She grinned again, rocking her head from side to side as she smiled.

"Yes, I am. A little. Surprised?"

He was surprised. Was she flirting with him? Was this for real? Could this girl really want to get to know him? He thought to himself, 'I'm going to be praying to crash every time I fly now!'

"A little. Why are you trying to embarrass me?"

She raised and lowered her shoulders in a quick, jerky motion as she said, "I don't know. I just think it's kinda cute, the way you're acting."

Did she say he was cute? Man, this day was just getting better and better, except for the plane crash and all.

He was about to say something, but stopped when he felt her shake a bit and tighten her grip on his hand. What's wrong with her now? She seems scared. Why?

"Do you hear that? What is it?" It was obvious that she had gone from flirtatious to frightened a second time.

He listened for a second and was just about to say he didn't hear anything, when there it was. The thump, thump sounds of helicopter blades cutting through the air.

"It's a chopper! Hey, it's the rescue chopper!"

The sound was very loud now, and it seemed to be just a little off to their left. They both had jumped to their feet and were looking up into those low-hanging clouds.

"It's over that way. Wait, shhhhhh." And he was listening. "It stopped. He is hovering in one spot. They're looking for us. Wait, he's moving again. He's coming this way!"

She still had a tight grasp of his hand, even though she was bouncing up and down on her toes as she looked upwards. "They'll never see us through those clouds. Will they? How can they?"

"Wait, listen. He's coming right for us. He must know we're here."

"But how?" she asks.

"I don't know. Wait." He looked at all the fire everywhere. Then it hit him.

"I got it. They have some kinda thermal detection system. They are tracking in on the heat from all these fires. That has to be it."

She looked at him and asked, "How would you know that?"

He never stopped looking up. "Late night TV. I watch shows about military aircraft, you know, helicopters and jets. All the time! The military develops things like that for the battlefield, but it always makes its way into civilian aircraft. It just makes sense that a rescue chopper would have something like that on it. Especially one that looks for people up in the mountains, like us."

"Do you think they'll be able to land and pick us up? Where will they land?" She started yelling, "Hey, Help, HELP. We're down here."

He was watching her point down at the ground as she again said, "We're down here." She finally noticed him staring at her. "What? They could hear me. Maybe?"

"They can't hear us yelling. Besides, he's a lot higher up than you think. Look at the tops of the trees. Lots of them are disappearing into the clouds. He'll NEVER be able to get low enough to see us. Hell, he'll never get low enough for us to see him. And land? Are you serious? A chopper can't land in here. This is all on fire, and he sure as hell can't land in the trees. They'd knock off his blades, and he'd crash. Like us. No, he's not going to be able to get us, but at least they know where we are now. I can't believe they found us this fast."

Just as he said that last sentence, he found himself hoping they didn't rescue them too soon. He wanted a little more time with Martha. He smiled. He liked that name. 'Ed and Martha' sounded good to him.

"He's moving again." She pointed up to where she thought the helicopter was, just above the trees. The sound of his rotors started to fade and they both could tell he was climbing.

"Oh no! Sounds like he's leaving. Why would he do that?"

Ed decided to try and console her. "Look. Doesn't matter why he left. He knows where we are now. That's the important thing. Wait, wait. Yes, I bet I know what he's doing. If we're in a deep valley, he has to go back up higher than the valley walls, so he can get a radio message out. That's got to be it! He's calling in our position, I bet ya!"

Ed had stopped moving and was tilting his head so one ear, then the other was facing upwards. "I can't hear him anymore. Martha, you heard him first. You have better hearing than I do. Can you still hear him?"

She didn't even hesitate. "Yes. You don't hear that thumping sound?"

"No, nothing at all. Can you tell if he's stationary, or is he moving away?"

She closed her eyes for a second. "No. He's not moving away. The sound is the same. He has to be staying in one spot. Maybe you're right. Maybe he's calling in our position." Then she tilted her head a little before saying, "Wait, WAIT. It's getting louder. The sound is getting louder. You hear it yet?"

"Yes, I hear it now. He's coming back down. Sounds like he is right over there. What's he doing now? Wait. It sounds like he is moving to the center of the field here." With his eyes intensely focused on the clouds above, he suddenly pointed.

"Look!"

They could actually see the chopper's skids protruding through the bottom of the clouds, and it was definitely moving to the center of the crash site. Finally the bottom of the chopper was visible and the blinking red light bounced off the trees that were not on fire. As it got closer to the center of the crash site and moved directly above the main fires, it suddenly dropped an extra foot. It appeared as if the fires were literally sucking the craft from the sky. They could see the bottom of the doors for only a brief second or two, before the skids began to shake from side to side. It was obvious that the chopper was struggling to maintain its height from the ground. The pilot must have reacted by accelerating forward and upwards. All they saw from the ground was the front of the skids dipping lower before the craft made a hasty retreat into the clouds.

She sounded very excited. "He was going to land. Did you see that? He was coming down. And you said he wouldn't try to land, but he was trying. I wonder why he stopped?"

Ed waited until she finally looked at him. "Why didn't he land? Really?"

He pointed at the burning mess in front of them. "You think that he can land in that?"

The sound of the chopper moving away stopped them from talking. They both looked up at the clouds again. They listened as the sound of the chopper seemed to move to the edge of the trees before following the treeline around the crash site.

"Ed? What do you think he's doing now?"

"I haven't a clue. Maybe he's trying to get a feel for how big the crash site is. I don't know."

They both stood there listening with all their might. As the sound of the chopper started to fade, she said "They're leaving? I can't believe they're leaving us? I know they couldn't see us, but surely they know we're down here right? If they have that thermal thingy you said, then it would detect our body heat, right?"

Ed's head fell to his chest, and he yelled "Damn it! I'm so stupid."

"What's the matter, Ed?"

"No, they couldn't detect our body heat. We're standing right in the middle of a burning field. I think those things work by differentiating temperatures."

"I don't understand. What does that mean?"

"It means that all he saw here in the middle of this field would be a big blob of color, because of all the heat being generated by all of this." He was waving his hands at all the burning debris around them.

"I'm so stupid. We had a perfect chance for him to see us. All we had to do was go out into the darkness around the trees." He was now pointing out towards the trees as he continued. "Out there. Our body temperatures would have stood out against the cold of the surrounding ground. He'd have seen us easily. In fact, I'll bet that is what he was doing. Don't you see? He was looking for people to be standing around the edge of this fire. Not in the middle of it like we are."

"So you don't think it's possible they know we're alive down here?"

He was looking at her and now realized that his outburst, though true, may not be the best thing for her to hear right now. How could he change the subject without answering her question? She was still looking up at the clouds as if hoping to see the chopper again.

"Well, anything is possible. Hey, it just dawned on me. For the few seconds we saw the bottom of that chopper. Didn't it look like it was painted camouflage?"

She glanced at him, then the ground before answering, "Yes. That's right. So what?"

"Well, that means it was a military chopper. We have the best military pilots in the world, and they have the best electronics in the world. So you could be right. They may have seen us with some kinda super-secret gadget that only the military has."

She had lost interest in staring up at the empty clouds and was once again smiling at him. "Oh, so you think they sent a military chopper after us for that reason? Then I was right! They *do* know we are here."

He decided it was best to let her think this, even though he doubted it himself. Why worry her with something they couldn't do anything about? The sound of the chopper was completely gone now, and they were left with the realization that even though their location had been found, help was probably still hours away. Maybe even longer.

All the excitement of the last few minutes had faded away, and they were standing there looking out at the darkness. Suddenly, she began to giggle. Low at first, but then it became louder until Ed finally said "What? You find this funny?"

"Well. I was just thinking. If he had gotten here sooner, maybe all those ghosts that were out there could have hitched a ride back to town!"

At first he didn't know how to take that comment. But under the circumstances, what she said was funny. He started to laugh too. They got louder and louder until they were again holding hands and silently staring up at the clouds.

Ed felt so happy and fulfilled at this very moment. Yes, he had experienced a major airplane crash and was now stranded somewhere in the mountains, but he didn't care. Not one bit. For the first time in his life, he had a girl that was holding his hand, smiling at him, and he felt completely comfortable talking to her. At least most of the time. His life had changed so drastically in these past few hours. The military won't be able to get to them for hours, and Ed knew this. That meant he still had a considerable window of opportunity with Martha. A chance to complete this bonding between them to a point that hopefully would continue after they were rescued.

"Ed? What were you thinking so hard about? Are you worried about something?"

"No. Well, of course I'm worried about the obvious stuff, but hey! We are alive and they know where we are. So we have to sleep on the ground tonight. Big deal. So what if they don't get to us until late tomorrow? Doesn't really matter. The fact is, they will get to us. We are OK."

"That's all good, but you looked like you were really going over something in your head. Were you?"

Boy, she was observant. What should he say now? "Well, I was just thinking that we are going to get hungry sometime tomorrow, but there isn't much we can do about that. I doubt that we can find anything to eat in this wreckage, but you never know. So we can look once the morning light comes. But I was also thinking that we are going to get thirsty and soon. So I was thinking that we could wait until it's light tomorrow, then find some clean snow. We could eat a little every now and then to get water."

"That's cool. We could do that! I used to do that when I was a little girl. Smart thinking, big boy!"

He saw her staring at him. Why? He was close to letting his usual panicky reaction force him to look away. But just as he started to turn his head, she reached up and gently placed her open palm on the side of his face. His mind raced and his fears grew as he thought to himself "Oh MY GOD! She is going to KISS ME!"

Just as he was positive that he was going to faint, she spoke so softly.

"Ed. Has anyone ever told you how absolutely gorgeous your eyes are?" Her face was only inches away from his. She was looking so intensely into his eyes, one would have thought that she was actually trying to see into his soul. "I have never, ever seen the whites of a person's eyes as clear as yours. You're killing me with these eyes of yours."

His tongue fumbled to find some kind of reply. All he can think to say was, "What?" His mind reeled as his ears heard that lame one word response. He thought to himself, 'Oh, no, I can't believe that I just said that in response to such a nice thing that she said to me. She's going to think I'm an idiot!' Yet, again she did exactly the opposite and was unfazed by his reluctance to talk much.

"I take it that nobody has. Right?"

He struggled to break free from his old habits that had always caused him to stand there and say nothing. It was at this moment, for some unknown reason, that he decided to change. He was going to talk to her just like he'd always talked to his parents when they were alive. He had always felt comfortable being himself with them. He never struggled for words or felt shy about saying what was on his mind. They had always accepted him as is.

He saw them both for a split second in his mind. They were standing together and smiling at him. It was as if they wanted him to know that they were happy for him. Yes, happy for him to have finally made a connection with a woman. As their image faded from his mind, he felt all his anxiety melt away.

"Nobody has ever told me anything that nice before. Ever! But, I have always had bloodshot eyes from working late on my computer or playing my video games. Are you sure you don't see any red in my eyes?"

"Like I said, I have never seen eyes as clear as yours. Except in newborn babies, of course."

"Martha. Could we sit back down for a while?"

She smiled and lowered her hand from his face. They both looked for a more comfortable spot to sit. Once agreement was reached as to where to sit, he held her hand as she sat first and then he lowered himself very close to her side. They were both smiling and looking around.

She said to Ed, "It's very nice sitting by this fire. Not too hot, not too cold, it's just perfect. Why don't we pretend that it's Christmas and we are just sitting by a large fireplace? I've always wanted to do that with someone. You?"

"Yes. I've always dreamed about the same thing. You know, it would be nice if you and I could maybe do that this Christmas. That is, if you'd like to?"

She squeezed his hand a little. "I'd like that, Ed. I'd like that very much."

Chapter 3

A RESCUE BEGINS

SAM WALKED TO the office door and looked in. He saw that Chris was typing away on his laptop, so he tapped on the doorframe.

"Excuse me," and he paused a second before adding "Chris."

Startled a little, he stopped typing and looked up at Sam standing in the door.

"Oh. Sorry, I hope you weren't standing there waiting for me to look up. I get kind of over-focused when I'm working. So, just for future reference, please just come on in or start talking. Otherwise, I may never notice you. Sorry."

"Hey, I'm the same way. At my age, it takes 10 minutes for my brain to register what my ears are hearing. Anyway, I just came by to tell you that the plane manufacturer's rep just called. He's checked into the hotel and is going to get some sleep. He just wanted you to know he was here, but he'd stay out of your way since there really isn't anything for him to do until we actually get in to see the site. He left his name and room number in case you wanted to call him.

"I also just got off the phone with the NTSB guy. He's also at the hotel. Said he wanted to stop and grab breakfast before he came up."

Sam has walked over to the desk and handed Chris two notes. "Here are their names, hotel phone numbers, room numbers, and their personal cell numbers."

"Thanks, Sam. You look tired, buddy. If you need to go get some shuteye, please go. I'll be fine. Thanks for introducing me to the tower supervisor. I'm sure that we can handle it until you get back. I have your cell number here somewhere." Chris was hitting Enter on his keyboard and looking for Sam's number. "Ok. Here it is. I can get a hold of you if I need to."

"Nah, I'm wide awake. Just like you, sir. I'll be good till sometime this evening. Then I'll leave for a while. I want to see that we get this rolling smoothly before I bug out for a bit."

"You sound a lot like me, Sam." Chris watched as Sam left the office and disappeared down the hall.

Chris went back to working on his 'To Do' list. The sound of big engines pulling up outside caused him to swing around and look out the window to see what was happening. Seeing a small caravan of trucks pulling up to the building, he jumped up and headed to the front door.

Sam was already there waiting.

"Sam. What do we have here?"

"Well, sir. It's two groups. These are the army reservists that I requested. They brought us six Humvees and those two large transports. Then those other guys are a logging crew that work the basin. The big guy with that cowboy hat is the owner. He's a good man. We'll need them to clear a path through the trees so we can get from the road to the crash site. You're not going to like what he is going to tell you, though."

"Why? What's he going to say?"

"Well, in a nutshell. He told me on the phone last night that he wasn't sure they could get that big tree cutter up there this time of the year. He's betting that the basin floor—he means the road - is nothing but mud this time of year. Says the melting snow probably has turned that road into mud three or four foot deep. The kind of mud that sucks things down. He doesn't think the army vehicles will be able to get past it, either. But they're all going to try. They're here to get some directions from us. I guess I should have told you this earlier."

The big guy with the cowboy hat and one of the reservists reached the steps outside. Sam jumped over to open the door for them.

"Come on in, boys! Get out of that cold."

Once the door was closed, the owner of the logging company shook Sam's hand.

"Morning, Sam. I brought a small crew, just until we get up there and see what we're looking at. They're all good men, and each one volunteered to help."

Sam turned to Chris. "Chris. This is Mr. Barthalomea Wilson." He was a tall man with a very stern look on his face. It was a look that he'd faced the world with for many years. A forceful, yet gentle man who was used to giving orders while caring very much for the wellbeing of those that worked for him. His face showed the signs of weathering, due to being in the field right alongside his men. This was a man that expected 100% from those that worked for him, but even more from himself. Yes, he was a hard man, but a fair one.

Chris extended his hand. "Morning, Mr. Wilson. I'm Chris Mathews and I'm really glad to have you here. I'd appreciate it if you could provide me a list of the men's names that are helping us with this. I want to make sure that every one of them gets an official thank-you when the time comes. I know it's a little thing, but I think that it's important.

"Oh, and if you would, please make sure the spelling of each name is correct. By the way, just call me Chris, and please pass that along to your men as well for me."

"Glad to meet you, Chris. Please call me Bart. Everyone else does. I think that Sam just likes introducing me that way, so he can impress everyone by saying my name. He never used to say it right and the family rode him pretty hard the first few years. You see, sir, I'm married to his wife's cousin."

Sam and Bart chuckled for a few seconds. Then Bart pulled a folded piece of paper out of his pocket and handed it to Chris as he continued to talk.

"I have a list of the men who are with me right here. I thought you might want it. These men are going to do everything they can to help you out with this, and it makes me feel good that you are already focused on acknowledging their contributions. Now sir, how do you want to kick this thing off?"

Sam interrupted. "Excuse me, Chris. I want to introduce you to Sergeant Martin from the army reserve base. She's in charge of the Humvees and heavy trucks."

She stepped forward and held out her hand. She was a stocky woman with long blonde hair that was braided and pinned up under her cap. Her eyes were bright and alert. It was easy to see that her military service had caused her to witness the horrors of war. There were two scars that ran downward from her right ear and disappeared beneath the collar of her uniform.

As Chris extended his hand, she spoke. "Just call me Sandy, everyone does. I picked these drivers myself, sir. Each one of them served at least two tours of combat duty in either Iraq or Afghanistan. Most of us saw both. I've been talking with Bart about what we're up against, and he may be right. All vehicles have their limitations and these are no exception. Just so you know. I also picked each of these particular vehicles because they were the only ones with winches on the front. So we'll get through, one way or the other."

Chris stepped back before speaking. "So, you and your men want a cup of coffee first?"

Bart spoke up. "Thanks for the offer, but both my men and the military here have our own in the vehicles. Even though the general consensus is we aren't going to find any survivors up there, I think we need to operate as if there is. At least until we know for sure."

Chris again stepped up to shake Sandy's and Bart's hands once again before saying, "I agree sir. Just remember. It is very important that nobody else gets hurt up there. I don't want anyone hurrying, taking shortcuts or working when they're too tired to think. Please pass this along to each of your men."

Bart and Sandy nodded in agreement. Bart turned quickly to open and hold the door for Sandy, then exited right behind her. Once the door was completely closed, Sam and Chris moved to the large front window to watch the caravan move out.

"So he's married to your cousin, huh? That means you know him very well, then. He seems like a determined man."

"Saying Bart is determined is like saying the sun gives off a little light."

"That's good to know, Sam. What about the sergeant? Know much about her?"

"A little. We've worked together twice before on finding and retrieving some stranded hikers. I'd say that she is a female version of Bart. In my opinion, we couldn't have any better than these two."

"How long a drive is it from here? You know, before they get to the part we are afraid of?"

"Oh, I'd say about two hours or so. Depends on how the road is going through the south pass. It's only a gravel logging road. I've only been on it in summertime. I can't imagine what it will be like after all that snow melted up there. I'll give them about an hour and a half before I get them on the radio. I'll let you know just as soon as they're through the southern pass."

"Sounds good. Oh, just one more thing. You think you can track down that chopper pilot for me? I'd like to talk to him about any ideas he may have to help us out. You know. In case Bart is right and they can't get through."

"Captain Tallmen? Sure, Chris. He gave me his cell phone number. I'll get right on it."

•••

Sam was just killing time in his office by catching up on his weekly field maintenance reports as the phone rang. "Messa Field. Sam speaking. Can I help you?"

"This is Captain Tallmen. You called and left your number."

"Oh. Captain, this is Sam up at Messa Field. The FAA investigator you met would like to ask you some questions if you have the time, sir."

"Sure. Your name is Sam, right?"

"Yes sir. Chris is the IIC you met. If you'll let me put you on hold for just a second, I'll transfer you to his office."

There were a few well-rehearsed beeps from the phone before Sam was speaking to Chris.

"Chris. I have Captain Tallmen on line two. Oh, by the way. His name is Louis, but he goes by Lou. Just push the blinking Line Two button on the bottom of your phone."

"Thanks again, Sam." There was a click as he pushed the Line Two button. "Captain Tallmen?"

"Just call me Lou, please. You are Chris?"

"Yes, sir."

"Sam said you had some more questions for me, sir?"

"That's right. We have a logging crew and some reservists on their way up to the site right now. The problem is, the owner of the logging company doubts they will be able to get up that one logging road. He says the melting snow will have turned it into three or four feet of mud. The kind of mud that will surely bog down even the Humvees. That's when I remembered something that you had said. When we were all talking back here in the office, you had mentioned you might have some ideas on how to get our men up to the crash site. I was wondering what you had in mind."

"Well, sir. I was thinking that if your men had some portable transponders, then they could give me the frequency and I'd be able to home right in on the signal. I could just drop through the clouds with certainty that I wasn't going to come down on top of a tree. Then I could pick up your guys and their equipment a few at a time, and ferry them up the valley. I'd just fly below the clouds along the roadway, provided that the tree line is out far enough from the road. If the trees were too close, then we could send some guys up on foot with a transponder and they could find a big, open area close to the site. Once they turned on the unit, I could drop down from the clouds right on top of them. It would be a piece of cake, sir."

"Wow, Captain. That is a good idea. The problem is that the reservists and the loggers have already left. They are over an hour from here now. It's my fault. I should have followed up with you the minute you mentioned it in the office."

"Not to worry, Chris! I took the liberty of having Sandy pick up a transponder for each of the vehicles she was bringing up to you. They already have them. So all I need from you is a call when you're ready for me and Willy to head your way. It might be a good idea if you have Sam call our base commander and get it all set up now. Then we could just hop on up to your field and wait there with you guys."

Chris was even more impressed with this pilot now than he was before. This guy had a real head on his shoulders and took the initiative for action all on his own. Yes, he liked this pilot a lot.

"Well, Lou. I am very impressed with your idea, and even

MORE impressed that you have this already in place. I wish more people were like you. These events are very stressful and people like you really make a difference. Thank you for taking it upon yourself to do all this."

"No problem, sir. I'm glad to be of help."

"I'll have Sam call your base commander in a few minutes. Thanks again, Lou." There was a cordial exchange of goodbyes before the two men quietly hung up. Chris immediately called Sam and asked him to contact Lou's base commander.

Once the phone was back in its cradle, he picked up his coffee and made his way to the large window that looked out at the mountain. The dark clouds hung low here also, and he wondered what the drivers must be facing up in Cantor Basin. He stared out the window while he slowly sipped his coffee. So lost in thought was he, that he didn't notice that Sam had walked up until he heard him say, "OK, Chris. Things are set and moving."

Slightly startled, he turned and saw Sam standing beside him. He still had that same unlit cigar and his large coffee cup with the big letters 'SS' on it.

"That was very quick, Sam. Thanks."

"Well, sir. Don't give me the credit. It was that hotshot chopper pilot. Did you know that he was talking to you on his cell phone while he was standing just outside his base commander's office? He already had this cleared with his boss."

Chris's eyebrows rose and fell before a large smile spread across his face. "I really like this pilot. God, he is one step ahead of us it seems. I wish he had been around on my last assignment. What a nightmare that was." Chris was amazed as he watched Sam talk without dropping that cigar from his mouth.

"Bad, huh?"

"Sam. You can't imagine the group that was assembled. Such talent, but damn! They fought and tried to 'one up' each other constantly. I wasted valuable time trying to keep them all calmed down enough to work together. "

"So, you see that happen a lot in your line of work?"

"No, Sam, thank GOD I don't. But when it does happen, it makes my life a living hell for months. All I'm saying, is that this pilot is a real breath of fresh air after my last gig."

"Gig? Tell me, Chris. You a musician?"

Again, a big smile raced across his face before he answered Sam's very observant question. "Why yes I am, Sam. Or, at least I used to be when I was younger. Played guitars and a little keyboard. It was fun, but I ultimately took a real job. These days, I play every chance I get. Met some old farts like myself and we get together from time to time. You must be one too?"

Sam finally stopped chewing on his cigar.

"I was, and still do it every time I get a chance. Love it. Play guitars too, but mostly just play the banjo now. Got into bluegrass and have been doing it ever since. We should pick a little once this thing smooths out some."

Chris chuckled. "Who knows? That pilot may just take over completely, and we can spend our days goofing off!"

• • •

A small caravan of vehicles was slowly moving along the only road in Cantor Basin. They had easily negotiated their entry through the southern pass, and had been off the paved roadway for over 30 minutes. There was enough light for them to see without their headlights, but each vehicle still had them on.

The first vehicle was a military Humvee. It carried both of the leaders who were responsible for the mixture of military and civilian personnel that made up this team.

Sergeant Sandy Martin was talking while she drove. "So, Bart. I hope you know the rest of this road as well as you did that stretch through the pass back there."

"Well, Miss Sandy, I've been loggin' this valley for over 50 years. I bet I could drive this road blindfolded."

"Now Bart. You promised to stop with the 'Miss Sandy' stuff. I need you to just treat me like any other guy you work with. It's taken almost eight years of my life to get these stripes and finally be accepted by the men I've been stationed with. I understand it's a generational thing with you, sir. But, for me, it's an acknowledgement that I'm just the same as any guy that wears this uniform. No disrespect for your generation, of course."

The older man was looking at her while she drove and talked to him. He couldn't really see the scars on her neck because of the low light, but he remembered what they looked like in the light of the building when he first met her. His thoughts strayed to a nephew that was killed in the same country that gave her those scars. He had always respected his nephew and now knew that this woman was a soldier that also deserved his respect.

"You're right." He said with a slight pause before continuing, "You've earned it, Sarge."

She glanced at him for just a second to smile before the rocking of the vehicle demanded her attention once again. With her eyes back on the dirt road before them, she continued to speak.

"When will we hit that first spot you were worried about being washed out? Soon?"

Bart now had one hand on the dash as he was leaning forward so he could see. "You need to slow down. Our first small obstacle will be right around that bend. There is a small bridge we built a few years back. You need to be ready to stop on a dime if I call out."

"You got it. Just brace yourself before you call out."

She was barely moving as she rounded the bend. The sight before her caused her to stop without needing to be told. Since her vehicle had come to a stop, every other vehicle in the column did the same. They both just sat there looking at what was before them, not wanting to believe their eyes.

There in front of them was a newly-formed creek that was over ten feet wide and looked to be several feet deep. It ran out of the tree line on the left and all the way across the road before disappearing into the tree line on the right. Looking into the tree line, they saw many trees that had fallen across the creek because the water had eroded the soil from their roots. Though the smaller ones had been swept downstream, the taller ones were wedged between the densely grown trees on the other side. Their loose ends were bouncing up and down as the water pounded them.

This was causing a large and eerie cloud of mist that resembled the base of a large waterfall. The sound of the rushing water was so loud inside the Humvee that they both had to talk louder just to be heard.

She snickered. "The way that water's moving, I wish I had a kayak. Man, that water looks like small rapids."

Bart was talking as he opened his door. "I was afraid of this."

Hearing his door open, she put the vehicle in Park and got out herself. The loudness of the rushing water could be heard inside the vehicle, but now it was almost deafening. He had walked only a few feet in front of the vehicle before stopping to assess what was in front of them. She slowly walked up to his side as she looked first to the left, and then to the right. Once she was beside him, they both just stood and shook their heads in disbelief. Sandy was the first to speak.

"So where do you think that bridge of yours went?"

Without taking his eyes of the roaring water, Bart answered "As fast as that water is moving. I'll bet it was washed out the south end of the pass and is on its way to Arkansas!" This statement brought a few seconds of laughter.

They were both startled by the sudden appearance of several of the others who had walked up to see what was going on. Each man had staked out his own small spot to stand and shake his head while observing this spectacle of nature.

Sandy turned to Bart and yelled, "We will NEVER get these vehicles across this! We are going to have to switch to Plan B." With that said, she motioned for him to come back with her to the Humvee so they could talk. He nodded his head in agreement and watched her as she turned to go back. After taking one last look at the water, he kicked the ground with his boot and turned to join her.

Just after Bart closed his door, she honked and motioned to the men still standing by the water. They all turned and began hurrying back to their rides.

"So, Sarge. What was Plan B again?"

"We have to go back and find a spot with at least 100 yards between tree lines. Then we are going to turn on a transponder device that will give the chopper pilot a signal to home in on. He will bring his bird right down on top of us. Then it's just a matter of ferrying all the men and equipment up the valley, but staying under the clouds."

Bart looked up to see how low the clouds were before saying, "How hard is it going to be to find a pilot that is willing to do this?"

"Already have one. It was his idea."

"I don't know anything about flying, but this whole thing sounds very risky. He'll have to have nerves of steel to do it and

ROCKs for brains to try it."

She smiled before adding, "He's very good! I've ridden with him twice and he can do things with that bird that you can't believe! And yes, he does have nerves of steel. You'll like him."

"I know a great place just five minutes back from here. It will be perfect. Lots of room for the trucks and the chopper to land. It will be perfect for a staging area. Let's get turned around."

Sandy picked up the mike. "We are going to have to go back a ways, guys. Come forward and turn around where I do." There were a series of "Roger that, Ma'am" comments that were heard over the radio as Sandy swung her Humvee in a lazy arc to turn back down the road. Each vehicle did the same until they were all back in one column and headed back down the road in search of Bart's field.

Once there, she pulled off the road and led them along the tree line before stopping. She and Bart exited the vehicle and started gathering all the others together. Sandy didn't hesitate to start passing out assignments to her detail.

"Now listen up, guys. I have to run back outside the pass so I can use the radio to get the chopper and tankers headed this way. Peterson. Pick a spot along the trees and get the tents set up. Then better get some fires going. Everyone is going to get hungry in a bit and it's gonna get cold."

She turned to look at Bart. "You're welcome to ride along, sir."

Bart called out to his men.

"Smitty, you're the foreman here. Help these guys get this camp put together. You all know what it's going to be like out here when it gets dark." Smitty replied, "On it, boss!" before he turned and led some of his men back towards their supply truck.

Bart stepped closer to Sandy. "I think I'll tag along with you, Sergeant."

They made their way back to her Humvee. Once inside, she had the vehicle in gear and moving the moment Bart's door was shut. They hit the dirt road and she accelerated faster than he was expecting. He looked out the window.

"What's the hurry, Sergeant?"

"Well, sir. I know that the chances are slim that anyone survived that crash. But I want to get up there as soon as possible and know for sure. I'd hate to think that somebody is hurt and hanging on, with us so close. Know what I mean, sir?"

Bart was leaning up against his door and looking at her as she drove. It was obvious that she was a person who put others' welfare ahead of her own. The more he learned about her, the more he respected her.

"Yes. I know exactly what you mean. Your speed is fine with me, just don't forget to slow down where I showed you all those downed trees on our way up."

"I was thinking about that, too. We slid pretty good coming through there. Good point. That should be about two miles back."

"I'd say that's about right. You mind me asking what kinda tankers you're calling for?"

"Fuel trucks for the chopper. He's going to burn a lot of fuel making repeated short hops up and down the valley. Lots of takeoffs. He'll burn a lot of fuel lifting off so much. We had three trucks about two hours behind us. We'll probably run into them at the pass."

Bart asked, "They're driving up on their own. I hope they don't get lost."

"Well sir. The lead driver is Corporal Roger Parks. He says he worked in this basin for three summers under you. Said he knew this place very well."

Bart smiled. "Roger Parks! I haven't seen him for years. Good kid. Always wondered what happened to him."

"He was excited about seeing you, too sir. But don't tell him I said that. Seems he really admired you. We were in the same unit in Iraq. We were riding in a Humvee together and got hit with an IED. That's short for an improvised explosive device, or long for a homemade bomb. Vehicle flipped twice. We shared some cracked ribs together. Got to know him pretty well in the hospital. You're right about him."

Bart asked, "How so?"

"He's a good kid. A good soldier. They wanted us to stay in the hospital for four days, but we insisted they let us go back to our unit on the second day."

Sandy noticed that Bart's face had lost all expression before he turned and just looked out the window. Finally he started speaking while he kept looking out at the passing trees.

"So you got hit with an IED. I had a nephew that joined the Marines. We lost him to one of those IED things. He was somewhere in Iraq just like you. My sister and her husband took it very hard. He was their only child."

They both rode in silence for over ten minutes, she driving and him staring out the window. Finally he noticed where they were and he spoke up.

"Pull over by that rock and stop. We're close to the pass entrance here, and high enough for you to reach the tower on your radio."

Sandy came to a stop right where Bart had pointed, and immediately called the tower.

"Tower. This is Valley 1. You copy?"

There was a few seconds of static on the speaker in the vehicle before a voice came booming out at them. "Read you loud and clear, Valley 1."

"This is Sergeant Martin. We have a message for Sam and Chris. We can't move any of the vehicles up the valley floor. They need to send for the chopper. Over."

"Copy Valley 1. Be advised that chopper is refueling here at the field and will be headed your way in 10 minutes. Pilot will contact you by radio when he is above you. Copy?"

"Roger, tower. Over." Sandy leaned towards the dash and was adjusting something when Bart spoke.

"Sergeant. It took us 35 minutes to get from the camp to here. That chopper could be there before we get back to camp."

"Yeah, I thought about that too, sir."

"What are you doing now?"

"Switching back to our tactical channel. I need to get Peterson to set up the first transponder so the chopper can find the camp."

"I want him to tell my men to start picking out what equipment they think will be best to carry up there on the first trip. They need to tell Smitty. He's my foreman." Sandy nodded at him, held down the button on the microphone and started talking.

"This is Valley 1 calling Valley team. Come in. Peterson, you listening?"

After almost a minute of static, they finally heard the voice of a man that was obviously out of breath. "Peterson here, Sergeant. We were putting up a tent. Had to run over here when

I heard you."

"Listen, Peterson. The chopper could arrive at your location before we get back. I need you to set up and activate the first transponder. Now remember what we discussed. Be sure there are no trees within 30 yards of the unit. Set the frequency to the first one on the list. Then keep your ears sharp. We are on our way. Copy?"

Again, the speaker spat out static before a voice poured out of it. "Copy that, Sarge. 30 yards and first frequency on the list. Over."

Sandy was holding up her hand towards Bart as she continued. "And find the logger named Smitty. He's their foreman. Tell him that Bart wants the men to start picking out what minimum amount of equipment they need to take up on the first trip. Over."

"Tell Bart that Smitty is standing right here with me and heard the radio. Anything else, Sarge? Over."

"No. Just keep your ears open for that chopper. He should be contacting you before we get back. Over."

"Roger. See you in a few, Sarge."

With the call completed, she turned the steering wheel as she accelerated back onto the road for the return trip. The level of urgency had risen substantially in the vehicle. Bart was the only one that said anything at all on the return trip.

"Well. I guess we will see if this hotshot pilot of yours is as good as he thinks."

• • •

A lone chopper climbed higher into the sky to clear the mountain peaks of the southern pass into Cantor Basin. There before them was the huge cloud bank. It had been trapped by the high mountain peaks that surrounded the valley below.

Willy was intently eyeing the clouds that they were about to fly into. He made a halfhearted attempt at humor.

"Those trapped clouds look like the fluffy white top of a really big cupcake."

Captain Tallmen knew that Willy's nervousness would disappear as soon as he was engaged with cockpit activities.

"Willy. Set us to the TACT ONE channel and get the ground

team on the radio. We are going to need that transponder activated."

Willy set the channel while talking, "Setting to TACT ONE frequency. Valley Team, this is Rescue One. You copy?"

After a brief few seconds, a voice was heard over their radio, "Rescue One. This is Valley Team. Copy."

Willy asked, "Is that you, Peterson? Where's Sandy?"

"Sandy and Bart went to the southern pass to radio the tower. They're on their way back to camp now. I bet you boys want a signal to find us by. The unit is on, and transmitting on the first frequency on your list."

"We should be over the southern pass in 60 seconds." Willy looked up just as the chopper entered the outer edge of the cloud bank. After a quick glance at the pilot, he focused his eyes once again on the scope that would show them the way to the transponder below. There was a soft beep, then a blinking green light appeared on the scope before Willy spoke.

"Peterson. We have you on the scope. Beginning our descent. How low are the clouds?"

Peterson looked at the foreman of the loggers and asked, "How tall you think those trees are?"

"I'd say it's about 80 feet from ground to where they disappear into the clouds."

"Rescue one. Cloud bottoms about 80 feet from ground. Over."

The chopper dropped out of sight and into the thick clouds. The intensity level in the cockpit would have overwhelmed most men, but not this pilot. Willy quickly glanced out of the corner of his eye and saw the pilot calmly focused on the scope. Again, their windows were completely sealed by the dull white clouds that surrounded them. The craft was slowly sinking ever lower as Willy called out their altitude, so the pilot could concentrate on navigating to the transponder below.

The pilot commented to Willy, "Tell them to keep an eye on the bottom of the clouds above the unit. I want them to call out the minute they see our skids."

"Peterson. We need all of your eyes down there. Look up at the clouds above the unit. Call out the minute you see our skids. Over."

"Copy Rescue One. We are all looking for you. Over."

Just as Peterson said that, he heard the sound of Sandy's Humvee as it came roaring into the camp. He glanced over in time to see it slide into place behind one of the trucks. She and Bart came running over to him.

Sandy said, "We've been monitoring your conversation over the radio." She then turned and looked up at the clouds like everyone else before saying. "Bart, 20 bucks says he'll drop out of the clouds within 10 feet of that unit."

Bart was staring up at the ominously thick dark clouds and shaking his head. "I'm not a betting man, Sergeant. I know the technology these days is out of this world, but looking at those clouds, I just can't believe he's even trying it. Either he's very good or just plain crazy!"

A logger who heard Sandy's offer of a bet spoke up. "I'll take that bet, Sarge. I don't care how good he is, or how good the technology is. There is NO way he will be within 30 feet of that unit."

Sandy answered without taking her eyes off of the clouds. "You're on, sir."

The pilot calmly said, "That unit is giving us the altitude of the camp, so we must be a little over 100 feet above it. Give them a heads-up on the ground. Our skids should be visible in a few seconds."

Willy immediately keyed his microphone. "Ok, boys. We should be visible in less than five seconds. Over."

All the men in camp were looking up at the clouds directly above the center of the landing area. Peterson's hand was poised with his thumb on the button of the radio. Slowly, two parallel metal bars dropped out of the clouds directly above the transponder. One of the loggers pointed at them. "There it is!"

The bottom of the chopper doors were coming into view just as Peterson pushed the button and said, "We see you, Captain. You're directly over the unit and no trees for 100 yards in all directions. Nice flying, sir."

The chopper cabin dropped out of the clouds and the pilot immediately switched to visual flight the moment he could see out of his window. His first reaction was to stop their descent and hover so he could look around. The men on the ground were witness to the strangest sight their eyes had ever seen. The chopper blades were still hidden in the thick clouds. With the entire body of the craft visible, it seemed to be just hanging motionless from the clouds. There were cheers and laughing from the ground teams as they all began to breathe a little easier. Slowly the pilot swung around to face the men on the ground. They watched as the chopper backed up about 20 feet so it would not land directly on the transponder that guided them here.

"Well, Mr. Willy. I'd say that went very well. What do you say we get her on the ground and find some coffee?"

Willy nodded. "Yes, sir. That sounds damn good to me, too!"

The pilot gently landed his bird just as he had done hundreds of times before. With the chopper resting back on Mother Earth, the two men were busy turning knobs and flipping switches as they went through their well-rehearsed dance of shutting down all the ship's systems. There were a dozen men cautiously standing just out of range of the still slowly-rotating blades. The Captain was closing his door as Willy rounded the front of the chopper and walked right up to him. "By the way. That was some damn good flying, sir. I mean it!"

"Thanks Willy," said the pilot as he looked around with a confused look on his face.

Willy noticed that and asked, "What's wrong, sir? You look concerned about something."

The Captain took a step towards Willy and slapped him on the shoulder. "It's not concern. It's pure relief. Well to tell the truth, I didn't really think this would work. I figured we'd bite the big one in the trees." He then laughed and walked off towards the ground crew.

Willy stood there for a few seconds with the Captain's words ringing in his ears. Then he spun and started running to catch up with him as he yelled, "What? What do you mean you didn't think this was going to work! Hey, man. I take it all back. You are just one crazy flying fool!"

The Captain snickered and kept on walking.

• • •

As Sandy accepted her winnings from the logger, she heard the sound of Willy's voice getting louder. She quickly tucked her spoils into the vest pocket of her fatigues before turning to watch the two flyers approach. The pilot had a big grin on his face and was apparently ignoring all of Willy's complaining.

"And another thing, buddy. Since it's my ass up there too, I think you need to show some courtesy by letting me know what is really going on. I don't think that is too much to ask. Do you, Sergeant?"

She held up both hands before saying, "Wow, I don't know what you two are talking about and I don't want to know." Her smile and playful demeanor signaled to the Captain that she would play along with whatever ruse he was perpetrating on poor Willy.

The Captain winked at her before speaking. "Seems Willy here thought this stunt was going to be a piece of cake. But just like you and I were talking about it yesterday, I wasn't sure it would work at all. So I told him. Who knew he'd get this upset?"

Willy stopped talking and just stared at Sandy for a few seconds. Then his face displayed a look of disbelief before he slowly started speaking again.

"Wait a minute. Sandy? You knew he didn't think this would work? My gosh! I've known you for a year now and you didn't think to warn me about this?" He shook his head and stared at her.

She tried to appear serious as she said, "I just thought that all you flyboys were crazy. It never dawned on me that you would be interested in how dangerous it was. My bad." Her blank expression only lasted a few seconds. Then she couldn't stand it any longer and a small laugh preceded a big smile.

Upon seeing her smiling and laughing, Willy squinted his eyes tightly. Then it hit him that the pilot was joking. He slowly wiped one hand over his eyes before smiling.

"Ha, ha. I guess you got me again. I really wish you wouldn't do that. I'm getting some coffee." He nodded his head at Sandy and left in search of a hot cup.

The pilot stepped closer to the sergeant and softly said, "You know. I bet he thinks I'm actually suicidal."

A huge smile spread across her face before she said, "I hate to tell you this, but we all think you're suicidal!"

He stared at her with an exaggerated 'What do you mean?'

look. Then he smiled and said "Come to think of it, I've been told that a lot over the years."

Sandy leaned closer and said, "Well. Everyone can't be wrong, sir."

He looked puzzled and then glanced down at the ground before quietly saying, "Maybe I am suicidal." Then his usual smile and demeanor returned. "Where's the coffee?"

Peterson called out, "Coffee is in that tent sir. And Sarge, I've been setting that other tent up to use as a command post. There are two tables and some chairs in there already." She waved and called out, "Thanks."

This said, she turned to Bart. "We need to start talking about how this is going to play out. Which of your men are going up first, and what equipment they need to take with them."

Bart looked around and called out, "Smitty! We need you over here."

The logger was helping some others unload equipment from the back of one of the trucks. Hearing his name, he turned and waved. Once his other hand was free, he came running over to Bart's side. "Yes, boss?"

"Did you get the men to start picking out the bare minimum of equipment for this first trip up?"

"Yessir. We have staged it all behind one of the trucks. It's in three small groups. You want to take a look at it and see if you agree?"

Bart talked to Sandy over his shoulder as he began walking away with Smitty. "Be right back, Sarge. I just want to take a real quick look at what they have picked out. Smitty and I will find you in a few minutes." He and Smitty walked quickly down to the second truck and disappeared behind it.

Sandy stood alone and surveyed all the activity going on in the camp. There were two loggers that appeared to be oiling the chains on several large chainsaws. She noticed that most of her men were busy putting up the last of the four large tents they brought up. The distinctive aroma of a freshly started fire attracted her attention to a lone soldier. He had finally gotten a large fire started about 20 feet in front of what would be the mess tent. The smell of coffee told her that Lewis had the big pot brewed already. The sound of pans clanking against each other told her that he was also setting up the galley to start cooking. This was good. These men were going to be hungry later, and hot food was what they would all need to get through the cold night up here.

As she was watching the fire roar to life, the pilot emerged from the tent with two cups of coffee. The cold valley air was causing a lot of steam to roll off the top of each cup. He approached and held one out for her. "Thought you might like this." Then he positioned himself by her side and started his own survey of the camp.

With both of them looking straight ahead, they began talking between sips of the hot liquid.

"Oh, that's hot! Corporal Lewis only knows one temperature for coffee. Lava!" She gently took another, smaller sip. "Captain. You mind if I ask you a question sir?"

"Shoot, Sarge."

"Why do you razz Willy so much?"

The Captain chuckled before answering. "'Cause I like him."

"You know he's never been in combat. I don't think he really knows how to take you sir."

"Yeah, I know. He was trained on active duty, but never left the States. He's been a civilian chopper pilot for over five years. He only joined the reserves so he could fly one of those babies." The pilot raised his cup in the direction of the chopper. "The reserve commander wants me to get him qualified as soon as possible. I figure this little outing should jump-start his training a lot! What do you think?"

"Yes. If you don't get him killed first."

The pilot turned his head to look at her, and she turned to look at him. He smiled as usual and said, "Well, maybe. But look at all the fun he's having!"

They both stood there laughing and sipping their dangerously hot coffee. Finally, Bart and Smitty emerged from behind the trucks.

Sandy yelled, "Grab some coffee and come on in the tent." Bart waved as he and his foreman headed for the mess tent. Sandy and the Captain turned to make their way into the command tent.

Inside they saw that Peterson had set up three long folding tables. One along each side of the tent and the third was dead center in the middle of the tent. There was a box of what appeared to be rolled-up maps sitting on one end of the middle table. The Captain stopped by the box and pulled one of the maps out of it.

"These your maps, Sarge?"

"No sir. I believe they must belong to Bart. His foreman was working closely with Peterson, so he'd know this was going to be the command post."

The Captain took a quick sip and then dropped the map back into the box. They both looked towards the tent opening as Bart and Smitty entered, carrying their cups of coffee. They walked to the table end with the box.

Smitty said, "When I heard this was going to be the command center, I brought your maps on in, boss."

Bart sat his cup down and started digging through the box before saying, "Ah. Here it is." He reached to the bottom of the box and began feeling around with one hand. Finally he smiled and pulled out a small leather bag. It was small, but its weight shook the entire table when Bart dropped it. The sudden loud bang caused everyone in the tent to jerk their heads in Bart's direction.

"Sorry! Slipped out of my hand."

Bart loosened the strap on the little bag and dumped out four small rocks. The Captain immediately reached over and picked one up to examine it.

"Is this what I think it is?" He was turning it around in his hand and looking closely at all sides of it.

Bart started laughing, "You'd make a poor prospector, Captain. That's Fool's Gold. Not worth a penny. I just use them for paperweights to hold down the corner of my maps."

When the Captain finally stopped staring at the stone in his hand, he looked up. Bart had already put the other three stones on the corners of the map. He was holding his hand out towards the Captain. "Trust me, son. It's not real." The Captain took one last quick look at the stone, and then slowly passed it over to Bart. He placed the forth stone on its respective corner before beginning to speak.

"Let me show you what we're looking at here." Bart put a finger on the map. "We are here. This is the road and here is the missing bridge. Now this is the only road in the valley, and it winds right up the middle of it. Goes all the way to the north face. As you can see, the tree line is a ways back from the road itself."

Hearing this, the Captain interrupted with a question. "Excuse me, sir. But exactly how far are those trees from the roadway?"

Bart kept his hand on the map while he answered him. "At least 30 yards on both sides. Plus you have 10 yards for the road itself. How much do you need?"

The Captain answered quickly, "I've flown through tighter spots. That will be plenty." Then he pointed to a spot on the map. "But that looks like they are a lot closer there and there."

Bart once again looked the Captain in the eye. "You're right, Captain. It's very close at both of those locations. Barely five yards away on both sides. I assume that is not going to be enough for your blades."

The Captain leaned his head out and directly over the map before speaking. "I'm not sure of the accuracy of this map. I just need to know how far till it opens back up."

Bart squinted his eyes at the pilot before replying. "I update this map at the beginning and end of every season. It's accurate." He then looked down before pointing to the first spot. "This is about 30 feet or less. You can see the road is straight, and you'll have a clear view of where you need to hop over to. It also opens up very quickly."

He then looked up at the pilot. "After seeing you fly that machine of yours this morning, I have no doubt that you can get by this spot, son." He then slid his finger to the other spot. "But here's the real problem. See how the road takes an immediate right? It travels about 50 feet before angling off left again. Then you have about 60 feet from here to here. You will not be able to see the spot you need to jump to. There will be no way to judge how far or where you're coming down."

Bart paused. "Looks to me like you'll have to pull another one of those stunts of yours like you did coming in here."

The Captain nodded in agreement. "Looks that way to me too, sir. I'll have to land before it and let someone walk through there to set up a transponder in the next open area. Then we'll hop over and pick him up before we scoot on up to the crash site. Well, of course we will be dropping your guys off on the roadway. They will have to hike through the trees for about a mile and a half to get to the crash site."

Sandy commented, "Looks good on paper. But the devil is in the execution, as usual. Do we know which men are going, and what they're taking?"

Bart looked at Peterson. "You're on."

"Right, boss. Well, yes we do. They are all ready and so is the equipment. They even have two small tents and some food, just in case we can't get them out before nightfall."

The pilot spoke. "I'll get them out of there. Once that transponder is in place, I can come straight to them any time they need out. I can also bring them anything that will fit inside the bird."

Sandy added, "I'm sending Williams too. He's an EMT in the civilian world and did two combat tours with us as our medic. Good guy to have along."

Bart added, "All of my men are trained in advanced first aid. I make sure they all recertify each winter while we can't work. Where we work, the closest hospital can be hours away. Your medic can count on each of them."

Willy stuck his head into the tent. "Captain. They topped off the tanks on the chopper. She's ready to fly, sir."

The Captain looked at Bart, "Have your men grab their gear and meet us at the chopper. Willy. Go on and get us through the pre-flight, but don't start her up yet. That land out there is not flat by the chopper. Means the blade tips are closer to the ground than is safe. I want everyone onboard before we let 'em spin."

Peterson looked at Sandy and spoke before he headed out of the tent.

"Sarge. I'm going to grab a couple of guys to help load the gear. I had them pick out more than they could carry. I thought they could leave the extra stuff at the landing site. That way we could start stockpiling things up closer to the crash site. You know. A little more each trip."

Sandy asked, "What about a tent to cover the extra gear? It will be just sitting out in the open."

Peterson answered her, "Small tent is going with them on this trip. All we need is for somebody on the next hop to set it up. Smitty and I decided that the first group is just going to take the medic and head on to the site. I know that everybody thinks there are no survivors and all. But it just seems they should hot foot it on in, just in case."

This comment triggered a few seconds of silence in the tent. Each person had their own gruesome mental picture of what they would find up there. The massive loss of lives will be almost unimaginable. They all knew this would be one of the toughest things they have ever had to do. What their eyes witnessed in the next few hours would be with them for the rest of their lives.

Sandy said, "Okay, guys. Let's do this!"

As each one exited the tent, they had the same thought. There is NO WAY they would find any survivors.

Chapter 4

A LITTLE 'WALKABOUT'

ED SLOWLY OPENED his eyes. How did it get so light so quickly? He couldn't understand it. He had just blinked, and it went from dark to bright. Had he fallen asleep? No! He knew for sure that he'd just blinked his eyes and now it was morning. How can that be? He saw that Martha was asleep so he sat up quietly. The sudden onslaught of morning brightness had him confused.

While he was pondering this thought, he heard Martha say "Good morning." He turned to watch her as she sat up beside him and started rubbing her eyes.

"Thanks for letting me sleep. I must have really been tired. I can't believe it's morning already." She leaned over towards him and slid one arm underneath his. Her other hand gently fell into his hand, and her head tipped onto his shoulder. "This feels good. Did you get any sleep?"

"I didn't think so, but I must have. It was so weird. One minute it is total darkness, except for the light from the fires and the next. Well, I swear I just blinked my eyes and it was light. I can't explain it, but there's something strange about it."

"Well, Ed. Hello? You were in a devastating airplane crash last night. Remember? Of course it feels strange. We could both be suffering from shock. Or maybe we have some type of post traumatic crash syndrome?"

Ed was still staring straight ahead with a very strange look on his face. Then her words began to sound plausible to him. He nodded as he realized she must be right.

"That's true. We both must have hit our heads several times. It's a miracle we both survived at all. What you said makes sense though." With this mystery solved, his eyes focused on the wreckage in front of them. "Wow! I didn't even notice that the fires have all gone out."

They both began looking around at the devastation. Only 40 feet away from them, they could now clearly see a huge impact crater from where the plane had hit. There were not any really big pieces of the fuselage to be seen anywhere. In fact, most of the debris was farther away from this big hole in the ground than they were. Now that it was light outside, they could easily see the mangled remnants of cabin seats everywhere. The ground was strewn with all sizes of what appeared to be pieces of aluminum that once had been the plane's skin.

Ed was focused on the tree trunks that formed an arena around them. He could see that every tree trunk was blackened from the fires, and most were still giving off smoke. Martha's attention had been drawn to a long ditch that stretched from the crater outward past them.

"I wonder what made this long ditch. Whatever it was, it was long." She had twisted part way around so she could see how far it ran.

Ed didn't even need to look.

"It was one of the wings." He was now twisting to look. "The engine should be somewhere close. Ah, yes." He was pointing now. "There's what's left of the one that was on this wing. Hmm. I would have thought it would have bounced farther than that. We must have come almost straight down for it to be so close."

Martha was now pointing at the tree line beyond the engine. "It may have hit those trees and bounced back."

Ed saw that there were several huge trees still standing. Each one was broken and splintered about ten feet up from the ground. The tops of two of them had fallen over, and were stuck in the branches of the trees behind them.

"I think you're right about that, Martha. The trees would have surely bent backwards before springing forward and throwing the engine back to where it is now. Makes sense to me."

She turned around and smiled at him. Her eyes were sparkling. "Thanks."

She was glanced at him while thinking that Ed was the first guy that had ever taken what she said seriously. He really listened to what she'd suggested, thought about it, and then acknowledged that she was right. She could really get used to being with this guy. He was different. She took a last look back at the engine, and that was when she saw what she had been so afraid of seeing. She gasped, put her hand over her eyes and said, "Ed! Look!"

He turned and saw her sitting with her eyes covered. "Look at what? What's wrong?"

"Behind us. Look to the left of the engine. Is that what I think it is?"

He quickly twisted around again to look, and there it was. A few feet from the engine was a mangled seat with an arm sticking out from underneath. His eyes fell upon Martha as she sat there with her head down. As he scooted closer and put his arm around her, he felt her shaking.

"Martha. Martha. It's going to be okay. You knew that this was probably going to happen. You aren't going to be able to avoid seeing things like that. There were over a hundred people on the plane. There have to be bodies everywhere around us. You have to be brave."

"I know," she said softly. "Oh my God! It just dawned on me that we were sitting here last night talking about the fire and Christmas. These bodies were there all that time." Her voice was breaking as she said, "We slept here and they were right there. I can't believe it!" She looked up at him with tears in her eyes. "I'm such a bad person. How could I be such a bad person?"

He was shocked to hear her say this. "You're not a bad person. Why would you think that? We survived. They didn't. It wasn't your fault."

"But I wouldn't let you walk around and look last night. Just because I was being a silly girl. How do you know that there wasn't someone alive and hurt out there? And I wouldn't let you walk around and see. I'm such a bad person. I was only thinking about myself." She had a blank look on her face now, and was staring down at the ground. Then her head jerked upwards and she looked at him.

"We should look around for survivors. Come on!"

He held her shoulders tightly and said softly, "We don't have to do that. I did it last night after you went to sleep. You suddenly rolled over and let go of my hand. So, I got up and looked around. I walked all over. I even walked around the tree line and stopped every few feet to listen. I never heard anyone moaning or calling out for help. Nothing. Then I came back over and sat down by you."

She looked at him and asked, "You went out into the dark by the trees? Weren't you scared? After what we saw last night? Are you crazy?"

Ed shook his head. "No. I didn't go into the dark. I thought about it, but didn't do it. Anyway. I never heard anyone at all. You and I are the only ones that made it."

"So you did see other bodies around. Didn't you?"

He paused for a few seconds. "Yes. I saw several scattered around. There seems to be a lot more of them on the other side of the crater. Don't know why. You really don't want to go over there. There are some really bad things over there. Since I didn't see the one by the engine, I would bet there are a lot more that I couldn't see in the dark. Maybe you should sit here and let me walk around now that it's light. Would you be okay with that?"

"You really wouldn't mind if I just sit here while you do that?"

"Of course not. I'll be right back."

She watched as he walked around. It was obvious when he had spotted a body. He stopped and moved his head all around as he was trying to make sure they were dead. Though he only looked for a second or two most of the time, he occasionally stopped a little longer. She wondered what he was seeing that made him hesitate so long. Once, he even knelt down for a few seconds before moving on. Whatever it was that he was looking at, she didn't want to know.

This went on for over 30 minutes before he was finally back by her side. Her curiosity about him kneeling was just too much and finally got the better of her.

"Why did you kneel down over there? What did you see?"

"It was really odd. There is a man, well, what's left of him. But he has a smile on his face. His eyes were closed and he was smiling. It was the strangest thing I have ever seen. Kind of looked like he was just asleep, and could wake up any minute." Ed's face showed his bewilderment as he recalled what he had seen.

"What did you mean when you said 'What's left of him'? Is part of him missing?"

Ed paused. "Do you really want me to answer that? It's not a mental image you need in your head."

With all the destruction that surrounded them, why would she want to know such a gruesome thing? Was it just human curiosity? She now realized what she had asked and shook her head 'No'. There was no way to escape the harsh realities of their current situation. She wondered if this was what soldiers on a battlefield went through after the battle was over. Even with her real fear of what she might see, she still found herself morbidly curious about the fates of the others that were on the plane. These thoughts were consuming her very soul and she desperately wanted them to stop.

All of her adult life had been filled with her wondering if she was depressed and if so, why? But here in this place, she finally realized what true depression must be like. Sitting and looking around, she now knew that she had never been depressed. In fact, she had been happy most of her life. But what she had been feeling for all those years was loneliness.

She had always wanted a man to share her time on earth with. Everyone wants someone to walk hand in hand through all of life's trials. Staring into Ed's eyes, she wondered if she had finally found such a man. The thoughts of her ugly surroundings disappeared and gave way to a smile. Then came a desire to cut up with him again.

"So he looked like he could wake up any minute? What would you have done if he'd opened his eyes?"

Ed smiled. "I'd have messed in my pants, and then ran!"

She playfully slapped him on the shoulder. "Now there's a mental image I didn't need either."

• • •

Again they were sitting side-by-side and smiling. Both knew that if they were discovered at this moment, the rescuer would think they had gone mad. After several minutes of silence, Ed finally posed a question.

"Are you getting hungry or thirsty?"

She thought a moment before answering. "It's odd, but no. I'm fine. You?"

"I'm fine, too." He looked up at the sky and then asked, "You cold?"

Shaking her head and smiling, she answered, "Nope. I feel fine. It must have warmed up once it got light."

Ed took a deep breath and clapped his hands together before saying, "Well, we can't just sit here all day. Want to go walk around a little? If we go straight back past that engine, we can get into the woods without you having to see anything, uh, unpleasant. What do you say?"

She was almost on her feet before she answered.

"Yes. Sounds like a very good idea."

He stood and started to brush off the back of his jeans when he noticed that there wasn't anything on them. A quick glance at the ground where he'd been sitting showed no sign of anyone having sat there. The spot was charred black, just like every inch of the ground around them was. "That's odd," he said, as he raked the ground with his shoe. "Look. I can't even stir the burnt ground with my foot."

Martha was now looking down and trying the same thing as she spoke. "That *is* odd. It must all be stuck together. What's going on?"

Ed made a deep throated 'Hmm' as he turned his head from side to side. Then his eyes lit up. "Stuck together. That's it. Maybe this ground has a lot of sand in it, and the intense heat from the fire melted it into glass. That's got to be it."

Martha looked up and added, "Maybe it's been holding the heat in the ground and that is why we aren't cold yet."

Ed was nodding his head as he once again made her day by agreeing with her assessment. "Yep, that sounds right." He looked at her and smiled. "Anyone ever tell you how smart you are, Martha?"

The dazzle in her eyes answered his question before her

words did. "Why no they haven't, Ed. Thank you for saying that."

"They haven't? You've made some very accurate observations around here. I can't believe you've never been told that before."

God, she liked this guy. "Oh, stop. You're going to make me blush."

With that said, she reached out and took his hand before they started walking towards the trees. Ed purposely positioned himself so that she couldn't see that hand sticking out from under that mangled cabin seat. He also distracted her by pointing in the opposite direction at something that really wasn't there.

Finally they were in the trees and away from the devastation of the crash. They were only a few feet into the trees when both felt a little relief to be out of it. Martha was the first one to mention it as they walked slowly in these more peaceful surroundings.

"It feels good to be out here like this, doesn't it?"

"Out here or do you really mean, out of there?" He points his thumb over his shoulder at the mess they were leaving behind.

"I suppose you're right. It was bothering me more than I wanted to admit. But it seems so nice to be out here. Nothing is burned out here, and there isn't all those little pieces of the plane around to remind us how we got here." She stopped and faced him before continuing. "I feel like a huge weight has been lifted off me. You?"

He looked into the trees behind her for a second, nodded 'Yes', and spoke.

"I guess I do understand what you are feeling. I don't think it was bothering me as much as you, but I do feel more relaxed out here. Yeah. I do." As he looked down into her face, he saw that her eyes had locked onto something behind him. Before he could even ask what she was staring at, she said "Oh, no." before running back towards the crash site. He spun around and shouted at her. "What? Where you going? What's wrong?"

She had run only a few feet back into the crash area before stopping to stare down at the ground. Ed came running up to find her looking at a small stuffed rabbit on the ground. She started talking without looking up.

"I talked with the little girl that had this rabbit. Her mother was taking her to a family reunion. She was such a cute little thing. So bubbly and full of life." Martha looked up and from side to side. "I wonder where she is. Did you see any children when you were walking around?"

"Yes, but they were all on the other side of the crater. I don't know why, but there are only a few bodies over on this side. The rest seemed to be bunched up on the other side."

Ed saw the sorrow in Martha's face. He wanted to get her away from all of this. He stepped closer to her side, placed his arm across her shoulders and tried to lead her back into the trees. She only took one step before stopping.

"I want to keep that little rabbit. Maybe I can find her family and give it to them." She turned to face Ed before adding, "Does that sound crazy? Tell me the truth. Does it?"

He was looking into her eyes and feeling something that he had never felt before. He'd been around people that were hurt before, but he never felt their pain. Why was her grief affecting him? He hadn't seen this little girl. He started to answer but found he was a little choked up. He hesitated before he spoke.

"No. I don't think that sounds crazy at all."

With that said she spun around, took a step, bent over and picked up the white furry toy. She held it gently in both of her hands. Ed was watching her face as she was smiling. It was a small smile, but a smile nonetheless. He was glad to see her emotions were settling down. She slowly lifted it up to her chest as if to hug it and that was when he saw it. He thought to himself 'Oh my GOD!'

There on the back of this fluffy white reminder of a little girl, was a bad sign of the fate of its previous owner. There was dried blood all along the toy's back. He stepped closer to try and take it before she saw it, but he was too late. Martha had noticed Ed's wide-eyed look and she instinctively turned the stuffed animal around to see what he was looking at.

Seeing the dried blood on it everywhere, she immediately dropped it. A few moments passed before she raised her hands in preparation for a blood curdling scream. Ed was helpless to do anything but watch. Everything went into slow motion from his point of view as he watched the little rabbit seem to slowly float down to the ground. Then the drawn-out sound of her horrified scream continued as she ran right past him and into the woods. His feeling of slow motion ended abruptly as he watched the fluffy toy bounce once on the ground before coming to rest with the bloodstain visible for all to see.

With his attention back to normal speed, he heard the full volume of her screaming. He turned to see that she was already several feet into the trees and running at full speed. Never being much for running, he had a hard time catching up to her. Her adrenalin had given her speed and stamina that Ed found hard to match. His legs were being driven faster and faster by his wanting to console her. But her legs were driven by a desire to get away from something terrible. This chase lasted for several minutes.

Finally her desire to run away had been replaced by a need to stop and cry. Ed found her sitting on a fallen log, crying her eyes out. She was holding her stomach with both hands while rocking back and forth.

Ed stopped just short of her and bent over to put his hands on his knees. Holding this position for just a few seconds, he realized that this action was more out of habit than a need to catch his breath. Actually, he didn't feel tired at all. How could this be? He remembers being winded just walking up a flight of stairs. Yet here he had just ran a small marathon with no ill effects? It must be the fresh mountain air or maybe his adrenalin was also in overdrive. Or maybe, just maybe, this girl was making him more of a man than he had ever been before.

While he stood there looking at her suffering, he felt a strange pain in his chest. Not a physical pain, but one that he had never felt before in his life. This mysterious pain grew more unbearable with every sob that she made. He didn't understand it, and he didn't know what to do about it. All he did know was that her tears were painful to him.

Slowly he approached the log, paused for a second and then sat down beside her.

All that came to mind was to say, "Martha. Please don't cry. I can't stand to see you crying like this. I want to help you, but I don't know what to do." After saying this, he sat there wondering what to do next. Then, without warning, she fell over and placed her head in his lap. Her crying had softened, but she was still holding her stomach with both hands. Without even thinking, he started to gently stroke her hair and spoke in the softest voice he had ever used.

"You go on and cry now. It's all right. Let it out. I'm not going anywhere until you're ready."

● ● ●

Almost an hour had passed while Ed stroked Martha's hair in silence. She had long since stopped crying, and had been lying there motionless. Her sudden movement caused him to stop, but her hand grabbed his before she rolled over onto her back. She held his hand to her temple and looked up at him.

"Thanks. I'm better now. A lot has happened to us since yesterday. I'm so thankful to have survived, but I almost feel guilty because those others did not. Does that make sense?"

"I know exactly how you feel. Those same thoughts came to mind each time I found another body last night. I'm sorry for them, really. But I'm alive, there is nothing I can do for them, and, well." He just stopped talking and looked away.

She tugged on his hand until he looked back at her again. "What? You started to say something else. Tell me. Please."

He smiled and stammered a bit. "Well, I , I , I, I don't want you to get the wrong idea. It's not that I am happy that the crash happened. It's just that, that . . . "

She was smiling. "What? Come on and tell me."

"It's just that I'm happy that the crash brought us together. I'm happy that I met you. I know that all these people have died, but I met you. There. I've said it."

She pulled his hand to her lips and kissed the back of it before saying, "I've had that same thought about you. Remember last night when I talked about us pretending to be sitting by a fire at Christmas? I was actually very happy to be there with you. I knew that fire represented the lost lives of all those people, but I couldn't help being happy to be sitting there beside you. I've been happy being with you all day today, too.

"You know, I can see what really hit me so hard about the little girl's rabbit. She was so precious and young with her whole life ahead of her. Now she's dead and here I am being happy about spending time with you. It's such a para.. para.. What's the word?"

"Paradox. Is that the word you are looking for?"

"Yes, paradox. That's the very word I was trying to say." To

Ed's total amazement, she kissed his hand once more then sat up and scooted right up to his side.

"Let's both agree on a few things. Okay?"

"Sure. What?"

"First. Let's agree that we both are sad about all the people that died here last night. Second. Let's agree that we both have the right to be happy that we didn't. I think it is only normal to be happy that you survive a catastrophe. Third. And this is a biggie. Let's agree that we are both happy that we have met. No matter that it was because of such a horrible accident. We have the right to be happy about this. What do you say? Okay?"

He thought a moment about what she had just said, then he slowly nodded 'yes' before speaking.

"I do agree with that. None of what you said is showing any disrespect for the dead. I think we still have to be solemn when we are around the crash site and bodies. But it is normal and okay for us to have fun other than that."

"Good! Then I'm ready to go back. I don't really want to, but we need to get back. That is where the rescuers will come. I hope they do come soon. The sooner I'm out of this place, the better I'll like it." She noticed Ed's face had lost his smile.

"What's wrong?"

He hesitated so long that she was just about to ask again, when he finally said, "I was just wondering about something."

"What?"

"Well. I've read about people that experience major traumatic events together, and often form a kind of bond because of it. But the bond's an illusion. Not real at all. They say it's just a coping mechanism our minds use to get through a really stressful experience. What if that is what we're feeling?"

She lost her smile as she took in what he had just said. Then her head began to shake from side to side as if she were saying 'No'.

"I don't think so. But even if that is the case, I don't care. I want to enjoy this feeling as long as I can. The only alternative is to be sad while we sit around waiting to be rescued. Real or not, I'd rather feel like this."

"Good. Me too."

They both got up and looked around before starting back.

"Ed? Which way did we come from? It all looks the same."

Ed looked around. With the low hanging clouds and all of these tall trees, there really weren't any good landmarks to go by. He thought about how he came running up to see her on that log. Ah yes, now he remembered. "We came from that direction. Come on." He held out his hand and she gladly slipped hers into his.

He said, "We couldn't have come that far. We should recognize sights along the way if we just pay attention."

She had a serious look on her face while they walked. "I don't know, Ed. I hope you're right, but every direction looks the same. All these trees are the same size, and each one stretches up into those clouds. Please tell me you used to be a Boy Scout."

"As a matter of fact, I was." What he didn't say was that he only went on one camping trip with the troop. All the older boys kept dropping his tent during the night because they thought it was funny. He had quit the moment they got home. Oh well. She didn't need to know that. He was sure they came this way, so all they had to do was walk for a while and they'd get back okay. How hard could it be?

• • •

They had been walking for over an hour now. The topic of conversation had started on what each one did for a living, but had quickly moved on to the people that they both had worked with. Each of them had been telling funny things that had happened or had been said by their co-workers. Each time Martha questioned if they were going the right way, Ed had quickly answered 'yes'. Though he tried to seem confident in his answer, she had noticed that he was also looking around more and more with each question she asked. Finally, she stopped.

She turned to him and playfully asked, "Are we lost?"

Again, Ed answered, "No. I'm sure it is just up here a little farther."

"But Ed? We've been walking now for over three times as long as it took to get to that log. I would think we would be back to the crash site by now if we were going the right way."

Ed stopped and turned around to face her.

"Martha. We were running full speed coming out, but we are walking and talking going back. We are probably moving at least one third of the speed we ran at. I'm sure this is the way. We ran straight out, so we are walking straight back. It's going to be okay."

Now she remembered something that was proof that they hadn't run in a straight line. With one finger tapping her lips, she was obviously trying to remember something as she slowly turned her head from side to side. She started speaking without looking at Ed.

"I just remembered that I turned left because there was a large tree that had fallen over and was stuck in the branches of two other trees. I turned because I didn't feel safe about running underneath that tree. I thought it might fall on me. Now I don't remember us walking past that tree yet. Kinda makes me think we're not going the right way."

She looked at Ed. His face was also showing signs of concern.

Seeing his questioning look prompted her to continue. "You saw that tree when we were running. Didn't you? And now that I mentioned it, you don't remember walking past it either. Do you?" She was not angry and her voice still sounded playful, but concerned. Though she really liked the fact that he listened to what she said, this was one time that she was hoping he wouldn't agree with her conclusion.

"I do remember that tree, and you turning left to run around it. And, no, we haven't walked past it." He looked down and lightly stomped one foot before mumbling "damn it". Then he took a deep breath before saying, "'I hate to admit this, but we may be lost. Everything looks the same, no matter which way you look. It's all the same."

She really didn't want to hear this, but at least he was honest about it. Though she was not angry, she did not feel playful any longer. Ed could hear it in her voice as she said, "I'm not blaming you, Ed. It isn't your fault. I was just thinking out loud."

Ed immediately spoke up. "I know you didn't say it was my fault. But it is! I'm the one that acted so SURE of myself. So sure that I knew which way to go. Now look what I've done. I've gotten us lost. The rescue people could be there right now, and they won't know we survived because of my ego!"

"No, no, no, Ed. It's not even remotely your fault. It's MINE! I'm the one that went running off into the woods like a crazy person. You were only running after me to try and help me. Now I've gone and got us both lost. It's my fault. You're just too nice to say so. But I know. Yes, I do."

There was an awkward few moments while they both stood there feeling that they were the one that was responsible. They were looking at each other, wanting so badly for the other to forgive them. The lack of conversation was only adding to the tension that they both were now feeling. Ed was really mad at himself, but his attention was being drawn to Martha's face. He could see that she was choking up and probably going to cry. What could he say or do to change the subject? He felt so desperate but nothing was coming to mind. Then he noticed a pair of rabbits sitting together and staring back at them. A sense of calm came over him.

He surprised himself when he pointed at the rabbits and said, "Look. If those two can survive out here, then so can we. Hey, we both survived a plane crash. I definitely think we can live long enough to keep looking until we find our way back. All we have to do is just keep looking. I don't know about you, but I was having a great time just walking around and talking with you. So why can't we just keep walking and talking until we find it? What do you say, partner?"

He was smiling and held out his hand towards her.

Martha smiled and took his hand.

"You're right. Sorry. We just need to keep going. But which way?"

Ed picked up a fallen tree branch and started drawing in the dirt. "We ran like this, then turned left and here is the log. I know we started back the right way, but we should have turned right somewhere. Agreed?"

Again, Ed was asking her opinion. She was so impressed with how he truly wanted to know what she thought. This one trait of his was attracting her to him more and more every time he did it.

"Yes, I see what you are saying, Ed. We both know we missed the point where we should have turned right. Since we don't know how far back we should have turned, what if we do this?"

She took the branch from his hand, making sure that her hand brushed his hand. Then it was her turn to draw in the dirt as she spoke.

"So we've definitely passed the point where we should have turned right. Let's just start going at a slight right angle from here, and hopefully we will come across our tracks. Then we can just follow them back to the crash site. Of course, we will have to keep our eyes on the ground as we walk. We don't want to miss the tracks or we'll go too far off in the other direction. What do you think?"

"Sounds good to me. In fact, I think that's a very good idea. So let's just start walking and talking." With one finger pointing at the ground, he added.

"But we need to keep our eyes on the ground."

She giggled, took a step. "Let's go, partner".

She really liked that he had called her 'partner'. Yes, she knew they were destined to be much more than just friends. She wondered if he knew it yet. No, he didn't have a clue. He's a guy. They were always blindsided by matters of the heart. This thought caused her to giggle for a second, which attracted his attention.

She disguised what she was thinking by saying, "Don't mind me. It makes me feel better now that we have a plan. So I'm just being silly again because we have things under control."

• • •

They had been scouring the ground as they walked for the first 20 minutes. Each one of them had taken their turn to talk about fond childhood memories of their parents. Martha innocently asked Ed to tell her about his experiences as a Boy Scout. Hearing her request, Ed suddenly stopped and turned to her before speaking.

"Ok. I have to tell you something."

Martha was confused by his sudden seriousness and she watched him as he continued speaking.

"I didn't lie when I told you I had been a Boy Scout, but what I didn't tell you was that I was only in the Scouts for a month. There, I've said it. I only went on one camping trip and it was a disaster. I quit two days after we came back home." He was now standing blank-faced in front of her, as if expecting her to say something.

She sensed that he was expecting a remark, but what? She finally said, "Okay. So you were only a Scout for a month and you only went on one camping trip. So what? I've never been on a camping trip. In fact, this is the first time I've actually been out in the wilderness EVER."

"So what? I wanted you to think I knew what I was doing. But I don't. I'm no mountain man."

She thought it was cute how he was acting like a little boy who had just admitted to something nobody even knew. Everyone tries to impress those they like. He was a good person. Wait a minute - he was trying to impress her. That meant he really liked her! A huge smile spread across her face. She reached out and slipped one hand underneath his arm, pulling herself tightly against his side. The look in his eyes was one of 'What are you up to?'

She finally said, "We both figured out what to do. We have a plan. I'm happy with it. Aren't you?"

He reluctantly answered, "Yes."

"So stop worrying about it. I like that we worked together and decided what to do. Like you said, we're partners."

He began to grin again before saying, "Yes, we are. I liked how we worked together too. Very much so! I just didn't want you to think I was something I'm not."

"Ed. I think I know exactly what you are. Who you are. And I like what I think."

Her smile had soothed his nerves and her comments had rejuvenated his spirit. They once again started walking forward while their eyes searched the ground for their earlier tracks. A few minutes later, Ed stopped very abruptly.

"Hey! These are tracks."

Martha's voice was loud as she said, "Yeah! I knew we would find them." She glanced at Ed, only to see he had knelt down and was studying the tracks. "What's wrong, Ed?"

"These aren't our tracks. They're too small. Look behind us at our tracks, and then look at these. These are the footprints of some kind of animal."

She nervously asked, "What kind of animal?"

"I'm not sure, but whatever it is, it's going that way." He pointed in one direction. As they both looked that way, their eyes zoomed in on a mother deer and her fawn. The animals were standing less than ten feet away from them. They were motionless and stared back at them.

"Martha. Don't move. I've always heard that a mother will charge if she thinks her baby is in danger. Be very still."

"I'm not going to move. I'm barely breathing," she whispered.

To their amazement, the fawn slowly walked closer and closer to them. The mother deer finally stomped one foot on the ground and the fawn froze. Then the mother slowly walked up to within inches of Martha. The animal sniffed the air several times and slowly leaned her head even closer to Martha.

Ed was so afraid that Martha was going to get hurt. He was seriously thinking about jumping towards the animal to try to scare it off or at least get it to go after him instead. Just as he was about to make his move, the doe turned and walked back past her baby. It looked first at Martha, then Ed one last time before turning away to follow its mother.

Ed was so relieved that the deer had moved on. He turned to look at Martha. She was still just standing frozen in place.

"Martha. It's over now. They are leaving. Martha?"

She was still, but looked as if she'd seen something. Then she pointed in the direction the deer were headed. "Look through the trees! It's a clearing up ahead."

Their eyes struggled to focus on the disappearing animals. The trees stopped just 20 yards from where the deer were. The animals had left the trees, and were slowly moving out into the clearing. Martha looked at him and he looked at her, before they both began walking quickly to the edge of the clearing.

Once they had left the trees behind, they both stopped and began surveying the huge open area.

Ed spoke. "This is not the crash site. Nothing is burned at all here. We must have missed our tracks again, and now we are too far this way. I can't believe it."

She raised her arm and pointed. "Look! That's a dirt road out in the middle of the field."

This revelation triggered a burst of energy from them both, and they ran out to the road. Once in the middle of the road, they both stopped and began looking both ways.

Ed said, "It's a road." He looked this way then that before continuing. "I wonder if it runs right down the middle of this valley."

Martha said, "I wonder which way we need to go. How can we tell?"

Ed was rubbing one hand on the back of his head as he thought. He began talking as if he were thinking out loud.

"I remember looking out the plane window, and seeing this valley that we were crashing into. It looked like one end of the valley had huge mountain peaks sticking up above the clouds, but the other end didn't."

She looked at him and asked, "So what does that mean?"

"Well. It could mean that the end by the mountain peaks would be higher than the other end. So, if we can figure out which direction the road is going downward, then we'll know which direction to go. It will eventually lead us out of the canyon and towards a lower elevation. That would also mean we could just follow the road to a farm, or even a town!"

Martha's excitement was now visible. "And we would be rescued! But both directions seem to be flat. How are we going to tell which way is down?"

Ed noticed that Martha was tilting her head to one side, as if she was listening to something far away. "What are you doing? Do you hear something? Is it that helicopter?"

"Yes, Ed. I do hear something. But it's not the chopper. It sounds like water."

Ed's voice now reflected the excitement he felt. "Where do you think it's coming from? If we can find it, then we'll know which way is downhill! Water always runs downhill!"

She was still trying to determine the direction of the noise. She took a few steps one way, stopped, and moved more to her right before pointing.

"It's coming from over there!"

They both began running in that direction. A few minutes later, they were standing beside a small creek of water. It was only two feet across and the water was merely inches deep, but it was flowing very rapidly in one direction. Now they knew which way was downhill.

Martha said, "Come on. Now we know which way to go!"

Ed asked her, "Are you thirsty? That water looks pure. It has to be from the melting snow. I'm sure it is safe to drink. Maybe we should drink a little before we go."

Martha had a quizzical look as she said, "Odd. I know I should be thirsty, but I'm not. I haven't had anything to drink since yesterday and I'm not thirsty at all. I should be. Don't you find that odd?"

"Not really. We are in a very cool environment. We aren't sweating, so we don't need water yet. I'm not thirsty either. I was just trying to plan ahead." With that said, Ed turned and motioned for Martha to walk with him back to the road.

Upon reaching the road, they both quietly turned and began walking in the direction that the water had been running in the creek. At first there was little talking and they both were walking slowly. Martha then began to hum to herself as her spirits were obviously beginning to liven up. Once her humming had started, it grew louder and louder with every few steps that she took. It was a current song from the radio that she had only heard twice before boarding their ill-fated plane. Her playfulness was recovering too and she eventually stepped close enough to Ed to bump hips with him in a half-hearted attempt to knock him off the road.

Though he was caught off guard by this sneak attack, he quickly recovered and said, "Look! There are those deer again." Martha immediately turned her head to look and that was when Ed carried out his Kamikaze attack. He actually bumped her hard enough to push her almost three feet off the road and into the knee-high grass. She stopped and stood there laughing before loudly proclaiming "REALLY?"

She glanced back at Ed, who was standing in the middle of the road with an absolutely huge grin on his face as if to say, 'Hey! Two can play at this game'.

While still laughing out loud, she found herself looking at this big guy and knowing he was completely capturing her heart. It was the first time she had seen him acting this playful and she found it utterly irresistible. His obvious lack of worldly ways gave him the innocent persona of a 10-year old. She wondered if she was falling in love with him as a prospective mate or just feeling her mother instinct kicking in.

Ed watched her intently to see what her next move would be. His expression was that of a happy child. Seeing her start to run towards him, he turned and took off down the road. She was amazed to hear him actually say, "Bet you can't catch me." Though she gained on him at first, he eventually pulled away from her. She slowed to a walk, expecting that he would as well.

Having noticed that she was now walking, he came to a complete stop and waited for her to get to him. Knowing that she was going to bump him again, he remained still and braced for the inevitable. Once the retaliatory bump had been rendered, they both were again walking side by side down the road. They scanned their surroundings, relishing their current feelings of contentment.

Without even looking at each other, they began talking again.

"I'm going to have bruises, you big OX!" Martha said as she reached out and playfully slapped his shoulder.

Before he realized what he was saying, he blurted out, "You started it, cutie." His eyes widened as he hung his head so she couldn't see his face. He couldn't believe he had said that. What if she didn't like it? Eventually he thought, 'I think she liked it. She's cutting up with me because she likes me. For the first time in my life, I'm sure that a girl likes me the way I am.'

Martha saw Ed's expression and she realized he was embarrassed for some reason. She decided to give him a break and change the subject.

"I wonder how far we should go down the road. As thick as the trees are, we will never see the crash site from the road. We are probably going to miss it altogether, you know."

Ed was still eyeing the treeline. "You're right. But the good news is that if we just stay on this road, it will surely take us out of this valley and we can find a farm or house, or little town. Something or somebody. All we have to do is just keep walking. Just let me know when you get tired and we'll stop for awhile."

She didn't feel tired at all. Always analyzing herself, she concluded that there are two main factors at play here, and they were keeping them both full of energy. First, she knew he was equally relieved to be away from the crash site and the bodies. Second, the excitement of their developing relationship was most definitely heightening their energy levels. She knew for a fact that it was affecting her. Her thoughts began to fast-forward to the ultimate climax of this drama, but she knew that now was not the appropriate time for that. Or was it? What could be more natural than a man and woman belonging to one another, out in the midst of nowhere? Isn't this the way it was in the beginning of the human march to populate the world? With these thoughts running rampant in her mind, she looked at Ed and could hardly wait for them to get to that stage of their relationship.

He looked at her, wondering what she was thinking. "Well, either I bumped you too hard, or you're still trying to catch your breath. Must be one or the other that has stopped you from talking. You too tired to talk?"

"I'm fine. I was just thinking. About, well, things."

"What kind of things?" he asked.

She found herself glancing at Ed and remembering her high school years. All her girlfriends had at least one boyfriend before graduation. She had spent many hours lost in daydreams as she listened to her friends talk about their special guys. They would say, 'He did this. He did that. We went here. We laughed at this.' How she had longed to have that special guy to do simple things with. Things like this hip-bumping escapade that she and Ed had just indulged in. It was fun, and would have been a perfect story to tell her friends back then. If only she had met Ed back then. She wondered if they would have been drawn to one another after a chance meeting. The lack of a boyfriend had been her biggest disappointment during her high school years.

"I don't mind telling you exactly what kind of things, Ed. If you're truly interested in knowing, I'll tell you."

Ed stopped walking and turned to look at Martha. Her answer had sparked his curiosity while setting off waves of emotions that begged him to be cautious. Though most of him wanted to know, there was that small, nagging part of him that was afraid of what she might say.

Even as he was inwardly wrestling with what to say, his newfound feelings for this girl overpowered his fear. So he answered with a wavering voice, "I think so. Ah, YES! I, I, I do want to know." Then he winced before adding, "I guess?"

Most of her girlfriends would have walked away from Ed for being so timid and unsure of himself. But not Martha. His childlike uncertainty was very appealing to her. She was about to begin telling him her inner most thoughts when something in the distance attracted her attention.

Seeing that she was looking past him and up at the sky, Ed turned to look for himself before asking "What now? What are you looking at?"

Chapter 5

A RACE TO A CRASH

A SINGLE HELICOPTER lifted off on a hurried mission to finally deliver rescue personnel to an isolated crash site. The collective belief shared by all was that there would not be any survivors found. Yet each team member secretly held a spark of hope in their heart that a miracle could have happened up there, and this spark was what drove the group to hurry to the site.

Bart and Sandy watched as the chopper slowly flew just below the clouds while it maintained an equal distance from the tree lines on both sides of the clearing. The chopper was following the road and it eventually slipped out of sight around the first bend. Even though they couldn't see it, their eyes were continuing to follow the motor's sound as it echoed through the forest. Finally, they could no longer hear anything.

"Well, Sarge? Now we wait."

"Yes sir. This is always the hard part. Those guys are busy getting there and time will pass quickly for them. But us? It will seem like time is standing still until we hear from them. This is the part I always hate."

Bart had both hands jammed into his coat pockets, looking down as he scraped the dirt with the toe of his boot. "I want to believe that at least one has survived, but my gut knows it ain't possible."

Sandy was watching him and commented, "It would take one hell of a miracle for that!" The sound of the chopper was completely gone now, and she looked up at the clouds one last time.

"Come on, Bart. I'll buy the next cup of coffee."

Bart looked up and smiled at her before saying, "Only if you let me get the next one." They walked back to the mess tent.

• • •

Both pilots were busy watching the distance to the tree lines. The captain was especially mindful that his bird was directly over the center of the logging road. It took them only 10 minutes to come to Bart's first mark on the map.

It was just as he had told them. The tree line was so close that they would have to hop over the narrow point by going up into the clouds and dropping back down on the other side. The pilot had stopped all forward motion and held the chopper in a perfect hover as he and Willy assessed their next move.

"Well, Willy? Looks to me that next clearing is about 300 yards straight ahead. What do you think?"

Willy was still looking as he spoke. "That might be cutting it a little close. It looks like that clearing is huge, and the map shows that the road goes straight for a good quarter of a mile after it comes out of those trees. Why risk it? Looks to me that we have plenty of room to overshoot, so why not say 350 or better yet, 400 yards?"

The captain was silent for a few seconds. "If you insist. Let's make it 400 yards. I'm sure the guys in back would appreciate us being responsible here!"

Willy quickly turned and glanced at the pilot before he said, "I'd appreciate you being responsible here. These guys haven't flown with you like I have! They still trust you completely. There is no need to scare the HELL out of them like you do me."

There was a small chuckle from the pilot. "You just don't want to have any fun. Do you?" Then with that said, he pulled the craft straight up into the clouds and slowly moved forward while watching his instruments closely. Finally, he again stopped their forward movement and slowly began to lower the bird earthward. Though the men in back were busy checking their gear, Willy and the pilot were intently staring into the clouds that completely obscured everything that was more than a few inches beyond the glass.

Finally, the isolation of the cloud gave way to the welcome sight of the open field below them. Willy was once again struck by the accuracy with which this pilot could fly. He had brought the chopper down directly in the middle of the clearing, and was almost exactly over the center of the road below. Willy shook his head before saying, "Damn fine flying, sir. You scare me out of my wits at times, but then you do something like this and make it look so easy. I have to hand it to you, sir. You're good!"

The pilot had already started forward again and was following the road as he replied, "Oh, shut up. You're going to give me the big head!"

Willy was already studying the map. "Looking at the map here, we have another 10 or 15 minutes before we hit that big nasty spot that Bart marked on the map. The one where we have to land and send somebody ahead on foot."

They continued to follow the road below. Both pilots were constantly focused on the distance to the tree lines on both sides of them. Finally they came to the spot where the road disappeared into the trees a few hundred yards ahead. The pilot brought the craft in for a smooth landing. The side door slid open and two of the men in back hopped out. One was carrying the transponder, and the other was carrying a hand-held radio. They both were bent over and hurried until they were out from under the rotor blades. Then the man with the radio faced the chopper, pushed a button and asked, "Can you hear me, guys?"

Willy's voice crackled out over the radio. "Hear you loud and clear. Just call out when you've planted the transponder and we'll be there in a jiffy to pick you guys up. Over."

The two men turned and began jogging down the road. As they disappeared from sight, Willy drew his finger along the road on the map. "Looks like they have a good hike to get to the next clearing. This will probably take them 20 or 30 minutes just to get out of the trees. If you figure another 15 minutes to get out into the clearing and set up the unit. Man, we are looking at 45 minutes to an hour before we can take off. Should we shut down and save the fuel?" Before he could turn to look at the captain, he heard the blades already beginning to slow. They went through their normal shutdown routine, and sat silently as the blades continued to slowly spin.

The captain finally commented, "I'll give them 30 minutes. Then we will spin her up and take off. We can climb up into the clouds and wait. Besides, they are going to be almost a mile away through all these densely packed trees. I'll bet we wouldn't even get the signal from that handheld sitting here."

Willy was nodding in agreement. "I hadn't even thought of that. Sounds good to me."

• • •

"Well, Captain. It's time." With that said, both men went through their

fine-tuned checklist and the chopper came to life once again. As they lifted off from the ground, the captain said, "Well, Mr. Willy. What do you say we go find our two wayward friends?"

No sooner than they had slipped up into the clouds, their radio sounded off. "Captain. We have the transponder up and functional. You copy?"

Willy responded, "We copy and we have your signal. We're on our way, gentlemen. Over."

It was literally two minutes later that the captain said, "This is Rescue One, and we are coming down on top of your signal now. Look up gentlemen. Same drill as earlier. Let me know when you see my skids."

"We hear you sir, but no visual yet." Then the other man patted the radio operator on the shoulder and pointed. "We have visual! You are directly above the unit and approximately 75 feet off the ground. You are right in the middle of the clearing. No trees for 100 yards in any direction, sir."

The pilot repeated his earlier maneuver and hovered just under the clouds. He slowly turned the craft in a clockwise direction until he saw the two men on the ground. Then he backed the chopper up 20 yards so he wouldn't come down directly on top of the transponder. Once on the ground, the two men hustled over and climbed back on their ride. The pilot immediately lifted off, centered his bird over the middle of the road, and began moving forward again.

"Willy. You have the crash site coordinates from our first night's trip up here. Let me know when we are directly parallel to the site and I'll set her down."

"Yessir. We should be there in just a few minutes now." He turned to look back at the other men. He was yelling, "Get ready to go as soon as we touch down."

Willy was watching the instrument readings and suddenly said, "Here! Take her down."

The pilot had them on the ground in just a few moments. The side door opened and two men jumped to the ground. They didn't hesitate, just ran off into the trees. One of them was holding a handheld GPS unit to guide them to the precise coordinates the chopper crew had logged the night before. The two remaining men in back moved quickly to unload all of the supplies brought up on this trip. In minutes, they had neatly stacked it all just a few feet off the road and placed the little tent on top of the stack. With this done, they shut the side door. One of them patted the co-pilot's window and waved. Then they both turned, picked up their supplies and began hiking towards the crash site. One of them also had a handheld GPS unit.

The pilot watched them disappear into the trees.

"Nobody ever says good-bye anymore. What is the world coming to? Let's go on back."

Willy was still looking at the trees where the two men had disappeared. "It's kind of sad. Nobody will even hear us leave."

• • •

Ed was still looking skyward and waiting for a response from Martha.

"Are you going to tell me what you are looking at?"

As Ed started to ask her again, she held one finger to her lips and went 'Shhh'. Ed looked from her face to the sky and hoped it was the helicopter returning. After several seconds of silence, he shrugged his shoulders and extended his arms as if to say 'What?'

Martha finally broke her silence. "I hear the helicopter, but it's very faint." She was slowly turning her head from side to side in an attempt to determine the direction of the sound. Finally, she pointed down the road in the direction they were walking. "It's coming from that way. We need to hurry. I think it's moving away from us now. It was loud at first, but now it's growing softer. Yes, it is definitely moving away from us now."

Ed took her by the hand and they both began to jog down the road. They hurried along for almost 20 minutes before she stopped and started listening again. Slowly her eyes dimmed, and she shook her head before saying, "It's gone. I can't hear a thing now. We've missed it."

Not wanting her to feel depressed, Ed said, "It will be back. At least we know that we're going in the right direction. Since it didn't come over us, it means that it came in and turned around to go back. This is actually good news!"

"I wonder why they turned around and went back? You think they went to get more gas?" she asked. Her eyes showed that she was somewhat concerned that they may have just missed an opportunity to be rescued. Ed was staring at her, wanting to again console her. But he was not sure of what to say, as usual. His words just slipped out.

"That's probably what is going on here. They're looking for the crash site and haven't found it yet. Don't worry. They will be back."

As they continued to walk along in silence, Ed was weighing whether or not to get back to the subject of what Martha had been thinking about. He found that he couldn't stand not knowing, so he asked.

"So? Are you going to tell me what you were thinking about? And before you ask me again, the answer is definitely 'YES'. I do want to know."

Since he was so much taller than she was, it was obvious to her that Ed couldn't see the sparkle in her eyes at his insisting she share her thoughts. Then just as she was about to start talking, a small sliver of embarrassment crept into her mind. She had never talked with a guy about such a personal subject. Her school years were full of loneliness, longing, and crying about what to do about both. Out of nowhere, she found the confidence to just start talking.

"I was thinking about my high school years. You know. Just

remembering how it was, and how it felt. Do you ever think about those days?"

Ed found himself not wanting to completely answer this question. He had always viewed himself as having been a total loser during those years. Somehow, Martha was making him feel like it was so far in the past now, that maybe he could and should talk out loud about it.

"Well. The truth is that I have spent years trying to ignore, no, trying to forget those years. My parents always told me those should be the best years of my life. They said that I was building memories that I would carry with me for the rest of my life. Well, they were right about those memories. The problem is that they were, for the most part, bad ones."

Martha was growing more comfortable with divulging her inner thoughts, since it sounded like Ed's high school years hadn't been all that good either.

"I had a similar experience myself, Ed. What made yours so bad? Didn't you have any friends?"

"Oh, of course I had some friends. They were good friends, actually. I had several that I had grown up with since I was four years old. We all lived next door to each other, and grew up playing together all the time. I was an only child and they were just like having brothers and sisters."

Martha watched him staring blindly ahead as he continued to walk along. He was most likely remembering and feeling his past. "Well, that doesn't sound bad. Sounds like you had some very good friends. What was so bad?"

Ed felt all those old childhood emotions of inadequacies and insecurity rush over him just as they used to. He was about to answer her and tell her the truth, but then it dawned on him that she wasn't telling him about her memories. Now she had him talking about *his*.

"Wait a minute. You were supposed to be telling me about what you were thinking. How'd this get turned around and be about me?"

Though she was somewhat unhappy with his tone of voice, he was right. She had started this by asking if he really wanted to know what she was thinking about. But when it was time to talk, she found it easier to get him to talk about his experiences than her own embarrassing high school years. Finally, she blurted it out.

"I never had a boyfriend in high school."

Ed stopped and turned towards her before saying, "What? How can that be true? You didn't want one? Why not?"

"Of course I wanted one. I wanted one really bad. The problem is, well, uh, actually I've never had a boyfriend in my life! There. I've said it. So what do you think of me now?" She was staring at him and he saw tears were swelling up in both of her eyes.

"Never?"

"No, never! So, are you, uh, are you . . . "

"Am I what? Come on, Martha. I'm not a mind reader. Am I what?"

Years of wanting to be wanted came rushing out in just a few words.

"Are you still interested in me?"

She was scanning his face for a sign of what he was about to say. If his response was negative, this was going to be a very bad day.

"Martha. Are you asking if it matters to me that you have never had a boyfriend?"

She had never been as nervous in her life as she was right now. "Yes," is all she could manage to say.

"Why would that matter?"

Now she was at a loss for words. How could he ask that? Did he not understand what she just told him? Are guys that blind to what this means?

"Why would you want a girl that nobody else wanted? Ever?"

Ed slowly nodded his head. "So I'd be your first boyfriend. The first one ever?"

Standing in front of him, she felt more vulnerable than at any other time in her life. She might as well have been standing totally naked in the middle of a completely filled football stadium at halftime. Her legs trembled as a smile grew on his face, and his eyes looked longingly into hers.

He slowly stepped closer until she was snuggled tightly against him as he wrapped his arms around her. "Martha. I've never been first for anyone. I like the thought of being your first boyfriend. I like it a lot."

They both were feeling things they had only dreamed about all their lives as they stood there in each other's arms. Martha looked up at him and was prepared for that first kiss. The one she had longed for her entire life. The one that she felt they had both been dancing around since the crash. The one that she felt was certain to happen now. Why was he hesitating? That's when she saw he was squinting, as if he was trying to focus on something behind her. Oh my God! It's a bear. What else could stop him from kissing her at a time like this? With a slight turn of her head, she saw it too out of the corner of her eye.

"Martha? Do you see something at the edge of the road down there? What is that?"

She was torn now. She wanted her kiss, but then again, she could see his attention had definitely moved on to whatever was near the road. With reluctance, she too felt the moment pass. She wondered how old she would be before Ed finally kissed her. One thing was for sure. The next time he was about to kiss her, she'd slip some blinders on him so all he saw was her!

• • •

Two men were silently working their way through the dense forest trees. One man had a GPS and was stopping every hundred yards or so. He was being followed by the reservist everyone called Doc. They were closing rapidly on the coordinates that the pilot and Willy had collected last night.

The logger named Fred had stopped again, but this time he didn't raise his GPS unit to look at it. Instead he called out, "Hey Doc! You smell that?"

The reservist replied, "Yes. How could I miss it? Smells like jet fuel and lots of burned wood."

"Yes, that's the smell. Every now and then, I get a whiff of burning rubber too. I don't need this thing anymore. We just need to follow our noses."

Both men saw the burnt clearing through the trees at the same time. Their pace quickened, and in a few seconds they burst into the open. Even though they had been preparing themselves for what they were going to find, they were both frozen in place by the magnitude of what was now surrounding them. They saw large numbers of body parts scattered throughout the wreckage.

There was the occasional complete body, but there were far more incomplete ones. Doc had seen large-scale death before during his two combat tours, but Fred had only witnessed the occasional accident victim during his years as a logger.

Doc noticed that Fred was barely even blinking as he stared out over the crash site. He knew that he must get Fred engaged quickly so that the work would prevent his mind from fixating on the dismembered bodies.

"Come on, Fred. We need to make a quick pass and look for survivors."

Fred was still frozen in place. "Where, uh, how do, where do we start?"

"Come on, Fred. I need you to go around the circle that way, and I'll go this way. We will meet on the other side. Obviously you only need to stop and take a hard look at the bodies that are intact."

"Man, I don't know if I can do this. It's too, too . . . man this is way too much for me."

Doc stepped in front of him to block his view of the scene for a second. "Look at me, Fred. Look at me! We need to get moving. You need to suck it up, dude. I need you, and I mean now! You go that way and remember what I just said. Only the whole bodies. Got it?"

He had his hand on one of Fred's shoulders, and he gave him a firm but slow push to get him moving. The logger started looking around and Doc started the other way. It took them about ten minutes before they joined up on the other side of the burn circle.

Doc was calm as he spoke to Fred, "Nothing on my side. You?"

Fred shook his head. It was obvious that he was still overwhelmed by what he was seeing. Doc felt sorry for him. He remembered his first time in combat. His company had two squads in a row blown apart—first by land mines, then grenades—during an ambush. That was his first time and it was bad. But even for him, this was much worse. There were the remains of children mixed in here. How could anyone be immune to this?

Doc was looking around before he spoke. "Fred. Look how all the debris is thrown out that way. I would think that more bodies could be out there too. What do you think?"

Fred was slowly coming to grips with the carnage and his mind welcomed the question. He looked into the tree line and saw an arm sticking up from the bushes. He couldn't believe his eyes. It looked like it was waving at them. He pointed and yelled to Doc, "Look! My God, there's somebody alive in the bushes!"

Both men broke into a frantic run towards it. They had to run around large chucks of metal and mangled seats. Having been a track star in high school, Fred easily leaped over most of the big pieces while Doc had to run around them.

Fred was easily the first man to the bush. He leaped over it and almost landed right on top of a small animal that was gnawing on a severed arm that had come to rest there in the bush. Seeing this, Fred could not hold it any longer and he began to vomit uncontrollably off to the side. Doc saw what was happening to Fred and slowed his run, because he could tell it was not good.

Doc finally had gotten Fred moved about 20 feet from the bush and had him sitting on a fallen tree trunk. A rush of motion behind them caused the two men to look at the tree line just as the other two rescuers appeared on the edge of the burn circle. They both had come to a complete halt, just as Doc and Fred had when they first arrived and saw the extent of the disaster. Doc was quick to yell out, "Over here! Come on over here!"

The other two made their way over to Doc's side. Rick immediately sat down and puts his arm on Fred's shoulders. They had been loggers together for almost 12 years now and it was obvious that Fred was his close friend.

Doc immediately said, "Rick. I need you to stay with Fred here while Riggs and I make a fast pass through the rest of this tree line."

Rick replied, "You can't possibly think anyone survived this? No way in HELL anyone could live through this. But, uh, sure, I'll stay with him. No problem."

He watched as the two reservists ran off to continue looking for survivors before turning to his friend. "Fred. Hey, man. It's me, Rick. You're going to be okay, buddy. I'm not going to leave you. Just take it easy and breathe man. Hey, this is some bad shit here! Just breathe, bro."

Doc and Riggs met up about 100 yards out into the trees. The debris stopped more than 20 yards back from that point.

They were standing there staring, first at each other and then at the mess back towards the center of the burn circle. They occasionally bent over and put their hands on their knees to catch their breath. Riggs was the first one to speak.

"Man this is some fucked-up shit here, Doc. I counted at least four kids' torsos back by the tree line. Damn, that is fucked up. I know you and I have seen death before and lots of it but, damn. Kids? I can't believe any man could ever get used to seeing this happen to children. It just ain't right man. What's God thinking when he lets something like this happen. Tell me. I really want to know, man."

"Hey Riggs! Now don't go philosophical on me, dude. Not now and damn sure not here. We've seen this all before. Both of us. Maybe not on this scale all at once, but we've both seen kids buy it before. I know it sucks, but I need you to keep your head on. Look at those two loggers over there. This is their first time to see this kinda shit. We have to get them out of the circle and back in the trees a bit. You know, get them away a little so they can collect themselves. You and I did the same thing our first time in combat. We have to let them both collect their manhood again. They'll be fine."

"You're right, Doc. You're always right. Come on. Let's move 'em back."

• • •

Bart and Sandy watched as the captain brought the chopper right down on top of the transponder again, performing his spin and backup before landing within three feet of where he'd landed the first time. Once the blades had stopped spinning, the two pilots exited the craft and exchanged some words with the fuel crew before heading to the mess tent for some hot coffee.

"Well, Sarge. I have to admit that your friend the pilot is a damn fine one for sure. It's amazing how accurate he is with that big piece of flying metal. I don't understand how he does it."

"I told you, Bart. He's as good as he is crazy. We're lucky to have him up here with us." As they both watched several men begin moving the next load of supplies towards the chopper, she continued. "Looks like Peterson and Smitty have things under control. You and I may just be out of a job, sir."

"We're both very fortunate to have some fine men working for us, Sarge. They will no doubt have this place running as efficiently as a major airport before we know it. I think I'll just walk out to the chopper and chat with them anyway. Care to join me?"

Sandy smiled at the crusty old man before commenting. "Old habits die hard. Don't they, Bart?"

"Yes they do, Sarge. That they do."

"Well, sir. I'd like to do that, but I'm afraid I need to stay close to the radio. The first of the men should be at the crash site by now. Once they assess the situation, they'll radio in. I'll need to drive back to that point by the southern pass and relay the news on back to the airport. That IIC man wanted to know as soon as possible about any potential survivors. Sam had also told me on the side that they will be mobilizing some forensic medical teams of some sort. They're just waiting till we have men on site and have more information about the situation. I suppose the pace of this thing is about to turn into a slow, methodical march from this point on."

Bart was shaking his head. "I suppose those medical teams will have the gory task of determining what part goes with what name. I really couldn't do a job like that. I can work from sunup till late in the night. I can work in heat and in cold. But there is no way I could ever do what those people are going to be asked to do. Absolutely no way." He started making his way towards the chopper to check on his men.

Sandy headed to the mess tent for another hot cup of coffee before planting herself by the radio in the command tent. She saw the captain and Willy talking to Corporal Lewis about what he was cooking for dinner.

She saluted as she passed them on her way into the tent. "Captain. Nice to have you both back safe and sound. Looks like they'll have your bird gassed and loaded soon. You'll just hop to the last transponder and back from now on, right?"

The captain replied as he turned to follow her in for more coffee himself. "Yes. Flight time is about 13 minutes. We'll shuttle all that designated equipment up there in the next three trips, and then we'll just sit up there until the men are ready to come back. It's going to get really boring really fast now. I'm planning on having Willy here, flying this back and forth on his own within the next two days. Then we can rotate on trips so each of us will get some rest between sorties. It's good training for him and safer for both of us."

Willy's eyes opened wide when he heard these plans. "Just one question, sir. When you say alternating, you mean we'll just swap out right and left seat positions. Right?"

The captain's steely blue eyes did not blink, and his expression was such that Willy knew that was NOT what he meant. "But sir. Surely you don't expect me to be able to pull off this miracle flying on instruments like you do. Do you?"

"Relax, Willy. It's actually easier than it looks. You'll pick it up in nothing flat. Trust me."

"But what if I don't, sir?"

The captain paused for a few seconds then he stepped closer to pat Willy's shoulder. "Then you'll crash."

He turned and continued talking as he left the tent. "Sandy. I'd only schedule equipment for the sorties that Willy flies. No need to endanger anyone else. I'll call the base and order a second chopper." He had stopped halfway through the tent opening, and was now looking back at them both. There was an evil grin on his face as he added, "Just in case."

Sandy was having a really hard time keeping her face expressionless though she was totally laughing on the inside. Willy's face was almost white as he asked her, "You don't think he's serious, do you? Well, do you?"

• • •

Doc came walking out of the trees and stopped a few feet in front of the two loggers. Fred and Rick were still sitting on the fallen tree where he had taken them to rest. Both men were smiling and seemed much more relaxed now.

Doc knelt down in front of Fred and looked him in the eyes as he reached out to take his pulse. "Fred. You look like you are feeling much better."

Fred's smile faded just a little from embarrassment. "I feel a lot better, Doc. Sorry about before. It all kinda, well it . . . oh, shit. You know what I'm trying to say, Doc. But I'm fine now. It won't happen again. What do you want me to do now?"

Doc patted him on the shoulder as he stood up. "You have nothing to be embarrassed about, Fred. This is not easy. This kind of death is hard to face, no matter how many times you see it. It takes a lot out of a man to see this."

Riggs came running up to them. "Doc. I ran the temp antenna up a tree and I have the radio all set up. We can transmit whenever you are ready."

Doc started walking as he spoke. "We need to get this over with. They are waiting for us to call in what we have found. This won't be a surprise, but it's damn sure going to be a letdown."

Rick and Fred followed the two reservists back to the waiting radio. Doc walked up and did not hesitate. He picked up the radio handset, held down the button and said, "Valley base. This is crash site. Come in."

It was obvious that the base camp had been eagerly monitoring the radio for their call because their response was immediate. "Crash site, this is Valley base. Doc. Is that you?"

"Peterson. It's me. I need the Sarge."

"Doc. Sandy here. What did you find?"

"Just as we thought. No survivors. Not a one. Over."

The mood in the radio tent had grown even colder than the evening air out side. Each man had known it was going to end like this, but at the same time, each one wanted to hope. It was only human nature to want at least one person to survive. But it was not to be. Not this time. Not in this place. Not for the passengers and crew of this flight.

Sandy saw the look on the faces of everyone around her. She shared their disappointment, but they all still had a job to do.

"Doc. I hate to ask this, but are you absolutely sure you didn't miss anyone? It's a big area up there. Do you think you took enough time to look around?"

"Sarge. We made two separate passes over the entire area. We followed the debris field out into the trees and then went on another 200 yards. Nothing. Riggs and I personally went back a third time to check the tree line around the entire burn circle. There are absolutely no tracks of anyone walking or crawling out of the area. I hate it as much as the rest of you, but there are no survivors up here. None."

"I see. What do you need from us first?"

"Sarge. We need to get all those smudge pots up here quick. We only have five more hours of daylight. We need to get some kinda smoking perimeter set up quick. We already have a critter problem. Just found one gnawing on something. It's going to be a long night. I don't think we want anyone, uh, I mean anything being drug off into the woods during the night. At least that's my take on it."

"Sounds good. We're on it. Keep your ears on. We'll give you a shout before the chopper flies your way. Over."

"Roger. Crash site out."

Sandy clapped her hands together very loudly. "You heard him, guys. Peterson. We need all the smudge pots you can cram on that chopper, and we need it done now. Then I want you to stage all the other pots at the landing site and start sending just them on each flight until they're all up there. I'll find the captain and explain the situation to him and Willy. They'll need to turn some fast sorties and we need to fit at least two new men on each flight. They are going to need a lot of extra hands up there to get this in place by nightfall." She could still be heard talking as she exited the tent. "We need to get moving, people. NOW!"

• • •

As Martha and Ed approached the mysterious stack of supplies at the edge of the road, she was still wishing they had kissed a few moments ago. She wondered why fate was being so cruel to her. They came so close, but then something always happened and the moment was lost. They both stopped together a few feet from the stack. While they stood there holding hands and staring at it, Martha asked, "What do you think this is?"

Ed immediately responded. "That chopper dropped off these supplies and then left. They must be staging this equipment here for the rescue workers to use."

Martha watched Ed turn his attention from one side of the road to the other. "Ed? Do you think they went back to get some rescue people now, and will bring them up on the next flight?"

"Actually, I'd say they dropped off some guys already, and they've gone on foot to the crash site." He let go of Martha's hand and began looking at the ground around the stack. "Yep. Here are their footprints. They lead that way towards the trees."

He was now pointing in the direction the footprints led.

Ed quickly moved back towards Martha and took her hand. "Come on! We need to try and catch up with them."

They both hurried, hand in hand, across the grassy field and into the trees. The trees were so close together that Martha was forced to follow behind Ed as he followed the men's tracks. Since Ed had his head down looking at the ground, Martha was busy looking through the trees in the hopes of catching a glimpse of the men they were following. "I wonder how many of them there are?"

Ed replied, "There are only two of them."

She giggled a little before saying, "Only two? What are you now, an Indian scout?" She had to stop abruptly, because Ed had stopped as well and was facing her.

"No, I'm not an expert tracker but I can see."

"See what?" she asked innocently.

Ed stepped to the side and pointed down at the tracks. "Look for yourself. There are two different tread mark patterns from their boots. There is a left and right boot with that waffle print there." He was pointing to one set of prints before moving his hand to point at the other set. "And here is a right and left print with a smooth bottom. See 'em?"

She did see they were different, and felt bad that she'd challenged him on his deduction. "I do see it. I'm sorry I made that crack about being an Indian scout."

Ed looked at her sincere expression before smiling. "No problem. I probably sounded more confident than I should have. Come on, let's catch up to them." He once again turned and started walking as he followed the tracks.

Just as she was about to start following him, she heard the faint sound of the chopper again. "Wait! I hear the chopper coming back."

Ed immediately looked back over his shoulder to see her looking skyward.

"Are you sure? I don't hear anything."

"You will in a minute. It's getting louder."

Eventually Ed's ears picked up the sound, and he looked skyward in its direction. "Yes. I hear it now. We should go back to the road."

Martha had already reversed course and was heading back the way they came. "I'm all for that! It will be so nice to get on the chopper and get out of here. Finally!" After a few hurried steps, she called out over her shoulder to Ed. "Come on!"

The sound of the chopper got louder and it was reverberating through the trees. As the blades chopped the air, the noise seemed to be coming from all around them. It suddenly grew softer, but they could still hear it. Ed was following Martha closely and said, "It's landed! We need to hurry and get to them before they leave again."

"Ed, I'm going as fast as I can. You know I want to get out of here too!"

After rushing through the woods in the direction of the sound, they finally saw the clearing through the trees. Martha summoned up a little extra energy and pushed herself harder towards the clearing. Finally! They rushed out of the trees to find an empty road before them, but no chopper in sight.

They both looked frantically for the huge machine before realizing that, in their haste to get back to the road, they had obviously drifted off course. This was why they didn't see the stack of supplies.

They stood there a few seconds before Ed pointed to his left and said, "The sound is that way!" He quickly grabbed Martha's hand before pulling her along in that direction.

"Ed! You're faster than me, so let go of my hand. You should run on ahead and stop them from leaving! Now GO!"

Martha watched Ed's face as he hesitated for just a moment while looking at her. She smiled to reassure him. "Go! I'll catch up. Now GO!"

Ed reluctantly released her hand before sprinting off in the direction of the sound. Martha ran after him, but she immediately started to fall behind. His strides were much longer and he eventually disappeared from her sight as he ran around the bend in the road. A few moments later she could hear him yelling, "Hey! Hey! Over here!"

As she rounded the bend in the road herself, her eyes beheld a sight that brought her to a complete halt. Ed was still running down the road while yelling at the top of his lungs, but the chopper had already lifted off. It had its nose down and was gaining altitude while headed in the opposite direction from them. The pilot couldn't possibly have seen or heard Ed as he continued to chase it down the road.

Martha found herself standing still, helplessly watching as the craft climbed higher. When it disappeared into the clouds, she noticed that Ed had stopped running after it. He was standing in the middle of the road, hands on his hips. Eventually he stopped staring upwards, head down as if he were ashamed of himself for letting it get away. She noticed that there were now two separate stacks of supplies—one on each side of the road. She wondered if Ed had even noticed that he passed right between them while chasing the chopper.

Once again her feet were in motion and she quickly reached Ed's side. She gently placed one hand on his arm and looked up at him as she said, "It's okay. They will be back soon. It looks like they are just bringing up supplies and leaving them here. We just have to be patient and they'll be back."

Ed twisted halfway round to look back at the stacked supplies. He startled Martha as he suddenly pointed at the trees. "Look! There are two guys off in the trees. Come on! We can catch them!"

Again he had grabbed her hand and was trying to pull her toward the trees. She began moving along with him, even though she couldn't see anything ahead. "I don't see anyone, Ed. Are you sure?"

"Come on. Come on! I just barely caught a glimpse of them. But YES! I'm sure of what I saw. They both had backpacks on too! That means they can't move as fast as we can. We can catch them easily. Come ON!"

Martha followed Ed as he hurried through the trees in search of the two men. After a few moments he stopped and looked from side to side. "I don't see any tracks but I know they were close to this broken tree here. Martha, can you hear anything?"

She closed her eyes for a moment to really concentrate. Ed was intently watching her face as her eyes flew wide open before she pointed to their right. "Over there somewhere. I can hear them talking but I don't see them. Let's go that way."

Ed started off in the direction she'd indicated. After they had moved about 30 yards farther into the trees, she yelled out,

"There they are! Hey! Hey! Fellas! Help! Over here. Help!"

To her amazement, the two men continued moving forward as if they hadn't heard her. She said, "That's odd. I can hear them, but they didn't hear me screaming. What are they - deaf?"

Ed motioned for her to keep following him. "They're just focused on where they are going. Besides, the trees are so thick in here maybe your voice doesn't carry. Also, I can't hear them. You have that super good hearing. Remember? Whatever the reason, they went that way. Come on!"

After they had walked for another 20 minutes without seeing them, she asked, "Are you sure they came this way? Shouldn't we have caught up with them by now? Maybe they weren't real. You know . . . like a mirage or something?"

Ed kept moving but pointed down to the ground beside them. "Oh they're real enough. If you look there, you'll see their tracks in the mud and snow. They may be getting away from us, but these tracks will take us right to them. We just need to keep moving."

Since she now felt that they were minutes away from being rescued, she relaxed and decided to have a little fun with Ed.

"Did you see that one guy was holding something up in his hand, as if he was using it to know which way to go? I wonder what that thing was?"

Ed never broke his stride as he answered. "It probably was a GPS unit. You know what that is, don't you? They make them for hikers just like they do for cars. Remember the first night when we saw the chopper over the crash site? Well, I'll bet he took a GPS reading and logged the position of the crash. Now these guys have input the coordinates into their GPS unit. It will take them right to the crash site."

Martha laughed. "We need one of those things. And YES, I know what a GPS unit is. I have one in my car. I use it all the time to find addresses in the city. They are very handy." She knew he couldn't see her shaking her head from side to side as she spoke.

Ed had noticed the sudden change in Martha's tone of voice so he turned to roll his eyes at her. "In your car? I don't have a car. I get everywhere I need to go by bus or the subway. You must spend a fortune on car payments, gas and insurance. I only spend $56.00 a month on a pass that covers both bus and train."

Martha was really getting playful now. "I know it costs more to have a car, but I like the freedom it brings. I come and go when I want. No schedules for me. Can you even drive, big boy?"

This remark actually made him stop and turn towards her. "Can I drive? Of course I can drive. I'm not helpless, you know."

She smiled at him as she stepped in close towards his chest and looked up into his face. "I never said you were helpless. Did I? No! So, why did you learn to drive if you don't have a car?"

"I drove my parents' car. You know, ran errands for them all the time. But when I moved out on my own, I just found it easier and less expensive to just do the mass transit thing. It was there. It was cheap. I'm cheap."

Martha playfully patted his belly. "Well, I'm not cheap. So I'll have to work on you about this, mister!"

Ed looked confused. "We need to keep moving. Don't you think? Or have you changed your mind about being rescued?" This time he was the one with a playful gleam in his eye.

To his surprise, she suddenly wrinkled up her nose and sneezed. This was not exactly what he had been waiting for.

"Bless you."

Martha's nose was twitching as she replied, "Thank you." Then she sneezed again before asking, "What *is* that smell?"

Ed breathed in deeply and then his eyes popped wide open as he exclaimed, "That's jet fuel. We must be right by the crash site!"

Martha and Ed both turned and saw that the crash site was within view, and there were men running across the burnt area.

Martha breathed a huge sigh of relief.

"Finally! Now we can be rescued!"

Chapter 6

TWO SURVIVORS?

ED AND MARTHA had crossed the last few feet of forest and were only inches away from stepping out of the tree line. Before them was the massive burn area of the crash site. They both had stopped walking, feeling as if some mystical force was holding them just out of sight. They seemed afraid to step into the freedom of the open area before them. Ed's apprehension of taking that next step was heightened by how hard Martha's grip was on his hand. He didn't have to look at her to know that, just like him, her excitement of being rescued had given way to this strange desire to wait in the trees. Without looking at her, Ed began to speak.

"I can't explain it, but I don't really want to go out there. Well, uh, *of course* I want to go out there, so they can get us out of here. But, well . . . " He stopped talking when she tugged on his hand. He looked down into her eyes as she began to talk in a soft, low voice.

"I know what you're feeling, Ed. I feel it too. Really I do. I can't explain it, but I feel exactly what you just said. I know that we both want to be rescued. But it's odd, this feeling I have."

"Martha, I do want to be rescued and get out of here too. But, I think I know what's at work here. I can't speak for you, but I know what is holding me back."

She took on her usual playful demeanor as she pushed tightly up against his chest. Her eyes were locked upwards on his eyes as she said, "Okay, mister. Spill it. What are you thinking is going on here?"

"Well, for me, I'm afraid that once we are surrounded by those men and whisked out of this valley, you will not feel the same about me. You know, you won't need me any more since you'll have others around you. I'm just afraid that it won't be the same between us. Like it has been since the crash."

Though her grip on his hand remained tight, her eyes softened as she looked at this big guy who had just told her he was afraid to lose her. How could this wonderful man think she'd just walk away from him like that?

"Hey mister." She softly poked her finger into his chest. "You don't think you can get rid of me that easy. Do you, SIR?" She stepped backward just ever so slightly, put her hands on her hips, and pretended to be outraged as she continued.

"So, I know what you're really thinking. You think that now you'll be rich from a settlement with the airline, and that you can use all that money to pick up really pretty women whenever you want one. Right?"

Ed's face displayed true panic as his ears relayed her words to his already worried mind. He tried to speak, but just mumbled. "Well, NO! Uh . . . ". Then he paused to try to convey a real sincere disbelief with his eyes before he continued. "I can't believe you would think that! I would NEVER do that. I meant what I said earlier." He was moving two fingers on one hand, back and forth as he pointed first at her, then himself. His eyes were locked on hers as he said, "I don't want to lose this feeling between us. I want it to last forever or longer if at all possible. I've wanted this my whole empty life." Ed was at a loss for any more words and it showed.

Martha realized that her little act had actually upset Ed. This was definitely NOT what she'd wanted to do. She knew just how to calm him down. A KISS! Yes! This was the perfect time and place. It would snap him out of it and give her what she had been longing for since she was six. Martha once again pushed her chest up against his. Ed's eyes were open so wide that he looked as if he had seen a ghost.

"Ed," she said softly. "I was kidding. I know you won't leave me. In fact, I'm counting on you being a major fixture in my future. I want you to always be around. You got it?"

Ed's face was slowly returning to normal after he realized that she had really just been kidding. He wondered why she had pushed her face up as close to his as she could, and had placed her other hand on the back of his neck. As she began to pull his face towards her, it hit him what she was about to do. His heart began to race as he realized what was about to happen. He thought it was going to happen earlier, back on the road, but the moment had passed when they saw the supplies just off the road ahead. He had longed for this since he was very young, and now it was finally going to happen. He started to close his eyes, but decided that he wanted to see her face when their lips met.

Suddenly one of the rescuers walked up right in front of them and stopped. He was only two feet from them, but he was facing the other side of the crash site. He paused for a second before he yelled out at the man on the other side of the circle.

"I'm back where I started. You?"

Then the man on the other side responded.

"Yes. See anything?"

The man by them yelled "No! What NOW?"

"Let's touch base with Doc and see what he thinks."

Then the man began running away from them. Ed and Martha were still pressed chest to chest, but their attention was now locked on the man running away from them. Martha feared that this kiss was once again postponed. Her emotions took an immediate tumble. Then Ed spoke without even looking down at her.

"Martha. It's time we get this over with. Let's do this!"

Her heart leapt into high gear and her emotions swelled as she assumed she was about to be kissed. But to her amazement, Ed didn't kiss her. No, he actually stepped away and towards the open area before looking back at her to say, "Let's get rescued!"

She mumbled, "Now?"

He had a big smile on his face. "Yes, NOW! I'm not afraid

anymore. We can do this and we will stay together. I know it!"

Though she was happy that he was so confident that their relationship would continue to grow, she couldn't shake the complete disappointment of not haven been kissed. Again.

Ed practically drug her from the trees and into a rather quick run to catch the two men. He called out, "Hey! Hey you guys! Stop! Wait up! Stop!" Ed was amazed how fast these guys were running away from Martha and him. Ed thought to himself, "Damn! These guys are in really good shape."

Even though Ed began to slow down, Martha suddenly became very determined to catch these guys and get their attention. They released each other's hand as Martha passed Ed in a flat-out run towards the rescuers. Ed stopped and smiled at the sight of Martha hustling along with her hair almost straight out behind her.

Just as she was about to catch them, the two men split off in opposite directions, ran another 20 yards and stopped. Martha's momentum kept her going until she finally stopped directly between the two men. Ed had a perfect view of the two men with Martha directly in the middle. She turned to the man on the right and wondered what he was staring at in the trees. Finally she just blurted out, "Hey! How about some help here? Hey, you! Look at me!" She was staring at him and wondering why he didn't turn and acknowledge her.

Just as she was about to yell at him again, he finally turned towards her, but didn't say anything. He was just staring at her.

She couldn't take this any more. What was this guy doing? She wondered if he was on drugs or something. The thought made her snicker to herself. 'Maybe he is, and that is why he can run so fast!' Martha had had enough of this silent treatment and said, "Hey buddy! Are you deaf? I've been yelling at you for five minutes and you just kept right on running."

The man finally responded. "Sorry." He held his hands out to his side in a big gesture and said "WHAT?" Then he just stood there looking at her.

She was really confused by this guy's actions. Her anger swelled rapidly before she began her verbal assault on this inconsiderate idiot.

"What? How can you stand there and ask me that? Are you

insane? Are you NOT here to rescue us? Well STUPID, I'm standing right here in front of you. RESCUE ME!"

Then he asked, "What are you doing over there?"

This really set her off and she began another tongue-lashing, "Look! I've fallen out the sky from, well, I don't know how far up, but it was way, way up, believe me. I've been stuck overnight with a bunch of dead people, got NO SLEEP, and I've been wearing these same clothes for three days now. I'll admit it. I'm a little bit cranky. But so would you be, dummy. NOW RESCUE ME!"

After saying this, she turned to make a frustrated gesture at Ed. He was standing where she left him, and he appeared to be staring behind her. She started to turn to see what he was staring at, but her attention was snapped back to the idiot she was trying to talk to because he had yelled out, "Are you going to tell me why you are over there? Do you see something?"

Martha's blood was beginning to boil at how absolutely rude this guy was. "Do I see something? Yeah! An ASSHOLE who lacks the compassion to be a rescuer. How did you ever pass the training? Surely they attempted to teach you how to console somebody that has survived a plane crash. You must have flunked every test they gave you. How did you ever pass?"

Again, he was just staring at her, saying nothing. Well she'd had enough of this shit. It was time to slap some sense into this idiot.

She had raised her hand and was almost to him when she felt somebody grab her from behind and stop her. She spun around to confront whoever had grabbed her. It was Ed.

He quickly moved his hands to her shoulders, looked her straight in the eye and calmly said, "Wait. Just wait. Okay?"

At this point, she really wanted to slap that guy. She tried to wiggle free from Ed's big hands. But he tightened his grip and slowly said, "Wait! Just wait a minute. Trust me. There is something going on here I don't think you understand."

She stopped wiggling and Ed released his grip from her shoulders. "Ok, now. Just calm down a little and let me explain."

Martha was struggling to calm down, but her blood was still in fighting mode. She took a deep breath and then spoke through clenched teeth.

"Explain quickly! I REALLY want to slap that idiot. I mean

I REALLY want to slap him. Can you believe the nerve of that guy? How can he talk to me like that? After all I, we've, been through?"

Ed had both hands out in front of him with the palms down. He was making a slight downward pushing motion with them and said, "Just wait. Please calm down and listen to me a second." He lowered his hands and stepped very close to her. Looking down into her eyes, he calmly said, "I don't think they see us."

Her mind reeled with Ed's words ringing in her ears. What was he saying? Had he lost his mind, too?

The frustration was evident when she asked, "Are you crazy? What do you mean they can't see us? That's nuts!"

Just as Ed was about to speak again, they both heard the other rescuer yell out, "I just saw Doc go running that way in the trees. Come on!"

Martha turned to look at the second man who had just yelled out. She noticed that he was directly behind her and about 25 feet away. Her mind raced to process all the information from this scene. She realized that she was standing directly in the middle of the two rescuers. They both were facing her.

Now Ed was telling her they didn't see her. How could this be? No, this was silly. They *had* to see her. How could they not? She was standing right between them. She turned her head towards Ed. She was about to speak when she caught a glimpse of the big idiot who had walked up right behind her. Before she could turn to face him, she heard, "Okay. Wait for me!"

Just as she completed her pivot and was facing the idiot, she realized that he was going to run right into her. There wasn't enough time to even scream at him and she braced for the impact. Every cell in her body seemed to dance with electricity as she blinked and he disappeared. He was GONE!

She looked down, then side to side, but he was just not there. She looked at Ed and noticed his eyes were as big as hers must have been.

"What just happened?" she asked. "Where'd he go?"

She saw Ed raise his eyebrows and tilt his head in the direction behind her. She allowed her head to continue turning until she was looking at the two rescuers running towards the trees. At this point, she felt her anger melt away and even thought she might lack the strength to stand another second.

She was immediately comforted by the feel of Ed's big arm softly falling around her trembling shoulders. After the two men disappeared into the trees, she slowly looked up into Ed's expressionless face. "What just happened?"

Ed paused before answering, "Like I was saying. I don't think they see us. From where I was, I could see that you were right between them, but they were making gestures at each other. Not at you. I could just tell."

Martha had a very confused look on her face as she asked, "But how did that guy get around me? I thought for sure he was going to run right into me. That's why I closed my eyes. You know, like a reflex. I guess he stepped around me before we hit. Right?"

Ed was shaking his head. "No. That is not exactly what happened. Did you not feel anything? Anything at all? Anything weird?"

"No. Well, sort of. I guess. I felt something, but it didn't feel like he ran into me. I just felt all tingly all over. I'd say it felt, well, kinda weird."

Ed chuckled and said, "Well it must have felt weird, because it looked as weird as HELL from where I was standing. Do you feel okay now?"

"What looked weird from where you were standing? What are you saying? I'm getting pissed off now! Tell me, what are you saying? How did he get around me?"

Ed hesitated and then cleared his throat before saying, "Well, he didn't go around at all. He, uh, well, I don't know how to say this." Ed really was not wanting to say it but Martha was giving him the sternest look he had ever seen so he said, "Brace yourself baby. He appeared to walk right through you." Then Ed just stopped speaking, leaving only his eyes moving as he searched Martha's face for a response.

She was motionless for a few seconds as she stood there, looking blank-faced at Ed. Then her head suddenly jerked and she blinked rapidly several times before she focused on Ed's face once more.

"Are you saying they are ghosts?"

Ed saw that even though she was looking directly at him, she wasn't seeing him at all. She was deep in thought and her face was expressionless. He knew that he had to be patient with her as she worked through the revelations of the last few minutes.

Martha began speaking as she turned to look towards the tree line where the two men had now disappeared. "So you're saying they're ghosts, and that is why they went into the trees. Just like the others we saw that first night? Wow! This is really freaking me out!

"I'll bet that since it's daylight, we won't see that big flash of light, but we should still hear that loud WOOOSH sound. Right? You know! When they, uh, move on like the others."

Ed looked at her for a few seconds before he bit his lower lip and began shaking his head NO. "I still don't think you understand what I'm saying, baby."

"Ed. That is the second time that you've called me baby. And don't get me wrong. I LIKE IT! REALLY! But, here's the thing I don't get. If you aren't saying they are ghosts, then what ARE you saying they are?"

Ed raked his teeth a few times on his lower lip, chuckled softly and said, "Well, and this is just my opinion at the moment. But I think they're the rescuers, just like we thought they were. It's, well, it seems that we . . . "

Ed was cut off by Martha.

"Are you trying to say that WE ARE THE GHOSTS? Are you OUT OF YOUR MIND? That's the most ridiculous thing I've ever heard. How can we be?"

She stopped talking abruptly, staring past Ed and into oblivion. A few seconds passed as she mentally reviewed everything that had transpired since they both walked out of the trees to chase down those two men.

Ed was intensely watching Martha, wondering what she would do next. He was so worried for her, but knew there was nothing he could do. She had to get her mind around all that had happened. He could only worry and wait.

Though it was only seconds, Ed felt that he had been holding his breath for hours before Martha took a very deep breath. She closed her eyes, held the breath for a second, then slowly exhaled. Her eyes opened just as she began to breathe normally again.

"I think you're right. In fact, I know you are right. We are the ghosts. We are not survivors about to be rescued." Her eyes were swelling with tears as her breaking voice said, "Because we didn't survive. Did we?"

Ed felt a pain in his chest that he had never felt before. It felt like his heart was breaking. Standing before him was a woman that he had come to care very much for in the hours since the crash. No. To say he cared very much for her was truly an understatement. Though he had never felt this before, he now knew that he loved her. This had to be the reason why her teary eyes were just crushing his spirit so much at the moment. He had always wanted to be in love, but to his amazement, he found that this really hurt.

"Ed. Can you just hold me for a minute or two? Really tightly. Please? I don't care if we are, well, you know."

Having said that, she exhaled and hung her head. She displayed her frustration with their new set of circumstances. Ed could only watch her and feel his heart break with the thought of her being in pain.

As he wondered what to say, she suddenly stood upright, lifted her head and sounded very confident.

"I don't care if we are dead. I need you to hold me. No. I WANT you to hold me."

Ed could tell that even with her emotions running rampant, she was beginning to find the strength to accept things and take control. She pressed tightly against his chest and he wrapped his arms around her, hoping to comfort her. Looking up into his eyes she said, "I know we'll get through this together. But right now I feel like I'm on overload, and I don't want to talk for a while. Okay?" Then she closed her eyes, lowered her head and rested it gently on his chest.

Ed could feel the tension slowly fade from her body and then she stopped trembling all together. The pain in his chest immediately disappeared as well. Feeling relaxed, he turned his head to one side and softly lowered it until his cheek rested on top of her head. "I'll stand here with you as long as you want, baby. We don't have to say a thing."

They hadn't been standing for more than a minute when a different man strolled out of the tree line on the opposite side of the crash site. Ed watched him walk about 30 feet into the crash circle before stopping. Ed was curious what the man seemed to be looking around for. Then Ed heard the man's deep voice say, "I know you're both here. I can't see you, but I know you're here. I heard you talking. I know she's scared. Don't worry, missy. It will all work out. These things always do."

With that said, he slowly looked around once more before he turned to walk back into the trees. Ed raised his head to better-focus his eyes on the man as he disappeared into the forest. He had a quizzical look on his face as he thought to himself, "Did that guy just say he heard us talking?" Once Ed realized he had heard the man say that, he wondered if Martha had also heard it. Glancing down at her, he saw that her head was still resting on his chest, and her eyes were still closed.

Martha looked so calm and peaceful that Ed decided not to disturb her. Though she was a dead woman, she was still his woman. He was content to stand there, holding the woman that he had spent his entire life waiting to meet. He softly chuckled to himself as he realized that he literally spent his whole life waiting for her, and had only met her moments before their deaths. He knew he was dead and felt he should be depressed about it, but he wasn't. In fact, he felt really happy at this moment. This being dead wasn't so bad. Not as long as he could be with Martha. He now knew that he would be totally happy spending eternity in this forest, as long as he was with her. He wondered if she truly felt the same.

He was certain that she liked him, but would her feelings for him withstand the test of time? After all, eternity was a very long time. Though he knew his feelings for her would be forever, he could only hope that hers would be, too.

• • •

Ed and Martha stood motionless for several hours. Not a word spoken. Martha never opened her eyes or made even the softest sound. Ed had never once closed his eyes or lifted his cheek from her head. They had stood there, locked in a comforting embrace. There, of all places. The very crash circle they had woken up in after the event that had taken their lives.

At first there was only the two of them and the debris from the crash. But, over the last hour, more and more equipment had been delivered just to the edge of the circle. Ed was content to watch the men as they moved about, performing their given tasks. Every time one of the men would yell across the circle at another, Ed would glance down to see if Martha had opened her eyes. She never did. There was never any facial movement at all. No outward sign of her hearing anything at all.

Ed wondered if this was sleep or something else. Could this be what dead people do in place of sleep? He noticed that she wasn't breathing. There was no gentle movement of her chest. No, there was nothing. She had absolutely no expression at all on her face. She hadn't moved a muscle. Well, so to speak.

It eventually dawned on him that he wasn't breathing either. He found this fact intriguing. He wondered what it would be like to walk under water. He would love to do that in some of the lakes he'd visited with his parents as a child. Maybe he could find his father's watch. It had a loose wristband, and had fallen overboard while they were on that ferry boat ride. That had been a great trip until his dad lost that watch. It had belonged to Ed's grandpa, and would have been his watch one day. Ed made a mental note to talk to Martha about going to that lake. That was, if they could leave this place.

Were ghosts allowed to leave the place where they had died? He and Martha had walked several miles away from the crash site before they had realized they were dead. Maybe that is just a misconception from Hollywood. Man, there was going to be a big learning curve for the both of them. They were going to have to reconsider what being dead meant. But that was all right. They had nothing but time now. There would be plenty of time to really get to know each other, and to explore the boundaries of this new state of existence. They would figure out the rules together.

Ed's train of thought was shattered by a sudden rush of wind, followed by the noise of a chopper hovering just inside the tree line on the opposite side of the circle. He hadn't even noticed that the cloud cover had risen with the temperature. Now he could actually see the tops of the trees, and then some.

There was a huge crate dangling on a cable beneath the chopper. On the ground, two men were standing with their hands up while a third man was obviously guiding the pilot to help him position it directly over the other two. Slowly the chopper lowered the cargo until the waiting men could grab and hold onto it until it was safely on the ground. The cable was released, and the chopper climbed till it was out of sight.

Ed was so fascinated by all the activity that he was startled when he heard Martha's voice. "What's going on? What are they doing? When did that chopper get here?"

He glanced down and saw that she had raised her head just a little. She was also watching the activity across the circle.

"Well, the clouds have risen and now they're high enough for the chopper to start dropping supplies right here, instead of on the road."

Martha looked straight up. "When did that happen? How long was I out? Have we just been standing here all this time?"

"Yes, we have. I'm not sure how long it's been. There's been a lot of activity on the ground for a while, but that chopper just got here. It dropped that load in less than two minutes, and was leaving when you woke up."

She turned to look at Ed again, then laid her head back against his chest. "I just want to close my eyes a little longer." Then she very softly added, "Okay?"

Ed put his cheek back on top of her head before answering, "Of course it's okay. We'll stand here as long as you want, baby. As long as you want."

Martha had closed her eyes and stopped moving instantly, but Ed had kept his eyes wide open for over an hour as he watched the activity of the rescue team. They were busy pulling smudge pots from that big crate the chopper had dropped off. He watched as they filled each one with a thick black fuel before taking them just a few feet out into the trees. They were placing these pots every few yards around the entire crash circle.

Ed could hear the men talking about how much smoke these pots would give off. They were all wondering if the smoke would really keep the small animals from coming around to scavenge on any body parts that had not been recovered by nightfall. Once this task was done, they all abandoned the circle for other tasks beyond the tree line. Ed found this lack of activity boring. There was nothing for him to watch, so he slowly closed his eyes.

• • •

The sound of men yelling drew Ed's attention. It took his eyes a few seconds to adjust to the artificial light that was now everywhere within the circle. From what he was seeing, he must have been out for quite a while. The dark of night was everywhere else, except in the circle, as there were now four huge portable light generators positioned on opposite sides. Though the entire circle was well lit, the light seemed to just stop right at the tree line. It looked as if there was a solid black wall that surrounded the circle.

Once Ed's eyes had completely adjusted, he could see the faint flickering of fire off in the trees. These fires were obviously from the smudge pots, since they were equal distance from each other and encompassed the circle completely.

Ed's attention was drawn to a young man that darted out of the dark and turned in their direction. As he jogged right towards them, Ed realized that he was going to run right into them. A quick glance down at Martha's face showed her eyes were still closed. She looked so peaceful. Ed wondered if he should take a step back and pull Martha out of this man's path. But she just looked so peaceful that he hesitated. He looked up just as the young man was about to slam into them. But instead, he disappeared.

Ed knew that the young man had just passed through them both. It was as if every cell in Ed's spirit body had suddenly been given an electric shock. Not a massive one, just a very strong tingling sensation that only lasted a second. Now he knew what Martha had felt when that other guy had walked right through her.

He was thinking 'That wasn't so bad'. Then Martha lifted her head and said, "Wow! I just had the strangest dream." She was rapidly blinking and gently shaking her head. "I think my entire body is tingling. I know this feeling."

"Well I'm tingling too. We just had one of those guys run right through us."

Martha stood upright and stepped back from Ed. She was trying to get her eyes to focus as she slowly looked around the circle.

"When did all this stuff get here? How long was I out this time?"

Ed also looked around the circle while answering, "Well, to tell the truth. I don't know when it all got here either. I closed my eyes, and it was all here when I opened them again."

Martha's eyes were beginning to focus in the light. "Well, these guys have obviously been very busy. How did they get those big lights in here? Did I sleep through the chopper dropping them off?"

"Well it looks like we both did. How do you feel? Are your eyes adjusted to the light yet?"

She finally noticed the flickering lights out in the trees. She tilted her head just a little and squinted as she was trying to see past the edge of the light, beyond and into the trees.

Without any warning, she screamed extremely loud, turned and stepped back tightly against Ed. With her face buried deep in his shirt, Ed heard her muffled voice.

"Hold me! Hold me tight. Are those lights in the trees here to take us now?"

Ed felt her trembling uncontrollably in his arms. He held her tighter in an effort to reassure her.

"What light? What is coming to get us? Talk to me, Martha. What?"

"The lights in the trees. You don't see them? Are they here for us like they were for those other poor souls that first night?"

Now Ed understood. She thought the lights from the smudge pots were the lights they saw take the spirits of the people that first night. She was shaking so hard he thought she might fall down.

"Martha. Martha! Those aren't lights. They're smudge pots. They give off smoke. The men put them out there to try and scare off wild animals."

Finally she lifted her head and she didn't appear to be shaking as much as before.

"Smudge pots? Where did they get those?"

"That was what was in that first big crate the chopper delivered. When you went back to sleep, I watched the men unload them. Then they fueled each one and spaced them around the circle before lighting them. I only know what they are because I was listening to them as they put them out there."

Gradually, she got the nerve to look back over her shoulder and into the trees at the flickering lights.

"Well, I'll take your word for it now, but I'm NOT going out there until daylight! You know. Just in case."

Ed's attention was now on the dark tree line, but he wasn't looking at the smudge pot fires. He was slowly looking around the tree line, wondering if it would ever be safe for them to go into the dark. He said, "You know, you might have a good point there. We never went out into the dark that night. Remember? Maybe that is why we didn't get taken that first night. You think?"

Martha was still shaking just a little when she answered him.

"What? I don't know what to think right now. I don't even want to talk about it any more. Not now. Maybe in the morning, when it's light again. Right now, it just seems way too creepy to me."

Ed was still surveying the darkness at the tree line as he added, "I agree. This is way too creepy for me too."

"Ed? I remember that first night. I really enjoyed just sitting with you by the fires. Maybe we can just do that again. Okay?"

Ed looked into her eyes. "We can do that. I'd like that. In fact, I'd like that very much."

"Great!" she said. Her eyes were beginning to display that little twinkle as a smile appeared on her face. She turned to look around, and then pointed to a section of ground. "Look! That is where we sat that first night. We won't have a fire, but it looks like we'll have plenty of light." She was pointing at all the portable light generators that illuminated the crash site.

Ed was relieved to see that she had stopped shaking and her mood was beginning to lighten up. "We can pretend that there's a fire."

Martha wrinkled her nose. "It won't be hard to imagine a fire since we'll have the smell of those smudge pots keeping us company." She started pulling him by his hand. "Come on, Ed. Let's get comfy!"

Ed happily followed her over to their spot, and helped her sit down first before taking his place beside her. He hadn't been seated for more than a few seconds when he noticed her eyebrows were raised, and that she was looking from side to side. "What's wrong?"

She looked around one more time. "I think you're on the wrong side. You should be over here." She was pointing to her opposite side.

Ed was still smiling, but inside, he was wondering if she was serious. Surely she didn't expect him to get up and move over there. What was the point?

"Well?" she said.

"Well, what?"

"Come on, you big goof, move over here."

She was smiling and pushing his arm upward, as if trying to help him stand up.

Ed couldn't believe she was serious. Then he recalled how his guy friends used to tell him silly things that their girlfriends would insist they do. He also remembered them saying that it was best not to resist and just go along with them. Yes, this had to be one of those times his friends had been talking about.

He didn't understand why, but he rose to his feet. She never let go of his hand as she gently guided him to where she wanted him. Then he sat down in what she considered his correct position. He still couldn't believe it made that big of a difference which side he sat on, but obviously she did. She was smiling, her eyebrows high on her face.

Her head began to slowly nod 'Yes' as she said, "See! Now isn't that much better?" Then she quickly scooted tight against his side and slipped one arm beneath his. Then she placed her other arm on top of his and stretched her hand out flat before laying her head on it. Ed felt her still nodding as she softly added, "This is perfect. Just like that first night."

While nothing was being said, Ed's mind replayed what had just happened. He kept wondering why she made such a big deal about which side he sat on. Then he recalled how his friends had always told him he was lucky not to have a girlfriend. They said girls were hard to understand at times. He now knew what they meant.

He also recalled how one friend had told him a secret to getting along with women. He had said, "If it doesn't really matter to you, but it does to them, then do it! Just do it! It's not worth trying to understand why or getting into an argument over it. It may be silly, but for whatever reason, it isn't silly to them. So it's not being 'whipped' like other guys say. No, it's just necessary if you want to have a peaceful relationship with a woman."

Ed's train of thought was broken by Martha, who was looking up at the lights.

"I wonder if they'll leave those lights on all night. God, I hope so. I don't like the thought of sitting here in the dark all night with those lights dancing in the trees. I don't know if I can take that."

"Well, you're in luck! I happen to know for a fact they are going to be on all night. I overheard one guy telling the others to make sure they completely filled the gas tanks on each of the light generators. He said he didn't want the lights going off in the middle of the night. Plus, they were hoping that the light would help to keep the little animals away."

Again, she was nodding her head in agreement. "Great! So, what do you want to talk about first?"

Ed shrugged. "I don't know. What would you like to talk about?"

"Well, first of all. I was wondering what all those black plastic bags were over there on the other side. Did that stuff come out of the crate, too?"

Ed hadn't even noticed the bags until she pointed at them. *Oh no*, he thought. They were body bags. How was she going to take this? How could he answer her without getting her all upset again? He hesitated for a moment, then decided to answer calmly.

"They are body bags, Martha." He scanned her face for any sign that she was going to be upset or cry again. To his amazement, she did neither. Her smile was replaced by a calm, reverent look.

"Oh. I guess they're lining them up to start taking them back for identification. How sad. You know, it just dawned on me. These men must be dealing with all kinds of feelings about what is all around them. I don't see how they can do it. They must be very special people to do this. I couldn't do it."

She had Ed thinking about it as well. "I hadn't thought about it before you said that. You're right, though. When you were asleep, I watched one of those guys throwing up out in the trees. Then he just stayed kneeling down for quite a while, before one of the other guys came over and helped him up. They stood there for a few minutes talking, and then they walked off together. I can't believe how wrong I was. I just thought that he had gotten sick. I didn't realize that it could be from what he was seeing."

Ed started to say how bad he felt about not having even considered why the man was sick. But there was sudden movement on the other side of the circle. Two men emerged from the trees, carrying yet another body bag. They walked over and gently laid it beside the rest of them. They stood there for just a second as if they were saying a short prayer. Then they turned and hustled back into the trees.

Martha said, "I wonder if they're going to work straight through the night?"

"Yes, they plan to. I heard them all talking earlier. They're hoping to bag all the bodies they have found so far, and get them inside the circle. The pilots are sleeping right now, and they want to be ready when they wake up. They will be bringing the next shift of guys up to take over, and take these guys back to their base camp to get some sleep."

Both of them seemed compelled to stare at those black plastic bags neatly lined up in a row.

She said, "It seems so sad to think that each of those bags represents a person that lost their life here. We saw their spirits get taken by that bright light, and tomorrow we will see their bodies get taken away to who knows where." Then she turned to him and added, "But we're still here. We know we're dead, but we still have some kind of existence. Right?"

"Well. That we do. I don't know what it is. But we are still here. I see you and you see me." He reached up and brushed his hand across hers before saying, "I feel you and I guess you feel me. Don't you?"

"Yes, I do. We are linked together for some reason. We aren't alive, but we are something. I don't know what, but we are something. We are more than what those others were. Well, maybe not more. But we're definitely in a different state."

Ed was rubbing his forehead with the one hand that wasn't currently pinned to his side by Martha. He had so many questions and ideas flying through his mind that he couldn't keep them all straight. He had been wondering about their status the entire time that she was asleep.

"I agree. There is something or some reason that we were

not taken that first night like the others. It was so odd. We could see them, but they apparently didn't see us. We knew then that we couldn't be seen by the other dead people, and now we know that we can't be seen by the living either." He had stopped rubbing his forehead. With his eyes closed and his head tipped so low that his chin was almost on his chest, he slowly began shaking his head 'NO'.

"You know. It just doesn't make any sense. None at all. I keep coming back to one basic question."

"The question of why?"

He opened his eyes. "Right! You read my mind. WHY? I just feel if we could figure out the 'WHY', then we would have a better chance of controlling our fate here. Or does that sound as crazy to you as it does to me, now that I've said it?"

"No. It doesn't sound crazy at all. In fact, it makes complete sense. We have to figure out why. But how? We can't ask anybody. And even if we do get it right, how will we know?"

"Well. I don't really know much, but I do know one thing." He smiled and lightly chuckled at her. "It appears that we'll have plenty of time to figure it out."

She smiled and her eyes changed from a little sparkle to that of a beautiful dark-blue lagoon. Just like they had several times today. He knew that she was thinking about kissing him again. Of course he wanted to kiss her too, but HEY! They're dead. It just can't be the same as if they had done it while they were alive. Or can it? After all, he can feel her and she can feel him. Oh, what the HELL. He decided he was all for it too.

Her face lost all expression and her eyes changed to that of a cat stalking its prey as she slowly moved her face towards his. Only an inch separated their lips this time as she whispered, "We have nothing but time to think, and to do other things as well."

Both had closed their eyes. Just as their lips were finally going to make contact, there was a sharp and very loud SLAP that sounded like thunder only a few feet from them. Their eyes snapped open as they both instinctively turned towards the sound. They saw that two men had dropped a large wooden pallet directly in front of the black bags. Martha was so startled that she had one hand on her chest. She thought to herself,

'Even in death, loud noises scare the heck out of me.' She didn't know what Ed was thinking at this moment, but she damn sure knew what she was thinking about right now. Yep! Once again, these guys have managed to stop her from getting a kiss. THE KISS! What was up with all these guys? Were they somehow unconsciously working together to keep her from getting KISSED? This was beginning to really get annoying. Then it dawned on her that these guys didn't even know she was here. But she didn't care. She had to blame somebody and they were HERE! Her agitation came across as she blurted out, "Now WHAT? What are they doing now? Can't they be a little more quiet over there? They just don't give any thought to how much noise they are making. They . . . "

Ed had gently placed two fingers on her lips to hush her rant before he said, "Martha. They don't even know we are here. You know?"

Even though she felt a little foolish, she couldn't help acting a little childish as she said, "Okay, okay, okay.. I know!" She was waving both hands in small circles in front of her as she continued.

"It's just that this whole DEAD, can't be seen thing is, is, uh . . . well, I just keep forgetting about it. It's still new to me. It seems that you have fully embraced it but it obviously hasn't sunk in with me yet." She put both hands out in front of her like a traffic cop. She took a deep breath in, and slowly breathed out.

"There! I'm better. It needed to be said. I did. I feel better."

Ed started to say something else, but the stern look in her eyes convinced him to drop it and turn his attention back to what those men were doing on the other side of the circle.

"What do you think they are doing, Ed?"

"Well. I bet they are going to start stacking those bodies on that pallet. If you look, they've already attached some cables to the corners of it. They'll use those to hook onto the cable hanging from the belly of the chopper. That's how they're going to get those bodies out of here. I bet they are building some more out in the woods right now. They'll have them all loaded up and ready for the choppers in the morning."

"How are they going to keep them from falling off in flight?"

"Well, if you look beside the pallet, it looks like they have a bunch of black nylon straps to secure them with." Ed was straining to focus his eyes on the straps on the ground by the pallet. "Yep. That's what they are going to do. Bet ya."

"I wonder why they just don't load them into the chopper?"

Ed has a small smile as he replied, "Well, two good reasons come to mind. They can get more bodies on the pallet than inside that chopper. But I'll bet the real reason is that the chopper can't land here because of all the plane wreckage. So that means they'd have to carry each body on foot through the woods and back to the road. I don't think that's really an option here. Do you?"

She just sat there looking at him for a few seconds. Then she sighed, rolled her eyes and lightly hit him on his shoulder. "Okay! Smarty pants!"

Ed faked like she hit him so hard that it knocked him over on his side. She immediately slapped him on his backside. "Hey! Don't point that thing at me mister! You sit back up like a proper gentleman. If we are going to go through time together, then you need to start showing some manners."

She was laughing and so was Ed as he quickly sat back up. Martha didn't hesitate to assume her usual spot. She was pressed hard against his side with her arm and hand on opposite sides of his arm. Slowly replacing her head on his shoulder, she asked, "So what do we talk about now, big boy?"

"I do believe that the topic was 'WHY'. Maybe we need to keep talking about that."

"I agree, but I just don't have any ideas. I don't even know where to start."

When Ed didn't reply for a few seconds, she lifted her head, leaned forward a little and saw that his gaze was completely fixated on that pallet. "What are you thinking so hard about?" she asked.

Ed started nodding his head. He finally said, "I want to get on that pallet tomorrow and ride back to their base camp." He turned to her with wide eyes and said it even more excitedly, "Look. We both should get on the pallet and ride back to their base camp!" He was really nodding his head 'YES' now.

She squinted and tightened her lips before saying, "I'm not so sure that's a good idea."

"Oh, come on! It will be fun! Besides, it's not like we can get killed or anything if we fall off. Aren't you at least a little bit curious about their base camp?"

"Oh my GOD! You're serious? Hey buddy! I maybe dead myself, but there is absolutely NO WAY I'm going to get on that thing with a bunch of bodies. NO!"

Ed's face lost all expression as he simply asked, "Why not?"

She hesitated as she fumbled to formulate her response.

"Well, before you say something like 'Hey! It's not like they're going to bite us', I know that. But I'll just say this again. There is NO WAY you are going to get me on that thing . . . " She shook one finger from side to side in front of him before saying, "NO! Absolutely NOT!"

Ed started to repeat his 'why' again, but stopped when he realized that she wasn't going to change her mind. He turned to continue looking at the pallet without saying another word.

After a few minutes of silence, she thought she heard something. Was that humming? Was he humming? Leaning forward just a little, she saw he was still staring at the pallet, smiling and now HUMMING? Oh, this wasn't good! She knew he was still getting on that thing and flying it back to their base camp. Would he go without her? Would he? Oh NO! He wouldn't do that. Leave her here all alone. Would he?

She knew that she better come up with a valid and logical reason for him NOT to go. But what? She was almost panicking as she tried to think of a good reason. Then it hit her. It wasn't a perfect reason, but it was a reason. Without even realizing she did it, she blurted out "AH HAH!"

This sudden proclamation caused Ed to jump, and then turn sharply to look at her.

"AH HAH WHAT? Gee! You scared the HELL out of me!"

She giggled softly, then began to explain.

"Sorry! I just thought of something. Interested?"

"Well, I am now! Spit it out."

"I just don't think that we are supposed to leave this area. How do you know that it's Okay? Maybe we should stay here for a little while longer. Just until we get used to this whole dead situation. Besides, how do you know we *can* leave?"

Ed was squinting now as her words rolled around in his head.

"Well. Obviously we don't know. I can't believe there is anyone who's going to get mad at us if we go off." He chuckled a little bit. "What can they do to us? We're already dead."

"Yes we are. But we can still feel things. Can't we?"

"Wow. You're right." He now looked like a kid that had just been told he couldn't go to the park and play. It was a good reason, but he still wanted to go, and she saw in his eyes that he was not giving up on this. She really needed to add another good reason, but what? Then it hit her.

"I'm not going anywhere on that thing. And you've told me several times now that you aren't going to leave me alone. Have you changed your mind already?"

Ed took one last glance at the pallet before his shoulders dropped a little. "Yeah. You're probably right. It was just a thought."

They both assumed their normal sitting positions. As her head settled on his shoulder once again, she let her smile slowly drift away. Yes, she had won this small battle. But in her heart, she knew it wasn't over. He really wanted to go. She wondered if she was being fair by not letting him go, just because she didn't want to. All she was thinking right now was that he was not going to leave her. She liked that.

Chapter 7

RESCUE TO RECOVERY

THE SOUND OF birds squawking in the treetops finally caused Martha to open her eyes. As they brought the new day into focus, she found that the clouds were completely gone. They had been replaced with a clear, dark blue sky that was ever so slowly yielding to the bright light of a rising sun. She had slept through yet another night in this field of destruction.

She looked to see if Ed was awake, but his eyes were shut and his face was expressionless. Her first thought was that he actually looked dead. A soft laugh led a smile across her face as she thought, 'Of course he looks dead. He is!'

As the light claimed more and more of the sky above, she couldn't help but feel some joyful anticipation of what was obviously going to be a beautiful day. Well, at least weather-wise, that is. Her smile disappeared as she began thinking of how nice it would be if this were all a dream. Yes, just a scary bad dream. But she was still glad she had met Ed.

Why didn't she meet this nice man in time to share life among the living? She was never one to pity herself and she wasn't going to start now. Dead or not, she had finally met the man she had always hoped for. He was what she had always wanted, and now she had him. He was right here beside her. She had a firm hold on him and she wasn't ever going to let go. NEVER!

She found it odd that she could feel so content with her head resting on Ed's shoulder when, just 40 yards away, there were so many black bags. Each one represented a lost life. Was she evil to feel this way in the presence of so many unfortunate others? How could she be happy in a place like this? Then she snickered at herself. *Wait a minute! I'm dead too!*

There were now five pallets on the other side of the circle. Each one had six black plastic bags neatly strapped down. The cables from all four corners were now securely fastened to a large silver ring. She guessed that the cable from the belly of the chopper would have a big snapping hook that would attach to the silver ring. She couldn't believe that Ed actually wanted to get on one of those things and be dragged through the open sky to God knows where. And to think he actually thought he could talk HER into doing it too! He must have hit his head pretty damn hard in the crash to think that!

One man was starting to shut down the big light generators. It was now light enough to see more than 20 feet into the trees. She clearly heard one man tell another that the chopper would be here in 20 minutes for the first load. Seemed they were also bringing up a second chopper and it would be in the valley by noon. Yes, they had definitely moved from rescue to recovery.

Their efficiency had really transformed the circle during the night. It now looked like a big industrial work yard. Equipment was neatly staged in various locations, and the men were all working together as if this was just another day at the yard.

She was intrigued that there didn't appear to be a single boss; a man who would stand back and tell the others what to do. No, they all were working in pairs and appeared to make joint decisions as they moved about their tasks. She wondered why some looked like lumberjacks and some were dressed in military fatigues. It didn't seem to matter though, and she was fascinated by it all.

Two more men emerged from the trees carrying yet another black bag. They placed it with the others. Even with the five loaded pallets, there was a growing excess of black bags patiently waiting their turn to start a journey home. A journey she and Ed apparently were not going to make for a while. That is, if she could keep talking Ed out of going on a joy ride in the sky. She still couldn't get over him wanting to get on one of those wooden flying carpets. Must be a guy thing.

There in the distance, she now heard that slow thumping noise in the sky. She was amazed that she could hear it, but none of the living people heard it yet. Of course, Ed never heard it either until it was almost on top of them. She looked at him and jokingly thought, *He's a disgrace to all dead people.* Then she thought, *What if he's the first deaf dead guy?*

This made her actually laugh out loud, but she caught herself quickly. Her reflex was to put her fingertips over her mouth and glance down to see if she had woken Ed. And she had.

Ed had just one eye open and was staring right at her.

"What are you laughing at?" Then he looked up at the sky and asked, "And what is that thumping noise?"

Her face went blank as she asked, "You hear that?"

Ed now had both eyes wide open and a very quizzical look on his face.

"Of course I hear that! What do you think I am? Deaf?"

Hearing this response from him made her completely lose it and she fell over on her side laughing out loud. Then Ed innocently commented without thinking, "You're getting kinda loud there, missy. You're going to wake the dead."

Ed was totally confused as to why his comment had sent Martha into an even louder state of laughter. She was actually rolling on the ground with tears in her eyes now. Eventually she held one hand up and shook it at him before saying, "Please. Don't say anything else. You're killing me here!"

Not being totally awake yet, Ed accidentally added even more fuel to her laughter by saying, "I can't kill you. You're already dead."

Now she had rolled over on her back and was holding her stomach with one hand while pointing at him with the other one. She spoke between laughs and gasps for air, "Stop! No more! Please!"

Ed just stared at her and wondered what had gotten into her. He watched her laugh for a few more seconds. He finally concluded that whatever was up with her, it must be what she needed. Maybe she just needed to laugh. It could be just a big release of pent-up emotions from the last few days. Whatever it was, he felt it was probably the best thing for her right now.

The chopper was directly over the circle now, and the activity on the other side drew both of their attention. Ed was calmly sitting and trying not to look at her any more, for fear something would set her off on another loud burst of laughter. But try as he did, he couldn't help but wonder what in the world had gotten into her. She slowly regained control and got back into her usual position by his side. He noticed that she was biting her lower lip while glancing sideways at him, then quickly looking away. Yep, he'd noticed the childish grin on her face and knew she could break out laughing again at any moment.

The men began a well-rehearsed dance with the chopper. They guided the newest arrival of supplies to its chosen spot on the ground, and freed it from the chopper's cable. It amazed Ed and Martha how quickly they had the first pallet of bodies hooked up to the cable and the chopper on its way.

Martha said, "Boy! Those guys are fast! It's like they've been doing this their whole life. There they go." She gave Ed a few seconds to comment, but he didn't. Looking to see why, she noted that his eyes were once again fixated on that pallet that was sailing out of sight beneath that chopper. She knew what he was thinking and her good feeling quickly disappeared. She nudged him softly in an attempt to get him to snap out of it.

Ed's eyes remained glued to the pallet until it was out of sight. He was still looking at that point in the sky when he mumbled, "Yep. There they go. Fast."

"You still want to go. Don't you?"

He turned his attention back to her, but he hesitated before he answered softly.

"Yes. Yes I do. I'm sorry, but I do. I know we discussed it last night and you have a good point about not going. You're probably right about us not being able to leave this spot. But I have to admit it. I do."

She couldn't believe she was about to give him the green light, but he'd get around to this point eventually on his own.

"Well. I've been thinking about it too. Not that I'm going on that thing! No, I'm NOT! But as far as us not being able to leave this spot, I overheard those guys talking about us only being a few miles from the base camp as the crow flies. Now if that is true, then maybe."

Ed's excitement at her apparently changing her mind caused him to interrupt her. "Maybe what? Come on, out with it!"

She gave him one of those 'SLOW DOWN' looks until he finally took on the look of a scolded little boy. Then she continued.

"If you recall, we walked several miles away from here. Remember? Well, actually we ran first, then we got lost and then we walked back. But the point is this. We must have been several miles away at some point. When we finally found the road, we must have walked at least a mile and a half getting back to that stack of supplies. Remember?"

Ed felt as if he was about to come out of his skin as he jumped to his feet and began talking while he paced back and forth in front of her.

"Hey! You know you're right. I forgot about that. We must have been at least two miles away or more. This is GREAT! Those guys said that the chopper would be back in 30 minutes! I'll just get on and ride it back. Then, and this part is totally optional, I could get off at the other end. You know, just to look around and see what all is going on there. Then when the chopper comes back the next time, I'll hop on and ride back here to you. What do you think?"

She tilted her head and faked clearing her throat.

"So now you want to just get off and walk around down there. Really? And just leave me here alone with all these boring LIVE guys? I don't think that is what we were discussing. Let's see. It takes 30 minutes to get there and you get off. Then the chopper comes back here and that's another 30 minutes. You add 30 more minutes for it to get back to the base camp again, and then 30 more for you to get back here. Hmm? That sounds like you now expect me to hang around here ALONE for over two hours! Is that what you are saying?"

Martha was now standing, and they were both nose to nose. Ed's face showed he was busy adding up the times in his head. Once he had the calculation verified, his face lit up.

"Yes! I'd only be gone about two hours! That's not so bad."

"Not so BAD? It's TWO HOURS!"

"But, baby. What's two hours when you're dead? We are talking about existing like this for eternity. So two hours will go by in a blink. Besides, what could go wrong?"

She stiffened her back. "Go wrong? Oh, I don't know." Then she stepped very close to him.

"Let me see. I was on a plane that fell out of the SKY. I watched a bunch of ghosts walk into that bright light. Then I found out that I was DEAD! Gee. What could go wrong?"

Again, her words stopped him from pacing back and forth so he could think.

"Hmm. Those are all good points. Very true." He hesitated for a moment. Then he got a huge, childish grin on his face, shuffling his feet like a kid trying to talk his mom into letting him go anyway. "But it is only two hours. Just two." He held up two fingers and repeated "Two".

Martha still didn't like the idea of him leaving her alone for so long, but she had to admit that he was pretty damn cute right now. He was acting like a little kid, but he was *her* little kid and she knew she must let him do it. She stepped in closer and pressed against him. Maybe this will be that moment she had been waiting for? It would be a perfect time for him to kiss her!

"Ok. But you better be back on that next flight. You got it, mister? Two hours!" Then she held up two fingers just like he had, "Two". She was bracing for her reward, the elusive KISS.

Ed's face lit up. He failed to read her body language all together; instead, he turned to run over to the other side of the circle.

Martha's reflexes were fast and she grabbed him by the arm. "Where are you going?"

"I better get over there and get ready. I don't want to miss it."

"Get ready? Are you kidding me? It's going to be an hour before it gets back."

"Well, uh, I know that. But you said it yourself. These guys are fast!"

• • •

Since Ed had been so keyed up about getting to ride that pallet, Martha knew she would never get him to sit back down and cuddle until the chopper returned. So she had suggested that they walk around the circle and just talk until the chopper got back. Ed eagerly agreed, as long as they walked around on the other side of the circle where the men were waiting for the chopper. So that was what they had been doing for the last 40 minutes or so.

Martha felt obligated to continue trying to talk him out of going, even though she knew it was a useless endeavor.

"You still sure you want to ride on that thing?"

"Are you kidding? I can't wait! This is going to be soooooooo cool! You really should come along. Come on, Martha. Come with me."

She pointed her finger at him again. "I told you NO! There is no way you're going to ever get me on that thing. So drop it. You can get on it and risk falling off, but I'm not."

"I'm not going to fall off. There is absolutely no way I'll fall off. And if I do, so what! I'm already dead."

"I still think it's a bad idea. Something could happen. You don't know for sure."

Ed got a playful look in his eyes. "I know what you're really afraid of. You think I'm going to fall off and land on my head. Don't you? You think the jolt will bring me back to life and I'll leave you for a live girl. RIGHT?" He was standing with a cocky smile on his face.

"You wish! I'm just afraid there are things that we still don't know about this dead thing we have gotten into here. Until we do, why push it?"

Ed's expression softened and he stepped closer to her.

"Look, Martha. I spent my entire life being afraid to do so many things. I knew I was missing out on experiences that I would one day wish I'd done. But I was too scared to try them. And I was right about later realizing that I should have done each and every one of them. So you see. I just have to do this. I have to."

"Well, if you fall off that thing, don't expect me to show you any sympathy."

Martha stopped in front of several large, unopened crates and tried to read the labels on each. She knelt down and tried to peek through a hole in one of the wooden slats.

"I wonder what all this stuff is? These labels are no help. I can't see what's in here. It is all wrapped up in black plastic, or maybe it's a tarp of some kind. I can't really make it out." She stood up and motioned at Ed. "Come on. Maybe you can see something."

Ed didn't even look in her direction. His eyes kept jumping from the sky to what appeared to be the next staged pallet for the chopper to transport.

"No need for me to look. You have better hearing than me, and I'll bet you have superior eyesight too. If you can't tell, I'd do no better."

She couldn't help but think how much he was acting like a little kid who couldn't wait to open that first present on Christmas morning. Every time she started to move, he was obviously trying to steer her closer to that waiting pallet. She was enjoying the look in his eyes as she intentionally walked in the opposite direction from that pallet. She never thought of herself as a bad person, but this was kind of fun. He saw her walking away from it, and he had a panicked look on his face. Then she would stop and fake left, then right, before turning back around to let him lead her closer to his goal.

Then it dawned on her that she was toying with the very guy she had waited her whole life to be with. Why? The only good answer she could come up with was because it was so much fun.

Martha was so caught up in her thoughts that she hadn't noticed that Ed had stopped following her. He was standing between her and the pallet. Obviously he thought if he didn't move any more, she wouldn't go any farther away. She was about to prove him wrong when the low thump of the chopper blades became audible.

She turned to tell him to go on and get over to his precious ride, but Ed was already standing by it. He rocked from left foot to right foot, never lowering his eyes from the sky. Two men came out of the trees to assist with the chopper's arrival. One of the men actually walked right through Ed but he didn't even react to it. No, he was totally focused on the sky.

The large flying machine appeared over the circle, and the well-choreographed process of unloading began. It took less than a minute for the newly-arrived crate to be lowered to the ground and unhooked. The moment it was unhooked, one of the men hustled over and picked up the big silver ring that held the pallet's corner cables. The other man held onto the hook as he walked it over to the pallet. The two men worked quickly to attach the hook to the silver ring. The moment that it was secured, one man started walking backwards, giving the pilot a thumbs-up gesture.

The pilot slowly lifted his craft to take the slack out of the cables. Once all four cables were straight and tight, the man signaled the pilot that he was good to go.

Ed stepped onto the edge of the pallet and placed each hand on a corner cable. He looked over his shoulder at Martha, wearing the biggest grin she had ever seen. Wow! It suddenly dawned on her that she had expected to get a goodbye kiss right before he got on that thing. Damn it! It was too late now. *Oh well,* she thought. He'd be overjoyed when he returned, and that was when he'd be very easily maneuvered into that kiss. FINALLY!

Martha watched as the pallet rose faster and faster into the sky until it cleared the treetops. The chopper swung its tail around until the big bird was facing the same direction it had just came from. She couldn't help but think that Ed really looked kind of dashing as he stood on the fleeing platform. She was just about to lose sight of him due to the trees, when it happened.

She heard Ed yell "HEY!" before his hands were pulled from the cables, and his body began to tumble backwards. He flipped end over end several times before she lost sight of him. She realized he had fallen into the trees more than eight football fields from where she was.

She started running as fast as she could in Ed's direction. In her haste to avoid running through one of the men, she side-stepped him, slamming into a tall narrow crate that was standing upright on its end. To her amazement, it toppled over on its side. She noticed the two men jump as it bounced on the ground. She didn't give this incident another thought as she rushed into the trees to find Ed.

She ran for a few minutes before she started to catch glimpses of Ed through the trees ahead. She saw him stand up twice, stumble around and then fall back down. Is that laughter she heard? He had just gotten up on his feet for the third time as she rushed to his side and grabbed his arm. He gladly laid it across her shoulder and she guided him to a fallen log so he could sit down.

Halfway there, he looked at her and blurted out, "You see that SHIT? Whoa!"

He had rocked his head back as he spoke, and they both almost went down. She didn't know how, but she found the strength to hold him up long enough to get him seated on the log. He immediately bent over and placed his elbows on his knees. His head quickly fell into his open hands.

"Baby, are you all right? Please tell me you're all right. Speak to me, Ed. Please say something."

After a few agonizing seconds, he said, "I think I hit every limb in that tree on the way down. But I'm ok."

"You scared the HELL out of me, baby. I told you to be careful. I just knew you were going to fall off. I told you that you would!"

Ed slowly lifted his head just enough so she could see his eyes.

"That's twice you've called me baby. And I think I like it. Really! But I didn't fall off."

"What? So you jumped off? Are you out of your damn mind?"

"No, no, I didn't jump off, silly! Something pulled me off. I can't explain it, but it felt like something just pulled me off."

"What? What are you talking about? What pulled you off?"

"Well, it was more like I hit the end of a rope. I stopped, but the pallet kept moving. Man, that was weird!"

Ed began turning his head from side to side, as if he were trying to crack his neck to loosen it up. Then he dropped his head back into his hands, and let out a muffled moan.

"So you were pulled off by some invisible rope? And you hit every tree limb before falling on your head. Right?"

Ed sat up straight and tried to focus his eyes on Martha, but with some difficulty. He was visibly wobbling around on the log as he answered.

"Rope. Limbs. Head. Sounds about right." Then he just fell backwards off the log, his feet straight up in the air. She couldn't see him but she heard him laughing. She couldn't believe her ears.

"Oh my God. I'm dead and I'm in love with a crazy man!"

This made him laugh even louder. After a second or two, she was getting a little annoyed by his laughter. She stepped around the log, looked down at him and saw that he was blinking his eyes while he was laughing loudly.

"I'm just curious. Earlier, you made a remark about what I was really afraid would happen if you fell on your head. Remember? Well you did fall on it, so I'm just curious."

She bent at the waist to put her face directly over his. "Do you feel alive now?"

• • •

Martha sat down on the log to wait for Ed to recover, her wrists crossed and comfortably lying in her lap. Her legs were crossed as well, with one foot gently moving back and forth. She looked like someone who was simply enjoying a day alone in the woods. Occasionally she would glance back over her shoulder to see how Ed's recovery from his fall was progressing. If he wasn't already dead, she would have been more concerned about how long it was taking him to recover. It was obvious that his laughter was the reason his eyes were tearing up.

Not ever having had children of her own, she wondered if this was how a mother felt when she waited for her child to snap out of a tantrum. Finally, there was a stretch of time that was blissfully void of laughter. She resisted the urge to look back at him or say anything at all.

The peaceful silence was broken when Ed announced, "I'm done now."

Her continued silence caused Ed to quietly rise to his feet before he stepped over the log and sat down beside her. Once seated, he leaned forward to look at her face. She immediately pivoted on the log so that she was now looking the opposite way and had her back to him.

"I know you're mad at me. I get it. Really! But I'm fine now. Besides, you can't kill a dead person!"

She spun around quickly. "Well, dead or not, it seems there are still consequences for stupidity! It's taken you almost an hour to get back on your feet."

"So I fell off. I'm fine. Nobody got hurt. What's an hour? I paid for it."

"You're not the only one that paid for it." She had turned to face him before she continued. "I had to listen to you laugh like a madman for way too long. I'd say that I also paid plenty for your little stunt."

"You're not going to let this go, are you? Is this going to be one of those things you always bring up when you get mad at me about something?" He was mainly focused on her face, but he also noted her stance. One foot was slightly farther back than the other. Her arms were crossed over her chest, and she had a non-flinching stare that was just pounding him right between his eyes.

Then he noticed that twinkle in her eyes. Wait a minute! She wasn't mad. Damn, she'd done it again. She'd faked being mad and he had fallen for it. He squinted as he smiled. "You're not mad. Are you?"

She held out as long as she could before she returned his smile. "No! But I should be, you big goof!" She reached out and hit him on his arm before stepping around him to walk off. He rushed to catch up with her before he spoke.

"I'm glad you aren't really mad at me."

She asked playfully, "Oh yeah? And why is that?"

"You're the only dead person that talks to me!"

• • •

The walk back to the crash site had been fun. Ed would reach over and quickly tickle Martha's ear then run a few steps ahead. Once he slowed to a walk again, she would attack him with a small ghostly twig that she didn't remember picking up. Ed would laugh and dance around her, egging her on to try and hit him. All the time he would be saying, "Come on. Hit me. Go ahead. You can't hurt me. I'm dead!"

Before they knew it, they were back to the circle. Though Martha was hot on his heels, Ed had again stopped just a few feet short of the circle opening. Martha also stopped the moment she realized where they were. They both were standing there as if some unseen force was holding them. Their attention fell upon two men that were sitting on two crates. The men were taking a break while they waited for the chopper to get back.

Ed and Martha decided to eavesdrop on their conversation. One of the men was a logger and the other a guardsman.

The guardsman asked, "So . . . what's the story with this Vic guy of yours?"

The logger chuckled before he answered. "I guess you heard the others talking?"

"Yep. They seem to think he is psychic or something. I don't know that I buy all that stuff. You?"

"Well." The logger paused for a few seconds before he shook his head once or twice. "You know. I used to think just like you. Now? Well, I just don't know. But I do know this. Vic has told us some things that later came true."

The guardsman seemed very interested now. "What kind of things?"

"Well. We used to have a guy named Ray Martinez that worked with us. One day Vic came up to Ray and asked if he was going to see his mother that Saturday. Ray said no, because he was going to help a friend work on his car. Vic got right in his face and told him he really needed to spend the day with his mom. Ray actually pushed Vic and told him he wasn't interested in his crazy talk. After Ray stormed off, I went over to make sure Vic was okay. He told me that Ray's stepsister was going to show up at their mom's house and that they were going to have a very heated argument. He said the stepsister was going to try and hit Ray's mom."

The guardsman stood up and stepped closer to the logger before speaking in a low voice.

"So . . . what happened then?"

"Well, I don't know why I did it, but I went and talked to Ray. He just laughed and told me that he didn't even have a stepsister. Well, I felt like a fool then, so I just dropped it." The logger paused a little too long for the guardsman.

"And that's it? Are you kidding me? Come on, out with the rest of it."

The logger looked around then he leaned closer to the guardsman before also speaking in a low voice.

"Ok. Get this! The next Monday rolls around and Ray doesn't make it to work. We held the truck up for 40 minutes waiting for him. Nobody answered when we called his cell or his apartment. So we left without him. The next day, Ray shows up and he has a bandage on his head. We asked him what happened, but all he would say was that somebody hit him with a cane. Since his mom used one to walk with, we teased him the rest of the morning about her hitting him for cussing in her house. He never said a word. But we all saw him talking to Vic at lunch. They both went off and sat a long ways away from the rest of us. Ray wouldn't tell anyone what Vic and he had been talking about. We bugged Ray the entire afternoon, but nothing. He wouldn't say a thing."

The guardsman chimed in, "So why didn't you just ask Vic?"

"I did, but Vic told me it was personal and he couldn't say."

"So, what did you do?"

"Well, I used to bowl on Saturday nights with Ray. He and I always drank at least one pitcher of beer a game. I just waited for him to get drunk and talkative."

The guardsman was so caught up in the story that he was shifting his weight from foot to foot. He looked like a tennis pro waiting to return his opponent's serve. "So what did he say? Who hit him?"

"He told me that he didn't believe anything that Vic had said, and that he was still going to go help his friend work on that car. He got into his car that Saturday morning and headed to his friend's house. There was a city crew working on a busted water line and they were detouring all the cars several blocks off the main road. It dawned on him at one point, that the detour had put him just a few blocks away from his mom's house, so he just went on by just in case.

"When he got out of his car, he immediately heard angry shouting and things breaking inside his mom's house. He ran in and this crazy lady came out of nowhere. She hit him in the back of the head with his mom's cane before he wrestled her to the ground. He could see his mom on the floor in the other room. He couldn't let go of the lady to call 911, and he really didn't know what to do. But the neighbor had heard the noise too and saw him run into the house, so she called the cops.

"Ray said he was just holding her down and trying to talk to her when the cops came running in through the open front door. It turned out that she was his stepsister. She had mental problems from birth and Ray's mom eventually had her committed because she couldn't control her. All the doctors had said she would only get worse and more violent as she got older. Ray was just a baby, so they never told him. Seems his mom used to slip away several times a year to go see her, but she didn't even recognize her mom half the time."

"So how did she end up at the mom's house?"

"She had been put on some new kind of medicine, and eventually sent to a halfway house just a few blocks from the mom's house. His mom had been going to see her at the halfway house, and had invited her to come to her house for lunch that Saturday. Things were said and it all got out of hand."

The logger stopped talking and the guardsman stopped rocking back and forth. A few moments of silence finally ended with the guardsman saying, "Damn! That's the weirdest story I've ever heard. So this guy Vic is for real. Weird!"

Ed and Martha had been so caught up listening to the men's conversation that they had not noticed the sound of the chopper until it was almost overhead. They both stood in the trees, watching the men unload and reload the chopper. The big bird soon disappeared from sight and the sound faded into silence.

The men slipped back into the trees to continue their work. Ed turned to talk to Martha.

"That story was very interesting. I'll bet Vic is the guy that heard us talking the other night. It has to be him."

Martha looked up at Ed with a questioning face.

"What guy heard us? When?"

"The night we found out that we were dead. You had just closed your eyes a few seconds before he stepped out of the trees. He walked a little ways out into the circle and stood there looking around. Then he said that he couldn't see us, but he knew we were there because he heard us talking."

Martha interrupted Ed's story, "You didn't tell me about this! Why?"

"I just forgot about it. Nothing sinister here. I just forgot. Honest!"

"Was that all he said?"

"No. He also talked directly to you. Called you 'Missy'. Said that you shouldn't worry because things always work out."

"And that is all he said? Promise?"

"I promise. That was all. Then he went back into the trees and I forgot all about it."

"So we need to find him and talk to him. He might know things that can help us understand our situation better. What did he look like?"

"I think we do need to find him, but I really don't know how to describe him. They are all dressed about the same you know. The real question is where is he?"

Martha thought for two seconds, then grabbed Ed by the hand and started towards the trees.

"Come on! Those two guys were talking about him, let's just follow them and see if they take us to him."

Ed nodded in agreement. They hurried off into the trees to catch up with the two men. They followed them until they came to a small, man-made clearing. It was obvious that the loggers had created this small area by taking down enough trees for room to set up a few tents. There was a fire burning in the very center of the circle. They had stacked some crates of supplies on the opposite side of the site.

Martha let go of Ed's hand and stopped to look around.

"Why would they make this area so far from the crash site?"

Ed was also looking around. "Well, for one thing, the smell of jet fuel isn't as bad over here. But, I really bet they didn't want to mess up the crash area any more than they had to. You know, for forensic research of the crash."

"But then why didn't they stack the bodies up here? Come on, mister know it all?"

Ed shook his head before he answered.

"Think about it. The bodies are part of the forensics. So . . . their being in the circle doesn't hurt anything. Besides . . . look around. This is a very small circle and these trees must be around 90 feet tall. That means it is hard for the chopper to lower things down into this place and also to pull them up. They would swing and hit the trees. Not good!"

Martha grinned as she stepped over and once again playfully hit him on the arm.

"Ok smarty! I get it. Makes sense that the big circle is better suited for it."

Just then the flap on a tent swung open, and four guys filed out one after the other. Martha looked at them, then turned to notice that Ed was staring at each man's face.

"So? Which one is he?"

Ed was shaking his head. "Hmmm . . . . I don't know. That guy there looks like it could be him, but then again, so does that guy there. I can't tell."

Martha rolled her eyes.

"You mean it? You really can't tell? I've never met a dead guy like you before. You're hearing is terrible, your eyesight is obviously not any good either, and now we know your memory is shot! I'm worried about you, Ed. You're falling apart."

Ed looked right at her but didn't speak. Instead, he mouthed the word 'WHAT?'

"Hey, big guy. Don't give me any attitude. You may be dead, but we both now know that a good whack on your head messes you up for a while." She smiled and shook a fist at him.

One of the two men they had followed to this circle called out, "Hey guys. Where's Vic?"

Hearing this, Ed and Martha immediately stopped playing around. They focused their attention on the four guys and waited for one to answer.

"Vic? He was here just a second ago. But I don't know where he went."

One of the other men was picking up a small wooden box as he commented, "Nature called and he went to take care of it."

Martha immediately asked, "What's he mean 'Nature Called'?"

Ed chuckled to himself and knew exactly what he was going to do.

"Come on, Martha." He started walking between the tents towards the trees.

"Hey! Where we going?"

Ed never looked back because he knew that Martha was following him.

"Hey! I asked you a question, mister."

Ed kept walking as he motioned for her to catch up and walk beside him.

"Come on. Vic is this way."

"How do you know which way he is? They never said. You're going to get us lost again you know."

"The guy that said 'Nature Called' nodded his head in this direction. Obviously my eyesight was good enough to see that!" He glanced at her quickly just to add, "Dead and falling apart, huh? Well I'm still more observant than you."

"Ok, Ok. But what does that mean?"

Ed couldn't believe she didn't know what that meant. And

he thought he led a dull life. How could she not know what that meant? Oh, well. This time, he was going to get her but good.

She was about to ask Ed for the fourth time when he suddenly stopped walking. Her eyes followed the same path that his eyes were looking. There, standing in the woods just five feet from her, was a logger urinating on the base of a tree.

She shrieked as she covered her eyes. "I can't believe you didn't warn me! This is just damn embarrassing! You wait until I get my hands on you!"

She spun around and uncovered her eyes, only to find that Ed was not there. Then she heard his laughter and turned to find him standing over by the logger. She again shrieked and covered her eyes.

Ed laughingly called to her, "Hey! I'm over here. Come get me. Are you deaf? I'm O-VER HERE!"

She was too embarrassed to open her eyes, so she just stood there not knowing what to do.

Ed was really rubbing it in now. "WHOA! You really should come over here and take a look. Better hurry . . . he's almost done."

"This isn't funny, Ed. Not at all."

Ed had a huge smile on his face. "Not funny? Oh yes it is! You should see yourself. I do believe you are blushing. Not bad for a person with no body and no blood. Hey! You can open your eyes. We're all covered up. You missed it!"

"If I open my eyes and you're lying to me, well I'll . . . I'll . . . "

"Come on. He's leaving!"

She turned and saw the man slowly walking back to the tents. Ed was walking beside him and waving one of his hands in front of the man's face. She hurried over to them and paced the man on the opposite side from Ed.

She pointed a finger at Ed. "That was not cool. Nope. Not cool at all."

"May not have been cool, but it was hilarious watching you try not to look!"

"I can't believe you let me walk into that. And stop sticking your hands in front of his face. It's just rude."

"Rude? You're kidding me, right? He doesn't even know we're here. How can it be rude?"

Martha stopped walking. Once Ed did too, she said, "This

can't be Vic. He didn't hear us talking and he doesn't see us either. It's the wrong guy."

Ed turned to watch the man as he moved through the trees.

"I think you're right. He can't be him. Can he?"

Martha poked her finger into Ed's chest as she walked past him to follow the logger back to the tents. Ed stood there looking at the ground for a second. Then he smiled and turned around to follow after them both. He mumbled under his breath, "Well . . . it still was funny!"

• • •

The man entered the circle with Ed and Martha only a few feet behind. He passed between the tents and walked straight towards the fire. One of the other men raised a hand. "Hey, Vic. Back so soon?"

Hearing this, both Ed and Martha stopped cold in their tracks. Martha was the first to speak.

"Did you hear that? He called him Vic. How can he be Vic?"

Ed's eyebrows were raised, and he was intently staring at Vic.

"Well . . . He must be Vic. And now that I look at him, I think he is the guy that said he heard us talking that night. But . . . I . . . I just don't get it. Why can't he hear us now?"

"Are you sure that's him? I mean, take another look. If that is him, then I'm really confused here." She was studying Ed's face as Ed studied Vic.

Vic held his hands out over the fire for a few seconds before rubbing them together. "Hey, Rob. Is that coffee ready yet?"

Ed immediately spoke up.

"Yes. I'm positive now. That's the guy. I recognize his voice loud and clear." Ed turned towards Martha, "Yep. That's him. But . . ."

"Well if that is him, something is very wrong. Why can't he hear us now? This is just too crazy." She held her hands out to her sides. "Now what do we do?"

Ed hesitated for a few more seconds then slowly walked over and sat on one of the crates on the other side of the circle. He watched Vic then shook his head. "Damned if I know. Got no ideas here."

Martha walked over and took a seat on Ed's crate. They both

spent the next hour watching Vic. He had drunk several cups of coffee as he stood by the fire just staring down at it. The other men did the same. They all shared a jovial conversation about their private lives back home.

Eventually, two of them said they were going to go wait for the chopper. They noted that it would be dark soon, so this would be the last chopper of the day. They dumped their coffee on the fire before walking off into the trees.

Martha and Ed had been sitting, listening and watching. Occasionally one of them nodded their head for a few seconds and then later the other one did. They hadn't said anything since they sat down on the crate. When Vic suddenly said he's going to go take a short nap, Ed and Martha followed him into the tent.

There were six cots and Vic lay down on one in a corner. He was asleep almost immediately after his head hit the pillow. With nothing else to do and no one else in the tent, Martha sat down on the closest cot near Vic. She watched him sleep, while Ed paced back and forth in the center of the tent. He finally stopped and sat in a folding chair by a small folding table.

There was a pen and writing tablet on the small table. Ed stretched out his hand over the pen. He squinted his eyes a little and then grunted softly before letting his hand fall to the table. His gaze never left the pen. Then he raised his hand above the pen once more and repeated his last actions. Martha watched him do this four times before she finally asked, "What do you think you are doing?"

"I'm trying to move this pen with my mind. Why?"

She snickered aloud before saying, "Oh really? Move it with your mind. You must be OUT of your mind, because you don't HAVE a mind anymore. You're dead, remember? No body, no mind."

Her comments were not deterring Ed from trying it yet again. And once again the pen remained motionless. His hand fell to the table but Ed's eyes never left the pen.

"I know that. But there has to be a way for us to interact with the living world. You know. A way for us to move material things. There just has to be a way. I can just feel it. And before you say it ... Don't!"

"Don't what?"

"I know you. So don't tell me I can't feel it because I'm dead. Besides, I didn't mean it literally."

"Ed. We're ghosts now. Do you really think we can move material things now? Come on. That's just impossible. It can't be . . . "

Hearing Martha stop talking in mid-sentence caused Ed to look at her. She was staring straight ahead and her eyes were moving without seeing anything. He knew she was intently studying something in her mind. It must have been a humdinger of a memory. As she sat there replaying it over in her mind, Ed wanted to know what it was.

"Martha? What are you thinking so hard about?"

Without even looking at him, Martha began to talk.

"When I saw you fall off that crate and tumble through the air. I couldn't think of anything but getting to you, and were you going to be all right. Stuff like that. So I just took off running full speed and almost ran right into one of the men in the circle. I didn't want to pass through him, so I sidestepped him. He was so close to a crate that I actually hit it with my leg. Now that I think about it. I remember it fell over. Yes. That's right. I hit it and it fell over."

"Are you sure that the guy didn't knock it over and you just thought you did it?"

"No. I'm positive. I hit it and it fell."

Ed's excitement caused him to jump to his feet and start pacing again.

"Ok! Now we're onto something. How were you able to cause it to fall? What was different? Something had to be, because now you would just walk right through it."

"I have no idea. All I know is that I was so scared that something bad had happened to you, and I had to get to you as fast as I could."

Ed stopped pacing and snapped his fingers very loudly. "That's it!" But before he could get his thought out, they were both startled as Vic suddenly sat up and asked, "What?"

Vic blinked his eyes a few times and then he looked around the tent before mumbling softly, "I must have been dreaming." He yawned, then lay back down. He started snoring almost the moment his head hit the pillow.

Ed had a huge smile on his face as he rushed over to pull

Martha onto her feet.

"Did you see that? I know what is going on now. Come on, let's walk outside a bit and let this guy sleep. He is obviously exhausted. Come on."

He led her out of the tent and over to the edge of the tree line. The other men must have gone back to work because they were all gone. They both hopped up on a crate of supplies. Ed's excitement was apparent and Martha was smiling at him, because once again he reminded her of a cute little boy.

"Ok. I know you're just about to pop, so tell me what you're thinking."

Ed turned a little and pulled one knee up on the crate. Now that he was facing her, he took a big choppy breath in and pushed it out quickly.

"Ok. Here goes. I think that when we're excited we must put out some kinda kinetic energy that actually can affect material things in the living world. Think about it. You were excited when you knocked over that crate. You must have been boiling over with emotions. Right?"

She slowly nodded yes.

"And the night he heard us talking was the night we realized we were dead! I remember you screamed and you were shaking. I was very wound up and scared too. So we both must have been giving off gobs of emotional energy." Ed paused because he saw a question rising in Martha's face.

"You were scared? I didn't think you were scared at all. You didn't show it."

"Believe me. I was very scared. I didn't like the idea of being dead any more than you did."

"Well, if you were scared, why didn't you show it?"

Ed looked away for second, then up in the air before he finally focused his eyes on hers. "I'm not good at talking about my feelings. I've never been good at it. But I want you to know. I just want you to bear with me a minute as I try to put it into words. Ok?"

"Ed, I'm the same way. At least I always was before I met you. You . . . you . . . well, I just find it so easy to talk to you. I wish you felt as easy talking to me."

Ed reached out and took her hand in his. He placed his other hand on top of hers. He spoke softly.

"I do. I really do feel very comfortable talking to you. I could NEVER talk to anyone like this before. Especially a pretty girl like you. So it isn't that I can't talk to you. It's just that I have never done this before, so it's awkward for me. Understand?"

She glanced down at his hands holding her hand. The smile on her face spread even more and there was a dazzling sparkle in her eyes as she placed her other hand on his. She looked up into his face and sighed very softly before she spoke.

"I do. I really do. And by the way that was the sweetest thing anyone has ever said to me. So you think I'm pretty?" She was softly moving her hand over his.

"I think you are more than just pretty. I think you are the nicest girl I've ever met. Not that I've met that many. I just can't tell you how glad I am that I met you. I feel different with you, and I don't mean the dead thing either. I feel like you see me, you know, inside. Not just this big dumb outside of me. In fact this is exactly why you probably didn't think I was afraid. I was very afraid the moment I realized that those two men didn't see you standing right in between them. Then the guy behind you turned and looked right in my direction. He didn't see me and I could tell he didn't. That's when I really knew we were dead. Boy, that was scary.

"But then I saw you and I couldn't help thinking how it was going to affect you when you figured it out. So, I ran over to you and I guess that is when I stopped being scared. Or more to the point, I forgot about me being scared because I was worried about you. I just didn't want you to be scared, but I knew you were on the verge of finding out. I just wanted to be there, you know, close to you. Is any of this making sense?"

He noticed that she had slowly leaned over towards him. His mind was racing. 'Oh my GOD! She's going to kiss me. I hope I do this right. I wonder if my breath smells bad. I haven't brushed my teeth in days. Oh, what the hell.' He leaned in too.

Just as they were about to finally touch lip to lip, they were startled by a very loud and excited voice from the tent. Vic yelled, "Damn it! Damn it!" and then burst out of the tent while putting on his coat. He rushed right up to where they were sitting on the crate. He slowed down just a few steps from them, but kept moving. He was looking in their direction but not directly at them. His eyes darted from left to right for just a few seconds. Then he clearly made a grunting noise and broke out into a full run as he reached the tree line behind them.

As they both watched Vic disappear into the trees, she felt Ed start to stand up. She couldn't believe this was happening again. She was finally about to get kissed, and now here they go again. Something always happened to distract them. She decided this time it was going to happen. She reached out with her hand and grabbed his arm. His head slowly turned back around and the moment their eyes met, she spoke.

"No! We know where he's going and we can find him later. You are going to kiss me and you are going to do it NOW!" Having said that, she realized she must be blushing.

Ed shifted his weight as he sat back on the crate before smiling at her.

"Hmm. So you want me to kiss you?" He was smiling as he awaited her response.

She sheepishly said, "Yes I do. I think this is a perfect time. Don't you?"

Ed had his lips only a breath away from hers as he said, "I've waited my entire life to hold you like this. I can't think of anything else I'd rather do. Or any place else that I'd want to be. And there is absolutely nobody else I'd want to be with, but you."

Their lips fell softly upon each other's. Martha had slowly wrapped one hand around his neck and was gently holding him as if she never wanted him to leave. He had responded by tightening his arms around her as if to say he would not. The kiss lasted only a few seconds, but it fulfilled the single most important desire they had both sought since puberty.

Though their lips were now separated, they both continued to stare lovingly into each other's eyes. Ed's thoughts were many. He was studying every inch of her face to capture a mental image of how she looked at this very moment. He began to envision a wonderful eternity of being with her. But Martha had only one thought, and it could be expressed with one simple word. A gleeful happiness spread across her face and her eyes sparkled as she softly said, "Finally."

Chapter 8

THERE BE GHOSTS HERE!

HAVING FINALLY ACHIEVED their first kiss, Ed and Martha found themselves contently sitting on that magical crate and silently staring into each other's eyes. Ed softly stroked her face, and then they kissed again. Then she did the same to his face before kissing him back. This was a blissful and passion-filled event that both of them had longed for their entire lives. Neither of them cared that they had not experienced this while living. Instead, they were both so overwhelmed with the newness of this wondrous feeling that they lost track of time. Moments turned to minutes, and minutes turned to hours.

Having just savored another long kiss, he was once again staring deep into her eyes. She was staring back and began to lean in for more, when her facial expression suddenly changed. Seeing this, he sat back and wondered why. Her eyes were focused on him, but he knew that she was not seeing him. What was she doing? Then she spoke.

"You hear that? It's a chopper coming our way."

"So?"

"It sounds different. Deeper. It isn't the same chopper!"

Ed began looking around and noticed that night was falling.

"Gee, when did it start getting dark? How long have we been here?"

She smiled at him and her eyes reflected an inner happiness as she spoke softly. "I guess we got caught up in the activities and lost track of time."

Ed's face showed only signs of peace and contentment as he also softly replied, "Guess we did. And you know what?"

"What, ED?"

"Time is nothing that we have to fear now. Ever!"

She slowly leaned towards him and placed her forehead gently on his chest. "That is so true. I have eternity now to spend with you. I could just sit here forever. I'm so happy."

"Me too, baby. Me too." He ever so gently placed one open hand on the back of her head, and lovingly pressed it against his chest.

Both had their eyes closed when a very large helicopter passed directly over them. The sound caused them both to sit back and look skyward. There was a huge craft with a considerably larger payload headed to the crash site.

"Ed? That isn't the usual chopper we've seen coming up here. It's huge."

Ed jumped up from the crate, extended his hand to help her up and excitedly said, "That's what they call a sky crane! It's a heavy lifting chopper. Man, that's big! Come on!"

He practically yanked her to her feet in his haste to get going. Once her feet hit the ground, she pulled her hand from his and began straightening her clothes.

"What's the rush, big boy? You almost pulled my arm off!"

Ed's focus was still on following the chopper. He didn't take his eyes off the sky so he didn't see that she lacked his sense of urgency. She still yielded to his will and began following him as he raced to follow the chopper's flight path.

Noticing that they were not running directly towards the crash site, she asked, "Ed? Why aren't we going towards the crash site?"

"I'm following that chopper. I don't know why it isn't headed towards the site. Maybe they have another site now for supplies. Who knows? But I'm going this way."

Though she questioned the direction, she knew that she wouldn't hesitate to go where he went. It didn't matter anymore.

She had totally accepted the fact that she would follow him wherever he went. He was hers and she was his. They belonged together. It had taken her a long time to find this man. Her man. She was again smiing as she thought to herself, "We stay together!"

• • •

Ed and Martha noticed that the new chopper had circled around to the right of the crash site, instead of the left like the other choppers. Whatever it was carrying was in a very large crate. They were very curious as to what it could be.

They both ambled up to a lone tree at the edge of the crash site. Ed was first to the tree, then Martha arrived and put her hands in their usual place around Ed's arm. Before them were two new guardsmen that must have come up in one of the last chopper trips. They were busy motioning the chopper pilot where to land his crate. This was when Ed noticed that just off to the left was one of the plane's engines. Noticing that there were huge cables attached to it, he pointed to it and said, "That's why they have this big chopper up here. They're going to drop that crate and pick up that engine to take back."

Martha was intently watching while nodding her head. "I didn't notice it until you said that, Ed. I bet that is exactly what they are about to do."

While Ed continued to watch them, they unhooked the crate and quickly began to hook up the cables from the engine to the cable from the new chopper. Ed really loved being this close to the action that he had previously been limited to watching on late night TV. This was SO much better than anything he had ever seen on his large flat screen TV back home.

Martha was looking for the other engine's whereabouts when it dawned on her that most of the smaller debris from this side of the crash circle was missing. Where did it go?

"Ed? Have you noticed that they have picked up almost all of the little pieces of the plane on this side of the circle?"

Ed was still caught up in watching as they began lifting the huge engine into the sky. His response was more of a grunt. "Un-huh". Then as the engine slowly cleared the tops of the trees, the chopper executed the usual turn to the south and disappeared from sight.

With the show now over, Ed turned to her and asked, "What did you say?"

Realizing that he hadn't been paying any attention to what she had said, she rolled her eyes at him, let out an exaggerated sigh and repeated, "I SAID! They have picked up all the little pieces of the plane on this side of the circle. Look AROUND!"

Ed hesitated as her words sunk in, then he began glancing around at the ground. "Wow! They have really been busy!"

She had now noticed something else had changed. "Ed, I don't see any body bags anywhere. Have they already taken them all back?"

Ed's head lifted a little so his eyes could scan the far side of the circle where all the pallets of bodies had been lined up for transport. "You're right. They are all gone." He slowly rubbed his fingers through his hair as he turned to face her.

"That kinda makes sense, though. They would get all the bodies first before starting to pick up the parts of the plane." He was smiling as he drew closer to her.

She said, "Well I sure hope they found them all! They're moving really fast. They could miss something and that just wouldn't be right."

Ed looked at her and started to speak slowly. "Martha. These guys are professionals and we've watched them move very slowly around here, and way out into the trees. I'm sure they've found everyone." He paused as he noticed her face take on a blank stare. What was going on in her head now?

She had no expression on her face as she faintly said, "Then they've taken our bodies out of here, too." Her eyes were open wide as well as her mouth. She was softly panting as if she couldn't catch her breath.

Ed watched helplessly as her eyes darted from left to right, ground to treetop. His heart was breaking as he stepped up against her and placed his big arms around her. She was still trying to move her head as he gently took a hand and pulled her to his chest.

"It's all right. We knew this was going to happen. I know we didn't talk much about it, but we knew this was going to happen. It's going to be okay, baby. I got you. I got you."

As she settled down, Ed could feel the tension leave her body.

He heard the two guardsmen talking about getting something to eat before coming back to open this crate. Maybe with no activity over here for a while, she would soak up the silence and be rejuvenated back to her old self.

They stood there for several hours, not moving or talking. They were quickly becoming more and more oblivious to the amount of time that was passing. Ed watched as one of the new guardsmen appeared and powered up all the huge lights that were spread around the circle. Then he disappeared back into the trees on the far side.

Ed had apparently drifted off himself, but was suddenly awakened by Martha moving her head to look around. She eventually pulled free of his arms and stepped a few feet away. She stood there looking around until Ed spoke.

"Are you okay now?"

She looked around at him, paused and nodded. "Yes. Yes, I am."

He was relieved to hear her answer. "I am so glad. You really had me worried the way you were looking around, but not saying anything."

She was just kidding as she said, "Yeah, like you listen when I talk to you."

A playful grin spread across her face as she squinted her eyes and began walking towards him. She was pointing her finger at him.

He smiled and began a hasty backwards retreat around the tree as she said, "You didn't pay any attention to me when I was talking to you, mister. Remember?"

Ed was smiling with his hands up in surrender while he continued to back up around the tree. She suddenly reached out to grab at him, but he stepped quickly behind the tree. His foot went into a hole at the base of the tree, and he fell backwards.

It all happened so fast that she let out a little yelp as she watched her guy take a tumble. She rushed over to him.

"Are you okay, baby? What happened?"

Her concern evaporated quickly when she heard him laughing. It was the same laugh she'd heard after he fell off the flying pallet the other day. Her expression changed to a stern look as she said, "Are we going through this again?"

He laughed even harder as he watched her exhale and hang her head. "You're hopeless, mister. Just hopeless."

He held one hand up and asked, "You want to help me up? I think my foot is stuck in this hole."

"Yes I'll help you up, you big goof! It's a good thing you're dead. You could have broken your leg in that hole."

"I know. It all just happened so fast. Hey! There's something in the hole. Feels like something soft."

"Well get your foot out of there. It could be a small animal, and it might bite you!"

Now Ed playfully rolled his eyes and exhaled before saying, "Bite me? Really?" He made a gesture with both hands before adding, "Plane crash, dead, GHOSTS! Ring a bell?"

She leaned over and was trying to quickly help him up as she said, "Stand up here so I can slap you!"

Once on his feet, she hit him on his shoulder and he pretended he was going to fall down again. But he almost did step into that hole again.

"Woooow! Almost did it again."

He stopped and bent over the hole. He reached down to move the grass so he could see into the hole, but his hands just passed through the grass.

"What are you doing?"

"I want to see what I stepped on in here."

"Please be careful. Dead or not, I don't want some little critter to dart out of that hole and scare me to death!"

Hearing what she had just said, Ed cut his eyes at her and she uttered softly, "I know. I know."

Ed had knelt down and was looking into the hole when he suddenly exclaimed, "OH NO!"

Martha quickly stepped up behind him and was trying to look over the top of his head at the hole. "What is it? What do you see?"

She was forced to step back as Ed stood up and turned to face her.

"Well? What is it? Tell me!"

He rubbed one hand down from his forehead and over his eyes before saying, "You know what we were talking about earlier?"

"What? Earlier? We talked about a lot of different things earlier. What are YOU talking about NOW?"

"Remember when you noticed that all the body bags were gone?"

She froze and her mouth dropped open.

"No way. You gotta be kidding me. You telling me there is a body in that hole?"

Hearing that, Ed shook his head. "A body? In that little hole? What?"

She sighed a little before she replied, "For a minute there you had me worried.

Don't do that! Now tell me what is in there."

"It isn't a body. But it *is* a hand." After saying this, he was bracing himself in case she overreacted again and he had to catch her. But to his relief, she just stood there staring as she processed what he just told her.

"A hand. A whole hand? Really?" She paused. "If you're making this up, I really am going to slap you!"

"I'm not making it up. I can't believe this."

She started to get really agitated again.

"See. I told you they had gotten in a hurry. But, NOOOOOO. You said they were professionals. Remember? That is exactly what you said. I remember I said they were in too big of a hurry, but you defended them and said they were PROFESSIONALS." She stood and gestured in the air with both hands, as if she were adding quotation marks before and after what she'd said.

Ed tried to calm her down. "Martha, please calm down. It's no big deal."

"No big deal? A part of somebody, THEIR HAND, is in that hole. Now it won't make it back to be buried with whomever and we can't even tell these guys it's over here and down there!" She was standing with her finger pointing to the hole.

"Well, if you don't calm down, maybe Vic will hear you, and come running over here and find it."

As Ed said that, both of them noticed movement out in the circle. They both turned their heads slowly, and saw that one of the guardsmen was standing by that crate with his eyes and mouth wide open. He was staring right at them and his face had gone completely white.

They both knew that he saw them, so their first reaction was to hide behind the tree. Once there, she whispered, "You think he saw us?"

"Well, YES! Did you see his eyes bugging out? Poor guy!" Ed laughed softly.

"So why we hiding, Ed?"

"Well, uh, HEY, I just followed you! I'm not hiding. You are."

"What are you? Two years old?"

"Look, you were very emotional and that was why he saw us. We should step back out and call or wave for him to come over, so we can show him the hand."

She couldn't believe this was his big plan. "You want to give this poor guy a heart attack? GHOSTS! HELLOOOOOO!"

Ed thought about it for a moment. "Well, he's already seen us. We could just step out there and point behind the tree. He'll get the message. He may not come over here now, but I bet he will tomorrow during the daytime. Curiosity is a strong motivator. Don't you think?"

Just as they were both about to step out from behind the tree, they heard a voice. Like little children being caught where they weren't supposed to be, they both slowly peeked around the tree.

The first guardsman was still standing there looking in their direction, but they could tell he couldn't see them now. They were looking around from the opposite side of the huge tree while he still stared at the other side. They noticed that a second guardsman was standing very close to the first guy. He was talking firmly but softly.

"Bob? Are you okay, buddy? What you looking at? Hey, buddy. You OK?" He placed a hand on Bob's shoulder, and it seemed to snap him back to reality. His eyes darted frantically from his friend, and then back to the tree. He did this several times before the other guardsman again asked, "Bob? Hey buddy. You okay? Come on, man. Talk to me."

Finally Bob looked at his friend's face and questioningly said, "I, I, I thought I saw something out there. I don't believe it, but maybe I did."

"Bob. What did you see? A bear?"

"No." He was still obviously in a real state of shock.

"Well, then what did you see? You can tell me, man. What was it?"

"There were two people over there by that tree. Just standing there. I could see them. HONEST! Two of them, right there!" He was pointing to the tree.

"I believe you, Bob. Hey, it was probably a couple of those loggers. You know there are a lot of us out here now." He turned and glanced at the tree his friend was still pointing to. "That tree?" Bob was nodding with exaggerated movements.

"Bob? You want me to go see what they're doing?"

Hearing this, Bob immediately grabbed his friend's arm and said loudly, "NO!"

"Okay. What's going on, buddy?" The friend was looking at the tree again as he asked, "Why don't you want me to go over there?"

"Believe me. They weren't loggers, and you don't want to go over there."

"Hey, man. You're beginning to freak me out here. Are you sure it wasn't a couple of loggers?"

"Trust me. They weren't loggers. And you don't need to go over there. In fact, let's get out of here now. I want to go back to the others. Come on!"

"Bob. Wait a minute. If they aren't loggers, we need to find out who they are."

Bob was really agitated when he said, "Look, it wasn't loggers. Okay? One of them was a woman!"

The friend stood up very straight and looked at the tree again.

"A woman? You sure? How can that be? Are you telling me you saw two possible survivors? MY GOD, MAN, come on. We need to get over there NOW!"

Bob jumped in front of his friend and grabbed him by the shoulders, leaned in towards his face before he spoke.

"Listen to me. LISTEN TO ME! They weren't survivors. Get it? You get my drift? They were not us, and they were not survivors."

"Wait a minute Bob. What are you saying? Who else could they be? There aren't any campers out here."

Bob repeated himself. This time, he spoke loudly and slowly. "They didn't survive anything. GET IT?"

Looking at his friend, he slowly put his arm around Bob's shoulder and started walking with him. "I got it, Bob. I understand now. Come on. I'm with you now. Let's just go back to the others and sort this out. Come on, buddy. Walk with me."

Ed and Martha watched in silence as the two men walked to the other side of the circle and disappeared into the trees.

"Ed, I feel so bad that we did that to that poor man. He is so confused and scared right now." She turned to Ed, took both of his hands and looked up into his face. "We have to really work hard at never letting this happen again. Can you imagine what we'd do to a kid if we accidentally appeared to one? We could scare that kid for life. Agreed?"

With no hesitation, he said, "Agreed. Totally."

She leaned up against his body and put her head where she felt so very secure, on his chest. He was her rock. He was her safe harbor. He was her MAN.

As usual, they stood motionless together for over an hour. Her eyes were closed as he held her against him. Once again, they were totally at peace with their situation. Yes, it was all tolerable as long as they were holding each other. Ed was thinking that death wasn't so scary, and he was so very glad to have her. Eternity here in the forest seemed like it could be a good thing. It could be a happy thing. Why would they ever want to leave? With that last thought, came a sudden realization that it was totally dark and they were standing just outside the light of the circle. He thought, *OH MY GOD! We need to get back into the light.* He didn't want that big flash of light to happen and snatch them away to who knows where.

He forcibly pushed Martha from his chest, but held onto one of her hands and started pulling her back into the circle. She opened her eyes and was about to yell at him, when she too noticed their position within the dark tree line. Without uttering a word, she knew what he was doing and her feet took flight to keep up with him. They didn't stop until they were completely in the center of the circle. Still holding hands, they stood there looking back into the dark at that tree.

"Sorry if I scared you. But it just hit me that it was dark and where we were. Sorry."

"Hey! I'm glad you did. I had my eyes closed. Don't be sorry.

I'm glad one of us was awake and aware."

"So what do you want to do now?"

Martha shrugged her shoulders and began looking around before she spoke.

"I don't know. What do ghosts usually do for fun on a Saturday night?"

Ed quickly asked, "It's Saturday night? Are you sure?"

"I don't know, silly. It was just a joke. In fact, I don't really know what day it is. You?"

Ed rubbed his chin as if he were checking his beard growth and thinking at the same time. "You know that is a good point. I have no idea what day or time it is. AND I DON'T CARE!" He laughed a bit. "You know? When we first realized we were dead, I wondered what it would be like to not be on the clock. I remember wondering if we would get bored with nothing to do and all the time in the world to do it."

She stopped smiling before she spoke. "Ed. What are we going to do?"

"Well, we can try to find our spot and sit until the morning." He started looking around.

"No, silly. I don't mean now. I mean, like, what are we going to do when all of this is over?" She was waving her free hand around, gesturing. "They're moving fast. You said it yourself."

Again she faced him as she held both of his big hands. "They are going to get this all cleaned up, and then they're going to leave." She pressed against him and looked down. She was silent for a second before she asked so very softly, "What will we do then?"

Ed felt a slight shiver go through her. He really hated it when he knew she was worried. What would they do? What could they do? How would he know? This was the first time he had been dead too!

"Well, I really don't know what to do either, baby. But we still have some time to think about it." He used a folded finger to gently raise her head up. He looked down directly into her concerned eyes. "And don't forget the most important part. You are not alone. We have each other. It makes me feel better. In fact, it is why I act like I'm not worried. Because I'm NOT!"

Her eyes once again sparkled as she smiled at him. "I'm so

very thankful that I found you. You are right. VERY RIGHT! We have each other. Let's find our spot and sit."

They both started looking around. Though the ground was still charred in places, most of the burnt areas had been plowed under by all the foot traffic from the men picking up bodies and debris. Their constant moving of those crates around the circle had also added to the earth looking like normal dirt once again.

Ah yes, but that smell. The area still reeked from thousands of gallons of jet fuel that had soaked into the ground after impact. Most of it obviously would have burned away. Still, enough had been left in the ground that it stung the rescuers' eyes when they were directly in the center of the circle. This was one fact that escaped Ed and Martha.

"Ed. It all looks so different now. I can't tell where we sat the first night. Can you?"

He realized that the usual landmarks within the circle had been erased. So he began looking farther out towards the tree line to triangulate their position.

"Well, I'm thinking." He was looking first back over his shoulder and then to their right. "That is where that engine was. The one they just took out of here. Remember?"

She looked and nodded. "I agree." She noticed that he was looking to their right. "And where you are looking is where that group of people with those kids were all standing. Before they, uh. You know, the light and that sound."

Ed realized she was struggling with the memory of all those lost souls that were taken that first night. "Yes, I agree. That is where they all stood. There." He was pointing now. He slowly lowered his arm and pointed to a spot about ten yards away. "That should be just about where we sat that first night. Don't you think?"

She knew that he was only trying to be so accurate for her sake. He was a really good man and was only doing it because of her memories of their first night together. Why couldn't she have met him while they were alive? They were so perfect for each other. He was so perfect for her.

"Yes. That looks about right." She started walking over there. "Come on, big boy. Come sit with mama!" She giggled like a little girl as they walked over to their spot. It might not be the exact spot, but it was their spot now.

He held her hand as she sat down first. Then he sat right where she was patting the ground for him to be. He had barely sat down when she scooted right up beside him, placed her hands in their usual spot on his arms, and approvingly surveyed the area. "This is it. It's perfect!"

Ed was happy that she was smiling and calm. He didn't want to disturb the peaceful moment by talking, so he just sat and looked around. But she decided to talk.

"It occurred to me that we should seriously talk about what happens when they are done and leave."

Ed was immediately apprehensive about starting this conversation. But it had to happen, and they had all night to talk. He reluctantly replied.

"Okay. But where do we start? How do we start?" Then his demeanor softened as he looked her in the face. "I just don't want you to get upset again. You have to promise me that you won't do that. It breaks my heart when I see you get nervous or worried. Really hurts me. That bothers me more than you know. I don't want you hurting."

She smiled and sheepishly responded, "I promise. Well, at least I promise I'll try." Noticing how intently he was looking at her, she quickly added, "I promise!"

"Okay. So, they get done and we see that they are packing up all their equipment. We have to make a basic decision here you know. Do we stay here and watch them leave, or do we go with them?" He shrugged his shoulders a little.

She continued to look at him but hesitated a few very long moments.

"Two very logical and obvious choices. The first one seems fine. I enjoy being with you. The thought of spending eternity wandering around this forest with you sounds nice. It really does." Ed knew that her pause meant there was a 'BUT' coming. "But, it seems that eventually we would both get bored. Don't you think?"

Ed wore a small smile as he thought a moment before he answered. "You're probably right. In fact, I know you're right. After all, we are talking about eternity and I'm fairly certain that is a long, *very* long time!"

Seeing him snickering, she lightly poked him on the shoulder. "Okay, you big goof! I know it's a long time. Of course it is. So it sounds like we both are thinking about the second option then."

"Going with them. But that brings up a real BIG question, doesn't it? Can we really leave this place? Remember what I told you about being pulled off that pallet when I tried to go back with them the other day?" He glanced at her. "I'm telling you. I didn't fall off. I was pulled off. Really!"

"So what did it feel like? I mean, describe it to me. What do you mean pulled off?"

He took a deep breath and stared straight ahead. "Well. Like I said before, it was like I hit the end of a rope and was yanked off. No! Wait a minute. I wasn't yanked. I was stopped." He snapped his fingers and turned back to look at her. "That's more like it. It was a sensation as if I was stopped from going any farther away."

They both were staring straight ahead now. Both sat in silence for several minutes. Occasionally they shook their heads ever so slightly as they thought. Two minds were rapidly processing several ideas in search of those that were feasible. What could be the reason? Why was Ed prevented from riding back with that chopper?

They had sat in silence now for over 20 minutes. Both of them were afraid to say out loud what they were actually thinking. Still looking straight ahead, they both uttered softly at the same time, "We can't leave."

It took a few seconds for them both to realize that each had said the same thing at the same time. They instantly looked at the other's face, but Martha spoke first.

"You think that's true? We can't leave this place? EVER?"

Ed had that childish grin on his face as he said, "Seems like it. But why?" He turned towards her again and gestured with his hands as he spoke. "But why? Why would we be forced to stay here? It just doesn't make any sense."

She giggled aloud before speaking. "Make sense? Are you kidding me? We're both dead, but obviously not governed by the same rules that took all those other ghosts to where ever it took them. Why were we left here? And also, according to you, those other ghosts didn't see us or acknowledge you yelling at them.

What's up with that?"

Ed just sat there listening to her. After a few more seconds of silence, he slowly started talking.

"Well. Those are all good questions. I just don't know what to think. And I don't know how we go about finding out what we can and we can't do? Maybe we have to just start trying different things and see what happens. We don't really have any other choice in the matter. But we're going to have plenty of time to work through it all. It looks like we have to find the answers ourselves. Agree?"

"Wish we could have been able to talk to those other ghosts. But that ship has sailed." She shook her head while continuing to wrestle with her thoughts.

Ed got a very quizzical look on his face and Martha asked, "Okay. What are you thinking? I can tell you have an idea, so spit it out, big guy."

"Well. You know we do have somebody we can talk to."

They both grinned widely as they spoke at the same time. "VIC!"

• • •

The guardsman who had walked Bob back to the tents had seated him on a log by the fire. All of the coffee mugs were lined up on a small table by the fire. He picked one up for Bob. He used the big potholder from the table to fetch the coffee pot from its perch on the big stones at the edge of the fire. He rinsed the cup out with just a dash of hot coffee and poured it out on the ground. After filling the cup completely with the super-hot liquid, he carefully placed it in Bob's hands.

Bob didn't even acknowledge the cup in his hands. He just sat motionless and stared into the fire. All of the other men knew, judging by Bob's lack of expression, that something serious had happened. Several of the men followed Bob's friend over to the tent, patiently waiting their turn to enter behind him. Once inside, one of them whispered. "What happened?"

The friend looked at each of the concerned faces, exhaled slowly and whispered back. "Bob, uh, well he, he saw something. At least he seems convinced he saw it. Or should I say them. Oh, HELL! This is going to sound crazy."

One of the men quickly asked, "Bob saw somebody? Really? Out here? Who could he see?"

The friend replied, "He says he saw two people out at the edge of the tree line around the crash site."

Another man jumped in, "Two people? So what? It had to be one of us. You know how many of us there are running around here now."

A second man stepped in and said, "But hold on a minute. When did he see them?"

The friend replied, "About 20 minutes ago."

A different man spoke up. "That's impossible." He looked around the group before finishing, "Other than you two, all of us have been here for almost an hour now. We've been eating and talking. Nobody could have been over there."

The first guy chimed in, "Wait. Wait a minute. Vic left over half an hour ago to go on one of his evening walks. Like he always does."

The second guy added, "But Vic was alone and he walked off in the opposite direction from the crash site. You all know he walks to get away from that place. Says it makes him uncomfortable to be over there. It couldn't have been him and he's alone anyway."

The friend shook his head 'NO' and the other men stopped talking to let him speak.

"Look, guys. It couldn't have been Vic."

One of the men asked, "How can you be so sure?"

The friend snapped back, "Bob said one of them was a woman!"

There were a few moments of silence as all the men stood looking at each other, puzzled. Finally the second guy said, "A woman. Out here? That's not possible. There's nobody out here but us!"

The friend continued, "I asked him the same question and made the same comment. I then thought maybe, just maybe, he had seen some survivors."

A different man entered the conversation for the first time. He excitedly said, "SURVIVORS! Are you crazy? There aren't any survivors out here! Nobody survived this! Impossible. Plus, we've been here for days. All of us." He looked around at the other men. "Have you seen any signs of survivors walking around in the area? Have you? Or *you*? This is nuts!"

The friend calmly stepped in. "Look. I don't believe there are any survivors either. But here's the kicker. Bob was adamant that they weren't survivors either. He even stressed it to me by saying, 'These people didn't survive anything! Get it?' "

All of the men fell silent. They just stood looking at each other or the ground. Several of them coughed nervously as they snickered and looked around. Finally, the biggest guardsman in the group laughingly said, "Well. If he saw, or thinks he saw, what I think you are insinuating, then that would definitely explain why he's acting as he is."

Most of the men laughed softly while shaking their heads, except for one. He was the youngest of the loggers. Most of these men towered over him, but all had come to respect his work ethic. Still he exhibited his youthful side as he actually raised his hand before joining the conversation.

"Uh, what exactly are you all thinking? Are you talking about ghosts? Really?"

One of the older guardsmen calmly replied, "Look, son. Look around at all the crap we all have seen in the past week. All the carnage and death. The mangled and severed bodies that were here. Son, it was just a matter of time before somebody, one of us, any of us, had this happen to them." He stepped into the middle of the group. Look, I've seen death on the battlefield many times. More times than I wanted. And I've seen what it can do to people's minds. I had a shrink tell me that this is usually a coping mechanism for the human mind. A way to make sense of and deal with the reality of death that one sees." He looked around the group before he continued, "We all know Bob is not crazy. But he believes that he saw whatever it was he saw. We just need to be supportive and let him work through it. I served two tours in Afghanistan with him, up in the mountains. I know from personal experience that he's a strong-minded guy. He'll work through it. He's my friend."

He looked around again at all of them, nodding at each one of them before finishing, "You all know him. He's the kind of guy that has your back. No matter WHAT! So, let's have his on this."

Bob's friend spoke up. "I agree. Bob is a hell of a strong man. He has the spirit of several men. He'll get through it with our help. However, I do think we should get Doc to talk to him. Just in case."

As they all quietly shook their heads in agreement, Doc spoke up from behind them all. He had entered the tent undetected due to the intensity of the conversation. Every head turned at hearing his voice. They instinctively parted to let Doc walk to the center of the group.

"Hey guys. I heard most of what you were saying. Just didn't want to interrupt." He was looking around at each of them, then looked right at Bob's friend.

"I was out back of the tents when you and Bob got back. Heard all the laughing and chatter stop all of a sudden, so came around to see what was going on. Several of the others outside pointed me to Bob sitting by the fire. I could tell he was kinda withdrawn for some reason. Tried to get him to talk, but he just stared at me and kept saying it was nothing. Then somebody motioned to the tent so I came in here. Wow, interesting conversation going on. I served with him over there too. He's a strong guy. But I've never seen him rattled like this. Doesn't mean he won't or can't get over it. Just means this, whatever it is, really looks bad."

The young logger asked, "But you think he'll get over it, right?"

The entire group was silent and all eyes were focused on Doc. He glanced around before saying, "Well, I hope so. I mean he should, but . . . "

The friend quickly jumped in, "But what? Come on Doc. What?"

Doc paused for a second. "Well, I'm only trained in patching up wounds. You all know that. But I've been taught a little about the mind, of course." He held out both hands towards them all to emphasize, "But only a little. This is really out of my area."

Again the youngest logger spoke. "Come on, Doc. Everyone here trusts you. But what?"

Doc rubbed his hand over his mouth then exhaled loudly before going on. "I've seen men withdraw before. It happens when the mind goes on overload. Yeah, most bounce back when given enough time. They work through it on their own. Which is, of course, the only way they ever really come back. They have to deal with it in their own way and on their own terms.

"But what worries me about Bob is that he isn't upset. He doesn't appear nervous. Like having a twitch, or his legs bouncing constantly. He's not wanting to talk about it either. No, he appears calm. But that doesn't mean he is calm on the inside. It doesn't mean that he is accepting what he saw, either."

He paused and looked in the direction of where Bob was sitting outside the tent as if he could actually see him. "And this is where I am concerned. He has a ton of conflict going on inside. He's questioning what he thinks he saw. His eyes may not have really seen it, but his brain thinks they did. He is struggling with what he believes is possible, and what he thinks he saw. In my opinion, he's really going to withdraw more if we don't keep him attached to reality."

The huge guardsman spoke. "And what does that mean? How do you bring a guy back to reality when he thinks he saw something that even *he* doesn't think is possible?"

Bob's friend said, "Well, we all know he openly questioned any talk about ghosts. He always said that it was impossible and only children believed in it. You all have heard what he thinks about the stories about Vic."

Doc continued, "Well, we all heard him say that. But to answer the question, I think we keep him attached to reality by talking to him. Don't ask him what he saw, just talk to him. Don't even ask him how he is doing. Make small talk. But and this is a big but - don't ask him about controversial things. Complain about the food instead. Joke about it. Say things like you can't wait to get back home to get a hot bath. Stuff like that.

"The goal is to get his mind off what he's wrestling with. His mind just needs a break. But don't feel like somebody has to sit with him all the time. Give a few minutes alone between each of you visiting with him. We just don't want him sitting there and getting lost in his own thoughts for long periods of time. That's what I'm thinking."

Bob's friend asked, "What about getting him back to camp? You know, out of here. Maybe the chopper could come get him tonight?"

Doc shook his head before saying, "I'll call base camp and let Sandy know what is going on. But personally, I think he needs to stay here and sleep tonight. In the morning, we can see if he is willing to do some work in the crash site. If he is, then that would be best. If he goes back there in the daylight, he'll probably get over it faster. Things always look different in the daylight."

The huge guardsman added, "Well. Since we aren't supposed to talk to him about what he saw . . . " He pointed at several of the loggers, "Maybe one of you guys could ask your friend Vic not to go around him. I'm not saying Vic is a bad guy or would do anything wrong. I'm just saying that if Bob sees him, well, he could get agitated. We know he's heard about Vic."

Doc immediately said, "Not really." Everyone in the tent stared at Doc. "Look. It might actually be good for him to see Vic. In fact, now that I think about it, I think that would be perfect."

The big guardsman looked confused as he asked, "But I thought you said we shouldn't push him on what he saw. Just make chit-chat. Remember?"

Doc nodded as he continued. "That's right. You're right. I said for us not to ask him about it. But the best thing in the world is for him to want to talk about it. The key is to get him to bring it up. Vic would be just the ticket!" Doc snapped his fingers and smiled, nodding rapidly.

Someone said, "So Doc. How can Vic get him to talk if he can't ask him about it?"

Doc really displayed some heightened energy as his words rushed out of his mouth. "Don't you see? It's perfect. Just perfect. All Vic has to do is grab some coffee and stand by the fire where Bob will see him. We all just back way off and leave them alone. You know. Give them some space. We tell Vic not to say a thing. Just stand there and drink his coffee. Maybe get him to act like he's tired. Yes. This could work out just fine."

A second guardsman asked, "But how do you know Vic won't say something bad to him if he starts talking? You said not to challenge him. Remember?"

Doc didn't hesitate to respond. "I wouldn't worry about Vic. He's a smart guy. He's a really good guy. I've talked a lot to him up here over the last few nights. About this very subject, too. He's not going to say anything that would hurt Bob. He's a good guy. Trust me!"

The young logger looked very confused. "Doc. You believe in ghosts? Is that what you're saying?"

Realizing what he'd said, Doc looked at everyone before he answered.

"What? Look. Everyone has an opinion on this stuff. I have mine. But it's just mine. So, let's not worry about that now. Bob is the only focus we all should have at the moment. Okay?"

Bob's friend asked, "So, Doc? Are you going to get with Vic and explain all this to him when he gets back from his walk?"

Before Doc could answer, a guardsman stuck his head inside the tent to say, "Hey, Doc. Vic just came back into camp. Bob's watching him like a hawk, and you know how he feels about that guy. You better get out here before something happens."

Before he exited the tent, Doc told all the men, "You guys tell all the others to back off from the fire and give us some space." He then started to leave the tent, but stopped suddenly right in the opening. What he saw happening was just amazing to him. He couldn't have planned it any better.

All the other men outside had gathered around the tent where Doc was. He motioned for them to come on in. Vic had gotten a cup of coffee and was standing on the opposite side of the fire from Bob. Doc saw Vic was actually yawning like he was tired. Bob was watching Vic's every move. Wow, this was as if Vic knew what happened and knew the plan.

Doc watched what was playing out by the fire. Everything was going just like he had described to the guys in the tent. What a stroke of luck . . . then the thought hit him. Doc shook his head. He realized that there was no way Vic could possibly know what was going on. He scratched his head and said softly to himself, "There is no way he knows. Or is this guy for real?"

Chapter 9

NOT EVERYONE SEES GHOSTS

BOB WAS WATCHING Vic's every move. Vic was standing with his eyes closed. He opened them to take a sip of hot coffee, then closed them as he tilted his head back, trying to pop his neck. Occasionally, he slowly rolled his head from side to side. Bob could actually hear the bones popping. Then Vic just stood motionless for almost a minute before repeating the entire procedure. After watching this for a few minutes, Bob found himself tilting his head back also. To his amazement, his neck popped as well - so loudly that it drew Vic's attention and a comment.

"I feel the same way, Bob. I'm beginning to wonder if I'm getting to old to do this any more." He looked across the fire at Bob and took another sip of coffee. "Problem is, this is all I know. Didn't set out to be a logger. Just sort of happened. Know what I mean?"

Bob nodded as he sipped his coffee. He never took his eyes off Vic.

"I do know what you mean. I'm a high school football coach in my real life. Was in the Army right out of high school, but went to college on the GI Bill when I was discharged. Started teaching and got married. Then when we were about to have our second kid, it just seemed normal to join the National Guard to make a little extra money.

"But then New York was attacked, and we were all mobilized because of Afghanistan and Iraq. I served three tours in all before getting back home to stay. They called it 'stopgap'. Fancy way of saying they were changing the agreement, and I wasn't going home. But it all worked out in the end. Came back, worked hard and I'm the head coach now. This is the first real activity I've seen in the Guard since my unit stood down from active duty."

Vic took a quick sip. "Bet you saw some really bad things over there. Glad you made it back."

"Thanks. Yes, I saw some really bad shit happen to lots of people. Ours and theirs. But I never saw so much of it all in one place before I came here. You?"

"Nope. I never served in the military at all. I've always respected those that do serve, but I just don't have it in me to hurt another person. I've never even hunted or killed any kind of an animal. I just think I'd have gotten myself killed, or even some of my own guys." He took another sip and then looked up at the star-filled sky.

"I started college after high school but then took a summer job as a logger. I went back the next semester, but quit halfway through. Found I really liked it out here." He looked at Bob. "I just find it more peaceful out here away from the city. I like people and all, but there are complications being around them. Anyway. I've been a logger for so many years now that I don't think I could ever do anything else. But to answer your question, NO. I cut down trees for a living. I had no idea what to expect when I volunteered to come up here and help." He took a few big deep breaths, and then exhaled slowly before going on.

"I have to admit it has been a real struggle for me up here." He pointed his coffee cup at Bob and said, "Man! I gotta hand it to you guys. I don't see how you carry on. Day after day up here. It's getting to me. I never thought of myself as a quitter, but I'm ready to get out of here. I don't think I'm going to be able to ever forget the stuff I've seen up here. How about you?"

"No, sir. It's really hard to forget the truly gruesome sights I've seen. Don't think you ever really can forget, but I've managed to put them in a box and label it the past." Bob stood up, sipped his coffee, then gestured towards Vic with the cup. "But to tell the truth, I know now that this is going to be much harder to deal with. That was a war, and those sights were expected. This is a true accidental disaster. I don't know why, but I'm really having a harder time trying to get my head around all of this."

Vic looked around slowly. "Where did everyone go? Are they all in that tent? Wonder what's going on in there?"

Bob sipped again before he looked down at the ground for a minute. "Well, they're probably talking about me."

Vic studied Bob's face for a second before he broke into a smile. "Well, if you pissed somebody off, I wouldn't worry about it. With all the tension we're under up here, it was just a matter of time before it got to somebody. Don't worry about it, Bob. Hey, as quiet as they are in there, they can't be too mad about it or we'd be hearing some loud voices."

"Nobody got pissed off about anything. But I guarantee you they're in there, talking about me."

Vic had a questioning look on his face as he stared at Bob. The two men stood there looking at each other. Then a loud roar of laughter came rolling out of the tent. Bob and Vic both looked over at the tent, but all the men were still hidden inside.

Vic waited till Bob had made eye contact again, then he asked, "Did you play a joke on somebody, or did they play it on you?"

Bob's demeanor changed immediately, and he sat back down by the fire. He sipped the coffee and just stared into the flames silently. Vic waited for Bob to look up at him, but he continued to stare at the fire in silence.

So Vic decided to fake a yawn. "Well, sir. I'm going to call it a night." He poured his remaining coffee into the fire, then walked to the table and left his empty cup on it. "It's been good talking to you, Bob."

Bob watched as Vic walked away. His eyes followed him until he disappeared into his sleeping tent. Then he sat there staring at Vic's tent for a few more minutes before he slowly turned back to the fire.

Doc had been peeking out of the tent at the two men by the fire. He watched as Vic went to his tent. He was discouraged that

Bob didn't stop Vic from leaving. Doc had really hoped the two men would talk a lot longer than they had.

He was just about to go out and talk to Bob himself. As he began to open the tent flap, Bob suddenly looked over his shoulder again at Vic's tent. A second later, he jumped up, poured his coffee into the fire, left his cup on the table and headed towards Vic's tent. Once Bob disappeared into Vic's tent, Doc spun around to face the men behind him. With a tightly clenched fist, he made a pounding motion and whispered "YES!"

• • •

Vic had unrolled his sleeping bag on top of his cot. His boots were off and stood neatly side by side, just within arm's reach. Though for different reasons, both the guardsmen and the loggers all did this as well, so they could quickly reach them in an emergency. With his personal reading light switched on and book in hand, he was settling in to do some reading before sleep. He was almost in position when Bob stepped into the tent and addressed him.

"Uh, Vic? I hate to interrupt you but I was wondering if I could talk to you about something? But now that I see you're reading, it can wait till tomorrow. Sorry."

Vic didn't hesitate. "Hadn't started yet." He motioned to one of the two

folding camp chairs in the tent. "Sit down. This book is a little slow for me anyway. My brother's wife gave it to me several months ago, and it really isn't the kind of stuff I read. But it was the only book in my apartment that I hadn't read yet. Truth is, I'd rather talk than read it."

He laughed as he watched Bob pull the chair closer to his cot before sitting down. Once Bob was situated and had made eye contact, Vic said, "Ok. What's the topic? I'm wide open and not a bit sleepy." Bob sat there biting his lower lip and fidgeting nervously. He was obviously trying to compose his thoughts.

Vic said, "I take it this is going to be a serious conversation. Have I done something to make you uncomfortable?"

Bob immediately responded, "No! Not at all. It's just, well, I don't know how to say this without sounding like I'm losing my mind. Of course, I guess, I could be losing it. For real. I'm not sure if, well . . . I think I did, but I just can't believe I did. You know what I mean?"

Since Vic first saw him sitting by the fire, he had guessed that Bob wanted to talk about something. The real question was how to get Bob to open up. Even though Bob was here in his tent, it was obvious that he was still not able to say it out loud.

"Bob. Other than our conversation by the fire a minute ago, you and I haven't really ever talked. But now that I've talked to you out there for a few minutes, I can tell that you're struggling with something. Most people find me easy to talk to, but not everyone." He laughed a bit. "But you came this far. Spit it out, man. What's the worst that can happen?"

Bob quickly said, "You could think I'm crazy. *That's* what could happen."

"I doubt I'll think you are crazy. You may not know it, but there are those that think I'm crazy too!" Again he laughed.

Bob sat up very straight. "But I've heard those things about you. And, I'm sorry to say, I actually thought . . . well, I found it hard to believe what they said about you. But something happened tonight and well, that's why I'm in here."

Vic calmly asked, "What do you mean something happened? What?"

Bob was on the edge of the chair. He slowly shook his head before blurting out, "I saw something. At least I think I did. No, I'm sure I did. But I can't believe it."

"Ok. You have me interested. What did you see or think you saw?"

Bob closed his eyes and tilted his head straight back. He breathed in very deeply, then slowly exhaled, opened his eyes and leaned towards Vic before whispering.

"I saw somebody by the crash site earlier."

Vic was quick to ask, "Who?"

"Actually it was two people. A guy and a girl." Bob exhaled a short puff of air, "Wow, I can't believe I even said it out loud. But there it is. I must be nuts, right?"

"A guy and a girl? Are you sure? How old did they look? What would they be doing out here?"

"Well, I'd say they were in their late 20s or maybe early 30s. It looked like they were standing there talking. Their backs were to me. But it was obvious that they were talking and pointing down at the base of a tree. God! I still can't believe it."

"So, did you talk to them? Ask them who they were, and what they were doing out here?"

"Well, NO!"

"Why not? Were they too far away?"

"No! They were actually very close to me. Maybe 20 feet or so."

"So what were they saying? You must have heard them if they were that close."

Bob thought for a second. "Now that you mention it. I didn't hear anything. Nothing at all. Now that's odd, too. You're right. I should have been able to hear them. This whole thing is just way too weird."

"Maybe they were whispering. That's why you didn't hear them. But I still can't get over a woman being out here. Did you recognize the guy?"

Bob began to fidget in the chair again like he wanted to say something but was just afraid to for some reason. He finally said, "There's something I'm not telling you."

"Okay. Why aren't you telling me?"

"It's not because of how crazy it'll sound. And believe me, it will sound crazy. It's just that I still don't think I entirely believe it myself. But I saw it. I know I did. They were there. But not totally there."

"Okay. Let me get this straight. You think you saw two people who were there, but not there? What does that mean?"

"Ok, but if you ever tell anybody I said this, I'll call you a liar to your face. Well, I really won't but you get my point." Vic nodded yes and Bob continued. "They were fuzzy-looking."

"Fuzzy-looking? Was there smoke over there? How could you tell one was a girl?"

"Look. Fuzzy is the wrong word. They were transparent. I could see them both clearly, but I think I could see through them. Especially when they moved really quickly." Bob had paused and was intently watching Vic's face for his reaction.

Vic sat up on the cot and slipped both feet into his waiting boots. He leaned over and placed his elbows on his knees. He glanced down at the ground for a second before saying, "I think

I know what you're talking about now, and why you're talking to me."

Bob suddenly sat up straight in his chair and placed one hand out in front of him, like a policeman stopping traffic. "No. No. If you think I'm here jacking with you, you're wrong. Really wrong."

Vic looked up, but kept his elbows on his knees. "Bob. I know you're not jacking with me. Trust me."

"You do? Well that's good! But how?"

Vic had now sat straight up and had his arms extended with his hands still on his knees. "Well, it's simple. You see, I heard a guy and a girl talking in the crash circle. I didn't see them, but I heard them loud and clear. I've known they were here ever since. So what do you think about me now? Am *I* crazy?"

Bob's face was expressionless as he sat looking at Vic. Finally he spoke.

"Well sir. If you had told me this before today, I'd have helped them lock you up." He leaned back in his chair, rubbing his forehead. "But since I saw what I saw, I don't doubt anything now. I still can't believe it, but I can't deny what I saw. They were right there in front of me. So when did you hear them?"

"About an hour after we got here that first day."

"The first day! What were they saying?"

"You really want to know?"

Bob blinked his eyes several times before saying, "YES!"

"I was out in the tree line, just about 15 feet from the edge of the burn circle. I kept hearing a guy and girl talking. I would stop making noise and listen, but then they would get quiet. This went on for about 30 minutes. Then I could hear them for sure, not clear enough to know what they were saying, but I knew I was hearing a girl. That's when I walked over just to the edge of the tree line to look. At first I was excited because I thought they were survivors. Man, what a story they could tell! But I couldn't see anyone. So I just stood there listening. Eventually I heard them clearly enough to make out what they were saying."

Bob's eyes were wide open and he was hanging on Vic's every word. "So what were they saying? Go on!"

"Apparently the guy had realized that they were dead, but the girl was just coming to grips with it. It sounded like they both had been walking around here since the crash, and didn't realize that they were dead. When we showed up, something happened in the circle between those two, and two of us. That's when the guy realized what was really going on. Sounded like she was very upset and he was trying to console her. I distinctly heard her ask him to hold her tightly for a while. I couldn't believe what I was hearing. He told her they could stand there as long as she wanted. Then they both stopped talking altogether."

Bob's excitement got the better of him. "So what did you do then?"

"Well, while I stood there waiting to see if they would talk again, it suddenly hit me that, dead or not, this girl was scared. I looked around the circle and noticed nobody was around but me, so I decided to say something to them. So I stepped out into the circle a ways and told her not to worry. Said I knew she was scared, but that things like this always work out. I stood for a minute and looked around, but didn't hear anything else so I left."

Bob was shaking his head as he spoke. "But you only heard them? You never saw them?"

"Not everyone sees ghosts."

"But I did. Why me? After what I heard about you, I would think that this kind of thing happens to you all the time. Does it?"

"No. Not at all. This is really my first encounter with ghosts."

Bob was becoming more relaxed. "So what is it that has everyone so convinced you have special powers?"

Vic laughed out loud. "I don't have any special powers. What has happened to me all my life is that I get visions of things. They just come to me all of a sudden. No warning, nothing. It just happens. It used to freak me out so bad as a kid that I wouldn't go outside to play with my friends. I spent most of my time alone in my room. My parents assumed I read a lot. But what I was really doing was writing down these things I was seeing. The pictures in my head were so vivid that sometimes I would vomit. My mom always told me not to worry about it. She said I was just one of those kids with a nervous stomach. She said I'd outgrow it. It wasn't until a few years later that I came across a news article about a murder that had happened in another state some years ago. The details seemed so familiar, but I couldn't remember where I had heard it. Then at the bottom of the article was a picture of this man and wife. I almost shit in my pants. REALLY!"

Both men laughed and Bob said, "I had that same thought when I saw those two!"

They both laughed some more until Vic continued. "I knew this picture. So I tore that page out and went running home to dig out my old notebooks where I wrote all my visions down. It took me 20 minutes to find it. But finally, there it was. I had written this exact account of the murder in my book. I had even drawn the picture out. It wasn't that good of a picture, but it clearly showed the man and woman holding this red and blue vase. I had even colored my picture the same way. That's when I started to understand and accept this crazy gift God has given me. Now how crazy does this sound?"

Bob smiled as he shook his head. "Well. I have to admit. I don't feel as crazy as I did." His smile disappeared and his expression softened.

"I really appreciate you talking to me Vic. I feel so VERY much better now after you sharing your own experiences with me like this." Vic could tell that Bob's tenseness had completely disappeared, as he was sitting back in his chair and looking forward without seeing.

"You know, Vic? When I saw those two, I wasn't scared at all. Not scared of them, at least. It did make me very nervous, but I don't know why exactly." He looked downward, while slowly turning his head from side to side. "It just felt like everything I thought about life - everything that was possible and not possible - it was all wrong. It was like there was no gravity in my life all of a sudden, and I was adrift in a sea of doubt. You know? That was the hardest part. Trying to figure out for myself what was still true." He looked up at Vic before he finished. "At least true for me. You understand what I'm getting at?"

"Bob, I understand totally! Look, buddy. I've dealt with this weird stuff in my life since I was a young kid. You've been dealing with it for how long? Two or three hours, maybe? Personally, I'd say you appear to be handling it exceptionally well for such a short time."

"You said you've known they were around here ever since that first day. Have you heard them again? Where?"

"I hear them all the time. I think they walk around and watch what we are doing. Seems to me they're very curious. It's not like they stand around listening to our conversations. It always sounds like they stand off away from us and just watch. Most of the time I can't clearly make out what they are saying. But I do hear them, like mixed in with all the other background noises from our daily activities."

"Man, I'd love to hear what they are saying. Wouldn't that be cool? To be dead and know you're dead, but still walking around. And with each other! Man, this is just mind-blowing!"

Vic nodded his head. "I'm curious what they're talking about too. Very!" He paused and glanced at the tent opening as if he were making sure nobody was listening or about to enter. "That's the real reason I walk around at night alone. I go over to the burn circle to listen to them."

Again Bob interrupted. "But you always walk out of camp going away from the crash site and you come back into camp from that direction."

"That's right! I do it on purpose. And that is why I'm gone for so long. I have to make a big sweeping circle around the camp to get back to the burn site. I have to walk far enough out and around, to keep you guys here in the camp from hearing me and being able to tell which way I'm walking. It takes me almost 30 minutes to get to the circle and then 30 minutes to get back. I listen until they stop talking. Man it is absolutely incredible, what I've heard them talking about. I've always wondered about ghosts. You know? Like everyone does I'm sure. But now I get to hear them talking."

Bob was very excited now. "So you're finding out what ghosts know? Man, you gotta tell me this stuff, too."

"Well, actually, they don't know any more than we do. At least not these two."

Bob looked confused. "What do you mean they don't know? They're ghosts! They have to know. Don't they?"

Vic smiled. "Well, apparently not. They are confused about being left behind and why they weren't taken that first night."

This revelation brought Bob from a relaxed position to almost bumping foreheads with Vic. "Taken? Others? Oh my GOD! Of course. There were over a hundred something people on that plane. I forgot! That means that there are a lot of them walking around here." He looked around nervously before adding, "I hope I don't see any more of them."

"You don't have to worry about that Bob. You missed part of what I said. The others were apparently taken by some flash of light that first night. These two sat in the middle of the circle and watched it happen. That's why they always return to the circle before nightfall. They stay there in the circle all night."

Bob was eating this up. "Why in the circle? Because they died there?"

"Not really. I've heard them joking around about not wanting to be out in the tree line in the dark. So, I think whatever happened to the others must have happened out there. It's like they feel safe inside the circle. Actually, I think it may have more to do with the fact that we've been keeping the circle lit up all night.

It's the light!"

Bob snapped his fingers. "So that is why you fought so hard to keep the circle lit up at night when the guardsmen wanted to turn them off at night to save fuel. Isn't it?"

Vic snickered. "Yep! I felt sorry for them. And if the light in the circle was really what was keeping them from being taken, then I needed those lights left on. That way, they would still be here and talking. So I could hear them."

"Wow. This is just really odd, isn't it? We are talking about ghosts. Dead people. And you are worried about them being scared. Very odd."

Vic spoke very slowly. "Odd? I'll tell you what is really odd. This has been bugging me for the last two days, but I think I'm right. They talked about just meeting on the plane during the crash."

Bob once again interrupted to inject a comment. It was as if he were trying to impress Vic with his insight to the two ghosts. "So they didn't know each other before! That means they aren't just dead and experiencing a drastically new circumstance. They are just getting to know each other. Right?"

"Yeah, that's right. But it's more than that. As crazy as this whole thing already is, I think they are falling in love, too."

"Falling in LOVE! NO WAY!" Bob slapped both hands to his forehead and fell back in his chair. He was staring at the tent ceiling and laughed as he exclaimed, "This just keeps getting better and better! Ghosts in LOVE!"

"Hey, keep it down! You want somebody to hear you?"

Bob sat up abruptly, with a few fingers of one hand over his mouth. He raised then lowered his shoulders before he lowered his hand. After looking at the tent opening, he silently mouthed 'SORRY' to Vic.

Vic continued, "Anyway. I swear sometimes they just act like little kids, but everything else about them seems like they are older. You know, like the sound of their voices and the advanced ideas they discuss."

Bob shook a finger in the air. "You know! I thought that very same thing when I saw them. About being little kids, I mean."

Vic quickly asked, "But I thought you said they looked older? Like in their thirties or so?"

"I meant they acted like little kids. I forgot to tell you this part. They were just talking away and suddenly stopped. Both of them slowly turned at the same time and saw me watching them. We all just stood there staring at each other a few seconds. Then their eyes got really big and they zipped behind the tree.

"I was so scared that I just kept standing there staring at the tree they'd gone behind. Then the girl just barely poked her head around the tree and a second later, the guy's head snuck around just above hers. Their eyes were still wide open as they both slowly pulled back around the tree. They looked and acted like little kids that just got caught being somewhere they weren't supposed to be. And the look in their eyes as their heads disappeared after looking at me again. I couldn't help but think they thought I wouldn't know that they were still behind the tree. I would have laughed, but frankly, I was just too damn scared to move."

Vic had been listening and taking it all in. He slowly processed what he had just heard before he spoke. "Man, that is cool. And it goes with the feeling I was getting about them. But that seems like a lot of detail. I thought you said they were fuzzy?"

Bob briefly shook a finger in the air, "No, no, no! When they move, only when they move. They looked almost as clearly defined as you do. But just when they're standing still or barely moving. But man when they moved behind that tree, just a fuzzy blur!"

"But you also said that you could see through them?"

"That's right. But I didn't notice it at first. I just saw them so clearly. At first, I thought 'Hey! There are two people right over there!', but I started noticing that I could actually see the tree trunks behind them." He rolled his eyes. "And I mean RIGHT behind them! It was as if I could faintly see things through them."

"And that is when you got scared?"

Bob laughed as he pulled both hands up to his face and slowly wiped them downwards. "Scared? That's a MAJOR understatement! I was absolutely freaking OUT! BIG TIME!" As Bob fell silent, he saw that Vic was lost in thought.

"Vic? What are you thinking about now?"

"You said that at one point they had been pointing at the tree. So, I'm just wondering why? What would they be interested in that tree for?"

"Well actually, they were pointing at the base of the tree. Both of them did it at least once. And come to think of it, the guy almost fell down at one point. It was as if he tripped on something by the tree. That's when they both looked down at something."

Vic asked, "So what happened then?"

"Well. That's when they must have realized that I was watching them. You know how somebody will stiffen up their back and raise their head up slightly when they hear something behind them? They didn't turn around right away, but I could tell the moment they sensed they were being watched. And it was like a scary horror movie the way they slowly turned their heads to look at me. No expression in their faces. Just cold blank stares."

"Man! I know now why you froze. I don't think I could have run away either."

Both men sat there slowly nodding until Vic snapped his fingers. "HEY! We should go over there and look around that tree. Come on!" As he bent over to lace his boots, he heard Bob.

"NO! NO WAY, MAN! I'm sorry, but I'm not going over there in the dark. You can go, but I've seen enough of that place today. I'm not going."

Vic didn't look up as he kept on tying his laces. "Come on, Bob. You have to go with me. I don't know which tree you're talking about. You have to go."

Bob slowly bent over in his chair until his chest was almost in his lap and his face was level with Vic's.

"Vic. VIC! Look at me. VIC!"

Vic stopped tying the laces, but left his hands holding the uncompleted knot.

"What?"

"I'm not going, man. Not tonight." He slowly stood up while still looking Vic straight in the eye. As he took a step away from the chair, Vic finally let the laces fall to the ground. He watched Bob walk over and stop in the tent opening.

"But you'll go with me in the morning and show me that tree, right?"

Bob didn't turn around to look at Vic. He just nodded 'YES' before he disappeared into the night.

• • •

It was still totally dark at 5:00 in the morning. All the men were already eating bacon and eggs, some standing while others sat in camp chairs or on fallen logs. The pleasant smell of bacon and coffee permeated the still morning air.

Bob sat on a stump in a lonely section of ground as if he wanted to be isolated from the jovial morning voices of the other men. He was almost through eating when Vic finally emerged from his tent. He stepped into the morning air, stretched out his arms for a second and headed for the food. He noticed Bob alone on the other side of the fire, separate from everyone else. He nodded at Bob, who nodded back. With a steaming cup of coffee and a bacon-filled plate, he walked over to take his place on the one log that was next to Bob.

"Mornin' Bob! I slept like a rock, you?"

Bob placed his now empty plate on the ground before he took another sip of his favorite hot liquid.

"Morning. I did sleep well, but woke up about 30 minutes before they started cooking. Just lay there thinking about everything from yesterday." He motioned at Vic with his cup before he continued. "Including our little conversation last night of course. I guess you'll be wanting to get over there to look at that tree first thing this morning, right?"

Vic looked down at Bob's empty plate on the ground and

chuckled. "Well, I want to eat this first." He delicately balanced his coffee cup beside him on the log. Then he pointed at his full plate before he spoke. "I'm sorry about pushing you to go back over there last night. I just got carried away and wasn't thinking. Sorry man."

"Forget it. I felt kind of foolish the way I just left everything hangin' last night. Odd thing is that I was really getting into our conversation, and it bothered me to realize how quickly my attitude shifted." He shrugged and shook his head. "I don't know what came over me to act like that. Sorry."

Vic finished chewing and swallowed before saying, "Nah. It wasn't you, buddy. I said it last night and I'll say it again. I have been dealing with this weird stuff my whole life and you just stumbled into it yesterday. It takes some time to let it all soak in. It did with me! Even now, some things happen and just catch me so off guard that I still lose it. Really."

Bob was holding his cup with both hands to let the warmth spread through his fingers. The steam was still rolling up and over the lip of the cup, only to be stolen by the morning's light breeze. He was watching this happen as he began talking, but then moved his gaze to meet Vic's.

"Well, you might be right. It was very overwhelming at first, but I slept very well. I actually feel very good this morning. Bottom line is that I'm ready to go back over there now when you are. In fact I've been sitting here thinking about all you said last night. I'm actually getting a little excited to go see what they were pointing at." He reached down and picked up his empty plate before standing up. "I'm going to make a nature call and then grab another cup of coffee. Take your time, Vic. Be right back."

Vic had a mouthful of bacon, but looked up and mumbled 'okay' before continuing to scarf down his breakfast. Bob walked quickly over to deposit his mess in the dirty dishes tub on the table. He had barely disappeared into the trees when Doc darted over to confront Vic. He took Bob's spot on the stump and took a quick hit of coffee.

"So? What happened last night? How'd it go?" He was talking very quickly as if he were afraid that Bob might come back at any second. He looked towards the tree line where Bob had disappeared. "How's he doing? You think he's going to pull through it? Want me to do anything?"

Vic pointed a half-eaten biscuit at Doc and choked down an oversized bite of eggs. "Slow down, man! Take it easy. He's fine. Just fine!"

Doc laughed softly. "Sorry. I must sound like a crazy man this morning. But I hardly slept a wink last night, just wondering how it went with you two." He took a slower, considerably calmer sip of his coffee. "You say he's doing fine? That's great! I was really worried about him. When I first saw him he appeared virtually expressionless. He looked like he'd seen a ghost!" Realizing what he just said, Doc snickered before adding "No pun intended."

Vic hesitated putting the last strip of bacon in his mouth so he could add, "Bob and I are going over there where it happened. Just as soon as he gets back." He looked straight at Doc. "This is a good thing for him. We are going to check out something he said he saw."

Doc leaned in closer and whispered softly, "Really? What'd he see? Think it would be okay with him if I tagged along? So what'd he see?"

Vic's eyebrows were crinkled up as he stared at Doc for a second. "How much of that coffee have you had? Maybe you need to switch to decaf! Ya think?" With his plate now empty, he turned his full attention to his coffee. "Look. Whatever he saw or thinks he saw, it's up to him to tell you. Not me. And no, I don't think it is a good idea for you to try and tag along. Look. He's just beginning to open up to me. I think he's comfortable with talking to me.

"Trust me. He wasn't at first. Last night, there was several times I thought he was going to clam up and stop talking altogether. That would have been bad. I know you understand that. So, NO, you shouldn't go. Introducing anyone new into this, even you, could make him stop talking again. We need him to keep talking."

He took one last big sip of the coffee before he stood up to walk away. "You know as well as I do. If he's talking, then he's working through it. And that's what we want because that's what he needs."

Vic nodded his head at a silent and thoughtful Doc, before he turned to walk away. Doc was left sitting on his stump.

Bob emerged from the trees and walked over to where Vic had just deposited his dishes in the tub on the table. Not a word was spoken as the two men took off to the trees towards the crash site. Doc sat and watched them disappear, but mumbled to himself, "What'd he see?"

• • •

Not a word was said as the two men made their way through the dense trees of the forest. About 10 feet from the open crash site, Bob and Vic both instinctively stopped walking and stood motionless while still inside the trees. Two sets of intense eyes swept the burn circle from side to side. Finally Vic said, "I don't see anybody out here. Do you?"

"No. Nothing. You hear 'em?"

"No, Nothing at all. I don't think they're here." Having said that, Vic heard Bob exhale a choppy breath before he mumbled, "That's fine with me."

Vic slowly walked into the circle with Bob following him. Vic asked without looking back, "So, where were you standing?"

Bob started pointing as he sped up to pass Vic. "Over there. Come on!" Once there, Bob stopped and spun around a bit before pointing. "There it is. That's the tree right there!"

Vic was standing just behind Bob's left shoulder as he tried to envision the eerie sight that had been described to him last night. Of course it was almost completely dark when it happened, and now it was totally light. Still, Vic could just imagine how intimidating it must have appeared to Bob.

Vic uttered, "Well!" as he started walking and motioned for Bob to follow. "Let's go take a look!"

Bob seemed to hesitate just a second or two, then looked right, then left before he began to follow Vic to the tree. Once there, Vic turned to face Bob. He pointed, then spoke.

"This is the one? You sure?"

Bob had caught up and was now on the opposite side of the tree from Vic. Both men had their backs to the circle and were not yet close enough to look behind the tree. To Vic's amazement, Bob just stepped on around the tree and looked down.

"I don't see anything!"

Vic arrived at the tree and also looked down. He rubbed the foot-tall grass with his boot before he looked up at Bob. "You sure this is the tree? Positive?"

Bob took a quick look back into the circle where he had been standing yesterday. "Positive. This is the tree they pointed at." He then pointed to Vic's right and said, "The guy was standing right there and she was there. That's where they were, and this is the tree."

While Bob stared at the base of the tree and scratched his head, Vic took one step farther behind the tree and looked around. "Maybe it just appeared from your position that they were pointing right behind the tree. But they were actually pointing out here somewhere."

Bob watched as Vic was slowly moving around the open area behind the tree. Vic looked down as he brushed grass, broken branches and pine cones around with his boots.

"No. I'm sure they were pointing right here." He had his hand pointing down again at the base of the tree.

Vic stepped back over by Bob and looked down once more. "Well, there isn't anything there."

Bob sounded disgusted as he said, "So now you don't believe me?"

Vic's head snapped up to greet Bob's stare. "Wow! Where'd that come from? I didn't say I didn't believe you!"

"Well that's how it sounded to me!"

Vic realized that Bob was starting to doubt things again. "Look, man. I believe you! Again, you haven't dealt with this weird stuff as long as I have."

Bob interrupted, "And what does that have to do with anything? HUH?"

"Bob. You forget what we are dealing with here. You are conditioned to see things that are only in our realm of existence. Even though you saw them for a few seconds, you're forgetting that they are interacting with two different planes of existence: the one they're currently stuck in, and ours. It could be that they are only bleeding over into our existence a little bit. But they are mostly in that other plane. These two are somewhere in between our world and the next. They could have been pointing to something that we can't see because it's in their plane, not ours. That would explain why we can't see anything. It ain't here!"

Bob grabbed his forehead and rubbed his temples. He made a small grunt. "I'm getting a headache just thinking about all this." He backed up a few steps with his arms spread out to his sides. "It's totally light out right now. But all of sudden I feel like I'm back in the dark, just like last night. I understand what you are saying. Hey, it makes sense. I guess. No, I get it! I really do. But how in the world am I supposed to accept all this? Huh? HOW?"

"Bob. Answer me this. Do you think you saw them or not? It's a simple question. Yes or no, Bob. Did you see them?"

Without hesitation, Bob shouted, "YES! I saw them. They were right there. I SWEAR IT! RIGHT THERE!"

Vic laughed. "Well, SO DO I!"

Bob fell quiet, looking at Vic. Vic slowly walked right up until he was face to face with Bob. He stuck out his hand.

"Shake my hand, Bob. Shake it."

Bob was confused, but he slowly reached out and shook Vic's hand anyway.

Vic said, "I'm real. You know you are shaking hands with me. Right? RIGHT?"

Bob reluctantly replied, "Yes."

"Ok then. Think about what I'm telling you now. Just relax and think about it. You can't shake hands with these two. The rules that you've learned to take for granted since you were a child don't apply to the two you saw. Understand? You are used to applying those rules to everything you see or come in contact with. But the problem is that these two exist outside those rules. Oh, there are rules where they are, too, but probably a lot different. From what I've heard them say, I can tell they are struggling to understand their new set of rules. Just like you are struggling with when to apply our rules or their rules. In fact, they're probably a lot like you. They may be trying to use our rules in their new plane of existence. How confused do you think they are?"

After a few seconds of silence, Bob was completely calm again. "I don't know if I should be relieved or worried. What you said just now, well, it's starting to make sense." He breathed heavily in and out before he continued. "In fact, that would explain why they acted like they did when they noticed that I saw them. They probably couldn't believe it either. WOW! I wonder if I scared them?"

Vic started laughing. "I'll bet you did! I bet you scared the HELL out of them. Didn't you say that they darted behind the tree?"

"That's right. Their first impulse was to hide. Like kids." Bob saw that Vic was looking around. "Do you hear something? Is it them?"

"I hear somebody coming, but it's our guys. Not them."

"So what do we do now?" Bob was hoping that Vic had a plan, because he was just too damn confused by all of this to have one of his own.

Both men now faced the direction of the sound. It was obvious that some of the other rescuers were headed into the circle. Vic turned just his head to address Bob. "There is only one thing for us to do." He started walking back into the trees as he said, "We have to come back tonight and listen to them talk. Maybe they will mention what they were pointing at by the tree. It's the only thing we can do. So, come on and let's go get some work done."

Bob followed Vic into the trees just before the others walked into the circle. They didn't hear Bob say to Vic, "Come back tonight? In the dark? ME? You know where the tree is now. Why do I have to come?"

• • •

Bob and Vic's work suffered because they couldn't keep their minds on what they had been assigned to do. It was hard to stop their minds from thinking about their upcoming quest tonight. Yes, both men were only going through the motions of working today. Each man endured endless questions from their assigned work team members as to whether or not they felt well. There were similar questions as to why they seemed so preoccupied while going through their assigned tasks. Bob and Vic had both received minor bumps and bruises that day because they weren't paying close attention to what they were doing.

Bob's work team felt it was due to his rather odd event the night before. They all were aware that Bob apparently thought he had seen a ghost. Though they didn't believe he had, he was their brother in arms and therefore worthy of compassion on the subject. Most of them were not so sure they understood Doc's jubilation over Bob's private talk with Vic. They had all heard stories about Vic by now, but most refused to believe in the concept of a psychic. Still, they all totally trusted Doc and if he thought it was a good thing, they thought so too. The loggers, as a group, were definitely viewed now as much more than just competent workmen. They were teammates.

Vic's team members were very concerned as they watched Vic make silly mistakes all through the day's work. He dropped things prematurely and seemed to trip over the simplest of debris on the ground. They knew he wasn't himself, because he had always been a very nimble and sure-footed workman. He was clearly pre-occupied with something else. It was easy to see that his mind was on something other than his work. They all suspected it had something to do with the guardsman called Bob. Still, they were very proud that their friend was helping Bob. They all knew how each guardsman listened to what Doc said. So, it was very important having a trusted guardsman openly endorse Vic to his fellow guardsmen. Each logger now felt an ever-stronger bond was developing between them and the guardsmen. Yes! They no longer would view themselves as one of two groups involved in this tragic plane crash. No, they all were a team.

At long last, the work schedule for today was finished. All men, guardsmen and loggers alike, were very thankful to see the sun coming down on one of the last remaining days they would be spending at this tragic event. The echoes of hard work had all stopped, replaced with the sounds of men laughing as they made their way back to their tents and a hot meal. Soon the smell of coffee and steaks surrounded the men, which caused each of them to quicken their pace.

The guardsmen hit the camp just moments before the loggers. Both groups of men spilled into the camp area and quickly blended into one happy group of campers. Immediate pairings formed in previous nights, quickly took up conversations started the night before. This was a time of male bonding that would cement their common memories for a lifetime.

• • •

With food and drink in hand, Vic was the first to reach his isolated log seat. He sat down quickly and began the delicate process of balancing his coffee cup in a cut out on his log. Once accomplished, he turned his attention to the huge steak and baked potato he had painstakingly selected from the chef's table. As he took that first delicious bite, Bob appeared and took his place on the stump. The log he had pulled up last night to use as a table quickly became a resting place for his coffee cup. He didn't speak, but instead also chose to take a bite of his beautiful steak first. Several minutes of silence passed as they both indulged in their own flavorful bliss. With over half of each man's steak now devoured, only then did the conversation begin.

"So, Bob. I've been thinking about it all day. After we finish eating, we can both just walk out of camp together right in the direction of the crash site. Everyone knows why we're talking, so they will just assume that I'm making you go back there for your own good. It's perfect. Nobody will question anything. We can walk straight there instead of losing 30 minutes each way circling back around the camp. That means we can spend even more time at the edge of the clearing, listening to them."

"I was thinking the same thing. Man, it's a wonder I didn't cut off a finger or even a hand today. My mind just wasn't on what I was doing. I have to admit, I have some real mixed feelings about going over there tonight. I'm excited as HELL about hearing what they're talking about, especially if they talk about that damn tree. But I'd be lying if I didn't say it was making me very nervous knowing they were going to be right there, too. Do you think I'll be able to see them again, or was that maybe a one-time thing?"

Vic had finished his steak and worked on the baked potato now. He pointed his fork at Bob as he swallowed a big bite. "That's a really good question. Here's what I think." He scooped out the last of the potato, shoveled it into his mouth and sat the plate down on the opposite side of the log from his coffee cup. He was still chewing as he reached for his coffee.

He looked at Bob as he swallowed it down, took a sip of coffee and quickly glanced at the others to make sure nobody was headed their way.

"There are two basic probabilities here. One. They were in an emotionally charged conversation about whatever it was they had found by the tree. And, their emotions were so intense that it caused them to materialize. That's when you saw them. If this is the case, then I'd say you're in the clear unless they get all charged up again and become visible.

"Two. It could turn out that you, my friend, may just have a gift that you never knew about until now. Think about it! Like all of the intense emotional events that brought us here to start with. You've been living, working, breathing in this hyper-sensitive state for weeks now, and it activated your special gift. And if this is the case, brace yourself, bro. Not only will you see them. But you might start seeing other spirits as you encounter them when you go back to the real world."

Vic tilted his head and nodded rapidly a few times.

Bob had stopped chewing the last of his steak. He sat motionlessly for a second, staring at Vic. Then he choked it down before coughing once.

"Oh boy! That hadn't crossed my mind. Surely not? Not me? I don't want to start seeing ghosts everywhere I go! That would drive me crazy!"

"I'm with you, Bob. I didn't want this either, but I've come to the conclusion that I'm going to be this way when I go back home."

"Wait a minute. You mean you just started hearing the dead while working up here? Really?"

Vic smiled ruefully and shook his head again. "That's right, Bob. I never heard any voices before I came up here. And I've been to lots of cemeteries and funerals. So I'm positive that it just started up here."

"So, you just stared hearing them non-stop? Damn! I hope I don't end up like you."

"Well, to tell the truth. It didn't just turn on and keep going. Not at all. I heard them very clearly that first day. Just like I told you. But then over the next few days, I wasn't sure if I was hearing them faintly, or if I was just imagining it. Like, for instance.

One day I was out taking a piss, and I swear that I heard them again. Just ever so softly. Man, the hairs on my arms and neck were straight and tall. I zipped up and made a beeline back to camp. Odd thing is, I had this creepy feeling they were walking right there alongside me. But I got back to camp and then it just stopped. I just chalked it up to nerves. But the next day. I was out in the trees and the chopper carrying a load of bodies flew just a hundred yards away from me. That's when I heard it loud and clear. First it was him. Sounded like he was up in the trees. Then I heard her screaming from a distance. I think either he fell or jumped from the trees to the ground. Then I heard her screaming. Sounded like she was running and calling his name. Then it all was muffled by the trees, and I couldn't tell which way they were. You know how it is out here. You can be within 100 yards or less of somebody out here and not hear them talking. But anyway. From that day on, I've heard them a lot."

"So what is his name?"

"He is Ed and she is Martha."

Bob was obviously concentrating on something before he spoke. "I just had a thought. When we get done here, we could look up the passengers' list and see if there was an Ed and Martha that were seated by each other. Then maybe we could do some research and find pictures of them. After all, I already know what they look like!"

Vic froze. He was just staring blindly at Bob. "Man! That's a really good idea. Damn good IDEA! But I'm not much of a detective. I wouldn't know how or where to start looking for that kind of information. You?"

Bob smirked at him. "Hey man! We work here. You and I both know half the people working in those hangars where they have the bodies and records. Piece of cake!"

Noticing that they were both done eating, Vic started collecting his stuff. "Come on. Let's drop this stuff off and get going."

They both quickly dropped off the dirty dishes and headed off into the trees. Vic saw Bob looking back at the others. "Stop looking back. Just look straight ahead, or it will look like you have something to hide. We really don't need anyone following us."

Bob complied immediately. Once they were a good ways into the trees, Bob began talking again. "Are you sure they will be there?"

"Yes. Remember what I told you. They always come back into the circle before it gets dark. And it's dark, so they will be there. Trust me. Now we need to be very quiet from here on. Let's move slowly and keep as quiet as possible."

"Just lead the way, my friend. I'll follow you."

The two men walked in silence, taking deliberate steps so they would not make any noise as they approached the crash site. Bob watched for hand signals from Vic. The light from the circle barely reached into the trees. Vic motioned for Bob to follow him to a small stack of fallen trees that was only 10 feet from the clearing's edge.

They were just a few feet from their hiding place when Vic noticed that Bob had stopped. He appeared to be frozen as he stared into the lit circle. Seeing Bob like that, Vic knew that he could see them. Both would carry their own special gift back home with them. They would be able to detect wayward spirits that stray into the realm of the living.

Bob finally noticed Vic was frantically waving his arms and trying to quietly get his attention. He waved back and motioned for Vic to move on to the hiding spot. Once there, they both lay prone on the ground and each selected a suitable observation point through the fallen branches of their hideout. Bob was slowly moving his head from side to side in disbelief as he saw a man and woman sitting only 20 yards inside the circle with their backs to Bob and Vic. He turned to look at Vic, then pointed towards the circle, then to his own ear. Vic immediately nodded 'YES'. He slowly moved over to Bob until their shoulders were touching and began whispering.

"Yes, I hear them just fine. You see them? Are they the ones you saw?"

"Yes. That's them. Are they talking? I can't see their faces."

"Yes, wait." Vic bit his lower lip as he listened. "She's complaining about the few remaining crates being in their spot."

"Their spot?"

"Oh, forgot to tell you. She always gives him grief about them having to sit in the exact same spot."

"I'll bet she makes him always sit on the same side, doesn't she?"

Vic stared at Bob before answering. "That's right. How'd you know?"

Bob rolled his eyes. "My wife does the same damn thing. Drives me crazy. If you're right and they are falling in love, then I really should go talk to that guy."

"Why? What about?"

Bob had forgotten that Vic was a single guy, so he didn't know this stuff yet. "I need to tell him that it only gets worse the longer you're with 'em. After a while, he'll learn not to sit until she says it's okay. That's what I do!"

Vic faked a silent laugh as his head went backwards.

"Now she's saying that she's scared being so close to the trees. Says it makes her nervous."

Bob interrupts Vic, "I can see him point over to the right. I bet he just suggested they could move over."

Vic nodded. "Right again. She just called him a big goof. Said that's not their spot. He just said it was a spot like any other."

Bob didn't take his eyes off of them as he said, "Yep. I'll bet she hits him. And there it is! Poor guy."

"He just asked what was that for."

Bob was still focused on the two in the circle, but he was nodding his head as he said, "Yep. This guy has a lot to learn about women."

At this point, Vic was biting the fingers on his clenched fist so he won't laugh out loud. Between what the kids were saying to each other and Bob's comments, Vic was seriously wondering if he was going to be able to hold it all together. But suddenly, Vic's demeanor changed to one of intent concentration as he closed his eyes and tilted his head so that one ear was higher. He was just about to say something when Bob uttered, "Hey. They both are looking to the left. Wait a minute. She's pointing at the trees. Hold it. That's the tree from the other day!" Bob looked down at Vic. "Are they talking about the tree? Are they?"

Vic nodded 'YES' and then he motioned with his hand for Bob to be quiet.

"Damn. A hole. It's a hole. Wait. I don't believe it."

Bob leaned real close and asked, "A hole? What hole?"

"He just said something about a hole behind the tree. She wanted him to check it first thing in the morning. Sounds like there's something in the hole. Wait. Now they are talking about the fact that there are so few crates in the circle. They know we're almost done and wonder when we will leave. Oh no. I feel so sorry for her. She just said, 'When they go, the lights go. Then what will we do?' Man, she sounds depressed again. She's stopped talking. So has he."

Bob spoke again without taking his eyes off the two spirits in the circle. "Yeah. She just put her head on his shoulder. Now he's got his arm around her. Just leaned his head against hers." Bob watched them while Vic was listening. After several minutes passed, Bob said, "Looks like they're going to sleep. Do they do that?" He then looked down as Vic nodded 'YES'. Bob looked back at the two in the circle, only to feel Vic pull on his shirt and say, "Come on. It's over for the night."

The two men quietly eased out of the area without saying a word. They walked in silence all the way back to camp. There were only a few die-hard coffee drinkers still sitting around the fire. They never even looked up as Vic and Bob wandered in and grabbed a couple of cups of coffee before heading off to Vic's tent.

Once inside, they both pulled the two folding camp chairs closer together and sat down. The warm cups in their hands reminded them of how cold it really was up here at night. They had been so caught up in what was happening with the kids that they hadn't even noticed the temperature had taken a very sharp drop.

"So Bob. What do you think now? About your new powers?" Vic chuckled before taking another sip.

Bob was grinning from ear to ear as he said, "That was absolutely the most exciting time I've ever had in my entire life! It's just incredible. And to think, that I was so scared at seeing them. But now that I've seen them again, I'm not scared. And thanks to you, know what they are saying . . . well, they just seem normal. They act just like they're still alive."

"I know! I get so excited every night when I go over there and listen to them. I think all those same things that you just mentioned. It is remarkable, isn't it?"

Bob got a serious look on his face. "You know we have to go check for that hole in the morning, don't you?"

Vic also became serious. "Yes. I agree. But how? When?"

Bob suggested, "What do you say we get up and sneak over there while everyone else is eating?"

"No. That won't work. They don't usually leave the circle until it's completely light. Remember, they're afraid to go into the trees in the dark. Besides, I have a feeling that Doc is going to be watching us very closely tomorrow morning. If he doesn't see us, he'll come looking for us. And another thing, depending on what is in the hole, how do we justify finding it? Doc would surely ask why we went over there so early. That just won't work. We need another plan."

Bob snapped his fingers. "I've got it! Here, take my pocket knife. Everyone knows that I don't go anywhere without it. So, in the morning you tell Doc the truth."

"The truth? Are you nuts?"

"Look Vic. Tell him that we had been back to the circle. Say that you had made me go over there again. You know, just walking around and talking. Then tell him I'm missing my knife and I asked you to go with me to find it. Since you also knew where all we walked. What do you think?"

Vic was nodding his head YES, but then stopped and held out his hand with the knife in it. "But what is this for? Why give it to me?"

Bob was shaking a finger at Vic when he said, "In case Doc invites himself along. If he does, then you just walk past that tree, stop and call out that you found it. Then you bend down and feel around quickly for that hole. Actually, I'd do it with my boot first. No telling what's down there."

"I'm impressed, Bob. That's actually a very good idea. Even has a backup plan. I like it. In fact, I'll pick up a small branch while I'm walking around. I'll stick it in the hole when I bend down to act like I'm picking up the knife." With that settled, they both began sipping their coffee.

Then, out of nowhere, Doc suddenly stepped into the tent. He stared at them without saying a word. Both men looked up at him, holding their cups of coffee up to their lips, but not drinking. The steam from their coffee was whisked away with their breath.

Finally, Doc broke the silence with an abrupt question.

"Where have you two been?"

Not moving anything but their eyes, Bob and Vic glanced at each other briefly before looking back at Doc.

"I asked you two a question. What's going on with you two?"

Bob spoke from behind his cup. "Nothing. Just having some coffee. It's cold out there."

Doc squinted one eye first at Bob, then Vic. "I know it's cold out there. What I don't know is why I'm getting the feeling you two are up to something. Where were you guys?" This time he was looking right at Bob.

"Look, Doc. We were just out by the crash site. Why?"

Doc continued staring at Bob for a second, then he turned to Vic. "I just heard your guys talking about seeing a bear today. Know anything about it, Vic?"

Vic immediately adds, "A cub. There was a mother and a cub. Came really close to us today halfway between here and the road. So?"

Bob finally lowered his cup as he turned to Vic. "You didn't tell me anything about a bear. Why not?"

Vic started snickering and it turned into laughter so hard that he barely got the words out. "I guess I was caught up in the conversation I was in!"

Seeing how hard Vic was laughing, Bob soon joined in and the tent was filled with uncontrolled laughter. Doc stood there and patiently waited for them to regain their composure.

"I know you two are up to something. I do! I'm going to find out." He turned to exit as quickly as he had entered. Bob and Vic stared at the tent opening and heard Doc exclaim outside, "I'll find out. I will!" He barely took another step and there was loud laughter coming from the tent behind him. He passed one of the other men who said, "Sounds like Bob is feeling better. Eh, Doc?"

Doc continued walking and spoke without looking back. "Yes, he does. It's a damn medical miracle!"

Chapter 10

NOT EVERYONE UNDERSTANDS GHOSTS

IT WAS A super-cold morning and the darkness made it feel even colder. The general consensus of the camp was that the sooner the sun came up, the better.

Bob and Vic had been the first two in the chow line that morning, and they were already in their usual eating spots. They saw Doc chatting with the cook. He looked their way, then patted the cook on the shoulder before starting to walk in their direction. He walked right up and stopped at an equal distance from both of them before he spoke.

"So you are looking for me?"

"Morning, Doc! Bob and I wanted you to know that we felt bad about last night. We were just cutting up when you walked in, and didn't realize you were serious until it was too late. Sorry."

"I told you two last night. I know you're up to something. And I'm going to find out. I promise!"

"Doc. Vic and I were over at the crash site. Surely you know why. But, I'm good now. In fact, I'm real good. Vic helped a lot. So, it's my fault. I wanted to go back again after we ate last night. You know what they say about getting back on the horse after it throws you. I had to face it, and Vic went with me. No big deal. I'm good now. Honest!"

Doc had gradually relaxed, and appeared to be buying their story. "That's good to hear, Bob. Thanks, Vic. Really. Hey man, I'm sorry about last night too. We've all been working under a lot of stress for quite a while now. It's a good thing that we'll all be out of here in another day or two. I'm glad to see you're better, Bob."

Bob acted very casual as he sipped his coffee.

"I'd be a lot better if I could find my knife."

Vic jumped in. "Yeah, Doc. That's another thing we wanted to tell you. He dropped his pocketknife over there, but we couldn't find it in the dark. We're going to run over there and look for it once the sun comes up. Should be easy to find. I know exactly where we were when he realized he'd dropped it."

Bob added, "We could use another set of eyes if you want to tag along, Doc."

While Doc was focused on Bob's face, Vic's eyes widened with disbelief when he heard Bob invite Doc to come along. But he decided to play along, too.

"What do you say, Doc? Want to take a walk?"

"Well, I really can't." He looked at Vic. "One of your buddies got some deep wounds on his forearm yesterday. One of the trees fell and threw up some small branches when it hit the ground. It was just like shrapnel, and a piece stuck almost a half an inch into his forearm. Your guys did an excellent job bandaging him up on site, but they had me look at it last night. I need to check on him one more time before he goes out to work. You want me to get a couple of the other guys to go with you? I'm sure somebody would go help."

Vic shrugged. "Nah, I'm pretty sure I know the area it has to be in. But if we don't find it this morning, then we might get some of the guys to go back with us tonight with some flashlights. Thanks anyway, Doc."

"Well, ya'll take your time and find it. The workload's pretty light today and tomorrow. This whole thing is almost over. Later."

He turned and headed off looking for the injured logger.

"I'm done. You ready, Vic?"

"Yes, but just one thing. When we get a little ways outside of camp, let's run on the way over there. You up for that?"

"Be happy to. Anything to get warmed up a little more."

"Oh, and one more thing, Bob. Let's do a little dance over there. Let's act like we are looking around a minute or two before I act like I found your knife. I'm thinking that Doc is still suspicious. So let's just put on the act, just in case he's planning on slipping over there to watch what we're doing."

"I hate being this way with Doc. You know he's really a good guy Vic? But I agree. The less he knows, the better."

"Bob, I like Doc too. But I also know for a fact that not everyone believes in ghosts."

The talking and planning was over. It was now time for them to execute their mission. Both men made the routine morning dish drop on the table before they headed out into the trees. They broke into a run after they were sure they were completely out of sight, and that nobody was following them. Bob got his wish and eventually had to unzip his coat just a little because he was warming up too quickly. Once they got close to the circle, they slowed to a walk and entered the open burn circle. The warmth of the sun's rays were unobstructed and it felt good on their faces.

Bob quickly lined up on the tree they sought and Vic followed him back out into the trees. Vic followed the plan and he picked up a five-foot long branch to poke things with as he pretended to look for the knife. He casually slipped one hand into his pocket to fetch the knife, so he would have it ready for the final deception. The stage was set. Bob was acting similar, but using his boot to move things around on the forest floor.

Once he was behind the target tree, he poked the branch downwards twice before it slipped into the hole. He immediately called out, "Found it!" He immediately bent over to act like he picked it up. Then he added, "Wow. There is a big hole over here. Lucky it didn't go down in it."

Bob ran over and looked at Vic's branch sticking out of the hole.

"Anything in the hole?"

Vic moved the branch around and that is when they smelt it. There was a very distinctive odor of decaying flesh. "Wow! That smells familiar. Did we miss something?"

They were once again back in recovery mode. Both men dropped to their knees and began to pull up all the tall grass that was hiding the hole. Once the hole was completely exposed, they could see straight down to the bottom. It was a hand. There appeared to be a ring on it.

Bob said, "We'll have to get this catalogued. I hope the hell they haven't packed the cameras and discovery forms."

"I think they're packed, but the crates are still sitting back at the camp."

"That means the forms are, too. Now I wish Doc had come out here. One of us has to stay here while the other goes back for Doc."

Vic said, "I'll go. Be right back."

Bob grabbed his arm to stop him, then pointed to the other side of the circle. Two guardsmen had just emerged from the trees. They were assigned to wrestle one of the last two big chunks of metal back into the circle to be crated up.

"Hey Spike! Over here! A little help, guys!"

The two guardsmen ran over to see what Bob wanted. They looked down into the hole and then agreed to both run back to get Doc.

After they were out of earshot, Bob said, "We need to get our stories straight here. Doc's already suspicious. Even if I show him the knife, he's going to wonder about it. Don't you think?"

Vic was shaking his head. "Nah, why would he be curious? Curious about what? We found the knife *and* a hand. Are we good or what?"

"I hope you're right, Vic. But I just got a bad feeling about Doc. By the way. You haven't heard the kids talking have you? I haven't seen them. You heard anything?"

"Nope. I've been keeping an ear out for them, but nothing so far. Like I said. They've been leaving the circle every day when the sun comes out. And lately, I never hear them around where we've been working. Maybe they're bored watching us, now that we're only picking up the little pieces of the plane. Look at it from their point of view. It can't be much fun watching us pick up every little piece after taking a dozen pictures of the area. And then we fill out those stupid discovery forms. Hell, I get bored doing it. I damn sure wouldn't sit and watch somebody do it. Would you?"

Bob snickered. "You see, Vic. The fact that you couldn't sit and watch somebody else work just proves you'll never be a manager!"

Both men laughed as they began walking in lazy circles waiting for the others to get back with Doc. It took about 35 minutes before Doc and a few others returned to the circle. Bob and Vic showed him the hand in the hole. Then they got out of the way as doc oversaw two guardsmen as they began photographing the scene around the hole. Then one man respectfully lifted the hand out and gently placed it in a bag being held by another. The proper tags were made and attached to the bag. Then the numbers on the tag were written on the forms to log it and connect it to the photos.

Once the task was completed, Doc sent all those men back to camp with the hand and documents. Bob and Vic watched as he began walking over towards them.

"So you two find the knife, or just the hand?"

Bob pulled the knife from his pocket and held it out for Doc to see. "Yessir. It was right by the hole."

Vic jumped in, "The knife was on the ground right next to it. Another two inches and it would have fallen down in the hole. We wouldn't have found the knife or the hand."

Doc stared at them. "Lucky break, huh?" He paused for a second, as if he were trying to decide if this was all there really was to this story. "Well. I guess things like this happen for a reason. It's like you were supposed to find that hand. Good job. You have your knife. You both should find your teams now, so we can all get the last of our jobs done and go home tomorrow."

With that said, Doc turned and started trotting off after the others who had now disappeared into the trees. Bob and Vic waited till Doc was out of sight too.

"Bob, you up for coming back again tonight?"

"Damn straight. It's going to be hard to keep my mind on what I'm doing today. Just like yesterday."

"Me too." Vic pointed off in one direction. "My guys are that way. See you at dinner."

Bob nodded. They both ran off in the directions of their respective work teams.

• • •

Bob's small group was the first one back to camp. They all were walking leisurely until they heard some other men coming out of the trees. Just like schoolboys, they all hurried to get in line first. There was a lot of horsing around that evening. What had begun as a large number of strangers had morphed into a solid bunch of friends. Sure, there were several small groups that always consisted of the same two or three. But there were also those inevitable loners who moved between the groups on a daily basis. The conversation topics varied from group to group, but none were more secretive than Bob and Vic.

Bob was already comfortably seated on his favorite stump as Vic came to take his place on his usual log. It was human nature to incorporate daily rituals in one's life. They provided comfort and normalcy during the day. These were two attributes that people involved in stressful endeavors long for and need. As they always had done, the two men focused on their food. But the discussion of what they would do tonight slipped in between bites.

"So, Bob. You ready for tonight?"

"Of course! It's the only thing I've thought about all day. You?"

"Same here. You know? I don't think Doc was right this morning."

Bob looked up, "Right about what?"

Vic pointed his fork at the food table. "I heard several of the guys saying that they didn't get as far as they hoped today. Seems they didn't get either one of those last two big chunks of wreckage pulled far enough into the circle to start crating them up. So even if they do get them crated up tomorrow, there is no way they'll get both of them lifted back to the trucks. You know what that means, don't you?"

"That's good for us. Means we have at least three more nights to watch and listen to the kids. Good!"

Vic stopped eating and looked at Bob for a second. "I'm worried about the kids. I don't know if I can just turn out the lights and walk away." He shook his head. "It just don't seem right. I can't tell for sure about the guy, but the girl is scared. She talks about it all the time."

Bob had completely cleaned his plate and swapped it for the cup on his improvised log table. "That thought has been going through my mind, too. But what can we do? You said it yourself. They're stuck here in between our plane and the next. I just don't see how we can help them."

Vic wiped up the final drops of gravy with his last piece of biscuit before he popped it in his mouth. "All I'm saying is that we need to try and help them. At least to make the transition to wherever they should have gone."

Bob seemed reluctant to suggest something, but he did anyway. "I hate to say it, but maybe we've been keeping them here by leaving those lights on." He immediately held one hand out in Vic's direction. "Now look. I'm not blaming you for getting the lights left on every night. I know you didn't do it just so you could go over and listen to them talk. You're just human. You heard how scared she was of the dark, so you did something to help her out. Hey! I totally understand. I'm just saying that it may be time for them to, well, you know . . . move on."

Vic closed his eyes and was lost in thought. "You're right. I know you're right. It just seems like there must be another way. They're different. We both know that. They weren't taken like all the others. That just has to mean they're special. Like they have something else to accomplish before they can go." Vic had his cup and plate in hand as he stood up. "You ready?"

Bob did the same and answered with just one word. "Ready."

After depositing their dishes, they ambled off into the trees. Nobody paid any attention to their exit. The day's chores were all that was discussed on the way to the circle. Again, they went into stealth mode when they were within a few yards of their monitoring post. Bob poked fun at Vic by saying, "Don't forget to sit in your special spot. We need to start your training for when you get married."

This brought a smile to Vic's face as he took up his listening post. Bob was barely in place when he spoke softly. "Well. Even in death, this proves that habits live on. There they are. Same spot, and Ed's apparently learned which side is his." As usual, Bob never took his eyes off the two spirits while telling Vic what they were doing. "Looks like she has her arm tucked under his, and is leaning her head on his shoulder. Are they asleep already?"

Vic answered, "No. They are talking very softly. They know that those are the last two big pieces of wreckage. Damn. They are wondering how long before the lights go off and we leave. Oh, get this. She just asked him if he was positive the hand was still there when they left this morning. Uh-oh. Bet she hits him."

Bob confirmed the strike then asked, "What was that for? What did he say?"

"He told her he may be dead, but he wasn't blind."

Bob said, "Looks like he's goofing around. He just fell over like she'd knocked him down. Looks like he's laughing because his shoulders are shaking."

Vic quickly injected, "Yes he is. I can hear him. He's getting louder and telling her to stop. What's going on?" Vic was staring out into the circle at nothing, but wishing he could see what Bob saw.

"Yep. She's partially on top of him. Looks like she's tickling him. They seem to be having fun. I think you're right. They're falling in love!"

Bob's description of what was happening in the circle was forming a vivid picture in Vic's head. He was leaning a little too far over the bush they were hiding behind, when he lost his balance and fell.

Everything happened very quickly then. A branch that had been sticking out of the bush swung up and hit Bob in the side of the head with enough force to knock him face down in the dirt. There were three noises that had just occurred: The sound of the crushing bush, Vic's grunt as he hit the ground, followed by Bob's 'OUCH!' before he hit the ground. These did not go unnoticed by Ed and Martha.

At first, they stopped wrestling. They remained motionless for a second with Ed on the bottom and her partially on top. Ed still had hold of both of Martha's hands which he had captured in order to stop her from tickling him. But both of their heads were turned in the direction of the sounds. Eyes were peering into the darkness in search of the cause for the sounds.

Ed said, "Somebody's out there!"

Martha's voice clearly showed she was scared. "I don't like this."

Ed finally said, "I don't hear anything moving."

"Me either." Then she looked down into his eyes and

whispered, "Maybe they're hurt. I heard them say 'OUCH' rather loudly. Didn't you?"

Ed gently helped her off, and stood before helping her to her feet as well. She hid behind him, peeking around so she could see the tree line. After a second or two, she began pushing him from behind to get him to move a little closer to the trees. He allowed her to drive him closer, but slammed on the brakes when they were within 10 feet of the trees. Their eyes were scanning the darkness for any sign of who made the sound. The problem was they were looking too far out. Bob and Vic were only a few feet away.

"You see anything, Martha?"

She shook her head. "No." But as her gaze fell a little closer to them, she suddenly noticed the subtle shape of Bob's body on the ground.

She exclaimed loudly, as she pointed at Bob. "There! It's a man!"

Ed looked down. "He looks like he's out."

"No! Look! He's starting to move. He's rubbing his head. He's hurt. Should we help him?"

Ed looked back at her in total disbelief. "Help him? Really?"

"Well. We can't just let him lay there like that. Oh look, he's moving again."

Bob's head hurt like hell as he gently rubbed where that branch had knocked the crap out of him. Forgetting where he was, he instinctively sat up on his knees. As his eyes slowly began to focus, there came the horror as he realized that he was face to face with the kids. And they were looking right at him.

Martha asked, "You think he sees us?"

"No! He doesn't see us."

"But he's looking right at us."

Ed chuckled as he replied, "He doesn't see us. He's looking through us at the empty circle behind. No way he sees us!"

Bob didn't know what to do. His first thought was to raise his hand and say "Hi!"

Seeing this, Martha instantly yanked her head out of sight behind Ed. Bob watched as her hand quickly darted up and her fingers flicked Ed's right ear before disappearing back out of sight.

Vic remained still but heard Ed say, "OUCH! Stop it!"

Then Martha said in a very condescending tone, "No! He can't see us. He's looking through us, blah blah blah." Then she reached up and turned his head to one side before popping her head out to say, "Unless you missed it, he just said 'Hi!'"

Ed pulled his head from her grasp and looked back at Bob. "But he hasn't said anything else. I'm not sure he sees us."

A second voice came from the dark covered ground. "Oh, he sees you all right. But he can't hear you."

Vic slowly sat up on his knees and started brushing leaves from the bush off his chest. "But I can hear you. That's my department."

Martha poked her head around again. "You can hear us?"

"Yes, ma'am! Loud and clear. But I can't *see* you." Vic reached over and nudged Bob, who had finally forgotten about the pain in his head. He'd been able to piece together the gist of the conversation because of what Vic was saying.

"Uh. Well. I can see you both. But like he says, I can't hear you. Sorry."

Ed asked, "What are you two doing out here?"

Bob could tell that Martha was scared, so he attempted to console her. "Look, Martha. You don't have to be afraid."

She let out a high-pitched girlish squeal. "He knows my name. They're ghost hunters and here to kill us!"

Hearing her comment, Ed just hung his head and shook it for a moment before talking over his shoulder to her. "Kill us? KILL US? Duh! Dead, remember? Already dead!" He then looked back towards Bob.

"How do YOU know her name?"

Bob was staring at Ed. He knew he was talking, but he had no clue what was being said.

Vic finally said, "We know both of your names. Yours is Ed." Seeing that Vic was standing up, Bob quickly followed along. Vic continued, "My name is Vic and his is Bob."

Martha's head popped out again. "Vic? We know you!"

Bob noticed that Martha's head appeared when Vic introduced them both. But she was still standing behind Ed, which meant she was still scared. So Bob said, "Martha. I'm Bob. I know you're scared of the dark out here. So, if you would feel more comfortable, we could all come out into the light to talk. Okay?"

But having said this, he was at Vic's mercy as to what was being said.

Vic added, "Truth is, we are here to help. But Bob has a good idea. Let's all stand in the light and talk. We want you both to be comfortable."

He looked in Ed's direction. "What do you say, Ed?"

Bob watched as Martha reached up and started tapping on Ed's shoulder with one finger. "I think that's a good idea. Ed? He's right. I want to back away from the trees." She finally stepped out to Ed's side, took his hand and was trying to pull him back as she continued, "Come on, you big goof! Let them come into the light."

Ed gradually relented and turned to let her lead him back into the center of the circle. As they walked, Martha whispered very softly, "You hear what he said? They are here to help us. Isn't that great?" Then she quickly glanced back at the two men that were just now entering the light of the circle. She turned back around and whispered again, "But just in case, you stay between me and them. What if they try to grab me?"

Again Ed hung his head in disbelief at what she was saying. "They *can't* grab you. You're a ghost. Like me." He was just about to say something else, when they heard Bob speak.

"We can stand in your usual spot. Or we can all sit down and talk. Whatever you want to do."

Ed rolled his eyes. "Oh. Here we go." Then he looked her in the eyes as he asked, "You going to tell them which side to sit on?"

Seeing this, Bob immediately suggested, "We can sit on any side you want, Martha."

She instantly spun around and took a step towards Bob, but Ed grabbed her by the arm to stop her. She put her free hand on her hip as she spoke.

"Okay, Mister Bob! How do you know about our spot? And what makes you think I care which side people sit on? Huh?" Then she looked back at Ed who immediately commented, "Wait a minute. You always seem to care which side I sit on. Why do they get to sit wherever they want?" She pulled free from Ed's grasp and walked quickly past him to take the lead. She didn't look at him as she went by. "If you don't know why by now, I guess you never will, big boy." Ed stood still and watched her as she passed by.

Both men were walking towards Ed. Vic was bringing Bob up to speed as to what was being said. "She just asked how you knew about their spot. She also wants to know why you mentioned sitting on specific sides."

Bob stopped suddenly because he was within a foot of Ed. They were facing each other. Ed was looking at Bob, but obviously talking to Vic. "So this one sees us, but can't hear us talking?" Then he looked over at Vic. "And you can't see us, but you hear us. This is going to get confusing!"

Vic had taken one step too far, and was standing slightly behind Ed's right shoulder when he spoke. "Yes. That's right. But I can tell where you are when I hear your voices."

As soon as Vic made that statement, Ed glanced over his shoulder at Vic and said, "And how is that working out for you?" Then Ed spun around and took off towards Martha.

Vic jumped when he heard Ed's voice, because it made him realize that Ed was farther back and closer to Bob. So Vic quickly took one big step backwards. He glanced at Bob, then looked at the space in front of Bob before he started talking again. "Well, I didn't say it was a perfect method. I just meant that . . . "

Vic noticed that Bob had a funny look on his face, so he paused.

Bob asked, "Why are you looking at me, Vic?"

"I'm not looking at you. Be quiet. I'm talking to Ed." He motioned to where he thought Ed was standing.

Bob snapped, "No you're not!"

"Yes I am!"

"No you're not!"

Vic squinted at Bob. "He walked away. Didn't he?"

Bob was exaggeratedly shaking his head, his eyes wide open. He looked like a life -size, G.I. Joe version of a bobble head.

"Walked away. Gone. So you're talking to nobody!"

Vic let out a huge breath then put his hands on his hips and closed his eyes. "Ed's right, you know. This is going to get confusing."

Bob said, "Well, I've learned one thing. I can't read lips worth a damn!"

Vic opened his eyes and motioned for Bob to lead the way. "You're on. I don't know where they are."

Bob stepped around Vic. "Look at the bright side. You have your own personal seeing eye dog. ME."

Vic chuckled and patted Bob on his shoulder as he took the lead and blazed a trail over to the kids. Bob held out his arm to stop Vic from walking right into Ed, who had done exactly as Martha asked him to. He had positioned himself between the two men and Martha. Seeing this, Bob spoke.

"Ed, Martha. We are here to help. I know this whole experience must be very confusing for you. Well, it is for us too." Seeing Ed's mouth move, Bob looked over at Vic. "He wants to know what is confusing to us."

Bob nodded. "Well, besides the fact that we're standing in a forest talking to ghosts? Sorry! That was really just for my sake. Anyway. Just like you two are learning about your new plane of existence, we're learning how to deal with our new-found abilities."

Hearing this, Martha stepped in front of Ed to ask, "You mean you both just started being able to see and hear ghosts?" Noticing that she was in front of Ed, she quickly stepped back to Ed's side.

Again, Vic's voice sounded off from behind Bob. "That's right, Martha. This is new for both of us. Mine started that first day when I heard you two talking out here in the circle. But Bob's just started when he saw you both talking and pointing to the hand over by the tree."

Ed snapped his fingers as a prelude to speaking, but stopped to stare at his fingers. He was looking at Vic and said, "Did you hear that?"

Vic replied, "Hear what?"

Bob said, "Ed snapped his fingers. Did you not hear it?"

"No. I heard nothing. Just Ed asking if I heard that."

Bob said, "Ok. Everyone make a mental note of that. Vic can hear you, but not you snapping your fingers!" Then Bob looked quickly at Vic and asked, "What does that mean?"

Vic shrugged his shoulders. "How the hell do I know?"

Ed looked at Vic and said, "Hey. We don't need to be cussing in front of Martha. Okay?"

Vic immediately said, "Of course not. Sorry." He looked around as if he was searching for where Martha was. "Martha! I'm so very sorry. I've been out here with just a bunch of guys for way too long. It's a bad habit and won't happen again. Sorry."

Bob saw Martha shaking her finger at Vic and moving her lips. Before Vic could speak, Bob looked at him. "Let me guess. She just told you there's no excuse for cussing."

Martha started pointing her finger at Vic. "You said he couldn't hear us. How'd he know what I said?"

Vic and Ed both said at the same time, "He's MARRIED!"

Martha looked at Ed. Bob looked at Vic. Then Vic looked where he thought Ed was standing. "I know how I knew he was married. But how did *you* know?"

Ed chuckled. "My mother used to tell my dad that all the time."

Vic and Ed stood there shaking their heads before they both broke out in laughter.

Martha asked Ed, "Who's married? And what does that have to do with what I said? Hey mister. Why are you laughing?"

The more that Martha demanded to know why they were laughing, the more Ed and Vic laughed. Finally, in an attempt to really get Ed's attention, she poked him in the shoulder with one finger and said "Don't you ignore me like that, mister. I'll have you know . . . Hey! You two are getting a little loud now!"

Vic couldn't help but say, "And my mom used to say that to my dad! ALL the TIME!"

This revelation sent Ed and Vic into ever more laughter. Seeing that Ed was indeed ignoring her, she stopped talking and crossed her arms. Bob looked at Ed, then at Vic, then back at Ed. Finally he held out both hands towards Martha as if he was asking her what was wrong. Seeing this, she tightened her lips, squinted her eyes in his direction and barely was able to squeeze out one word.

"MEN."

Bob's eyes flew wide open as he pulled his head backwards. He spoke out of the corner of his mouth in Vic's direction. "Vic? Why is she staring at me? She looks mad, Vic. What did I do?

Did she just call me a name?"

Vic was holding one hand up at Bob and the other one hopefully at Ed. "Stop! No, really. Stop! Come on Ed. Stop it, buddy. My sides are hurting."

It took a few more seconds for Ed and Vic to settle down. Bob had hardly moved. Martha had been staring at him the entire time, ignoring the others. Bob was watching as both Vic and Ed held both hands up to their faces. He knew that Vic had stopped laughing, and assumed that Ed had too since his shoulders had stopped shaking.

Martha had noticed that Bob was not willing to make eye contact with her. She thought to herself, 'Huh! I must be getting the hang of this ghost thing. He can't even look at me, he's so scared!' She smiled at this new feeling of power.

Having regained his composure, Ed asked, "Where were we? I forget."

Vic immediately answered. "Let me think. Oh, yeah! You had just snapped your fingers, but you didn't say why."

Ed shook his head, then looked at Vic again before speaking.

"What I was going to say is that I recognize this guy now." He was pointing at Bob. Vic said, "Ed recognizes you now."

Bob said, "Yes, that was me. I'm sorry about just standing there and staring at both of you. But I just couldn't believe what I was seeing. It was a real shock."

Martha was getting braver as she stepped slightly in front of Ed and held her ground. Apparently she was no longer afraid of the two men. She was looking at Bob and spoke as she motioned for Vic to pass it along to Bob.

"She says they were also shocked when they realized you could see them. That's why they hid behind the tree. She said they're sorry they scared you. Says they felt very badly as they watched your friend take you back to the camp. She also said she is glad we found that hand. They were so worried that it would never be found, and that it wouldn't have been right. She said 'thank you' again."

Hearing this, Bob smiled and he nodded at her. "We're just as relieved as you that it's on its way home to aid in closure for the family."

Martha looked at Bob. "I know you can't hear what I'm saying, but it feels rude not to look at you as I talk. I know you see me. I can see it in your eyes. You watch as we move about. I really wish you could hear us. It would make this so much easier."

Then she turned to face Vic. "But you can hear us. So I probably should be looking at you. But you can't see us. So it's like, well, pardon me if this sounds crude. But it's like talking to a blind man, because you don't really watch me as I move about. This is really going to be hard. And I'm very interested in learning how either of you can really help us. How? What can you do?"

Bob saw that she had turned to face Vic, so he did as well. Vic was looking straight ahead, but unfortunately just off to Martha's right. "I understand how you feel, Martha. But we'll work our way through our communication issues together. That will fall into place as we get to know each other. But I do think we all need to spend our time talking about how to help you both. Bob and I don't really have any ideas yet, but we're committed. We are willing to do whatever we can to help."

Bob interrupted. "I do have one suggestion about the communication issue. It probably will sound stupid, but it's the best I got!" He paused for a second as he saw Ed's mouth moving. So he looked at Vic and waited for Vic to tell him what Ed was saying.

"Ed wants to know your idea. He says that at least you have an idea. He doesn't."

Bob started talking, "Ok. But remember, it's going to sound stupid. So, I was thinking that we should all sit down facing each other. Me and Vic side by side. Ed and Martha side by side. To help Vic, I could draw an 'E' in the dirt in front of Ed and an 'M' in front of Martha. That way At least Vic will know where to look when he is listening and talking to you. Might make it seem more natural." Again he paused for just a second. Then he saw that Vic, Ed and Martha were all nodding 'yes' to his suggestion. Not needing Vic to interpret, he continued. "Okay then. Let's all just sit down and get comfortable."

Bob again motioned for Martha to sit first. Seeing this, she immediately smiled at him and reached for Ed's hand as he helped her sit down. She glanced up at Ed and said, "See. Now he's a gentleman. Just like you. I like these guys, Ed. They're nice." Ed thought to himself, 'Good thing he's alive. I don't want her liking him too much.' Then he chuckled to himself as he realized that she really couldn't have him, since he was already married.

Once all were seated, Bob started talking to Vic as he reached out and drew in the dirt with his finger. "This 'E' is right in the middle of where Ed is sitting and the same with this 'M' for Martha." He quickly glanced up at Vic and said, "If you look up about two and half feet for him, and about two feet for her, you will be face to face with them." Vic nodded his head and immediately looked in Ed's direction. "Ed. How's this."

Ed responded, "Perfect! You're looking right at my face. Hey Bob! This is a great idea."

Vic said "Great! Bob, Ed likes your idea a lot." He then turned and said, "Martha? How about you?"

There was a slight pause as Martha blushed before answering. "Uh, Vic? Just a little lower, please." She was displaying her girlish charm as she glanced at Ed. "I'm not as tall as my big guy." Ed looked down at her with a smile. All of his recent thoughts of losing her to a married live guy seemed to just melt away. She was still his. He was safe.

"How's this, Martha?"

She smiled very big and nodded approvingly at Bob. "Wow, that's much better! Please tell Bob I also like his idea. Good job!" She was looking right at Bob and he could tell that she was pleased too.

Vic glanced at Bob. "Wow, this is much better for us all. I don't have to wonder where they are. This will make things a lot more normal." Then he smiled as he looked from face to face. "And I think we all agree that we could all use as much NORMAL as we can get."

Bob watched as Martha laughed for the first time. Her eyes sparkled as she smiled up at Ed. Bob noticed that her eyes looked just like his wife's. In that moment, he realized just how much he missed his wife and he lost all expression in his face. It was such a vivid mental picture that he became more homesick than he had been during his entire time up here.

Martha was first to notice that Bob had drifted away from the conversation and was suddenly lost in thought. "Bob?" Then she looked at Vic. "What's wrong with Bob?"

Vic asked, "Bob? Hey Bob! What are you thinking, man?"

It took a moment before Bob's ears checked in with his brain. "What? What did you say?"

Vic laughed softly, "Hey, man. We lost you for minute there. What are you thinking about?"

"Oh. Nothing. It's nothing. Really!"

Vic said, "Martha says it didn't look like nothing. You have another idea, man. Out with it!"

He's a little embarrassed. "Well. It was my wife. I mean, it was Martha's eyes, but they reminded me of my wife. It just hit me how long it's been. I miss her a lot." Then his eyes flew open as he looked at Martha. "Oh, I'm so sorry. I shouldn't have said that. Really sorry."

Ed didn't really understand what Bob was apologizing for. He wondered if Bob's comment was some attempt to flirt with Martha? But he quickly ruled that out when he saw the concerned look on Martha's face.

Vic started talking again. "Bob. Martha says she is sorry that we've all been away from home for so long. She is glad that you will get to go home soon to your family." Now Ed understood what was happening. Or at least he thought he did.

"But Martha, that's why I said I was sorry. It was inconsiderate of me."

Ok, Ed now knew that he had absolutely NO idea what was going on, so he asked Martha, "Uh, what was he inconsiderate about?"

Martha reached up and placed her open hand on Ed's cheek before softly saying, "He's talking about the fact that we can't go home to our families. Understand, baby?"

Ed slowly acknowledged that he understood. "Oh? But I don't have any family to go back to. I know you do." He paused as he continued looking in her eyes. "But, I don't." Then Ed turned to glance at Vic. "Vic. Tell him it's okay. I don't have any family to go back to. Just an apartment full of computers."

Martha was now looking in Vic's direction also. "And tell him that I have a sister, but we really weren't all that close. I lived alone just like Ed. Neither one of us had much of a life. In fact, as strange as it sounds, we both have more going for us in the personal department now that we're dead. So tell Bob, it's really okay. I'm very happy that I have Ed now. I may not be alive. But I'm alive inside more now than during my entire life among the living." She had her head against Ed's shoulder as she looked at Bob but talked to Vic. "Tell him. We are both happier now than we have ever been, and he should not feel sorry for us at all."

Ed was now looking down into her lovely eyes as he said, "Ditto! Tell him I feel the same way. Very happy! Before I met Martha, I was just going through the motions of living. I'm happier now than I ever was alive!"

Vic conveyed all that was said. Bob responded, "You were right. They *are* in love."

Martha again placed her open hand on Ed's cheek as she said, "You hear that, handsome? They think we're in love! Are we? Are you in love with me, Ed?"

Ed saw something in Martha's eyes that he had never noticed before. She was looking at him differently. Why? He felt some of his old, insecure feelings return, as this would be where he would always screw up a conversation with a girl. But he was amazed how calm he was. Looking into her eyes brought such peace to his soul.

"I can't lie to you, Martha. I've never been in love. So I'm not sure if what I'm feeling is love. All I know is that I feel different around you. I'm happy. For the first time in my life, I don't just feel good. I am HAPPY!" He paused to glance at the two men before looking back into her eyes. "I guess I do. No! I do. I know I do!" He smiled contentedly. "I do love you, Martha. I do."

Vic started to tell Bob what had been said, but was cut off by Bob. "No need bro! I got it from their eyes." He sat a little more erect as he spoke rather excitedly. "Okay! We need to get down to business and figure out what to do to help you two. What do you say?"

Ed and Martha looked like they were going to kiss, but Martha patted Ed's cheek as she jokingly said, "Hold that thought, big boy! We'll get back to this later. Trust me."

Ed edged just a little closer to say, "Really?"

It was obvious that she wanted to kiss him, but she pulled back slightly as she placed one hand on her chest, let out a little breath and said, "Oh, yeah! We are definitely going to be getting back to this later when they leave!" She sat up by herself, looked from Bob to Vic, then spoke. "Okay, Vic. Let's talk about it."

"Okay, then. So, let me ask some questions, for both of you of course. I overheard your conversation one night. You spoke of seeing other spirits go out into the trees and just stand there in the dark until something happened to them. And, by the way, I've filled Bob in on everything I've heard you both say. So I guess we need to figure out why you two were left? Agreed?"

Ed and Martha looked at each other. Then Ed answered for them. "Yes. We think that is a good place to start. Do either of you have any ideas?"

Vic pointed first to Bob before pointing to himself. "We both have talked about this. We're wondering if maybe it had something to do with you both staying in the light. But we also had some questions about that." Vic looked at Bob. "Martha said they thought of that, too. That's why they always come back to the circle before nightfall. Also says they've been worried about what happens when we take the lights out of here."

Bob nodded, then turned towards the kids. "Vic and I have an idea that our lights have nothing to do with it. Which would mean that you walking in the dark wouldn't be an issue either. But we have no way to prove it. Well, no safe way to prove it."

Again, Vic started talking. "Well, Ed. I heard you two talking about that night when the others were taken. Your wording was that the others seemed drawn out into the dark." Ed and Martha were nodding their heads 'yes'. Vic continued, "You also said that the other spirits didn't seem to see you. You two could see them, but they couldn't see you. Right?"

Bob said, "I can see them nodding 'yes'. So we wondered if you felt drawn to the darkness out in the trees and just resisted it? Or, did you not feel any need to go out in the darkness?" He watched as Martha's lips started moving. She was shaking her head 'no' as she pointed at herself, but she was nodding 'yes' as she pointed at Ed. Then she glanced at Bob briefly.

Bob said, "So she wasn't drawn to go there, but she says that Ed was. Then why didn't he go? Oh! He wanted to stay with her. Right?"

Vic was shaking his head 'no'. "No, no, no. She said they were curious what the others were doing out there, but she wasn't going out there to see. She said that Ed wanted to go out there and ask them what they were doing out there. Of course, that was before the big flashes of light started happening, and the others began disappearing with each flash. That's when Ed decided it wasn't a good idea to go out there."

Bob spoke up again. "So, neither of you were pulled to go out there. That brings us back to something that Vic and I also wondered about. Why weren't you both drawn to go out there? What was different about you? Oh, and we also decided that there is something else special about you both, because the others couldn't see you. It's like you were caught between the plane of the living and the plane of the dead. Of course, we all agree that you both are dead." He closed his eyes for second. "Your situation is just so hard to believe."

Vic nodded. "Ed says they agree!"

Bob continued, "Well, here is where Vic and I ran out of ideas. Obviously we need to figure out what is keeping you here."

Vic started nodding and Bob could see that Ed was speaking to Vic, then Martha spoke. Vic finally said, "I do remember that! So that is what happened. Let me tell Bob!"

He looked at Bob. "Remember when I told you that I heard Ed up in the trees, and thought he had fallen or jumped? And that I thought Martha had called his name? Remember?" Bob was nodding 'Yes'. "Well, it turns out that Ed here had gotten on one of the pallets with some bodies, and was going to fly back to check out the base camp. But he was yanked off the pallet. What I heard was him falling through the trees to the ground. Well, of course I only heard him yelling. I didn't hear any branches breaking or anything like that. Like when I couldn't hear him snap his fingers earlier. Any way. He says it was like he hit the end of a rope. He wasn't pulled off, but stopped from going any farther away. That is why they haven't tried to go anywhere. They don't think they can."

Bob's voice sounded depressed. "Man. That sounds like they are somehow locked in here. But what would be keeping them here? What?"

Vic said, "No Ed. We're out of ideas, buddy. What's next? I don't know, man. Not everyone understands ghosts!"

All four of them were silent for several minutes and then it happened. They were all startled by a new voice that sounded off all of a sudden. Out of nowhere, they all clearly heard a voice off to their right say, "It's not what. It's who!" They were all looking around frantically.

Bob asked, "Did everyone hear that?"

Vic said, "I did. Oh, and the kids say they did too." After a few seconds, Vic added, "That was what Bob and I call you two." Another few seconds and he added more. "Yes. We are both older than you two. Yes, Martha. We can tell that you are younger than Ed. Okay, Ed! We believe you. You are just a little older than she is."

Bob was looking right at Ed when he said, "Hey dude. Just a word to the wise. Don't get into discussions with a woman about her age. It will always end poorly for you."

Vic started talking. "No Ed. He doesn't know that because he's married. I'm not married and I know that! All guys know that." There was a very slight pause before Vic added, "Okay, Ed. Not all guys know that! I got it."

Bob snickered. "Yep. She hit him. Dude! I told you."

Vic said, "Ed says next time he'll take your word for it. No Martha, I don't know who said it. And yes, Martha. Bob heard it too. No, he can't hear ghosts. We told you that remember. And Ed, she's just excited. She's not losing her mind. Come on, you two. You are not helping."

Bob said, "That's right. I heard it. But I still don't hear these two. What do you think that means, Vic?"

Vic shrugged and was just about to say something else when Doc popped up from behind a crate that was only five feet from them. "That's because I'm not a ghost, you two morons!" He stood there brushing the dirt off his fatigues as he walked right up to where they were sitting on the ground. "I told you I'd find out what you were up to!" He looked down at the two men as they both began to fidget about like two schoolboys who had just been caught doing something they shouldn't. "You want to tell me what you two think you are doing?" Nobody answered, so he continued. "Okay. Which one of you junior paranormal investigators wants to tell me what you *think* you're doing?"

Bob didn't hesitate. He was looking up at Doc as he pointed a finger at Vic. Vic saw this gesture and slapped the extended finger before saying, "Oh no, you don't. You came out here on your own. You tell him."

Doc stood glaring down at them, but neither said anything for several seconds. "Okay. I see. So you want to play 50 Questions. Okay. I'll play. Who do you two think you're talking to?" He points over to where Ed and Martha are sitting.

Bob nervously said, "Nobody, Doc. We're, uh, uh, just talking."

Vic let out a rapid breath. "What Bob meant to say was that we are just talking to each other. Why, Doc?"

"Ok boys. So that's how it's going to be. Well then. Why are you both sitting side by side? If you were just sitting and talking, then why aren't you facing each other? Or did I walk into the middle of a lovers' retreat?"

Hearing that, Vic and Bob looked at each other. Noticing how closely they were sitting to each other, their eyes almost bugged out of their heads as they immediately began their guilty shuffle to put some space in between themselves. Seeing this made Ed and Martha both start laughing out loud, but they assumed that only Vic could hear them. Before Vic realized what it would sound like to Doc, he mumbled, "Not funny, guys,"

Doc pounced on him. "Who are you talking to now, Vic? Can't be me. You said 'guys'. That sounds like you are speaking to two individuals. Not just me."

Vic slowly rolled his eyes and became very still. Bob tilted his head in an attempt to keep Doc from seeing his face as he silently mouthed 'Shhhhh' at the kids.

Doc started in again. "Okay. Moving along. Before I crawled over behind that crate so I could hear what you were talking about, I watched ya'll do some very strange things while you were still standing. Yeppers! Sure looked like the two of you were standing and talking to someone. But your posturing and gestures, really looked like half of a conversation. What do you think about that? Vic?"

Vic slowly said, "I don't really, uh, know what you're talking about Doc. You can clearly see it is just the two of us. We were just talking."

"Well Vic. Then why were you laughing so hard? What about? Nah. Don't answer that. I don't need to know that. But I am very curious as to why you held your hand up in two different directions and kept saying, 'Stop! Stop! Really. Stop!'

Sure looked to me that you were talking to someone else than just Bob."

Again, Bob was fidgeting around like a kid expecting a spanking. Doc looked down at him. "And Bob? Was I dreaming when I saw you make a motion like you were inviting someone to sit down first. Huh?" He paused for just a moment before continuing. "Okay. We'll come back to that too."

Then Doc pointed to the two initials scratched into the dirt. "Oh, look. How cute! Two letters drawn in the dirt. What could they be for? Hummm? Maybe they mark the spot for two invisible guests? What? No denials? Well then, let me think. I bet those letters are initials for somebody. Of course, I think we all know that there aren't any BODIES connected to these somebodies. Anyway, I digress. So. I wonder what the 'E' stands for. Could be Ellen? Perhaps, Edith or Elizabeth? Nope? I bet it's a guy's name. Say, ah, Ed?"

Both Vic and Bob's head snapped upwards to look at Doc. Martha's mouth dropped wide open as she pointed her finger at Ed.

Doc continued, "Let's move on to the 'M', shall we? Ok then. I'll just go out on a limb and guess. Oh, maybe, MARTHA."

Hearing this, Martha squealed and covered her ears with her hands. Ed immediately pulled her tighter against his side.

Bob spoke with a newly-found stutter. "Da, Da, Doc. You're talking crazy, man. Come on Doc. Listen to what you're saying. There is a logical explanation to all this."

Doc was still talking in a sarcastic tone as he said, "Oh, I agree! I bet there is a very logical explanation for *all* of this!" He made a wide gesture with stretched-out arms. Then he suddenly pulled them back to his sides as if he was snapping to attention. "Wait! Did you just call ME crazy? CRAZY? What if I did THIS!"

Doc suddenly stomped his boot in the dirt right between the two letters and let out a blood-curdling scream. Martha threw herself backwards to get away and Ed quickly fell to her side with one hand up to protect her. Seeing how scared Martha looked, Bob sounded a little angry as he yelled out, "Stop! You'll scare them!"

Vic closed his eyes when he heard Bob's inadvertent admission that they had some unseen guests.

Doc's posture softened immediately. He stepped back from where the two letters were drawn on the ground. His sarcasm was also gone as he said, "So finally. The truth. Interesting that your impulse is to protect them. Very interesting."

Vic slowly asked, "Protect who?"

Doc almost sounded like he was asking a question as he said two words. "The KIDS?"

Bob stared straight ahead in silence as Doc looked down at the ground, just behind the two initials in the dirt.

Finally Vic spoke. "We might as well tell him, Bob."

Bob looks up at Doc and said, "Tell him what? Sounds like he already knows everything. How long have you been here? Why did you follow us? You're just going to make this whole thing a lot more complicated."

Doc says, "No. Believe it or not. I'm going to help you out here."

Bob looked at Vic, then back up at Doc. "Help us out? What are you going to do? Suggest a very good insane asylum?"

Doc hesitated for a moment. He looked at the faces of the two men, then glanced over where the supposed invisible guests were sitting. He ran a hand through his hair before he spoke. "A moment ago you stated that not everyone understands ghosts. Well sir, that is not entirely accurate."

Vic sat up very straight as if he were anticipating a particular answer and asked, "And?"

Doc grinned. "Lucky for you, someone here does. ME!"

Chapter 11

GRAMMA TAUGHT ME

SEVERAL MINUTES HAD passed since Doc's surprise announcement. Everyone was hesitant to be the first to speak, although their eyes were very busy darting from one to the other and back again. Bob looked at Doc, then Vic and then the kids.

Vic kept going over and over what Doc had said. Did he really understand ghosts? What exactly did that mean? How did he come by this information? Could he really help the kids? Everyone else had their own questions to ask, but they all realized this could be a good thing.

Doc finally ended the silence. "So, mind if I sit down and join the conversation?" He was looking directly at Bob and Vic. The two men glanced at each other before Bob motioned for him to sit.

Once on the ground with his legs crossed like everyone else, Doc looked right at Martha before saying, "Martha. I'm sorry for scaring you and Ed. It was an impulse move on my part totally intended to make Bob react." He glanced at Bob just as Bob asked, "Why me?"

Doc cleared his throat softly. "I could tell that you were becoming protective of these two. So I used that to get you to open up." Doc raised his hand at Vic to stop him before he could speak. "Martha. I don't need Vic to ask me if I can hear you. The answer is complicated. You see, I don't hear you with my ears like Vic does. I hear you in my head. And by the way, Ed, I wouldn't hear you snap your fingers either, but I would know that you did it."

Bob chimed in. "Well that's just great! Everyone hears the kids but me. This SUCKS."

Doc was still looking at Vic, but spoke over his shoulder to the kids. "Yes, Martha. I agree that there is no excuse for Bob to cuss."

Bob immediately hung his head. "Sorry, Martha."

Doc turned back to the kids before he spoke. "No. I can't see you. However, I do know exactly where you are, and that you are both lying beside each other. Ed is propped up on his left elbow, and you're on his right. But I just sense it. I don't actually see you. And no, Ed. I can't read your mind."

Vic couldn't stand it any more. "I don't understand, Doc. All this time I thought you were trying to find out if I was really a psychic. But you were pumping me for info on ghosts. Weren't you? Admit it!" Vic looked in the direction of the kids before saying, "I agree with Ed. Doc must not know everything about ghosts."

"No, I don't know everything. But I have been doing this much longer than you. The ghost part, not the psychic part. No, Ed! I'm not a psychic, and being psychic is not the first step. Trust me."

Vic calmly asked, "How long have you been doing this?"

"Since I was six." He paused and looked towards the kids as he asked, "What, Martha? Oh. Gramma taught me!"

Bob asked, "Your grandma taught you to speak to ghosts? How could she do that?"

Everyone focused on Doc as he started nodding his head.

"Ok. Look. She always played hide and seek with me as far back as I can remember. It was on my sixth birthday. We were playing in my room, when she grabbed her chest and fell over on my bed. I was a kid and didn't know what was going on. She held out her hand and I took it. She looked like she was trying to say something, but never did. Then she smiled at me and closed her eyes. I just stood there holding her hand, waiting for her to open her eyes, but she didn't. I thought she had gone to sleep so I crawled up beside her and went to sleep too.

"I was still holding her hand when my mom woke me up, trying to pull my hand out of Gramma's hand. I didn't understand why mama was crying and I didn't want to let go of Gramma's hand. Anyway, my mom made me sleep with her every night until about a week after the funeral. She didn't want me playing alone in my own room, either. I didn't know why. I started crying one night because she wouldn't let me close my door and play with my toys.

"She finally caved and let me close my door. I think she stood outside my door for a long time, listening to me play. I knew she was there. She used to always sneak up to my door to listen to what I was doing, but I always heard her. Eventually she stopped it. That is when I first heard my Gramma. She wanted to play like we used to. I guess it was because I was so young and I really loved my Gramma, but I never questioned her being there and wanting to play. I wanted to play too. So we did. Just like always. Until one night when my mom busted into my room and started looking around. Then she asked me who I was talking to. I told her 'Gramma'. She looked really scared and made me sleep with her again. The next day, we talked for a long time about it. She didn't believe that I was playing with Gramma. Said she was worried about me. Then I told her I could prove it. So I took her to my room. Put this red ball on my bed and pulled mom out into the hallway. I counted to ten and then we went in. I got scared because mom stumbled a little when she saw that the ball was gone, and she was holding one hand on her chest. Then she watched me look for it, and when I found it, we did it all again. She asked me if I was sure it was Gramma. I said 'yes'.

"As time went on, Mom would sit with me in my room and we'd talk to Gramma. Mom would ask questions, and I would tell her what Gramma said. Of course I didn't really understand most of it, because I was just six and simply repeating what Gramma said."

The moment Doc paused long enough, Bob asked, "So you still talk to her? Your Gramma, I mean."

"No. My mother came down with cancer my senior year. She suffered a lot. It's why I wanted to be a doctor. She died in the hospital three weeks after watching me graduate. I was holding mom's hand and Gramma's too when it happened. Mom just closed her eyes and was gone. Then I clearly heard my Gramma say, 'Your mom is with me. I have to go now. Goodbye, son. I love you.' It was the last time that I heard from my grandma. What? No Martha, I never heard my mother once she passed. Please don't cry, Martha. Yes. It was sad. But it was a very long time ago. Besides, my mom helped my Gramma go to where she was supposed to go."

Bob asked, "So you think we can help Ed and Martha?"

"Well, I think so. But I have a few questions first."

Vic suddenly spoke up. "I'm with Ed. What you said from behind the crate. You know? When you scared the shit out of us all." He immediately caught himself and said, "Yes, Martha. I know. No excuse. Sorry. Come on, Ed. Just say you're sorry, too. What? I didn't make you say that word! Ha! Serves you right!"

Vic looked at Bob and asked, "She hit him again, right?"

Bob just snickered and nodded 'yes'.

Doc laughed. "Take it like a man, Ed. She's a woman. What's that mean? Means she is always right. You'd better learn that quick before she bruises you! Huh? No, I'm not married. Why?"

Doc looked confused when Vic and Bob both burst out laughing. "What are you guys laughing at? Why'd she hit him this time? What's so funny?"

• • •

Doc waited patiently for the laughing to stop. He was very interested in why they were laughing. He realized it must be an inside joke, and definitely was why Martha hit Ed several more times. It seemed odd how Ed laughed louder when she would say something about him ignoring her again.

Doc was looking around when he made eye contact with Bob. "So, Doc? What you said from the crate." He noticed that Martha squinted her eyes at him. He held his hands out. "No, no. I'm not going to repeat that word. Promise!" Then he looked back at Doc. "You said something about it not being *what*, but *who*. What did you mean?"

"Well. You guys were talking about what could be holding the kids here. I was just saying that it probably isn't a what. The question is who is holding them here. So, Martha. You and Ed up for some questions? Good! So how long have you known each other? Just met on the plane? So did you both talk and realize that you had a common acquaintance? You know, somebody you both know at least fairly well? No? You didn't talk at all? Ed went to sleep right after you sat down? I don't think that his going to sleep was rude. You just said you didn't know each other. Wait. Did you talk at all before he went to sleep? Just started talking as the plane was going down. So you really didn't have time to talk about much at all before the crash, right?"

Hearing her 'yes' answer, Doc paused and shook his head as he looked down at the ground. Then he suddenly blurted out the next question. "Did either of you know anyone else on the plane? No? You either, Ed? Hmm. This doesn't make any sense. None at all."

Vic asked, "Why not?"

"Well, there are four main reasons why a spirit doesn't move on. First, they suffer a very violent death. Yes, Ed. Just like the two of you did. But this usually happens if they were murdered, or die in battle. That sort of thing. I don't think this applies to the two of you. I just don't think you two fit this pattern. I could be wrong, though." He shrugged before continuing.

"Second would be that they are very emotionally tied to a place. Somewhere they lived their whole life, and the source of lots of positive memories. Obviously this doesn't apply in this case. I doubt that either of you dreamed about this forest while you were alive." He paused to look at the kids before he asked, "Did you?"

He waited for an answer. "So you both said 'no'. What, Martha? Well I asked because it struck me that maybe both of you could have been having the same dream about a forest like this. If so, then that could be the bond that ties you together."

Bob asked, "It could be something that simple? Just a shared dream?"

Doc nodded 'yes' as he continued. "Sure! Dreams can be very powerful emotionally." He looked around a bit, then went on.

"A third reason would be that they feel so strongly about finishing something that they can't bring themselves to move on. But we're not talking about reading a book or watching a movie.

It wouldn't be something mundane like that. Yes, Martha. It could be that they wanted to experience something personal, and are sticking around until they do. That makes sense to me, too. But even if you both had wanted the same thing, you still have to have a bond between you that invokes that common desire. Right now, I just don't see this being what is holding you here."

"But the fourth reason is the most common. They are too closely tied to someone on this side. They may feel they love them too much to leave them. And of course, they could feel there is still something they still want to do for, or with them. The point is that they are completely focused on the other person, so they stay. At least that is what my Gramma said. What? Yes, Ed, it could be they are attached to an animal, too. Sure, like a favorite pet! But still, that something usually involves another person. Love is a very strong emotion.

"Ok. Let's do this. Ed, tell me what's the first thing you remembered after the crash."

Bob felt cheated as he could only watch as Vic and Doc listened to what Ed was saying. Doc suddenly spoke. "Wait! You just said that you were still holding Martha's hand when you first woke up? So, by 'still', you mean that you began holding her hand before the crash? Yes! Good. Here we go now."

Doc was now doodling in the soft earth with one finger as he was thinking. "Ok. So did you both try to talk at all while you were holding hands before the crash? Anything? Uh-huh. And then she laid her head on your shoulder. Wait a minute.

"Now Ed, this is really important. What were you thinking while she had her head on your shoulder? Do you remember? Yes, you have to be honest. Don't be embarrassed. I'm sure she already knows. That's IT! Has to be! Martha, same thing. What was the last thing you remember thinking about as you held his hand before the crash? Yes, you have to be honest too. That's IT!"

Bob couldn't stand it any longer. "What's going on? Doc? What are you thinking? Somebody tell me!"

Doc said, "Just a second, Bob." He was still doodling in the dirt as he thought. Suddenly, he erased the doodles by smoothing them over.

After brushing off his hands on his fatigues, he said, "Ok. Here's what I think. You both said that you had always wanted a real boyfriend or girlfriend. That is a very powerful emotion. Everyone wants that. You add the adrenaline-charged emotion of knowing you're about to die. That right there is one HELL of a strong bond! Oops, sorry, Martha."

Vic mumbled, "Way to go, Doc. I'd never have thought of that."

Bob asked, "But what does that mean? How does this help?"

Doc continued. "Well if I'm right, then they don't have anything to fear about being in the dark as long as they are together. It might be a good idea to be holding hands when we get to that part. Just to be safe. After all, they are here because they kept each other here. They both wanted so badly to experience the boy and girl thing, that they chose to stay. It's so they could be with each other in the only plane of existence they know. This one."

He looked towards the kids. "I agree, Martha. That is a very good question. I guess it will be for as long as it takes for both of you to feel satisfied that you got to live out this dream. Who knows how long that could be? I'd say that it is really up to you both. Huh? Ed, that is a scary thought, I agree. It would be bad if one of you became satisfied before the other."

The others could tell that Doc was hesitant to answer the next question.

"Well, I have to be honest here. It could happen. Yes, it could be that one of you could move on before the other. But you are both obviously very involved with each other. I have felt that for a while now. What? Yes, I have known both of you were around since about an hour after I got up here. Not as quickly as Vic caught on, but I knew. What? I wouldn't worry about that just now. Ok, yes! The one left behind could possibly be stuck here for a while. But that one would eventually be drawn to follow after the other. Yes, I'm sure."

Vic told Bob, "Martha just said at least she doesn't have to worry any more about what happens when we turn off these lights and leave."

Bob said, "I still don't believe it is right for all of us to just go home and leave them out here. It just feels wrong, and I don't like it."

Vic added, "But they can't leave, remember?"

Doc said, "Why can't they leave? Of course they can!"

Vic now shook his head as he spoke. "I don't think so. Did you hear Ed's story about being pulled off that flying pallet from under the chopper? He said it was as if he hit the end of a rope. It sounds like they're stuck here to me."

Doc chuckled. "If they stay together, they can go anywhere. Anywhere they want. I'm positive. If she had been on that pallet, they'd have made it to the base camp. Guaranteed."

Bob asked, "How can you be so sure Doc? I mean, you obviously know more than I do! But how can you be so sure about it?"

Doc smiled. "It's simple. I came home from school one day and my Gramma was sitting on my bed and she looked very sad. I asked her why. She said because she had tried to go outside, but for some reason, she couldn't leave the room. It was like she was a prisoner. But then I reminded her that she had chased me down the hall just yesterday. We both ran all the way into the kitchen. So she figured out she could go anywhere as long as I was with her. We started playing outside all the time. We went everywhere. She was bonded to me more than the room she died in. We had been holding hands, remember. If I left the room first, then yes, she was stuck there. But she could walk out with me, no problem."

Vic spoke up. "Me and Martha want to know how we can test this theory. She says that she isn't going to get on anything that flies through the air and risk getting pulled off like Ed did. No WAY!"

Doc looked over at the kids. "It will be easy to test this. Look, tomorrow when we're working, both of you walk out to the road. Yes, I know you know where it is. I'm just saying, go to the road. Then one of you stand still, and the other walk as far away as you can. I'll bet that at some point, the one walking away will be stopped. Just like Ed said. All you should feel is like you hit the end of a rope. You're just walking, not going fast like he was riding under that chopper. Thanks Ed! It is a good plan."

Vic looked around. "Look guys, we have been out here a long time. You don't think anyone will come looking for us, do you?"

Bob and Doc both shook their heads 'no' before Doc said, "I doubt it, but you're right about it getting late. We need to get back soon and get some rest. I don't want any of us being so tired tomorrow that we get hurt. We are so close to being done out here and going home. Let's get a good night's sleep and be safe tomorrow. Shall we, gentlemen?"

Everyone stood up to leave. Doc faced the kids. "It has been a real pleasure to finally get to actually talk to you both. And don't worry. This is going to work out just fine. Just hang in there. What? No, Ed. I've never heard of any ghosts coming back to life. But hey, anything is possible. Good night to you too, Martha. See you both tomorrow evening. What? You're welcome, Martha. I'm very glad that you aren't scared anymore. That's good."

Both Bob and Vic waved as they wished them a good night.

The three men jogged off and quickly disappeared into the trees. Ed and Martha stood there watching until they couldn't see them any longer. Slowly they strolled over to their spot and took their customary side as they sat down. She gently placed her head on his shoulder.

"I feel so much better. Don't you?"

"I'd feel a lot better if you would keep your promise."

She looked up at him and asked, "What promise?"

Ed's goofy smile returned. "You know when we were kissing earlier. You said we would definitely get back to that. Remember?"

Her eyes shimmered as she gently pulled his head towards hers. Just before their lips met, she said, "Oh yes! I remember that. I don't feel tired at all. How about you, big boy?"

Ed slipped in a few last words before he felt her lips on his. "Not at all. Feel like I could stay up all night!"

• • •

The smell of bacon and coffee wafted through the camp as it had every morning for all these weeks. At first there were only one or two voices heard from within the cold tents, but more and more voices began to emerge as these inviting aromas grew stronger in the camp. With boots on and rubbing their hands in the cold air, the men began to emerge from their tents to make their mad dash for the chow line. Cold and hungry, each man stood patiently in line for their turn to shovel as much as they could on their plate before returning to their favorite breakfast spot.

Bob and Vic were just a few steps from the front of the line when they noticed that two "claim jumpers" had commandeered their secluded spot this morning. After filling their plates and topping off a cup of coffee, they began their selection of a bigger group to sit with. They both participated in the customary morning conversations.

Once they had both sat down, Doc passed by them with his plate full, but he chose a different group to sit with. Bob and Vic knew that he was just doing as he always did each morning. It was his way of not drawing any unwanted attention to his new alliance with them. This way, their shared secret and goals would be safe.

One by one, the morning's meal was transferred from plate to stomach. Conversations ended with the usual trip to the table to drop off the dirty dishes. Every man cheerfully expressed his thanks to the cook and paid him a much-deserved compliment on how great the food was. The cook playfully responded to each with, "You're welcome! Now get out of here, you bum, or I'll make you do those dishes!"

Bob and Vic headed off in different directions after Bob said, "Work hard, but safe." They and Doc were thinking about the test that the kids were going to carry out today on the road. What they wouldn't each give to be there with them when they tried it.

• • •

Martha's eyes were open so she looked around, her head still comfortably resting on Ed's shoulder as usual. She felt Ed's cheek on top of her head. She wondered if he was awake yet. Though she wanted to look, she chose not to, fearing her movement would wake him if he wasn't. Besides, she was very content feeling his body against hers. She watched as the sunlight slowly reached through the trees and illuminated the ground around their spot. The day was upon them, and it meant they could leave the safety of the circle.

She began to feel a little anxious about the test they would carry out on the road today. Her thoughts were also of the three men that were helping them. Each seemed so nice. She was so very glad that they were helping. She trusted them all. To think that just yesterday, she and Ed were still wondering what they were going to do when the lights went out.

Calm came over her as she realized that everything was going to be fine. She and Ed had friends here, and these friends had brought options.

She was so caught up in her thoughts that she didn't notice Ed lifting his cheek from atop her head. His sudden yawn caused her to jump before she looked up at him.

"I'm sorry, baby. I didn't mean to wake you."

She responded, "You didn't. I've been awake and just looking around. Watched the sunlight spread across our feet. It's funny how you miss the little things like the warmth of the sun."

Ed wasn't totally awake yet, but he could tell that she had been thinking about pleasant experiences that were only granted to the living. He hoped she wasn't worried about the test today. Yes, that must be it. She usually was very bubbly first thing in the morning. This wasn't like her at all.

"Martha? You okay?"

She looked at him for a second. "Yes. I'm fine. It's just, well, I've been thinking."

"You mean you've been worrying. Haven't you? Why?"

"No I wasn't." Then she paused and her gaze traveled from his face to the ground. "Well. Maybe a little."

Ed lifted her chin up with his finger. "Just a little?"

"Okay! Okay! More than a little. I admit it! I don't know why? I'm anxious to find out if Doc is right. Just like I know you are too. It's just that up till now, right this minute, we've only been talking about what to do. Now, we will actually be doing something about it."

Ed spoke softly to her. "That's right. Today we start moving forward again. We have a plan. What's the worst that can happen? We find out he was wrong. So what? He's a really smart guy. He definitely has more ideas than I do. Besides, we're still together. Nothing changes that."

"And that is part of it. I've been so very happy here with you, Ed. I love our walks and talks during the days. I look forward to sitting here beside you every night. We've been doing it every day and it feels so normal now. I could be perfectly happy staying right here and doing this for eternity. All I need is you, Ed. Just you."

"Wow. That's a heavy topic for so early in the morning." He said this with a smirk. "But I do understand. And I feel the same way too. Totally!" He pulled his shoulder a few inches away from her, so he could twist slightly and look directly into her face. "But if Doc is right and we don't have to stay here, then just think of the possibilities! We can go all the places we've both dreamed about when we were alive. We will see them together." She watched as he got that goofy look again and she knew he was going to crack a joke. "Martha. So what if we're dead. Who cares? Look at the bright side. It won't cost us a dime!"

After a few seconds, a smile slowly returned to her face and her eyes again sparkled as she looked at him. He was her man. He would always be her man.

Seeing her smiling, Ed asked, "Ready to go find out if Doc is right?" She nodded 'yes'. "Good! Today starts the rest of our lives." She giggled.

He added, "You know what I mean. Now let's get going."

Ed jumped up and held out a hand to help her up. He turned and led her off towards the road, but she resisted. Sensing that she wasn't moving yet, he looked over his shoulder to see why. She took her free hand and turned him back around. Once he was facing her again, she zoomed up against his chest and reached up to pull his head down. "Hey, mister! Where's my morning kiss?"

There was that smirk on his face again. "I didn't forget. I was sparing you the pain."

She looked puzzled, "Spare me? What pain?"

His smirk changed to a smile as he replied, "The pain from all that kissing last night. Your lips have to be sore. Mine are!"

She kissed him and then immediately poked him on the shoulder. "I'm going to give you something that hurts, goofy!"

Ed stepped back as he said, "Oh no you don't, young lady. No poking this early in the morning!"

"And who is going to stop me? You, mister?"

He was already turning to run as he said, "I don't have to stop you. I just have to outrun you!" Two steps later he yelled, "Can't catch me!"

She took off after him, but knew that she would never catch him since his legs were so much longer than hers. They dashed through the forest on their way to the road. A few times she actually got within an arm's reach of him. But he quickly held out one arm to grab a passing tree and pulled himself around so he ended up behind her. The moment she was in front of him, he would tap her on the back of the head before taking off in a different direction. This childish game of tag was played until they both saw the road. It stretched out of sight both ways, to their left and right.

Ed had stopped to wait for her to catch up. He pointed to their right as he said, "That section of road is relatively straight for almost two miles. It will work just fine." He then pointed back to the left. "You can stand over there and I'll take off that way. You don't have to do anything. I'll go out as far as I can."

She looked at where she was to stand, then at the road where Ed was going to run. "You think that this will be long enough?"

Ed also glanced from one end of the road to the other. "Well. It looks to be longer than the distance from you standing in the circle, and where I was pulled off that pallet under the chopper." He turned to her and held out his fist in front of her. "You ready to do this?"

"Yes." She bumped her fist against his. As he took off running towards the road, she called out to him. "I don't want you to be running, Ed. I don't want to be pulled down when you get to the end of this rope of yours!"

"Got it!" Once he was on the road, he slowed to a fast walk and watched her over his shoulder. She was now standing right in the middle of the road where he had wanted her. He was too far away to see her expression of concern, but he was sure it was there. She couldn't help but wonder if she would feel a jerk as he hit the end of this imaginary rope. Just in case, she staggered her feet apart to brace herself.

Ed was trying to visualize the distance that he had been from Martha when he was pulled off the pallet. Sensing that he must be getting close, he slowed to a virtual crawl, then turned and walked backwards so he could keep his eyes on her. It dawned on him that she hadn't felt any tug when he was sailing through the air on that pallet. Still, if he pulled her over or caused her to fall forward, she would never let him hear the end of it. He rubbed his shoulder in anticipation of being poked by her should that happen.

He saw that she was really a long way away. The thought entered his mind that Doc might be wrong. But then it happened. He was completely stopped. No matter how hard he tried to take another step, he couldn't. His eyes strained to see if she was being moved at all as he pushed against this force that was stopping him. He didn't see her moving at all, so he turned around and pushed forward as hard as he could. Then he heard her yell 'Hey!'

His first thought was that she had been pulled down. He could almost feel her hitting him now. But as he spun around, he saw that she was standing and waving at him. He called out, "What?"

"Are you stopped? Why aren't you moving anymore? Was Doc right?"

He was amazed that he was actually leaning backwards, yet this mystical force was holding him upright. He thought, 'How cool is this?'

He yelled back, "Yes. Just like Doc said. I can't go any farther. Not at all!"

With the test successfully concluded and Doc's theory verified, he started running back to her. His excitement grew as he got closer to her. Then he noticed she was bouncing up and down on her toes as she clapped her hands. She was smiling and her long hair was bouncing in the sunlight. She looked like a young girl cheering for her boyfriend as he ran for a touchdown. This must be how jocks felt back in high school.

He ran up, lifted her into the air by her waist, and started turning around in a slow circle. Her feet couldn't touch the ground but she cared not. Her arms were wrapped around his neck, her head tilted backwards. Never had either of them been as happy as they were now. His circles slowly stopped. She lifted her head to face him. Only an inch separated their noses. Smiles of joy quickly turn to looks of longing and then came the kiss. Lips that had been denied companionship in life were now blissfully content to have found those of another.

As all things do, this kiss ended as well. He slowly lowered her back to earth. She slipped from his arms but still held his hand tightly. She started swinging her arm and his followed along. "So, should we go tell Doc?"

"Why not? Everyone likes to be told they're right!"

She smiled and stopped swinging their arms. As she stepped in close to his chest, her hand released his before she said, "But this time . . . you chase me!" Suddenly she pushed him backwards with both hands. He was completely caught off guard by this, and stumbled as he struggled to regain his balance. She never looked back as she laughed very loudly. He wondered if she heard him as he yelled. "That's cheating! I'm going to get you!" She easily beat him to the tree line and disappeared from sight. Her laughter made it easy for him to know which way she was running, even though he had lost sight of her in the trees. Finally he saw her, and knew he would catch her in just a few moments. Then, to his amazement, she just stopped. He came up beside her and stopped as well.

"Why'd you stop?"

She pointed off into the trees. Ed saw that Doc and several other men were apparently taking a break. They were all sitting on fallen tree trunks and joking with each other. As they stood there watching the men, Doc looked in their direction before saying loudly, "I'm glad it worked!" The other men looked at him. One asked, "What worked? Why are you yelling?" Doc laughed and replied, "Sorry, I meant that everything is working out and we could get out of here soon. Just got excited. Aren't you guys ready to go home?" They all agreed and returned to their conversations. When nobody was looking, Doc glanced in the kids' direction and nodded before he also rejoined the conversation.

Ed and Martha took Doc's cue to leave. She immediately punched him and said, "You know you'd never have caught me if I hadn't stopped."

"Oh, come on. I was about to tag you and you know it."

Before he knew what happened, she tripped him and he stumbled until he caught hold of a tree. He didn't see her run off, but he could clearly hear her call out "SUCKER!"

They had a blast chasing each other as they searched for Bob and Vic. They wanted to make sure every team member knew of the successful test. Once Bob was found, it was easy to get his attention. When he was looking at them, they put on a small skit so he would know what happened. Martha acted as if she was holding onto a rope tied to Ed. He simulated not being able to run away. Then they both turned to face Bob before they gave him four thumbs up. He nodded that he understood and they continued on to search for Vic. Bob smiled as he watched them chase each other into the trees. He was happy because they were happy.

They found several small groups of men doing various jobs before they finally came across Vic. He and two other loggers were busy clearing a new path for something. The kids watched the three men as they dragged the last freshly cut trees off the path. Martha was very close to Vic when she whispered, "Hey, Vic. It worked. Doc was right. Just thought you would want to know. Have a nice day now. See you tonight. And nod if you heard me." Vic immediately nodded. He then heard Ed. "What are you whispering for? Nobody else hears us but him. Sometimes I really worry about you, girl." He then motioned for her to come on before saying, "Bye, Vic." She followed Ed as he trotted off into the forest. Vic smiled, pleased at how happy the kids sounded. Then he returned to his work.

The kids spent the rest of the day frolicking all over the area. First she chased him, then he chased her. They both were shocked when they realized that it was starting to get dark. Martha reached out and took Ed's hand. "Walk me back to the circle, big boy."

Ed replied, "Love to!"

They made their way back into the circle just as one of the guardsmen was turning on all the lights. Once that task was done, they watched him head back to camp to eat. They performed their well-rehearsed routine of going to their special spot and sitting down, each on their proper side. Now all they had to do was wait for their friends to come over tonight and tell them what the next step would be.

• • •

Vic and Bob had made sure that they were first in line for dinner. It was the only way to insure they got their favorite eating spots this time. They barely said anything until after they were seated and each had downed at least two large spoonfuls of hot chili.

"You know, Bob? This is some of the best chili I've ever eaten. In fact, every meal up here has been unbelievably good." He was pointing the last piece of his biscuit at Bob as he added, "That cook of yours really knows what he's doing. I wish we had a cook like him up here when we're logging."

"Vic. Did you know the cook used to be a logger up in Oregon?"

Vic jokingly said, "Well if I were you guys, I wouldn't let Bart know about it. He'd try to talk him into coming back into the fold and working for us!"

Both men finished their meals before dumping their dishes in the tub on the table. They looked around for Doc, but didn't see him. "Bob, you want to wait for Doc?"

"No. He knows where we're going. Come on, let's go see the kids."

There was chitchat about things they heard the other men say today as they made their way to the burn circle. It was just the usual mix of comments about news heard on the radio today. Then they heard the unmistakable sound of someone running through the trees.

At first they couldn't see anyone. Slowly, the shape of a man could barely be seen out in the dark. Bob called out softly, "Doc? That you, Doc?"

"Yes." The shape turned towards them and ran up to them. Doc was breathing a little hard as he said, "Man, I wasn't sure I could catch up to you two. I was only halfway through my second bowl when I saw you guys go into the trees. I had to wolf that last part down a little too fast."

Bob chuckled. "You're breathing kind of hard there, Doc. Out of shape?"

Doc smiled. "No. That chili was DAMN GOOD, but heavy!"

Bob pointed to Vic. "Vic liked it too. Says he wants to steal our cook. What do you think about that?"

As they began their walk to the circle, Doc glanced at Vic and said, "You know, the cook used to be a logger like you. Anybody tell you that?"

Vic patted Doc on the back and said, "Yessir. Bob here was just rubbing that fact in. Says you guys would put up a mighty big fight to keep him!"

They all laughed and continued chatting as they walked the rest of the way to the circle. Once there, Bob called out to the kids, "Knock knock! You have guests!" Hearing the men coming, Martha pushed Ed to get him to sit back up as she whispered, "Straighten up that shirt. They're here."

Vic fell behind and followed the other two men to where the kids must be sitting. Doc saw him hesitate, so he pointed to a spot as Bob said, "That will work. The kids are right here."

As Vic was getting settled, Bob commented, "So, the test worked this morning. I know, you came and told me. I assume you told them both." He could see the kids nodding 'yes'. "So Doc? What's on the agenda for tonight?"

Doc scratched the top of his head. "Let's see. So we now all agree that the kids are tied to each other, not this place." He surveyed everyone's expression before he continued. "Good. That means that we only have one big question to answer. Can the kids walk around in the dark without being taken?" Again he looked around at each of them before he went on. "Well. You all know what I think." Now he was looking directly at the kids. "Your test this morning proves I was right about that. But I know you're bound to be nervous about this part. Unfortunately, there isn't a way to safely test this theory.

"Martha. I sense that you're more than just a little worried about what I'm going to suggest. So let me just get it out there so we can talk about it. Look, you and Ed will have to go out into the dark sooner or later. If it was me, I'd just get it over with tonight. But it's up to you."

Bob saw that Martha was already shaking her head 'no'. "Guys, I don't think she wants to deal with this tonight. Martha?"

She smiled at Bob, then looked up into Ed's face. "I can't speak for Ed, but Bob's right." She then looked right at Doc. "I'd be lying if I said I wasn't scared. I trust you Doc, I really do! But I just don't want to risk leaving Ed any sooner than I have to. I'm sorry to be such a baby, but I am."

Ed immediately added, "I'll go along with whatever she wants to do, or doesn't want to do."

She patted him on the chest and then leaned her head against his shoulder.

Vic asked, "So where does that leave us?"

Martha's voice broke up just a little as she asked, "Just out of curiosity, when will they be taking the lights down? Do you know for sure yet?"

Doc looked down at the ground. "Looks like we'll be packing them up tomorrow afternoon, and we're all going back the next day. Our part is done. I'm sorry."

Ed only got a few words out, "That means that . . . " before she interrupted him and finished his sentence.

Martha had closed her eyes and pressed her head very hard against Ed as she mumbled, "Tonight could be our last night."

Ed felt a shudder go through her body. "You don't know that." Ed nodded in Doc's direction. "You know what Doc thinks. He was right about the other thing. I bet he's right about this too! Come on Doc. Tell her!"

Doc hesitated. "I can't promise either of you anything. All I can tell you is what I think. That's all."

She let out a small sigh, then sat up. "I know that we are the only ones that can go through this. And we will." She turned her head to look back at Ed. "Together. We will do what Doc says and hold hands, and we will do this thing together. Right?"

Ed sat closer to her and said, "You're damn right! We will do it together. You can hit me now if you want."

She shook her head a little. "Not going to hit you Ed. It's all right this time." Then she rolled her eyes. "But don't do it again. There's still no excuse." He smiled and nodded that he understood.

Doc clapped his hands together suddenly. That brought all eyes on him. "Okay! Now that everyone is totally depressed, let's talk about some positive things. Shall we?"

Bob asked, "What positive things? Did I miss something?"

Doc spoke. "I choose to believe that I'm right on this. So we need to start making plans on getting the kids back home with us."

Bob saw that Ed and Martha were looking back and forth at each other before focusing squarely on Doc. Bob asked, "Excuse me. But what do you mean when you say 'taking them home with us'? Who's us?"

"Well, Bob. This is what we need to discuss. You said you didn't think it was right to leave them out here, and I happen to agree. So, since we now know they can leave, the real question is: where do they go from here? I say they go home with one of us. But before you panic Bob, I don't think it should be you. Not that you wouldn't take them in, but you have a family and you can't hear them." He then looked at Vic. "Now Vic, you're in a similar boat here. You have a live-in girlfriend and you can't see them. So even though I know you'd take them also, I think we can rule you out too. Now that just leaves me. But the good thing is that I live alone. Plus I can tell where they are, and what they're saying. I think it just makes more sense for them to come home with me. That is, if they want to."

He stopped talking and waited for a response from the kids.

"Are you sure you want us there, Doc? I mean, that is very nice of you to offer, but Ed and I don't want to be a burden to anyone."

"Oh nonsense! You both are more than welcome to hang out at my place for as long you want. Besides, it will give us a lot of time to explore other avenues of how to help you out."

Martha seemed unsure. "I don't know if we can let you do this, Doc. We appreciate it, but to take us into your home? And us being a couple of . . . well . . . ".

Ed smirked. "Ghosts? Are you having trouble with it yet again? We are ghosts." He looked at Doc. "It's not like we will be eating your food or messing up bath towels or anything. It will be like we aren't there at all. We'll be the perfect house guests. Invisible!"

Martha hit him.

"Look, Martha. Ed's right on all of that. No problem at all. What do you say?"

Ed was nodding energetically.

Finally she said, "Well. Just for a little while. And just until we decide what we want to do. Fair?"

"Ok! Then that's settled."

Bob raised one hand as if he were still in elementary school. "Uh, Doc? What are these other avenues of help you're referring to? You have more ideas? What?"

"Well, I do, sir. That I do." Doc held one hand out toward the kids. "Now don't read anything into what I'm about to say. Please let me get the whole idea out first. Okay?" The kids nodded. "Good! Seems to me that the next step is to find out exactly how you can move on to where you're supposed to be." Both Martha and Ed stared at Doc. "Now wait! Hear me out. I'm not saying you have to go through with it when we find out. I'm just saying that we should find out more about it. If nothing else, knowing about it is the best way to not let it happen. That is, of course, if you both want to stay in your present condition and plane of existence. All I'm saying is that information is power, and we need to go find out what we can about it. Understand?"

Vic picked up on something Doc had just said. "Excuse me, Doc. Did you just say 'go find out'? Reason why I ask is that it sounds like you want to take them somewhere. Where?"

Doc smiled. "Very perceptive, Vic. You're right. I want to take them somewhere, and hopefully we can see someone I kind of know. Sort of."

Everyone looked at each other, confused. Finally, the silence was broken by Ed. "Are we going to meet your gramma?"

"No, I wish I could still see and talk to her, but I can't. I haven't been able to communicate with her since my mother died and they both moved on. You see, I have limitations just like Bob and Vic. I am only able to communicate with spirits like you two. Those that are stuck between the living and the next place. Understand?" He looked around and saw everyone nodding 'yes'.

Bob asked, "So where you planning on taking them?"

Vic also asked, "And who are you taking them to see?"

"Both are good questions. I want to take them to Gettysburg."

Bob interrupted. "Oh yes. I heard you were a real Civil War buff and you go there all the time. But why there?"

Vic inserted, "I take it that whoever it is you want them to talk to is there in Gettysburg?"

"Right again, Vic. He's there, but I'll get back to that in a minute. Bob, I know everyone thinks I'm really into the Civil War, but actually, I just go there because there are so many souls trapped there. Are you aware of how many men died there in that battle? It is just amazing how many thousands of spirits are still wandering around there. They don't even know they're dead. I don't think most of them are even aware that they've been trapped there all this time. In fact, they don't even know how much time has elapsed since they passed!"

Bob asked, "So how long have you been going there?"

"I've been going there twice a year since I was discharged and became an EMT for the fire department. I would split up my two weeks of vacation and go about every six months. But I start getting three weeks of vacation this year. So I'll get to go every four months now." Vic seemed intrigued but hesitant to speak, so Doc said, "Vic? What is it?"

"I was just curious why you want to take the kids there. You must have a reason. Is it just to see this guy you know?" Now Doc was hesitant, so Vic repeated his question. "Well Doc? Is it?"

"Well, this is something that I was going to talk to Ed and Martha about at the house. I wanted them to help me with something."

Ed quickly said, "But it's not anything to do with your gramma. Right?"

"No, Ed. Nothing to do with her."

"Doc. Ed and I would be glad to help you any way we can. Right, Ed?"

"Oh. Uh, of course baby. I mean, yes, Doc we'd be glad to help. What do you want us to do?"

"OK, everyone. Here it is. Other than my gramma, you two are the only spirits that I have met who are spatially aware of your situation. Just like Gramma, you know that you are dead. Plus you understand that you are between the living and where you were supposed to go. See, most spirits that are trapped like you don't realize anything. I sense them and talk at them, but rarely do they know that I am talking *to* them. Understand?"

Bob said, "I can see that. But where does this friend come in? What's his deal in all of this? And how is he going to help the kids?"

Doc cleared his throat. "Well, he falls into a much different category."

Vic spoke up immediately, "Wait a minute. Are you saying this friend is a ghost too?"

"Well, yes. But the problem is that he doesn't think he is dead. In fact, he thinks I'm the ghost! Really! And it bothers him when I show up and start talking to him. He says he must be losing his mind. He even told me once that at least all the other ghosts he sees have the decency not to scare the HELL out of him by talking! Sorry, Martha. His words, not mine."

Vic asked, "I'm afraid I still don't get how he can help the kids. What do you think he knows?"

Martha spoke out decisively. "It doesn't matter why Doc wants us to talk to this guy. He must have a good reason and that's good enough for me. I'll do it, Doc."

Hearing her commit, Ed agreed too. "Yes! Me too Doc. Count us in!"

Doc waved his finger in the air towards the kids. "Thanks to both of you, but I need to tell you the rest of it. I don't want you to talk to him, because I think it will help you." There was a real silence for a moment before Doc continued. "You see. I want to see if you can help him. Okay?"

Ed asked, "Help him? How? We can't help ourselves. If it weren't for you, Doc, we would end up spending eternity here in these woods. So what makes you think we can help him?"

"That's a good question. Here's my thinking. In his mind, he's still alive but surrounded by ghosts. He knows that he is different from all the other spirits so he is convinced that he is still alive. But he also knows that he's different from me. He just thinks I'm a very special ghost because he can see and talk with me. So what I'm hoping is that he would be able to tell that you two are like him. Therefore, he would assume you were alive and he would engage in conversation with you. My hope would be that given enough time for conversation with you, he would ultimately realize that he is dead and then he might move on."

Again Vic interrupted. "That sounds feasible. But are you about to suggest that Ed and Martha spend time trying to get those thousands of souls there to move on? That would take forever."

Doc was strongly shaking his head. "Not at all! All the others are soldiers. They are stuck there because they met a very violent end. They seem to play out the same scenarios over and over. I don't have any ideas on how to help them. Yes I sense them and know what they're thinking, but I can't communicate with them like I do the kids.

"But Mr. Gruber is different for some reason. See, he wasn't a soldier, he was a farmer. I'm not sure I even have his story correct. He's told me several odd and random pieces of it. It's like his memory is not all there, and he doesn't know what actually happened to end his life. The best I can piece together is this. He was milking a cow when a stray cannon ball hit his barn. The loud noise made the cow jump and it killed him. I think he loves his farm so much that he just stays on to take care of it. That, and the fact that he doesn't believe he's dead."

Martha had a tear in one eye as she spoke. "Doc, I would be very happy to talk to Mr. Gruber if you think it will help." Ed added, "Where she goes, I go. So me too."

"Thanks, you two. I really appreciate it."

Bob mentioned that it was very late and they should get back. Everyone stood to leave and Doc thanked the kids again. Bob watched as the kids walked off to sit in their special spot before he trotted the few feet it took to catch up with the other two.

Vic and Bob asked questions about Gettysburg all the way back to the camp. As they came out of the trees, Doc said he needed to check that injured logger's bandage on his way back to his tent. Vic and Bob joined a group of men by the fire for one last cup of hot coffee. They all stood around the blazing fire and exchanged jokes. The laughter was extra loud tonight because everyone knew that tomorrow was their last full day here. Yes, the recovery was complete and they would all be going home.

After about 20 minutes of small talk, Vic said he was heading to bed. Bob was having too much fun cutting up with the others, so he went to get another cup of coffee to fight off the cold. A guardsman named Simmons got to the coffee at the same time Bob did.

"Hey, Bob! I didn't see you after supper tonight. Where've you been?"

"Oh just out walking about. I'm getting kind of excited about this ordeal coming to an end. You?"

"I'm ready to get home too. Lots of people around here seem to be excited tonight."

Bob sipped his coffee and chuckled. "Well that excitement is going to make guys do some strange things in the next two days, I bet!"

"Yep, it's already started. Didn't you see Doc bolt out of here a few minutes ago?"

Bob quickly asked, "What do you mean Doc bolted out of here. What happened?"

"Well several of us were playing cards in the back tent when Doc came in to check that logger's bandage. But he wasn't there. He'd tagged along with Mikey to go shut off the lights at the crash site. That's when Doc just took off running into the woods."

Bob poured out his coffee, ran over to put his cup on the table and hurried over to Vic's tent. He just stuck his head in and saw that Vic still had his boots on.

"Hey Vic! Get up! We need to get back to the circle."

"Why? What's up?"

"Come on, man! I'll tell you on the way."

Vic grabbed his heavy coat and put it on as the two men rushed out of the camp. Once a few feet into the trees, Bob said, "We better run. Some guys went to turn off the lights. Doc heard about it and he took off after them. I didn't see him leave. I just heard about it two minutes ago."

Vic immediately started running full speed alongside Bob. They heard some voices up ahead, so they slowed down to see who it was. It was the guys who had turned off the lights, and they were returning to camp. "Hey! What you doing out here, Bob? Evening, Vic."

Bob said, "Evening, gents. What you been doing?"

"Oh, I forgot to turn off those lights like Sandy had told me to do this afternoon. So I went out and shut 'em down. Hey, did you know Doc just came by here too? Said he forgot a tool on one of the crates, and was hoping to catch us before we shut down the lights."

Vic calmly asked, "So where is Doc? Did he go on to the circle anyway?"

"Yessir. We offered to go help him find it, but he said he knew exactly where it was. He told us to go on back without him. Said he was in no hurry and might take his time getting back. Wanted to clear his mind, he said."

Bob said, "We'll that's what we're doing too. We're just out walking to clear our minds as well. It's hard to believe we'll all be home in about 48 hours or so." He and Vic started walking off towards the circle as Bob spoke over his shoulder, "See you guys at breakfast!"

Bob and Vic had to fight the urge to take off running again. They didn't want to appear too anxious to get to the circle, so they walked slowly until they were well out of range to be heard. Then they both broke into a run all the way to the circle. As they burst into the circle, they could see Doc standing there in the dark. He was rubbing his head with one hand and slowly turning around as he looked off into the trees.

Vic asked, "Bob, do you see the kids anywhere?"

"No, Vic. They aren't out here in the circle anywhere. You hear them?"

Vic shook his head. "No. I don't hear anything at all."

The two men walked up and stopped just a few feet from Doc.

Doc looked at the two men, lowered his arm to his side and said, "Well, boys. The lights were off for about 30 minutes before I got here. Looks like I may have been wrong. I can't sense them anywhere. I just don't get it. I was so sure they'd be okay."

Bob said, "Hey, Doc. Don't beat yourself up over it. It's not your fault. We all knew it was bound to happen sooner or later. They knew that."

Vic was still tilting his head to one side then the other in the hopes of hearing the kids. "I still don't hear them. But aren't you two being a little premature? We don't know that they were taken. For all we know, they could be walking around out in the trees. You don't know."

Doc was obviously upset as he kept saying, "I just don't get it. It just don't make any sense. They should have been okay. I was so sure."

Bob said, "Vic's right. We don't know anything yet. Look. Let's split up and go about 30 yards into the trees, and then walk all the way around the circle. We'll meet back up here in the middle."

No further talk was required as all three men turned and jogged towards the trees in different directions. After about 25 minutes, Bob was back in the center of the circle, wondering where the other two were. Then Doc showed up with Vic right behind him. Bob said, "I didn't see or hear anything. You guys?"

Vic and Doc shook their heads 'no'. Then Doc said, "Well, the lights have been off for about an hour now. Looks like it's over. Damn it! I just don't get it."

Bob patted Doc on the shoulder. "Looks like it's out of our hands now, Doc."

Vic patted Doc on the other shoulder. "They were happy. We have to remember that. Come on, guys. Nothing left to do but go back to camp. It's over."

Reluctantly, the three started walking for the trees. Nobody was talking and their mood was very depressed. They walked in silence except for the occasional utterance by Doc, "I just can't believe it." They were almost back to camp when Vic and Doc almost jumped out of their boots. Bob didn't know what had scared them, but he jumped when they did. Vic and Doc were staring right at Bob as Vic said, "Not funny, dude!" Doc snapped at Bob too. "Yeah man! Not cool at all!"

Bob was wondering what they were talking about. Then he saw movement right behind Vic and Doc. Finally he pointed behind the guys and yelled, "There they are!"

Vic and Doc both heard Martha start laughing before they could turn around. Ed's goofy laugh quickly drowned out her laughter. Then he said, "Man! You should have seen how high you two jumped when I screamed 'BOO'! It was hilarious!"

Doc said, "That was you, Ed? You hollered 'BOO'?"

Vic added, "We thought it was Bob that did it."

Martha was very excited as she started speaking. "See Ed! I told you they'd be scared. You were right though, your voice was better!" She looked at Doc and said, "It was my idea. I wanted to be the one that screamed 'BOO', but Ed was right. If you'd have heard a girl's voice, you'd have known it was me. Wouldn't you have?"

"Martha and I were afraid you'd hear us or sense our presence before we could get close enough to scare you. But Martha said you'd all probably be depressed and therefore distracted. That is what we were counting on. AND IT WORKED!"

Bob didn't know what was being said, but he was so happy he said, "I am so glad you two are okay! I wish I could hug you both!"

Doc said, "I'm so sorry, kids. I swear we didn't know they were going to turn the lights off. When we found out, we all ran over here as fast as we could. But you were gone. Man, I felt so bad."

Vic asked, "So what happened? Where have you both been?"

Ed shook his head. "Nothing happened! That's what."

Martha spoke. "We couldn't believe it when those two guys darted out of the trees and just turned off that first light unit. Then all we could do was sit there and watch them walk around turning off the others too. Then they just left. I was so scared. But my big guy just kept telling me that he believed in you, Doc. So after a few minutes, Ed asked me if I felt anything. I said no. We sat there for almost 20 more minutes before we figured we might as well walk around. Why not? We were already in the dark."

Ed took over telling the tale. "So we walked out about 20 feet or so and just stood there. It was a little nerve-racking but nothing happened. Then she pushed me and took off running, and I chased her. We ran off that way. But you guys probably came in from the other side of the circle, right? That's why we missed you."

The three men all noticed how much Martha reminded them of a young girl while telling her story. She bounced from one foot to the other as she spoke. Her eyes sparkled in the moonlight as she explained how Ed almost caught her, but he tripped over a branch in the dark and fell. She got away, but he did finally catch her. Eventually they decided to walk over to the camp to scare them, but they weren't there. They started back to the circle and that's when they heard the three of them coming. Martha really wanted to scare them. So she and Ed hid in the dark just off the path until the men were in the trap. It was a great plan and she was very excited that it had worked so well.

When she finished the story, Ed said, "So Doc, you were right after all. We owe you, Doc!"

Bob asked, "Do you two want to come back and spend the night in our camp? The fire burns all night so the whole area stays lit up. It's really kind of pretty."

Martha walked over to Ed and patted his chest lightly before she took his hand. "Thanks Bob, but we aren't afraid of the dark any more. So we're going back to our spot." She tugged on Ed's arm to get him started walking. "Come on, big guy. They need their rest."

Ed looked at her. "But I don't really feel sleepy at all. In fact, I think I'll be up all night."

She kept him walking and giggled. "I know you will, Ed. We both will be."

Hearing what she said, Doc started towards them as he said, "Uh, Ed? Martha? Can I have a private moment with you both? Please."

Vic tapped Bob on the shoulder and motioned that they should leave the others. Bob nodded and followed him off into the woods.

Doc waited a second before clearing his throat. "Now, please excuse me for saying what I'm about to say. It's very personal, but I have a thought that I need to share with you both."

They both faced Doc. He hesitated, then started talking again.

"Remember when I told you that you both would probably be here until you have satisfied the emotions that are holding you here?" They were both nodding so he continued. "Now I'm not asking you anything because it isn't any of my business. I just want you to think about something." He hesitated again but finally summoned the nerve to say what was on his mind. "I'm fairly confident that your desire to experience the girl - boy thing is what kept you here. If I'm right, then you may not want to let your passion get away from you tonight. Do you understand what I'm getting at?"

Ed looked lost as he asked , "Martha, do you know what he's talking about?"

Martha rolled her eyes at Ed then looked back at Doc before she whispered, "You don't have to worry about that, Doc."

Doc really felt embarrassed as he realized that Martha may have taken offense at the suggestion that she may not be a 'good' girl. "No! No! I wasn't saying that you would, uh, you know. I was just saying that, maybe, caution might be best at this time. Sorry."

She giggled a little before she whispered very softly, "If that was going to happen, then we would have gone over already." Then she winked at him. "But we're still here." Then she raised her eyebrows and smiled as she turned to take Ed's hand again. She waved bye to Doc over her shoulder. Ed gleefully let her lead him back towards the circle.

Doc watched them disappear. As he turned to go back to camp, he said, "I bet Ed really loves the dark after tonight."

Chapter 12

NOBODY BRINGS GHOSTS HOME

SMALL RAYS OF sunlight were beginning to dance on the tops of the tallest trees. However, total darkness still reigned supreme on the forest floor. Martha and Ed still slept in the final embrace they had shared last night. Ed was on his side and she was tucked close with her head upon his outstretched arm. His nude body was draped along her side, while she had a gentle grasp of his arm as it rested across her stomach. He had one leg over hers and her free hand sat atop his raised hip. Starting as two individuals, they had now been peacefully interwoven into one. A state sought by all that live had now been granted to two that had passed into a middle existence. Not living and not totally gone, they and their love existed here in this spot that they called their own.

Back at the camp, the signs of a new day had slowly begun to manifest. Bob, Vic, and Doc chose to quickly scarf down their breakfast and accept only one cup of coffee. They rushed to ditch their dirty dishes and headed off into the trees. All the other men were just beginning to line up for breakfast. It was a quickly-paced run through the trees on their way to the circle. The morning air was exceptionally cold, due to its nightly abandonment by the heat of the sun. Somehow, the cold on their faces seemed to invigorate them - or was it their eagerness to greet the kids again? All three were equally excited as they burst into the clearing of the circle.

Vic surprised the other two when he suddenly stopped and held out both arms to force them to stop also. Doc and Bob leaned forward over Vic's outstretched arms and were attempting to see his facial expression. Doc asked, "Hey man! What's wrong?"

Vic simply said, "What's going on? I can see them." He looked at Doc as he pointed to the two motionless figures in the middle of the circle. "I see the kids."

Bob's voice boomed in the silent darkness. "Ed's not dressed! Is that Martha's leg?"

Doc was also looking in the direction of the kids. He was amazed as well, for he didn't sense where they were as usual. This time he actually saw them for the first time.

"What's going on here? I see them too! I mean, I see them with my eyes. I don't get it."

Bob added, "They look very good. Don't they?" He turned to Doc, excited. "What the hell? Vic even sees them. Are we all going nuts now, or what?"

Doc held up his hand to stop Bob from talking and said very loudly, "I knew it! I just knew they were special. No! More than just special. They are truly different and unique from any other spirits I've encountered."

He was now pounding his fist into the open palm of his other hand. "I knew there was something about them. I just knew it!"

His fist made several loud, sharp pops that echoed around the tree-lined circle. Hearing this, Martha raised up to look over Ed's body and in the direction of the sound. Her eyes popped wide open as she clearly saw the three men standing and staring at them. She glanced down at herself, thankful that at least she still had on her shirt. There was no need to look at Ed, because her hand on his naked hip meant he was still *au naturel*.

She did what women throughout the ages have done when they have been caught in a semi-dressed moment. She screamed at the closest man. "ED!"

Ed opened one eye and smirked as he always did. "Hey. Nice shirt! You should wear just that more often."

She never looked down as she slapped his bare hip. With her eyes still on the men, she pointed to the pile of clothes behind Ed. "Get dressed! Quick!"

"Why?" He was slowly looking up at the trees before he continued, "It's still dark out." This was when he allowed her eyes to lead his in the direction of the men. Even though he now saw the men, he still had not grasped the exposed situation they were in.

Still unconcerned, he calmly said, "Wow. The guys got here kind of early."

She again slapped the bare skin of his hip. "Quick, my panties!" Then she slapped him yet again as she pointed. "The pants, too!"

Hearing her rapid requests, he instinctively looked down to survey her bare legs as they disappeared up under that one lonely article of clothing that she still had on. As his mind finally recognized that she wasn't totally dressed, his next thought was to look at himself. Seeing he was totally naked, he spun his head to look at the men before loudly saying, "OH SHIT!"

All three men clearly heard Ed's rather colorful shout. From Vic and Doc's point of view, both of the kids instantly disappeared. Bob was shaking his head as he turned towards Vic. "Did I just hear Ed yell out 'OH SHIT'?"

Vic answered Bob's question while never taking his eyes off where the kids had been sleeping. "Ah. Yes he did. Right before they disappeared."

"Disappeared?" Bob looked back to see Ed grab the pile of clothes and yank Martha to her feet with only one hand. They both dashed behind the nearest crate. "What do you mean, disappeared? They just ran behind that crate. Looks like we surprised the HELL out of them! Come on, guys. Turn around and let them have some privacy as they get dressed. You know they have to be embarrassed!"

Vic and Doc followed Bob's lead. They all turned their backs towards the center of the circle. Bob noticed that both of the others were exceptionally quiet and blindly looking straight ahead. "What's wrong with you two? Come on now! They know it was an accident. How could we know they'd be naked? Besides, they knew we were coming back this morning."

Vic said, "I saw them. Just as I can see the two of you. But how?" He turned to look at Doc. "I saw them very clearly. In fact, too clearly! They looked real. But then they disappeared. Is this how it started for you when you started seeing, or sensing, the spirits? Did they come and go like that for you too at first?"

Doc had closed his eyes and tipped his head downwards just slightly. He almost looked like he was praying. His lips tightened as he very slowly began moving his head from side to side. Now, with open eyes, he glanced over at Vic. "I saw them too. With my eyes, just like you did." He sounded confused as he continued. "I know I saw them with my eyes at first. But just like you said, Vic, they *did* disappear. I lost them from my view but I sensed them again with my mind. Like before."

Bob was confused as to why both his friends were acting so strange. "What is wrong with you two? I'm telling you. They didn't disappear! They picked up their clothes and zipped behind that crate."

Vic said, "But you've always seen them, Bob! I didn't! And now I can't see them again."

Doc looked at Vic. "That's right, Vic." Turning towards Bob, he asked, "Did they look any different at all to you, Bob? Think about it! Was anything different?"

Bob chuckled. "Well they weren't dressed. That was different. I don't know what you want me to say? They were easier to see, I guess."

Doc's voice intensified as he spoke. "What do you mean, they were easier to see?"

"Well. They were, uh, more clearly defined? Not fuzzy. OH, DAMN!" His eyes popped a little wider open. "You're right. Now that I think about it. They were easier to see because their bodies seemed almost real. Or more like they were solid." He snapped his fingers. "Yes! That's it!" But then the firmness of his voice tapered off as if he were watching a video of the scene in his mind. He almost sounded like he didn't believe what he said when he commented, "They looked real."

Vic asked, "Doc? What's going on?"

Doc replied, "I don't really know. It's not like I have ALL the answers. I need to think through this." He looked at them both before saying, "But they are special. Very special."

• • •

Martha was completely dressed while Ed still needed to put on his shirt and shoes. Once she made one last tug on the bottom of her shirt, she reached over and slapped Ed's backside since he was bent over tying his first shoe.

"Hey! What was that for?"

She was pointing at him. "You'd be dressed too if you hadn't been just staring at my bare bottom so much!"

"I can't help it! I like looking at your naked rear end. Everything about you is beautiful. HEY! I'm a guy!"

"You think I'm beautiful? All of me?" The beginnings of a smile appeared on her face, but then in an instant, it retreated completely. "We'll talk about this later." She leaned closer to him. "What are we going to say to them? How am I supposed to look them in the eyes now that they've all seen me, well . . . " She grabbed a handful of shirt and finished, "Wearing nothing but this?"

Ed finished tucking his shirt into his jeans. "I'm dressed. Happy?" He then looked in her eye. "Ok, first of all. You are whispering again." He looked to the left, then the right before he asked, "WHY? No one's here but us, babe."

She squinted and began to raise that dangerous finger of hers. He reacted by quickly crossing his arms so each hand could cover a shoulder. "Uh . . . no poking in the dark. Remember the rules."

"What rules? Oh, so you want a rule that says no poking anything in the dark. You sure?"

Ed thought for a second. "Okay. Rule modification. No poking in the shoulder except in the daylight." His huge smirk displayed how proud he felt that he had outsmarted her at last. So she poked him in the stomach. "Hey! No poking."

"You didn't say anything about your stomach." She shrugged. "Your rule!"

Their conversation came to an abrupt end as they heard the three men slowly walking up on the other side of the crate. First Martha's head crept up over the top of the crate and then Ed popped up with a huge smile as he said, "Hi guys!"

Bob said, "Martha. We are so sorry. We didn't mean to embarrass you. Forgive us?"

Vic added, "We really didn't see anything anyway. Really!" He looked at Doc who nodded a big 'YES'.

Bob rolled his eyes as he bit his lip. It was obvious that he didn't want to make eye contact with Martha. Seeing this, Doc punched Bob on the arm before saying, "We didn't see anything. Isn't that right, Bob?"

She couldn't help but think that Bob was innocently cute. His eyes were wide as he rapidly shook his head in very short up and down motions. Eventually he offered a squeaky little grunt as a form of acknowledgment. She moved quickly to end Bob's embarrassment.

"That's good! Let's just pretend that this never happened. Ok, gentlemen?" Bob immediately lost the tension in his shoulders and lets out a sigh of relief.

As she smiled at Bob's response, Ed whispered in her ear. "Do I have to pretend it never happened, too?" A sharp elbow in Ed's ribs brought a muffled yelp.

She glanced at Ed. "I thought you didn't like whispering?"

Ed simply replied, "Got it!" before he began to rub his side as he smiled at her.

Doc stepped up closer to the kids. "They brought up two more choppers to help close down this site. That means that everything, including personnel, will be air lifted out of here today. So I am offering again for both of you to stay with me."

Ed slipped his arm around her shoulders. She smiled at all of the men, but mainly focused on Doc's face. "Are you sure you want to do this, Doc? I mean, really sure?"

Ed commented, "Nobody brings ghosts home."

She again asked, "Are you sure, Doc?"

"I'm absolutely positive, Martha. You and Ed will be very welcome in my home. Of course it doesn't offer the open spaces that you have out here." He motioned around the circle with one arm.

Martha and Ed laughed for a moment before Ed said, "We decided last night to take you up on your offer, Doc. We want to say 'thank you' to all of you for everything you've done, and anything you do for us in the future. You're good people. But, we wanted to make sure you understand that at some point we will be leaving you. We may move on to our next destination. If we stay here in this 'between worlds' existence, we have decided that we will still go our own way and sightsee for as long as we can."

She stepped closer to Doc and quickly said, "But we promise to help with Mr. Gruber as long as you want us to." Then she stepped back by Ed's side before saying, "If we do go sightseeing, we were wondering if it would be okay for us to visit each of you occasionally?"

Three voices answered at the same time. "Yes!"

Doc said, "Since that's settled, let's get to the reason the three of us came over so early this morning. We don't really know when each of us will be catching our ride back to the base camp. So you can just jump on a flight with whomever you want, and we'll all regroup back at the other camp. Then we all have to get back to the airfield where they are reassembling the airplane you were on. They are still trying to understand what brought it down. Anyway, from the base camp, Bob and I will ride back in one of the guard trucks."

Vic added, "But I'll be riding with the other loggers since I work with them."

Doc again took over the conversation. "Now I've had a friend bring my SUV up to the airfield. So all five of us can ride back to town together from there. There's one more thing. We may not be able to leave the minute we get back to the airfield. I heard that there may be some kind of debriefing for each of us by the FAA investigators. None of us really knows what that is all about, but I was told it should only take about an hour or less for each of us."

Ed perked up. "Hey, guys. I don't know about Martha, but you can take all the time there you want. I would be very interested in watching them reassemble that plane."

Martha immediately shook her head at Ed. "I'll go look at the plane with you. That's fine." She turned to look back at Doc. "But I don't want to see any bodies. OK Doc? No bodies. Please!"

Doc quickly said, "The bodies have all been transported back to the city and most back to their families. All that's left there is the wreckage."

Martha spun to look at Ed. "Don't! Don't say a thing." She playfully pointed her finger at his belly.

Ed covered his belly button with one hand. "I'm not going to say I told you they'd all be gone, because that would be rubbing it in." He moved his hand from guarding his navel up directly in front of his mouth. "Oops! I guess I just did. Sorry!"

She poked him in the stomach.

There was the unmistakable sound of a very large number of happy men coming through the trees towards the circle.

Bob said, "Looks like it's time to go to work, gents!"

• • •

All of the men were energized, since they were each anxious to get home to their own beds. The work was progressing very rapidly. The entire campsite had been stored in small crates, and each crate was in the circle by 10:00 that morning. There were several teams of men stacking these neatly on large wooden pallets. Once a pallet was full, it was carefully crisscrossed with yellow nylon straps to ready it for the short flight back to base camp.

Eventually there were six pallets ready for shipping so a radio call was made to activate the choppers. The designated ground team swung into action the moment a chopper was heard in the distance. It would arrive over the circle, a cable would be lowered, and it would be attached to a pallet in less than two minutes. With a motion from the ground crew, the pilot would raise the bird into the sky and disappear from view.

Most of the men stopped to watch this spectacle the first time or two that it happened. But after that, they barely noticed. Only those with hats would still stop working so they could keep them from being blown off. Occasionally, men were caught carrying something with both hands and not able to secure them in time. So the frequent chopper visits were often followed with men running into the trees to recover their hats.

This provided the kids with a never-ending floor show of activity to watch. Of course, they were busy darting around in the trees as they chased each other with endless laughter. Apparently the kids were betting on whose hat would be next to visit the trees. Bob and Doc occasionally smiled as they watched the winner get to spank the loser's bottom. Afterwards, they would both happily scurry off into the trees again.

Martha took a great deal of pleasure in repeatedly sneaking

up behind Vic and yelling 'BOO' by his ear when he least expected it. It happened several times until he jumped so high that his workmate asked him, "What happened, Vic? See a ghost?" Of course this triggered one of Ed's laughing attacks that ended with Martha poking him in the stomach. She then turned to yell back at Vic, "Sorry, Vic! I won't do it again. Promise!" Then she chased Ed back into the trees.

At 2:30 in the afternoon, the circle was totally empty. As the sound of the last chopper faded into the distance, the men headed back to the road. There, the choppers could land to pick them up for their ride back to the base camp.

Only Vic, Bob and Doc remained behind in the empty circle. Soon the kids made their way out to them. Bob saw them walking up and commented, "You two seem to be having a lot of fun today."

Ed snickered before saying, "Well, Martha still hasn't realized that she can't catch me!" She responded with, "Yeah, yeah, yeah. What makes you think I really wanted to catch you?" She flashed a quick smile before she turned back to face the guys. "So, what's the plan now?"

Doc said, "Well, we all need to head to the road. That's where the choppers will be picking us up, a few at a time. If we walk slowly we can all ride together." He looked over at Martha and Ed. "You two ready to get out of here?"

Ed and Martha both lost all expression in their faces as they looked back at the now empty circle. Ed finally said, "It's hard to believe what has happened here. I lost my life here in a fiery moment." He shook his head a few times before he turned to look into Martha's eyes. "But it brought me to you. I'd do it again without even flinching. Do it in a second!"

She stepped closer and hugged him tightly. "Me too. Me too!" She eventually turned her head away from everyone, but they knew it was a tear that she wiped from her face. Slowly turning back to face them, she reached down and took Ed's hand. "I am, uh, I mean WE are ready to go now."

After two steps were taken, Ed said, "Martha? Since they always call us the kids, why don't we see if these OLD GUYS can keep up?" She glanced back to smile at the men before they both broke into a full run. Seeing them speed off in the direction of the trees, Bob yelled out, "Who you calling old!" The three men gave chase.

Bob watched as the kids took turns looking back at them occasionally. But only Vic and Doc could hear the childlike laughter coming from the two semi-departed entities ahead of them. As they cleared the trees, they all saw two choppers sitting on the road with rotors spinning. One man was holding a clipboard and standing outside of the first chopper. As he saw the last three men running towards him, he checked off their names then pointed to the last chopper. Doc waved his hand and then pointed to the second chopper as well. Seeing that they were running towards it, the man took the last seat in the first chopper and quickly buckled up.

Doc reached the second chopper right behind the kids, and motioned for them to get in. The co-pilot was watching but only assumed Doc was waiting for the other two men. Bob took the seat right by the kids, and pointed to another seat for Vic to take. Doc sat by Vic and turned to give the co-pilot a thumbs-up. He watched to make sure that the co-pilot turned his attention back to the front.

Bob could tell that Martha seemed a little bit scared, because her hands were clasped tightly to the edges of her seat. Her eyes were open wide as she nervously stared out the open door. The pilot increased the engine speed to lift off. The pulsing sound of the blades beating the air made her look straight up at the ceiling. Doc had also noticed she was obviously scared.

Ed was the exact opposite. He was definitely enjoying the ride, and had a smile that stretched from one ear to the other. He had his arms crossed in front of his chest while he was looking out the open door. There was a youthful sparkle in his eyes and he resembled a 10-year old boy excited about his first chopper ride. Eventually he noticed that Doc was waving his hand at him. Ed turned to see what Doc wanted. Doc pointed to Martha's hands, which had an ever-tightening grip on her seat. Seeing this, Ed immediately unfolded his arms to place one behind her and rested his free hand on hers. She didn't dare release her grip on the chair to hold his hand. Instead, she leaned back against his arm and smiled nervously at him. Luckily, the pilots couldn't hear her sudden scream as the chopper leapt into the air. Bob didn't hear it, but he saw it. He laughed a little until she looked at him with a mixture of fear and anger.

They flew into a clear, bright blue sky, the crash circle becoming barely visible as they gained altitude. Doc saw that the kids were both stretching their necks in hopes of seeing the circle from the air. He reached over the back of his seat and tapped the co-pilot on the shoulder, then hollered out, "Sir! Can you take us once around the site?" The co-pilot nodded then talked into his headset.

The chopper flipped sharply over on its side as the pilot veered to make a pass around the crash site. Again, the pilots were spared Martha's scream as her view out the open door was now straight down at the ground below. Though they were smiling at her, neither Doc nor Vic dared laugh. Eventually the chopper leveled out again and her scream gave way to the loud sound of wind rushing in through the open doors.

Even the pilots were captivated by the site of the huge, elliptical shape that had been carved out of the thick forest on that fateful night. From the air, it was easy to see that it wasn't a circle at all. It was wider where the wings hit. Due to the plane coming almost straight down, the tail section had actually fallen very close to the wings. So this side of the area was shorter than the debris field in front of where the wings hit. The forward momentum of the crash had spread debris almost four times farther in front of the wings during the event. More trees had been destroyed in this forward area than in the tail area.

Everyone was silently staring at this massive area of devastation caused by the impact and the following firestorm. With all eyes on this huge reminder of a violent end to a 40,000-foot fall, no one noticed that Martha had released her grip of the seat and was finally holding Ed's hand.

The chopper slowly completed its circle then headed back to camp. Everyone watched until the circle was completely out of sight. Each knew that they would never forget what they had been thinking in those last few moments. But only Doc heard Martha's thoughts as she took her last look at that special place. 'There goes our spot. No, it will always be OUR SPOT!'

• • •

The flight back to the base camp took only 10 minutes. Bart and Sandy had been rotating men weekly from the base camp to the crash site camp. However, these three men had requested to just stay at the crash site camp. At first, Bart and Sandy did not want to allow it, but eventually did for continuity's sake. At least that was the official reason. None of them had been back to the base camp in almost six weeks. Seeing the camp from the air for the first time since that first night, they could hardly believe how it had morphed into a small city. The landing zone now had a huge orange windsock installed to aid the pilots by giving them a visual of wind direction. They could see two other military choppers neatly tucked into separate corners of the large, flat landing zone.

The chopper that left just before them was still being unloaded. A guardsman holding a red flashlight in each hand stood alone in an isolated area of the zone. He had both arms straight out in front of him to direct the chopper where to land. The moment the skids were on the ground, the pilots began their shutdown sequence and the sound of the engines faded into a dying whine. As the ever-slowing whoosh of the blades echoed off the canyon walls, they exited the chopper one by one.

So many unfamiliar eyes made Martha say, "Don't mind us. We can get off by ourselves. You do what you have to, and we'll just follow you." The men followed along with that plan and started walking towards two familiar figures that were approaching them. Bart and Sandy smiled as they came closer to three men they hadn't seen for all these weeks.

Bart grabbed Vic's outstretched hand and shook it vigorously while patting him on the shoulder. "Good to see you, Vic! You did a very fine job up there. You did our crew proud!"

Vic smiled. "Thank you, sir! It feels good to finally leave that place. I can't wait to get home."

Sandy was also smiling as she said, "Bob, Doc. Great job, guys! The base commander wanted me to tell you both that he's put in good words for you. All the way up the chain. And I mean up to the really big brass!"

Bart said loudly, "The first coffee's on me, gentlemen. And if anyone's interested, I have a special sweetener back in my tent. Some say it has a bit of kick to it, but it will definitely stop the cold dead in its tracks! If you want to taste it, drop by the big red tent after supper. You're all welcome to come. It's good to have you all back!" With that, he turned and walked by Vic's side in the direction of the campfire.

Sandy waited until Bart and Vic were well out of earshot. Then she said, "I want to warn both of you about that sweetener of Bart's." She was smiling widely. "Bart talked Nick into having a little of that last week. Took him two days to recover!" She was chuckling as she rubbed her hands together in the cold air. "So if you go, you do so at your own peril."

They all were laughing loudly as they headed back to the mess tent for some hot coffee. She started filling them in on the schedule for closing down the base camp over the next few days.

Once they reached the mess tent, she said, "You guys go get some coffee and try to relax a little. Now we've cleared out a tent for both of you and Vic. It's right over there behind the mess tent. Bart's probably told Vic by now. All of your personal belongings should already be inside the tent. The three of you are on immediate rest and relaxation orders as of now. I'll send Peterson to round the three of you up after supper tonight. Bart and I have something you're all going to want to hear." She gave them a shortened version of a salute before she began walking towards the other end of the camp.

Doc motioned for Bob to go in first and he did. They quickly fetched a cup of their own. Once filled, they decided to go back outside to drink it. As they took their first sips, Vic came walking out from between a long line of trucks. He glanced back over his shoulder several times to look at one of the trucks, then smiled as he strolled on over to stand by Bob.

"I see you both already have a cup of coffee. I need one too. Be right back."

Before he could walk off, Doc asked, "Know where the kids are?"

Bob shrugged before saying, "I've been looking around for them, but I don't see them anywhere."

Vic chuckled. "Well, they're over by the trucks. I heard them just now when I walked by."

Bob asked, "Is that what you were laughing about?" Seeing that Vic was nodding 'yes', he said, "I can't see either one of them. What are they doing?"

"Well. It sounded like she was on the far side of the really big one. Evidently Ed is up inside looking around. He kept telling her about all the cool things that are in the back, and he wants her to look. Of course she is scolding him and saying something about he was going to get arrested. Last thing I heard was him saying something about nobody being able to put handcuffs on him because he's dead."

Bob choked a little on his sip of coffee. "Yep. Ed is just a big kid with new toys to look at!"

Doc added, "Sounds like Martha is going to have her hands full trying to keep Ed in line."

Vic made a sweeping motion with one hand. "So much here for a boy to look at. Martha might break her finger on the boy before the night's up!" He patted Bob's shoulder as he stepped around him to enter the tent. "Be right back, guys." Barely a minute passed before he emerged from the tent holding a steaming hot cup of his own. "Man, this is hot!"

Doc started shuffling his feet to keep the circulation going. "I was thinking we all should walk out into the trees and talk. We can stroll through the trucks and pick up the kids on the way." He headed out and the other two followed behind him. They walked through the trucks but didn't see or hear the kids at first. Then came the unmistakable 'Ouch!' from Ed before Martha was heard saying, "Hey guys, we're over here!"

Ed hopped out and then helped her down before they both ran over and followed the men.

As they made their way through the camp, Ed kept pointing at one thing after another. He was truly a child in an Army wonderland. Though Bob couldn't hear him, he saw that Ed's head was on a constant swivel so he knew he must be talking. The others heard a constant chatter of, "Oh, WOW! Look at that!" or "I have to check that out!"

Of course, every time he tried to wander off, Martha quickly grabbed his shirt and pulled him back in line. Only once did he offer enough resistance that she ultimately grabbed his ear before saying, "Oh no you don't, mister. Now stay with us!"

Ed shoved his hands into his pockets. "Where we going? Why do I have to go?" He tugged on Martha's sleeve and they both stopped walking to face each other. "I don't see why I have to go. Martha, you go. I'll agree to anything you decide. I just want to look around. Okay?"

"Ed. If we are going to be a couple, we have to make decisions together like a couple. You'll have all night to mess with this stuff!" She pointed haphazardly around at several things. "Look, Ed. Just come hear what the guys want to talk about. For me?"

He tilted his head backwards, but was really looking at the last stack of equipment they had just passed. His attention slowly came back to her face. "You promise? I can look around all night long?" She nodded 'yes'. Then he quickly added, "And you're going to go with me, right? I want you to see it all too. Okay?" She nodded her head 'yes' and he smiled as he jumped back in line. Vic had to bite his lip to keep from laughing because two steps later, Martha whispered to Ed, "This is why they always call us kids. It's not me, it's you!"

They were out of the camp and approaching that turn in the road that led to the missing bridge. The sound of fast moving water was becoming more and more audible. Ed asked, "Are we near a river?"

Vic responded, "Yes. It's a real mess around the corner up there."

Doc had stopped walking and was about to suggest they were far enough away from camp to talk safely. But before he started talking, Ed ran past him. "Sounds like a lot of water! It's just around the bend you say? I want to take a look." He was still running as he looked back and yelled for Martha to come on. She rolled her eyes. "He's going to be the death of me!" Then she giggled at what she had just said. "Sorry!" was the last thing they heard before she ran off after Ed.

Vic said, "That boy has an endless supply of energy. Doc, you sure you want them living with you?"

Doc motioned for the other two men to catch up with him before he started walking again. Once Vic and Bob were by his side, he said, "I was just wondering that same thing. But I should be okay. I doubt that she'll be able to keep him in the apartment long. I bet they're off exploring most the time."

It only took the kids three or four minutes to disappear around the bend, but it took the three men over 20 minutes to walk around the bend and catch up to them. They strolled up alongside Martha and stopped. Everyone stared at the rushing water that was now twice as wide as it was when they saw it that first night. The sun was melting more and more snow every day, adding an ever larger volume of water that raced through the valley to exit the southern pass.

The logjam that replaced the old bridge was still there. It too had grown to a massive pile of interlocked logs. For the most part, the innermost trees were wedged motionlessly in place. Only a few latecomers to the jam were still free enough to have one end bobbing up and down in the rushing water. They all stood silently, watching and listening to this impressive display of nature's monstrous power.

Occasionally Martha would loudly protest that Ed was getting to close to the edge of the water. Of course he would turn to yell back that he understood. But like a moth drawn to a flame, Ed was compelled to get even closer. Martha was finally relieved to see Ed stop. He was as close as he could get without being in the water. She commented over her shoulder to the men, "Well, the big goof has to stop now. There isn't anywhere else to go!"

With her words still hanging in the cold air, they all were totally caught off guard when Ed casually jumped onto the log pile. She was so petrified with fear that she didn't say anything. Without any hesitation, Ed turned around and sat down. There was a huge smile on his face as the log bobbed up and down. He then scooted backwards until he was only a few feet from the end. First one arm was slowly raised up in the air and then the other. Though the crashing sound of the water made it impossible for them to hear what Ed was yelling, each felt certain that it was something like, 'Look, Mom! No hands!'

The log that Ed was riding began to move farther up and down with each new movement. Without warning, Ed was flipped backwards almost 20 feet in the air before falling into the rolling white water. He was swept off at an incredible speed. Martha's instinct was to run after him, but Doc's voice froze her in place.

"Martha, STOP!" Her face displayed pure horror as she looked back at Doc. "Just stand still! Remember the test? He can only go so far from you." Now Doc was motioning with both hands for her to just stand still. In a flash, Ed had been taken out of sight around the bend in the river. Doc was now standing right in front of her.

"He can only go so far. You're helping him get out of it by just standing still. He can't drown. He can't get hurt. Think about it? He fell from the sky off that pallet and hit the ground. Remember? He didn't get hurt then, and won't be hurt now. Okay?"

Her eyes showed how concerned she was, even though she was nodding that she understood what Doc was saying. "It's just hard to watch him do stuff like that. I love him, Doc!" Her eyes were so intense looking. "He's what I always wanted. I just can't lose him now. Not now!"

Though all the men knew that she loved him, it was only now that Doc realized just how deep that love was. They both turned to look as Bob yelled, "Over there in the trees! It's Ed!"

Hearing this, Martha bolted around Doc to run towards Ed. Her arm bumped him and he was pushed aside. She didn't look back as she yelled, "Sorry about that, Doc!"

Bob stepped towards Doc and asked, "Did she just bump you? Looked like you felt it? Did you?" Doc started rubbing his arm where she came in contact with him and watched as she reached Ed. Since he didn't answer, Bob continued. "Doc? Is this normal? I mean, should you have felt her run into you like that?"

"No, Bob. Uh, I mean, yes, I felt her bump me. But, NO, it's not normal. It just means that they are so very unique. And before you ask, NO, I don't know what it means."

Vic joined the conversation. "We all know they're special. Maybe we just don't know how special! Seems to me, they are not that far removed from our side. It's odd that they are still able to interact with tangible things here. I wonder why?"

Bob interrupted, "Yeah! That's right. Like how the water took Ed and moved him downstream, just as if he had a real body."

Doc studied the two men. "Sounds like both of you are thinking along the same lines as me. But the real question is: Why are they affected by our solid existences? I was wondering how the water was pulling Ed, too. But when Martha bumped me and I felt it, well that really has me wondering now."

Bob joked, "Well, maybe Ed will get his wish and they will come back to life."

Vic looked at Bob. "You forget. We never found their bodies. That means they were some of those that were right in the middle of that massive fire. Totally cremated. I heard there were 14 bodies missing. Supposedly their ashes are all mixed into that massive blob of melted sand, plastic, and metal that was in the very center of the site. What a thought."

Bob looked down at his feet as he raked the ground with one boot. "I try not to think about that." Then he looked up quickly to add, "I still can't believe they were actually thinking about us digging that huge blob out of the ground! What was that all about?"

Doc said, "Well, they meant well. Somebody back there probably thought it was possible to separate out ashes or bone fragments, something that could be sent back to the families for burial. But when that scientist actually came to the site to examine it in person, he knew it would be impossible."

Vic added, "Plus, I hear that one of the engineers had estimated that blob could weigh more than three tons! The choppers would never have been able to lift it. Still seems sad that those remains will be just left out here for the forest to grow over. Nobody will ever know they're here. It's all so very sad."

Bob spoke up, "I guess neither one of you heard? There's talk that the state may erect a memorial out here. I guess the State Park Service will take care of it. Sounds like the airline is going to kick in some money for it, too."

Vic looked very surprised. "Really? I hadn't heard that, but I like it. These people should have a marker of some sort. Yes, I like that a lot. It will be perfect since there will never be any trees growing out here again. Too much fuel and hydraulic fluid is in that ground now. I doubt that anything will grow out there for hundreds of years."

Doc was looking at the kids as he said, "You two keep all that quiet. The kids don't need to know their bodies were never found. It doesn't make any difference anyway."

Vic was the only one who couldn't see that Ed appeared to be laughing as he fell to the ground in front of Martha. She was now standing, bent over at the waist while she shook her finger at him. The three men walked over to join the kids in the trees. Once there, it was considerably easier to talk. The trees muffled most of the sounds of the water crashing through the distant logjam.

Ed was now holding both hands up at Martha and was promising that he was done with the log riding for now. She motioned for him to get up and join the coming conversation with the guys, but he said, "Nah. I'm kind of tired. I'll just lay here and listen. Okay?"

In the time it took her to walk over to stand with the guys, Ed had stopped laughing and even appeared to have fallen asleep. She took one last look over at Ed, then stepped into position to complete the circle they all had formed. "You will have to excuse Ed. Looks like he went to sleep or whatever it is we do."

Doc took control of the conversation. "Does anyone know what Sandy and Bart want to talk to us about after dinner? She told me they were going to round us up after we eat tonight."

Vic snapped his fingers. "I do! Bart told me already. Seems the Governor is going to have a big ceremony after this is all totally done. He plans to recognize all of the people that did the recovery and stuff. But he also told me that the three of us are going to get special recognition. Somehow it just sounds wrong to me. Don't know about you guys, but it just seems like that takes the focus off those that lost their . . . " He stopped talking and looked at Martha. "Sorry, Martha. I wasn't thinking."

She smiled. "No need to be sorry, Vic. We died. It is what it is. For what it's worth, I think they should recognize all the people that worked on dealing with this mess. Especially you three."

Bob asked, "Did he say why they set the three of us up in that tent together?"

Martha gave out a little girlish squeal. "I know this one! Ed and I overheard that Sandy lady talking to a guardsman by the trucks. She said that you guys were flying back to the air base at first light in the morning. He was supposed to make sure some bird was ready to go. I don't know what they are doing with birds up here, but they must be through so they are sending them back. It sounds like we get to go along too!"

When Vic told Bob what Martha said, he started to laugh but stopped cold when she glared at him. "What did I say that was so funny?" Bob didn't need Vic to tell him what she said.

Doc quickly explained, "They call the choppers birds because they fly."

She was nodding her head. "Oh? That makes sense. I didn't know that." Then she looked over her shoulder at Ed as she said, "I said the same thing to Ed. Hmm, come to think of it, he was laughing too. He never would tell me why. Remind me to poke him when he wakes up!"

The three men were looking at each other for a few moments before Doc said, "Well, it's starting to get dark. Maybe we should all wander back and see if the chow line is ready."

Martha told them she would get Ed up and come find them. They all watched her for a few seconds as she walked towards him. Then they slowly turned and began walking back to camp. After a few steps, Bob said, "Think she'll get after Ed for laughing at her bird comment?" His words were still in the cold night air when Ed was heard, "Ouch! What's that for?"

Vic said, "There's your answer, Bob. She didn't waste any time!" They all laughed as they disappeared into the rapidly advancing darkness.

• • •

When the camp came into sight, they saw the chow line was already forming. They broke into an eager trot in hopes of securing a prime position towards the front of it. As always, meal time was full of the usual light banter and jovial conversations that helped solidify a group into a unit. They had all endured very cold conditions as well as grueling 12-hour workdays. Those that had worked exclusively at this base camp had been spared the gruesome memories of seeing the bodies scattered around the forest floor. They had only known the long hours of pushing supplies to the crash site and the reverence of handling the body bags as the choppers brought them back. But for those that had worked at the crash site, the sights and smells had formed indelible memories that they would carry with them for the rest of their lives. Though they were laughing loudly, it was there in their eyes. It could be seen in the small pauses in conversation and small glances at the ground from time to time. Each one knew that they had done something worthwhile. Yes, something that needed to be done, and done quickly. They were proud of their participation and of the newfound bond formed between all those around this campfire.

These calm moments of friendly chatter over a hot meal heightened the realization that they would soon be home. All spirits were extremely high due to this one uniting and well-deserved fact. They were going home!

As the tasty food disappeared from once overloaded plates, the men wandered off in small groups to continue their conversations elsewhere. Bob, Vic and Doc were no exception. They dumped their dishes on the table as always and walked a short ways out of earshot of the others. Vic asked, "You two see the kids anywhere? I don't hear them."

Bob and Doc were looking around as Bob said, "I don't. But if I had to guess, I bet we will find them by those trucks. You know Ed wanted to go back and look around."

Doc was nodding as he motioned for the two to follow him. "I bet you're right. Those trucks are kid magnets for sure. Ed's bound to have dragged Martha there by now." Doc and Vic were listening intently as they approached the trucks. Finally Doc said, "I hear them! Don't see them, but I hear them."

Vic said, "Sounds like they're on the far side of the trucks to me."

The three men walked around to the other side of the line of trucks and slowly started making their way down the line. They listened as they passed the cab of each truck, then they would quickly glance backwards to look inside the truck as they passed the end of it.

As they approached the third truck, they clearly heard Martha.

"Come on, Ed. I want to touch it. Turn around, you big goof!"

"You might not be able to handle it, Martha. This thing is big!"

The three men came to a silent and embarrassed halt. They were looking at each other as they were trying to understand what the kids were talking about. Whatever it was, it was highly suggestive and they all started smiling. Of course Bob had no idea what he was smiling about, but knew it must be something the kids were saying.

"Ed! Turn around and let me touch it."

"Ouch! Stop it! Okay, Okay! Here. Happy?"

Bob didn't know what was happening, but Vic and Doc appeared to be biting their lips to keep from laughing. Finally Vic let slip a small but audible snort before quickly clamping one hand over his mouth and nose. But the kids heard it. First Martha's head popped out from the back of the truck, and then Ed's emerged. "Hi, guys! You want to see what we found? Don't know what they are, but they're cool looking."

Martha added, "Yeah, and they are really big too! But Ed won't get out of the way so I can touch one. Doc, can you order him to move out of the way?"

Ed looked at her with a big question on his face. "Hey. I'm not stopping you from touching anything. Go on, touch away!" Then he jumped to the ground and walked over to the guys. Martha smiled really big before saying, "Be right back!" She disappeared for a few seconds. Then they heard her let out her customary little-girl squeal before saying, "This is so cool!" Then she reappeared and made a more graceful exit from the truck than Ed had.

As she walked up to them, Ed asked, "Hey Doc? Can you look at this stuff and tell us what it's for?"

Before Doc could answer, a guardsman appeared and said, "Oh. Here you guys are. Sandy and Bart want you three to join them in the big red tent." After Doc said, "We're on our way," the guardsman disappeared as quickly as he had appeared.

Martha said, "You want us to come along, Doc?"

But before Doc could answer, Ed's eyes lit up as he pointed, "Look! I didn't see that stack of stuff before. Come on Martha, let's take a peek." With this said, he was focused and gone.

Martha rolled her eyes at the three men before saying, "It's going to be a long, LONG night! He's like a kid in an Army candy store. Better go on without us!"

With Martha in hot pursuit of Ed, the three men headed towards the red tent. A few feet from the tent, Doc asked Vic, "Just in case. You do know about Bart's special sweetener. Right?"

Vic nodded, "Yes sir, I do. Bart's a nice guy and a great boss, but I doubt he has any living taste buds left at all. You two should be careful of that stuff. Oh, it's good and will kill the cold for sure. But if you aren't careful, it sneaks up on you quickly. One minute you are cold as hell, and the next you feel like you're some place like Hawaii! Be careful."

Doc sounded serious as he pointed a finger at them both. "Well, that's my point. We need to be careful here. Don't want to overdo it and say something we really didn't want them hearing.

Understood?" They all agreed.

Once inside Bart's tent, the men were each given fresh cups of steaming hot coffee. Then Bart performed a well-rehearsed ritual of topping off each man's cup with a little of his 'special sweetener' to help against the cold night air. Even though the three men already knew what to expect, they politely accepted the compliments and acted surprised at the news. An hour of happy laughter was shared by all attendees. As advertised, Bart's sweetener did the trick and not one of them felt the plummeting temperature when they finally emerged from the tent. Bob was the first to speak.

"I don't know about you two, but I think Bart really has something there with that sweetener he makes. Don't think I believe the part about his wife not knowing he makes it, though. I know I can't hide anything from my wife. Not that I have anything to hide from her, of course."

Vic snickered. "Oh really? So you are going to tell her about Ed and Martha the minute you get home then? Huh?"

Doc laughed as he added, "Well if you do, make sure she tells us which insane asylum she had you committed to! That way, we can come see you on visiting days!"

They all laughed as they walked towards their tent. As they passed the last truck, Bob suddenly said, "Hey! Is that Martha out there in the dark by that chopper?"

They all stopped to stare into the field where the choppers were parked. Finally Doc said, "What's she doing. Where's Ed?"

Bob interjected, "Well, my guess is he's in the pilot's seat since she's standing in front of it. Yep, there goes that finger."

Doc chuckled, "Looks like she is threatening our boy again. Let's go coordinate our leaving in the morning." As he turned to walk into the dark towards the chopper, the other two men shoved their hands deep into their pockets.

As they got closer to the chopper, they heard Martha. "You better not touch any of those buttons, you big goof! For all we know, this is the one we're going to fly on in the morning. I don't want to fall out of the sky because you messed something up in there!"

Ed's muffled voice could be heard replying, "Mess something up in here? How can I do that? Come on Martha, get in! It's really cool in here. Look at all these dials and buttons. I need one of these!"

"Me? In there? No WAY! I have no intention of getting on this thing until I have to. NO!" Hearing the three men approaching, she turned and said, "Doc! Tell him to get out of that helicopter. Is this the one we are going to fly on? Make him get out before he breaks something!"

Doc smiled. "Martha. He's right you know. He really can't hurt anything in there. Think about it. Did he have to open the door to get in?"

Bob said, "Tell her about the checklist the pilots run through before taking off. That should help."

Vic laughed at Bob, "You just did. She hears you. Remember?"

Bob smiled and shook his head. "Oh yeah! I forgot? Wow, that coffee is still with me."

Martha was staring at Bob with a quizzical look on her face. "What's wrong with him? Is he . . . wait a minute." She sniffed the air, "Is he drunk? You guys have been drinking! Was the pilot drinking too? I'm not getting on this thing if he was. I'll walk back!"

Nobody saw Ed as he slipped through the door of the plane and walked up behind them. "What's going on? Why is Bob smiling so big? Is he OK?"

Doc was holding both hands out towards Martha. "Nobody's drunk."

Ed immediately asked, "You guys are drunk? Won't you get court-martialed for that? Was it any good?" He stopped talking as Martha turned to stare at him. After a few seconds he asked, "What?"

She rolled her eyes and looked back at Doc. "Look. I just want to know if the pilot we'll be flying with tomorrow is drunk. Well, is he?"

"No. The pilots are all asleep by now. They have a busy day tomorrow." Doc paused, then added, "We are all going back tomorrow morning and you'll be fine. Ok? And I doubt very seriously that Ed could have changed any of the settings on the chopper."

Martha countered, "Why couldn't he? I knocked over that crate and then I hit you down by the river. If I can do that, why couldn't Ed mess something up? Huh?"

Ed looked shocked as he stared at her. "You hit Doc? Why?" Then he turned to look at Doc. "Did she poke you with that finger of hers? Hurts, doesn't it?"

Bob's head was tilted straight back as he looked up at the starry sky above. "Man look at all the stars! It's really nice out here. I feel really good!"

All the others stopped to look at Bob before Martha asked, "Exactly how much did he have?"

Though Vic was not as bad as Bob, he had a dazed smirk on his face too as he said, "Well. I know I had four shots of Bart's elixir, and Bob was doing two to my one, so that means. Uh? Let's see." He stopped talking as he pulled one hand from his pocket and started mumbling numbers as he moved his fingers.

Doc was looking at Vic as he said, "You had four shots? Are you crazy? Didn't we talk about this? I only had one shot. What's wrong with you two?"

Hearing that, Bob wobbled a little before saying with a slight slur, "Well Doc. You're just not a real coffee drinker like Vic and me!" Then he nudged Vic's shoulder and the two broke out into laughter.

Martha stopped staring at the two men and turned to Doc. "Are they going to be okay?"

"Well, I have a feeling they're going to pay for this tomorrow morning. Hey guys. Why don't you two head back to the tent?"

They both nodded at the kids before saying, 'Good Night' before walking away. They had only taken a few steps when Bob, thinking that he was whispering, spoke rather loudly.

"He didn't say which tent, did he?" Then Vic choked out a 'No'.

Hearing this, Doc yelled out, "Heard that! Not the red tent, you two. Go get some sleep."

As they were almost out of range, Vic was heard saying, "I agree. I don't think Doc really likes coffee at all!" With every step, their laughter faded into silence.

Doc turned back to face the kids. "I've been meaning to talk to you both about this bumping things and making them move. Do either of you have any idea how this is happening?"

Ed spoke up. "I think it has something to do with us being

emotionally charged about something. Or something like that. Why?"

"That would make sense, actually. Martha was trying to get to you both times. When she hit that crate, you had just fallen off that pallet under the chopper. Then when she bumped into me, you had just fallen into the river. I'd say that qualifies as emotionally charged on her part. What about you, Ed? Have you moved anything like that?"

As Ed shook his head 'no', Martha said, "Yeah, you did, Ed. You had to be excited when you fell in the river. And the water swept you away, remember?" She turned to Doc. "That counts, doesn't it?"

"Well, I thought so at first. But now, I think that is probably more a holdover from what you remember things working like on this side of death. Like, you walk on the ground and don't float above it. You run around fallen trees, and I've seen you both jump up on things and not fall through them. I'm really talking about you moving solid objects. You've done it twice but Ed never has."

Martha smiled. "Well, he's certainly been trying to do it. He tries to move things all the time. I hate to think of what he'd do if he could move or lift things when he wanted to."

Ed didn't see her smile. He was staring at that red tent and obviously thinking hard about something. "I know what I'd do if I could lift a cup."

Martha now noticed that he was focused on that red tent and her eyes widened. "Oh, no you don't, mister! Don't you even think about it." Then she reached over and grabbed a handful of his shirt.

"Hey! What did I say?"

"You can't even feel the cold, goofy. So you don't need any coffee, or anything else for that matter! Besides, even if you could lift it up. What then? You can't drink it, silly!"

With the realization of what she just said, Ed's shoulders dropped and he let out a sad grunt. But just as quickly as he realized he couldn't drink Bart's elixir, his spirits bounced back and he whipped his head around to look at the chopper. Without even looking at them, he started to walk back to the chopper door as he said, "You two don't need me anymore, right? I'll be right over here. Okay?"

Before Martha could say anything, Ed had slipped back into the chopper and was happily jumping into the pilot's seat. She watched him for a second, then looked at Doc. "So, where does this leave us in this conversation?"

Doc yawned, then smiled apologetically before he said, "Sorry. I guess that coffee of Bart's is getting to me too. I really just wanted to make sure you don't forget that we are leaving at first light in the morning. We'll be up and eating breakfast in the dark as usual, so just keep an eye out for us."

Martha glanced up at Ed in the chopper then back at Doc. "You go get some sleep, Doc." Then she pointed over her shoulder to the chopper. "We may still be right here when you guys get up! He's such a big kid at times!" Then her eyes sparkled and her expression softened. "But I do love him, you know. Big kid or not. I do love him so."

"I know Martha. We all know. See you in the morning." He nodded good night before turning to head off towards his tent.

Chapter 13

OUT OF THE VALLEY

IT WAS NO surprise that Doc was the first one up that morning. Although he felt slightly affected by Bart's sweetener, he took a great deal of pleasure in making as much noise as possible to annoy Bob and Vic. They both had moaned loudly before rolling over to wrap their pillows around their throbbing heads. Even this additional padding was not enough to silence Doc's intentional whistling combined with his banging and dropping of various objects. Finally, Bob and then Vic threw their pillows at Doc. Perhaps their aim would have been more accurate had they actually dared to open their eyes.

"Doc! We get it! So knock off the torture, will you? My head is pounding like a drum. As bad as I feel, Bob, you must be in pure hell. You alive, buddy?"

Vic had been slowly sitting up as he spoke. With his feet on the ground and his head now cradled in both hands, he mumbled, "Come on, Doc. Have a heart, man. Shhhh."

Bob had his head pulled down into his sleeping bag and his muffled voice was heard saying, "Am I dying? I feel like it. If I am, can somebody go ahead and just finish me off?"

Doc's head hurt too, but he didn't let it show. Besides, he was having too much fun tormenting these two fools. "I just can't believe you dummies drank more than one shot of that stuff. And after I warned you both! No, you deserve to feel like you're dying." He now had all his gear packed and stacked by the tent opening. "So if you two alcoholic deviates are expecting to find some sympathy, you're in the wrong tent! Now get up and get packed, gentlemen. We have to eat and catch our ride." He was now standing in the tent opening and was flapping the two panels that made up the tent door. The cold air rushed in and brought the smells of breakfast with it. "Smell that? Ah yes, coffee and bacon. That is your salvation that you smell. Now get up and rejoin the living. NOW!" He released the flaps as he disappeared into the early morning darkness.

Vic said, "It's a good thing for him that he left. I was tempted to get up and close the tent flaps in his face. What an ass!"

Bob had now partially emerged from the sleeping bag. "Well, you'd have been on your own, buddy. I can't feel my feet."

Vic made a halfhearted attempt at a joke. "What about your head?"

Bob immediately snapped back, "That I FEEL! Boy, do I feel THAT!"

The two men remained motionless for another few minutes before they finally made it to their feet and slowly began to collect their gear. Each wanted desperately to lie back down, but they doubted they would have enough energy to get back up. No, each movement to pick up something was a painful reminder that Doc had warned them. What would have taken them only five minutes on an ordinary morning took them almost 30 minutes in their current condition.

With their gear stacked on Doc's, they stepped from the tent. The cold mountain air actually opened their sinuses and slightly softened the pounding in their heads. The walk to the end of the chow line was just what the doctor ordered. They felt better as they waited their turn. Both men thought about skipping the chow and heading directly for the coffee, but a giant hole in their stomachs kept them from making that dash.

Doc had taken a seat on the log farthest from the fire and the chow line. He had been watching Bob and Vic as they continually rubbed their foreheads with first one hand, and then the other. He had done the exact same thing several times since leaving the tent. He realized that if he felt this bad from just one shot, those two must be in real agony. Even though he felt sorry for them, he smiled. He was not through torturing them yet.

He had not been able to catch a glimpse of the kids as he looked towards the choppers before sitting down. But now he could hear their voices coming from around the trucks. He was sitting and facing the trucks, so he only appeared to be looking out into the darkness. Then he saw Ed come running up the middle of the line of trucks and turn left before he disappeared out into the darkness towards the choppers.

Martha had just called out, "I'll get you for that! You just wait!" A few seconds later, she emerged from the middle of the trucks and stopped before looking both ways. Seeing that Doc was looking at her, she yelled "Which way?" and Doc nodded towards the choppers. As she waved 'thanks' to Doc, Ed's voice boomed from the darkness. "No fair! I thought we were friends, Doc!"

Doc sat watching as she disappeared into the darkness and was startled by Bob's voice behind him. "She chasing Ed already?"

Vic had already sat down on a log. "I wish I had their energy this morning!"

Bob added, "Back in the tent, I was thinking that being dead might be an acceptable alternative to this pounding in my head."

Doc snickered. "Still no sympathy here for you two. You both need to hurry up." He pointed to three guys jogging out towards the choppers. "That's the ground crew heading out to get the chopper ready. It will be light soon, and we still need to take our gear out there. Lucky for you two, you can nap on the gentle ride back to the airfield." He then stood up and walked towards the table to drop off his dishes before walking back to the tent.

Bob watched Doc walk away. "You know, Vic? I've seen that look in Doc's eyes before. He's a nice guy, but has a real mean streak sometimes."

Vic turned to watch Doc while speaking over his shoulder to Bob. "He's going to say something to the pilots. Isn't he?"

"Well, I know he wants to. But he may not, since Martha's going with us. He knows she's scared of flying."

Vic snickered. "Well, that works for me. You and I feel like we're dead, and we'll be saved from a bumpy ride by a woman that really is dead. Go, Martha!"

They ate in silence until they saw Doc pop out of the tent carrying his gear. Each man shoveled the remaining food from his plate into his mouth before choking it down with the last of their coffee. They walked quickly over to deposit their dishes before returning to the tent. They were only in the tent a moment before emerging with large duffle bags thrown over their shoulders, carrying smaller bags. They made their way over to Doc just as the first rays of sunlight hit the tail of the chopper. Only Doc and Bob saw Ed as he was sneaking around behind one of the trucks. Suddenly, Martha popped out the back and thumped him on his head. She screamed out, "Gotcha!" Then they heard her cute, little girl squeal as Ed rubbed his head and yelped, "OUCH!"

She leaned out and threw her arms around his shoulders as she jumped from the back of the truck. They both fell to the ground and lay there laughing. Slowly Ed stood before he offered her his hand to help her up. She stood and stepped right up to kiss him for a few seconds.

The sound of the ground crew starting a generator caused the kids to spin around. They saw the guys waiting for them, so they hurried out and stood with them.

As they ran up, Martha said, "Morning!"

Ed stared at Bob and Vic for a moment before he said, "You two don't look so well. Why are you holding your stomachs?"

Suddenly Bob said, "I need to take a short trip. Be right back."

Vic immediately said, "I'm with him."

Doc and the kids watched as the two men made a hasty retreat towards the latrines. Once they disappeared from sight, Martha asked, "Is that what happens when you drink alcohol?"

Ed looked at her before he asked, "You don't know?"

She replied innocently, "I never drank any. But I know that some of my friends got sick from drinking it. Maybe nobody ever told them what would happen."

Doc started laughing, "Oh, they knew better and now they're paying the price for ignoring my warnings. Let them suffer."

Without warning, Ed's curiosity got the best of him and he quickly wandered off to watch the ground crew get the chopper ready. Doc and Martha stood watching Ed as he followed the ground crew during their flight preparations. They chatted about a myriad of topics and failed to notice the two men returning from their adventures in the latrine. Vic and Bob walked up and took their places near their friends without saying a thing. They both were obviously still suffering the ill effects of Bart's sweetener.

Doc laughed out load as he looked at the two ill men. "Nothing like a nice boring ride back to base early in the morning. Eh, guys? Hey! This will make you feel better. You'll be new men by the time we get back to the field." This comment caused Vic and Bob to sigh as they stared at each other. They both knew that Doc was signaling that he had cooked up a rough ride with the pilots to make them sicker. Vic leaned his head down in Bob's direction and whispered, "We still have Martha."

The ground crew completed their work just as the pilots boarded the craft. Once a stack of equipment was stowed aboard the bird, all of the men's personal gear was secured inside as well. The pilots quickly ran through their pre-flight list. Finally there was an eerie whine as the motor began to spin the huge blades. One guardsman motioned for the others to climb aboard.

Ed was the first one to claim his seat and patted the seat next to him as he smiled at Martha. She was slowly shaking her head from side to side as she hesitated. Finally Doc said, "It's going to be a gentle morning flight. No bumps. Promise." She closed her eyes for a second, then slowly walked over and got in next to Ed. Seeing this, Bob and Vic did a fist bump as they both mumbled, "Go, Martha!"

As soon as they were all in their seats, one of the ground crew closed the door. Once again, Martha's hands were tightly gripping her seat. This was happily noticed by both Vic and Bob. Feeling safe from any pranks by Doc, they both relaxed and leaned their still-pounding heads back against the cabin walls.

The sound of the engine grew louder and louder until they felt the slight swing of the craft as it inched into the air. The chopper had to go straight up, since the canyon wall was behind them and the forest surrounded them everywhere else. Higher and higher they climbed until they were above the canyon wall. Without warning, the routine flight made a very different maneuver. The pilots usually just let the tail spin around a half circle to point the nose south towards the airfield. But this time the pilots let the tail spin not one complete circle, but two entire circles before dropping the nose to fly off. Then as they picked up speed they banked hard to the left for a few seconds, and then hard to the right before leveling off.

Martha was screaming at the top of her lungs. Due to this violent maneuver both Vic and Bob had sat up straight, their eyes were wide open. Vic heard her hideous screams while Bob could only see the obvious fear in her eyes. Vic hollered at Doc, "I can't believe you'd scare her like that just to prank us!" Both of them were staring in disbelief at Doc for his being so callous about scaring poor Martha.

Then they heard it. They couldn't believe what they heard. Slowly they turned to see that Martha was laughing even louder than she had been screaming. She released her grip on the seat and leaned on Ed as she said with a smile, "Gotcha!" Then she gave Doc a thumbs-up. Bob and Vic were totally confused as they now focused on Doc. He put one hand in front of the co-pilot who immediately gave him a high five.

Martha was still smiling as she said to Doc, "You were right. It was just like that carnival ride." Then she looked at Vic and Bob. "I hope this teaches you two a lesson about the evils of drinking alcohol."

Doc said, "Now, we can have that smooth ride back to base?"

Ed leaned down to look into Martha's eyes before he said, "I knew you could do it. Wasn't that fun?"

Martha replied, "It was fun. A little. But I don't want to ever do that again. Ever!"

Ed nodded that he understood before his attention was drawn to the sight out the window. They all watched as the chopper flew over the top of the canyon wall and the rock face of the mountain gave way to a valley that stretched to the horizon. Ed pointed as he said, "Out of the canyon!"

• • •

The rest of the flight was level and uneventful. Bob and Vic both slept during the remainder of the trip and missed the breathtaking blue skies. There wasn't a cloud to be seen in any direction. Finally, a small suburb of orderly houses could be seen adjacent to a sizable town a little farther beyond. Only the pilots and the kids were scanning the ground below for sight of the airfield. Ed noticed it off to their right and pointed it out to Martha. Moments later, the pilot gently laid the chopper over on its side to swing towards it.

There was a flurry of activity in the cockpit between the two pilots as they approached the airfield and prepared to land. Doc and the kids watched as the chopper followed the routine landing path as did the planes. When they were halfway down the runway, they followed a section of the tarmac to a lone civilian standing in front of a huge hangar. He had ear protectors on and held two red-tipped flashlights in his hands. With a few gestures from him, the pilot brought the craft to the exact spot needed and gently touched down. The civilian was already opening the chopper door when the sound of the engine changed to the customary whine as it began to slow.

The open door allowed them to see inside a massive hangar. The two large doors were both pushed back along opposite sides of the front of the structure. Martha's attention was totally on the activity inside the hangar. This prevented her from noticing that Ed was out of his seat and already exiting the craft. She called to him as she reached for his shirt, but it was too late and he walked a few steps before stopping. With both hands on his hips, he stood there surveying from side to side. He then looked back over his shoulder and motioned for her to join him. Doc smiled and winked at her before she hopped out and walked over to Ed.

The man holding the door spoke over the sound of the dying engine, "We will unload this gear for you." He then pointed to a single door at one corner of the hangar. "They're waiting for you men in the office over there." Then he looked at Vic and Bob, who were both still asleep with their heads resting on their chests. He smiled and commented "I heard that they worked you boys pretty hard up there. They look like they're really out of it."

Doc laughed and replied, "These two have had a very hard time!" He was out of his seat now, but forced to walk bent over due to the cramped ceiling. He punched each man in the shoulder as he passed them on his way out. "Wake up, you two knuckleheads! Ride's over!"

Bob immediately pulled both hands to his temples and kept them there as he lifted his head. The bright sunlight caused his eyes to blink uncontrollably before he said, "Damn! That's bright! Can't we come back tonight when it's dark?"

Vic's fingers were fumbling with something in his shirt pocket before they found and extracted his prize: sunglasses. Once on his face, he was heard saying, "This is going to be a bad day."

Doc smiled "Only for you two! They're waiting for us in the office over there, so get out, gentlemen." He stood a few feet away and waited for the two moaning men to exit the chopper.

Ed suddenly started pointing, "That's the plane wreckage back in there. This is what I wanted to see." Again, Martha's attention was elsewhere so she missed her opportunity to hold Ed back. She glanced towards Doc and rolled her eyes.

"It appears that we are going to be looking around in there. Take your time, Doc. I'm sure we will still be there when you get back." Then she lost her smile before she asked, "You sure there are no bodies in there? Promise?"

"They have all been shipped back. Promise." He smiled before he turned to lead the two hungover men to the office.

She watched as Vic and Bob fell in behind Doc to follow him to the office. She noticed that Doc was walking upright and with a spring in his step. But the other two both had their heads down and were gradually falling farther behind. She knew that the two of them were not feeling well at all. This bothered her because they were good men. With a smile on her face, she muttered, "I hope they never forget how bad they feel today. Maybe this will teach them not to drink."

Once the three of them disappeared through the office door, she turned to face the entrance to the hangar. Even though she had been assured that there were no bodies left inside, she was still nervous about it. She walked up to where she could easily see the entire inside of the hangar, and stopped just inches before actually entering. She carefully searched for black body bags, but there were none to be seen. But she still couldn't bring herself to take that last step and go inside the hangar. From here, she saw three basic areas.

To the left was a sea of metal fragments that appeared randomly scattered all over the concrete floor of the hangar. After a closer look, she could see that these parts were laid out in lines within small groups and sorted by size. There were small pieces all the way up to larger items like the landing gear.

Farther over, they were actually putting some of the plane back together. Martha couldn't believe how much it actually looked like a plane. These people really knew what they were doing.

To the right of the entrance were ten large tables with small parts scattered on them. One table was full of small laboratory equipment and several computers. A man was dipping a long cotton swab in some liquid and then rubbing the side of a piece of metal. It was about the size of a football, and Martha wondered what it could be. The woman at the next table was looking closely at all the small parts scattered before her. She occasionally picked one up and examined it closely with a magnifying glass before replacing it on the table and picking up another. Once again, she reached down and picked up a piece to examine it. After a few seconds, she walked quickly over to the man at the next table and held it in front of his face. She rolled it from side to side while holding the magnifying glass for him to view the object. He took the part from her hand and pushed back with both feet to propel his chair to the other end of the table. His shoes squeaked loudly as he stopped his chair directly in front of one of the computers. She quickly joined him, and looked over his shoulder at the computer screen.

Martha was completely caught up in watching these people and wondered what they were looking at. She didn't notice that Ed had snuck up behind her. He reached out and poked her in the side as he yelled, "Gotcha!" She jumped and screamed at the same time. As he stood there laughing, she stepped back towards him and slapped his shoulder. "You scared me, you big goof! Don't do that!"

"Why not? You looked so serious. What are these people doing? I didn't make it over here yet. But I saw you so I came on over."

"How would I know what they are doing? I don't know anything about airplanes."

Ed stopped rubbing his shoulder and took her hand. "Come on! I want to show you what I was looking at." She reluctantly let him pull her towards where they were rebuilding the plane. They walked around to the farthest side of the hangar. There in the corner, they had lined up all the seats that were still intact. Each seat was in order by its row and seat number. Martha slowly walked through what would have been the center aisle. She stopped at the end. "They don't have our row. I wonder why?"

"I noticed that, too. Seems they are missing several rows before and after our row. They must have been too damaged to tell what numbers they were." He pointed to a pile of metal against the back wall. "That pile is all that's left of a bunch of seats."

She walked over to stare at the pile for herself. These were smaller pieces of twisted and charred metal. No fabric was left, just the metal. After she looked for a few seconds, she turned to say, "Ours must be in here somewhere." After looking a few more seconds, she turned and walked back to stand in front of Ed. He noticed that she was thinking hard about something.

"What are you thinking about?"

"I was just thinking that if our seats were reduced to those small, twisted pieces, then I wonder what our . . . " but she was quickly cut off as Ed stepped close to her before he lifted her face up with his finger.

"Don't! Just don't even say it! Don't think about it. It's over and done, so let it go."

She glanced back over her shoulder to look one more time at that pile of metal and said softly, "But I was just wondering if they found . . . ".

Ed reached around and used his finger to gently nudge her face back so he could see her eyes. "Please, baby. Let it go. Okay? It really doesn't matter anymore."

"Doesn't matter? But they were our bodies. Of course they matter."

He saw the tears in her eyes, so he wrapped his big arms around her and pulled her in tight. She closed her eyes as she laid her head against his comforting chest. "Oh baby. I'm so sorry. I shouldn't have brought you over here. For that matter, I shouldn't have dragged you into this building at all. I'm sorry, baby. So sorry."

Although she had closed her eyes, Ed was intently watching all the activity that was going on in the hangar. He focused on four men as they picked up a partially reconstructed section of the fuselage and carefully carried it back towards the tail of the plane. They ever so gently placed it on the floor before they walked away. As his eyes followed them, he noticed several tables along the back of the hangar. The items on those tables didn't appear to be plane parts at all. He clearly saw a small and very battered piece of luggage.

Slowly his eyes roamed along the length of each table. Most of the stuff was too small for him to make out from this distance. Just as he was about to look away from them, something white caught his eye. He strained to make out what it was. Something about it seemed oddly familiar. It was white and fluffy, like a small stuffed animal. OH NO! His mind raced as he recalled her having picked up that little stuffed rabbit with the blood on it. DAMN! He knew he had to get her out of here before she saw it. He realized that she would absolutely fall apart again. Taking small half-steps, he slowly turned her as if they were slow dancing on a very crowded dance floor. Once her back was to those tables, he released her from his big bear hug and took her hand to lead her out of the hangar. She actually took the first step before she even opened her eyes.

"Come on baby. Let's get you out of here."

Seeing the bright sunlight outside, she smiled and quickened her step to walk beside him. "It looks absolutely beautiful out there. I wonder how long before the guys are done?"

They were finally outside the hangar and began to walk towards the building that the men had entered some time ago. Ed said, "I don't know. But it could be fun to go inside and see what they're doing. Want to go?"

Seeing that look in Ed's eyes, she knew there was no stopping him. "Well, I don't see how it can hurt. There are only three people in there that will even know we are there. But you better behave, you big goof! They are going to be having a serious conversation with the people in charge of the crash investigation. So we, meaning you, can't mess with them in any way. OK?"

Ed was holding each of her hands as he walked backwards. "Hey! Have I ever done anything like that?"

She rolled her eyes but said nothing. Ed stopped walking and let her run into him. "Ok. I get it. I'll be good. Really!" Seeing her raise that menacing finger of hers as if she was prepared to poke him, he said "Promise!" Then she tilted her head before slowly pushing her finger closer and closer to his ribs. "Okay, okay! I really do promise."

"You better! This is serious stuff and they are our friends now. We don't want to get them into any trouble. Okay?"

Ed paused before nodding, "Yes. I agree. Come on. I'll race you to the door!"

She watched him as he sprinted away. Slowly she began to follow him. By the time she had gotten up to a good running pace, she saw that he was about to go up the steps to the door. "Ed! They could be coming out of that door at any minute! Slow DOWN!"

As his foot hit the first step, he glanced quickly over his shoulder to call out to her, "So what? I'll go right through it."

At that very moment, the door swung open and a woman appeared. Bob was holding the door for his wife. His eyes almost popped out of his head as he saw that Ed was running up the steps towards her. Things happen very quickly in situations like this. Bob's instinct was to grab his wife's arm, and hold out his other hand to stop Ed.

It was obvious to Ed that his momentum was too great to stop. So he did the only thing he could think of. He dove over the short railing and disappeared as he sailed right through the wall of the building. Martha had stopped and was holding both hands up to her mouth as she shockingly said, "OH!"

Bob's head followed Ed's trajectory from the steps, over the railing and through the wall. His eyes stayed fixed on the exact spot where Ed pierced the building. His attention was still on that spot as his wife asked, "What's wrong? You're squeezing my arm, baby. What are you looking at?"

Hearing his wife's voice, Bob's mind raced in search of what to say. He hesitated before he turned his head back to look at her. He was trying to buy as much time as he could, trying to come up with a plausible explanation for his actions.

His wife saw that his eyes were wide open and wondered why he still hadn't answered her. "Bob, are you okay? Your eyes are so big. Did you see something?"

Bob was looking at her as he continued to stall by muttering "Uh . . . ". Looking over his wife's shoulder, he saw Martha standing in the parking lot, looking as surprised as he felt. He mumbled a little louder, "UH . . . ". Then he noticed Martha had dropped her hands to her hips and squinted, just like she does when she's about to get after Ed for something. Bob turned his head back around towards the wall and there was a head just sticking out. Ed looked up at Bob and said, "Hi! That was close!" Bob didn't hear him but saw the smile on Ed's face as his lips move.

Bob uttered even louder "Uh . . . ".

"Honey? Are you okay? You look like you saw . . . " Bob's wife was cute off by a voice from within the building. It was Doc, and he completed her sentence for her. "a GHOST?"

Once again, Bob stammered, "Uh . . . ".

Doc offered Bob a way out. "Wow! It sure looks bright out there."

Bob jumped on Doc's lead. "Yes! It's very bright out here. WOW! I can't see a thing!" He turned to look at his wife. "That's it. Yes, I couldn't see anything as it was so bright when I opened the door. I was, uh, I was afraid that you couldn't either. So I uh, that's why I grabbed your arm, baby. I didn't know if you could see either, and I didn't want you to take a tumble."

He was afraid that he didn't sound very convincing, but it was the best he could do. He intently watched her face for a reaction. Did she buy it? God, he hoped she did.

"Really?" She paused to look around. Bob hadn't taken a breath as he was so nervous. Then she slowly raised one hand to shield her eyes as she looked up at the sky. "Yes, it is very bright out here." Then she looked at her husband and smiled as she patted the hand holding her arm. "Thanks, darling, but you can let go. I can see just fine."

Bob reluctantly released his grip. "Well, okay. Just be careful, baby." She was on the second step before Bob stepped completely through the door. He looked back at Doc before he let go of the door. His eyes made a short and hopefully secret gesture to get Doc to look over at the wall.

Doc chuckled as he saw Ed's smiling head sticking out of the wall. "Well, this seems kind of weird."

Bob's wife was now off the steps and had turned around to face the two men. "What seems weird, Doc?"

Bob's eyes snapped wide open again and he stared at Doc as if to tell him to watch what he said.

Doc chuckled. "I just meant it seems odd to be back in civilization."

She responded, "Oh? I bet it does. You all have been gone for a long time." Bob was now by her side and she reached down to hold his hand. "I can't imagine what you all saw or how you got through it. But I do know this." She pulled herself up tight against her husband and quickly kissed him on the lips. "I am very glad it is over and you are back. I missed you very much." Still holding his hand, she turned and began to lead him to the car.

Bob let her pull him along, but asked, "Shouldn't we wait for Vic and Glenda?"

Doc smiled as he told them, "Nah, you two go on home. You've been separated long enough. Take care of that bum, Lisa. He's a good man."

"Yes he is, and he is all mine."

Bob looked a little hesitant so Doc added, "I'll wait for Vic and Glenda. I have nobody waiting at home for me, so I'm not in a hurry. They're in there talking to Bart, so there's no telling how long it will be until they are ready to go. You two go get reacquainted. Now get out of here!"

Bob and Lisa were laughing as they climbed into their ride. With Lisa in the car, he ran around to the driver's door before waving bye to Doc. He noticed that Martha had walked over to the wall and had grabbed Ed by the ear. Bob motioned over the top of the car in the direction of the kids. "Take care of those two!" He knew his wife would only think he was talking about Vic and Glenda.

Doc had watched as Martha swiftly walked past Bob and Lisa on her way to Ed. Before he could even turn his head to look at them, he heard Ed yell "OUCH!" Once Bob's car had driven away from the building, he knew it was safe to turn and look at the kids. Martha had Ed by his ear and pulled him out of the wall.

"See what happens when you don't listen to me, mister! You promised you'd be careful and behave. Then you go and do this!"

Ed now stood beside her. He stood up straight to break her grip on his ear. "That hurts, lady." he said with a laugh. "You sure are good at that. Are you sure you aren't a nun?"

"A what?"

Seeing the look in her eyes, Ed knew he was safer when he put some space between himself and that finger of hers. He was holding both hands straight out in front of her as if to keep her at a distance. His laughter filled the air as he asked her, "Excuse me, lady. But do you have a license to carry that weapon? Is it loaded? Do you have it on safety?"

She stepped up quickly and poked him in the ribs. "Ok mister funny man. I'll show you my license." She poked him again. "There, happy?" Then she poked him a third time. "Oh, I'm so sorry. I didn't realize it was loaded. Oops, and that darn safety seems to be OFF, too!"

The opening of the door brought things to a halt. The three of them turned their eyes to the door. Vic had opened it for Glenda, and she had stepped out. They both walked over to where Doc was standing.

"It was good working with you, Doc. I'm looking forward to seeing you again soon. We'd love to have you over for dinner one night if you're interested."

"I'd be crazy to turn down a home-cooked meal. Of course I'd be interested. You have my number now, so just let me know when to be there."

Glenda smiled at Doc. "Do you have a favorite food?"

"Ma'am, according to Vic here, you are a real serious chef. So whatever you choose to cook will be just fine."

She looked at Vic and smiled, "So you said I was a good cook? That was nice." She leaned in close to kiss him, and then quickly wiped her lipstick from his lips with a tissue.

Vic glanced over at Doc. "Let's try to do it before you go to Gettysburg again. Any idea how soon you'll be going?"

Before Doc could answer, Glenda turned to Vic. "If he's going to Gettysburg, why don't you go with him? You always said you wanted to go."

"But baby, we talked about us going together. Remember?"

"Of course I remember, but I also remember saying that I never had any big desire to go there. I was only going to be with you. But this way, you can figure out the really neat things to see and then take me." She hugged him as she said, "You can be my own personal tour guide."

Doc said, "Well, since they told me I don't have to go back to work until the first of the month, I'll probably leave the day after tomorrow. Probably won't work for you two. Remember, I don't have anyone at home that I haven't seen for two months."

Vic was shaking his head as he looked at Glenda. "No, I can't be home for just one day and leave her again. I'd lose her for sure!" He was smiling at Glenda as he pulled her closer. "And I certainly don't want to do that."

"Lose me? You're never going to be free from me! But you can go if you want too. Really! It's perfect."

Vic had a quizzical look on his face as he slowly shook his head. "What would be perfect?"

"I knew you wouldn't remember. I'm leaving day after tomorrow for Atlanta. I'm going to sit with my high school girlfriend's kids while she delivers her third child. I told you this several times. We discussed it, remember? Now she's counting on me being there to help. I have to go."

Though Vic was actually excited to hear that he was cleared for the Gettysburg road trip, he put on a very convincing show. He exhaled while he ran one hand through his hair, pretending to think it over. "Well, it's not the homecoming I was hoping for, but you've already promised her."

Glenda scooted up very tightly against his chest and whispered into his ear. "Oh, you are going to get a homecoming you'll never forget in about an hour. Then, you'll get another when we both get back. How's that sound?" She lightly nipped his ear lobe, leaving some very visible bright red lipstick behind.

Vic let out a low, manly growl before he said, "You know I won't be able to sleep the entire time you're gone?"

She nipped his neck and whispered one more thing. "You aren't going to sleep tonight either."

Another low growl was heard before he spoke with a slight stutter. "We, we, uh, we have to go, Doc. I'll call you tomorrow sometime."

Doc didn't know what she said to Vic, but he definitely saw the effects. Vic hurried to open Glenda's door, helped her inside, ran around and got in the driver's side. The sound of the engine coming to life was followed immediately by a short squeal of tires from too much gas pedal.

The kids strolled up and stood behind Doc. The three of them watched as Vic drove out of sight. Doc finally broke the silence. "There goes a man on a mission."

Ed looked puzzled as he said, "A mission. Is that why he's in a hurry? What mission?"

Doc chuckled softly as he waited for the inevitable yelp from Ed.

"OUCH! Hey, what was that for?"

Doc didn't have to look to know that Martha had rolled her eyes at Ed's question before she struck with that lightning-fast finger of hers.

Martha asked, "How we getting to your place, Doc?"

"That's my red SUV on the side of the building." He was pulling his keys from his pocket as he turned to walk towards it.

Ed's words still hung in the air though he was on his way to look over Doc's ride. "Wow. Nice! Can I drive?"

Though she tried to get to him, Ed was too quick and ran off to the car.

"Doc, is there any kind of medicine you can give a ghost to make him grow up?"

Doc chuckled again. "He is a live wire, isn't he?"

When they got close to the car, Doc hit the electronic hatch release and it slowly rose up in the air. Then he opened the back door and pulled out two small bags to clear the seat. He walked around and threw them in the back before he hit the button once more to lower the hatch. Ed let Martha get in first and slide to the middle. As she looked at the dash, her eyes were drawn up to the rear view mirror. It is the first time she had been in front of a mirror since the crash. She wasn't prepared to *not* see her reflection in it.

"Oh!"

Ed immediately jumped in. "What's wrong?"

"Oh, nothing. It just caught me by surprise when I didn't see myself in the rear view mirror. It's nothing. Really."

Hearing this, Ed had to lean over in front of her to make sure he couldn't see himself either. "Wow. That is so cool!" Then he looked at her before he said, "Now I can see you." Then he looked in the mirror. "Now I don't." Again he looked at her. "Now I can see you."

Doc smiled as he closed the door and walked around to the driver's side. Just as he reached for the door handle, he heard a muffled "OUCH!"

As the door opened the voices became clearer. "Why does it constantly amaze you that we are dead? Ed, this isn't healthy, baby."

"Not healthy?" Ed was looking at her with his typical blank look. "What do you mean, not healthy? Doc, do you think a ghost can be unhealthy?"

Doc slipped behind the wheel, closed his door and started the car before he answered. "I don't really know, Ed. But I'd say that if you keep pestering her like that, you're going to find out."

"You should listen to him, Ed. They don't call him 'Doc' for nothing."

The conversation stopped as they drove past the rows of hangars on their way to the main gate. Soon they passed one of the runways just as an old plane was accelerating to take off. This instantly caught Ed's attention.

"Hey, look! That's an old World War II fighter taking off there."

Doc glanced over at it before saying, "Yeah. That's a Hellcat. I've met a few of the guys that restore and fly those old planes. They have several out here. They are part of the Confederate Air Force, I think."

Martha quickly asked, "I didn't know there was a Confederate Air Force. Will we see more planes like that at Gettysburg?"

Ed never stopped staring out the window but said, "Doc, I'll let you explain this one to her. I'm tired of getting poked."

Doc was biting his lip to keep from laughing. Finally he cleared his throat and said, "Martha, they didn't really have planes during the Civil War. So, there really aren't any planes to be seen at Gettysburg."

"So why do they call themselves the Confederate Air Force? That's just outright confusing."

Ed was still watching that plane as it lifted off the ground and into the air. "And here we go. Be gentle, Doc."

"Well Martha, they aren't part of the U.S. Air Force. They are like clubs of pilots and airplane mechanics that ban together to save old aircraft. It's like a hobby and a mission. Their sole purpose is to salvage and restore these beautiful old machines for future generations to see. Make sense?"

Martha thought for a second before she answered. "I guess. It just seems like they should call themselves something like the 'Old Plane Dudes'. It would be a lot less confusing."

Hearing her comment, Ed did finally turn to look at her. "Old Plane Dudes? Really? Who would ever take their kids to see the 'Old Plane Dudes'?"

"All I'm saying is that they shouldn't use the word 'Confederate'. It makes it sound like it has something to do with the Civil War. That is why I got confused." She nudged Ed's arm with her elbow before having her attention also drawn to the sight of the old plane as it disappeared into the clouds.

There was silence as they exited the airport's main gate and pulled onto the highway. After a few minutes, Martha sheepishly asked, "Doc. Why didn't your girlfriend come meet you? You do have a girlfriend, don't you?"

"Well the truth is that I don't have a girlfriend anymore."

Martha waited a few seconds to see if Doc was going to say anything else, but he didn't. Finally she said, "I'm sorry, Doc. It was none of my business."

"It's okay, Martha. I had one, but it ended over six months ago. We were together for almost three years, but we just grew apart over time. At least that is how she put it before she moved out. I haven't seen her since. A friend told me later that she had moved to Chicago with an old boyfriend. Never saw that coming."

Ed said, "Well it's lucky for us that you live alone now. I doubt you'd have invited us home if she still lived there."

Martha nudged Ed's arm. "That's not a nice thing to say. You sound like it's okay that he's alone. He's our friend and you should be more sympathetic about it. Sorry, Doc. Ed obviously speaks before he thinks."

Doc was smiling as he said, "Don't worry about me. The truth is I should have known she wasn't happy. It was bound to happen eventually, and now it has. It's over."

Ed wanted to change the subject. "Where do you live? A house or an apartment?"

"I live in an apartment in the old downtown area of this little town up ahead. It's an old hotel that was converted into apartments. Each apartment was made out of about five hotel rooms. They are actually very nicely laid out, and lots more room than I need. Plus the whole downtown area has been renovated and there is a cool, big city feel to it now. My building is right in the middle of it all. There are several other apartment buildings, but mine is by far the coolest. Plus the neatest shops are all in my end of the little town. I have a bakery and deli on opposite ends of my street. Then there is a family restaurant, sub shop, two clothing stores and some kind of a computer gaming store on the other side of the street."

Hearing this, Ed sat up and leaned way over the back of the seat till he was almost able to see Doc's entire face. "What kind of computer gaming store? Do they sell games and electronics?"

"I think so. I've been in there several times. I bought my girlfriend's new laptop in there last Christmas. They also put a bigger hard drive in my desktop a few months ago. They do good work and are very friendly."

Ed was obviously very excited about this new revelation. "Well, just FYI guys. I'm going to be hanging out over there a lot."

Martha rolled her eyes. "Figures. The minute we get back to civilization I'm going to be a computer widow. Yep! Just another lonely dead girl that had her guy stolen away by a shiny, cold machine." She shook her head. "Maybe you can just take me back to the forest, Doc. It sounds like I'm going to be alone anyway."

Ed scooted close to her and put his big arm around her as he leaned over to look in her eyes. He slowly leaned closer and closer until their lips are almost touching. Martha had begun to close her eyes when Ed suddenly leaned back and smiled that big smile of his. "You're not ever going to be alone again, baby, because we're tied together. Literally!"

Martha's mouth fell open as she realized that Ed had just tricked her into thinking he was going to kiss her. She couldn't believe she fell for it. "Well just don't expect me to go over there with you just to watch you drool all over the place. You better just hope that rope we are tied together with will reach over there from Doc's apartment. If not, then you're standing in the street looking at your electronic heaven just a few feet away. What a pity!"

Ed's eyes showed that he was really considering the possibility that she could be so cruel. Then he got his usual playful smirk on his face. "You wouldn't do that to me. Would you, babe?"

Martha leaned her head on Ed's shoulder. "I love you Ed, but yes I would!" She slowly closed her eyes as Ed rested his cheek on top of her head. In a matter of seconds, they both fell silent.

Doc sensed immediately that the kids had drifted off to sleep. His instinct was to look in the rear view mirror at them, but he noticed he couldn't see them in the mirror. He had never thought about this. He wished he could see them, but he was driving and couldn't turn to look. With the kids asleep, Martha's questions about his girlfriend triggered a flood of memories. The rest of the drive was spent remembering all the happy times he had spent with Susan.

Just as he pulled off the highway to head into town, he began thinking of how long he had hunted for, and then finally found the perfect ring to surprise her with. The morning he was going to pick it up was the same morning she told him that they needed to talk. He was so excited that he replied to her saying he agreed, but had he to run an errand and would be right back. Then she called his name sharply and he stopped to look at her. That was when he saw the intensity in her expression and knew something was wrong. With one hand already on the doorknob, he heard her blurt out, "I'm moving out today".

For at least a month, those words were his last thought before falling asleep and the first thing he recalled upon waking in the morning. He shook his head a little as he recalled the weeks of wandering around like a zombie that had lost a mate. Leaving the television on for background noise in the apartment had become an everyday thing. He never really listened to it, but he heard the news flash about the plane crash up in Cantor Valley. He knew immediately he was going to volunteer to go. It was just what he needed to get his mind off her.

Yes, the irony is that Ed and Martha's tragedy ended their lives, but saved his. These thoughts swirled in his head as he drove. He eventually realized that he hadn't thought of Susan at all these past weeks. He smiled at this. The emptiness in his heart had been filled by his concern for these two unique entities seated behind him. Perhaps they were sent to save him instead of the other way around.

Doc had been so lost in his thoughts that he didn't notice that Ed had opened his eyes and was looking around. The sight of the electronics store caused Ed to suddenly sit up straight. "Hey! Is that the store you were telling me about?"

Ed's sudden exclamation brought Doc out of his daydream and woke Martha. Her head slid off his shoulder as he sat up and leaned towards the window to look inside the store as they passed by.

"Yes, Ed. That's the one. Does it look like the ones you used to go to?"

Ed had the look of a child who just run downstairs to see the presents on Christmas morning. His eyes sparkled as they danced across every word painted on the windows of the store. Knowing him as well as she did now, she quickly grasped his hand to keep him from just jumping out of the car. He turned to look at her. "What? Oh, I'm not going to do anything stupid. Just looking."

She had a look of disbelief in her eyes, and one corner of her mouth was scrunched up tightly. "I believe you, baby. But I'll just hold your hand in case you try."

Doc slowed and turned into an alley in the middle of the block. "That's my building to the right, and the parking garage is right back here." A few minutes later and they were parked inside. The kids slid out through the passenger side door and patiently watched as Doc gathered up his bags.

"There is a walkway right over there, and it goes straight into the building. But I'm one floor up."

Martha only relaxed her grip for a second, and Ed was off at light speed to be the first one on the breezeway. "I'll wait at the elevator. " He never slowed down, but turned around to talk as he was walking backwards.

"Doc. You do have an elevator, right?"

"Yes. The elevator will be to your left."

Ed quickly disappeared through the cars and into the hall that crossed into the apartment building. Martha walked beside

Doc and asked, "Is that stuff heavy? I wish me and Ed could help you with stuff like that." Then she giggled a bit and added, "Of course that would require Ed to hang around and not run off all the time. I just don't know what gets into him." She was making motions with her hands as she spoke.

"If I look this way, he goes that way. When I think I know what he is going to do, the big goof does the exact opposite." Then she got a little quiet before she asked, "Was it like this with your girlfriend? If you don't mind me asking."

Doc smiled at her, then looked away for a second before he slowly shook his head. He recalled doing the same thing sometimes with Susan. She would be walking slowly and looking at everything in each store's window. Not him. He'd walk off ahead of her to look at something that interested him. Maybe she would still be with him if he had stayed by her side more. Maybe if he had shown more interest in what she was looking at. He used to do it. He remembered walking arm in arm all the time when they had just started dating and even that first year they lived together. What happened to him? He loved her more every day, but now he realized that he had also became more willing to wander away from her. Was he responsible for her leaving? Did she think that he didn't care anymore? Wow! It could all be his fault that she left.

He glanced back at Martha before saying, "I don't mind you asking at all. In fact, I'm kind of glad you did. But to answer your question, Yes. I did the same thing to her. But I loved her more each day. Now that I think about it, I don't know why I did it."

"So you loved her? That means it must have hurt when it ended."

"Yes it did. I was going to pick up an engagement ring when she stopped me at the door and told me she was moving out."

"Oh no! And she moved out, even though you had gotten her a ring?"

"Well, actually she didn't know anything about the ring. It was going to be a surprise. But her surprise was bigger than mine, I guess."

"So what did she say about the ring? Surely you told her about the ring."

Doc was looking away from Martha now as he shook his

head and spoke. "No. Never told her about the ring."

"Why not? You really should have. It could have changed everything. She might have stayed. Why didn't you tell her?"

"Just didn't. Couldn't believe she would just leave like that, without even trying to talk about it first. I think I actually knew why she was leaving. You know. The real reason. But I just didn't want to face it."

"What real reason? What do you mean, Doc?"

"She was going back to her old boyfriend. A guy she grew up with. I found out later that they both had moved back to their home town."

"I'm so sorry I brought this up, Doc. It was none of my business. I'm so very sorry, Doc."

Doc smiled at her. "Don't be. I think this conversation actually is good for me. It's the first time I've talked about it out loud." He suddenly realized that he'd been talking out loud to her, and not even checking to see if anyone was around. He looked behind them but luckily they were alone. He pointed around the corner towards the elevator and she turned just in front of him.

Martha shook her head when they both saw Ed standing there trying to push the buttons on the elevator. He looked up and smiled. "I thought I actually did it just a minute ago. But it turned out somebody got on above us and went to the next floor. What a bummer!"

Ed stepped aside as Doc came up and dropped one bag to the floor. The sound of it echoed through the hall for a full second or two. The kids both sensed that Doc seemed in a hurry . . . or was he mad? They stared at each other for a moment while shrugging their shoulders as if to say 'what is wrong with him?'. Doc stood facing the elevator doors without saying anything. He never turned around to look at them and stepped into the elevator when the doors opened. They hurried in after him and took up positions against the back wall. Doc faced the panel and pushed his floor's button, then remained motionless until the doors opened again. He stepped out and walked straight to his apartment door. Once again, that bag made a loud sound as it hit the hall floor. His hand dove into a pocket and emerged with his keys. A quick flip of his wrist and the door was open. He picked up the bag and quickly stepped inside.

The kids quickly followed him in and watched as he threw the bags onto the couch before he circled around them to close the door. Then he leaned back against the door and breathed a big sigh of relief as he looked up at the ceiling. The kids stood in the middle of the room, staring at him as he rubbed both hands over his face while quietly moaning.

Finally Martha asked, "What's wrong Doc? Did we do something wrong?"

Ed quickly said, "I'm sorry. It was probably me, right?"

Upon hearing them, Doc immediately dropped his hands and started laughing. "No, Ed. It wasn't anything either of you did. Promise."

The kids both looked at Doc, then each other and then at Doc again. Martha quizzically asked, "Are you sure it wasn't something Ed did? See, even he knows he is annoying sometimes."

Ed's head snapped towards Martha. "Annoying? Wait a minute! Who you calling annoying? When have I ever been annoying?"

Martha squinted as she stared at Ed. "Never been annoying. Really?"

Ed had just opened his mouth and was about to speak when Doc suddenly cut in. "Okay, you two." He laughed a bit then continued. "Look. It wasn't anything to do with either of you. It was me. Not you. Okay?"

Martha turned to look at Doc. "But it felt like it was something we did. You suddenly stopped talking, and seemed to be rushing to get away from us. Why?"

Again Doc chuckled and then looked to the ceiling as he rubbed his face with both hands. Slowly he stopped laughing and dropped his hands.

"Look. It was me. I noticed that I was just walking along and talking out loud to you." He pointed towards Martha. "Remember? When it dawned on me what I had been doing, I got a little self-conscious. I wasn't trying to get away from you. I wanted to get into the apartment so we could be alone and talk. Get it?" He paused long enough to look at each of their faces. "Look. We've been out in the forest all this time, and there weren't that many people walking around us out there. So it was easy to watch out and make sure nobody saw us walking around apparently talking to ourselves. I have gotten so comfortable talking to you two that I forgot that nobody else can see or hear you but me. So when it dawned on me, I just panicked a little. Understand what I mean?"

Martha was nodding when Ed spoke out, "I gotcha, Doc. So you need to be more careful in the city, because there are a lot more eyes around that might see you. Don't want anyone thinking you're losing your mind, right?"

Martha playfully slapped Ed on his shoulder before turning to face Doc. "You big goof. He's going to need our help, too! We will all need to work together to not let that happen again. Right, Doc?"

Doc nodded. "It would be great if you both would help me on this. You have to remember that I see and hear you just like I do everyone else. So when I'm involved in what we're talking about, I easily forget that nobody else sees or hears you."

The three of them stood for a moment nodding their heads 'Yes'. Then Ed, his usually playful self, clapped his hands and asked, "So, Doc. Where are we going to sleep?" He chuckled at what he just said. "You both know what I mean."

Doc pointed to a door behind them and then started walking towards it. "This is the spare bedroom. It's not very big, so you may feel a little cramped at first. Sorry."

Doc had opened the door and walked in. Ed walked to the door, but stopped to let Martha go in first. She entered and Ed followed her. She said, "This is really a cute room, Doc." Then she saw a little stuffed teddy bear in the middle of the bed leaning up against the pillows. She let out that cute, little girl squeal. "That's so cute! It is just absolutely adorable. Your girlfriend must have decorated this room. Didn't she?"

Martha was fixated on the teddy bear but Ed was watching the expression on Doc's face. "You okay, Doc? What's wrong?" Hearing this, she turned to look at Doc, too.

Doc was staring at the teddy bear. Finally Martha asked, "Doc? What is it?"

Doc slowly exhaled before looking at her. "Yes, Susan decorated the room." He looked around as if he was admiring it for the first time. "You know, I never really thought about it, but she did a good job. She really did." He stepped towards the door before stopping to look back at the teddy bear. "But I gave her that bear for our one month anniversary after we moved in together. She said she'd never let it out of her sight. I found it on the floor by our bed right after she had taken the last of her stuff to her car. I thought she'd dropped it, so I picked it up and ran down the stairs to catch her before she pulled out of the parking garage. She barely rolled down her window when she pulled up and stopped by me in the alley. I said 'You dropped this' and held it out to her. Instead, she told me to keep it and rolled up her window before she pulled off. That was the last time I saw her.

"I just stood there for several minutes holding that stupid bear. I walked over to the dumpster to trash it, but I couldn't make myself throw it in. Finally I brought it back up here. I stood in the front room trying to decide what to do with it. Then I thought I'd just toss it on this bed in here. It's been here ever since." It was obvious that Doc wanted to get out of the room, so Martha said, "Well, you probably want to get cleaned up and rest. So, don't worry about us. We'll be okay."

Ed said, "Yeah, Doc. We'll stay out of your way for a while so you can get settled and such. She's right. Don't worry about us. We are very thankful that you asked us to come to your home. Really, man. Thanks!"

Doc stepped closer to them. "You are not in my way. You are my friends and I am very happy to have you here. Please, make yourself at home. I mean it. But don't think for a second that I don't want you here. I do. I mean it. Okay?"

Martha stepped a little closer to him and looked into his eyes. "We know, Doc. Believe it or not, Ed and I have talked a lot about how nice all of you have been to us. But when you asked us to come home with you, we realized just how good of a friend you really were. Thank you, Doc. Thanks for all that you have done for us, and what you're doing now. I just don't see how we can ever repay you."

Doc smiled. "Like I said. You're my friends, and friends help each other. You don't owe me anything, or anyone else. We're all very happy to help. And you're more than welcome to stay with me as long as you want to."

Ed had stepped up beside her and placed his arm around her shoulders. "She's right, Doc. Thanks, man."

Doc nodded before he smiled and said, "But, I am going to leave you both now and take your advice about cleaning up, then resting. See you both in a bit." He turned and closed the bedroom door as he left.

The moment the door was closed, Ed pinched Martha on her bottom and dove for the bed. "Ouch! I'll get you for that, mister!" But Ed was too fast and he rolled off the other side of bed to his feet. She pointed at him and said, "Ok. You stand still. Right there. You hear me, ED?"

Ed's eyes were shining as he laughed while he motioned for her to come on. She suddenly faked a lunge at him. The moment he started his roll across the bed, she sprinted back to the other side and caught him just as he stood up. He reacted by wrapping both of his arms around her and pinning her arms to her side. "Hey! You let me go right this minute! You hear me ED?"

"Not until you promise that you aren't going to poke me with that damn finger of yours. Okay?"

She wiggled a few more seconds before she realized that he was too big and way too strong for her. Ultimately she gave up and simply stopped struggling. Noticing this, Ed said, "Calmed down now? Promise me, no finger. Come on. Promise me." He leaned over and kissed her softly on the forehead. "Come on, baby. Promise me, no poking."

She looked up at him and softly answered, "I promise."

Just as he released her, she quickly shoved him and he fell backwards onto the bed. He laughingly asked, "Now what?"

She started removing her sweater as she answered, "We are alone in a very cute room with a heavenly bed. I think we can find a better use of our time then chasing each other around. What do you say, Ed?"

He turned his head to look at the teddy bear sitting atop the neatly stacked pillows. "Well. I think we need to find a way to cover up that bear. I don't want to be the one that teaches him about the birds and the bees."

Chapter 14

IT'S A GHOST SLEEP OVER

DOC FELT COMPLETELY revitalized after his long hot shower. He emerged from his room as he rubbed his clean-shaven face. It felt good to be wearing his old pajama bottoms and his favorite Gettysburg t-shirt. There was a new spring in his step as he strolled to the kitchen to get something to drink. Suddenly it dawned on him he couldn't hear the kids anymore. Odd, he could hear them laughing and carrying on the entire time he was shaving. He stopped and stood just at the edge of the carpet before stepping into the kitchen. He had his senses on full alert to anything coming out of the kids' room.

Just as he thought that they must have fallen asleep, he heard Martha say ever so softly, "Oh Ed. Yes, right there, baby." Now he felt embarrassed that he had been trying to hear what they were doing. With a slight blush, he stepped onto the cold tile and hurried to get a soda. He tried to be as quiet as possible so he didn't interrupt the kids. He thought to himself, 'Well, they may be only spirits, but at least somebody is having sex in this apartment again!'

With his drink in hand, he moved to his usual vantage point in the middle of the large bay window. From here, he could see his entire street from corner to corner. It felt good to be home, even if she wasn't here. It was odd how he didn't feel alone - not like he'd felt ever since Susan left. Maybe that was because he wasn't alone. He didn't know what type of ghosts they were, but they were here and he was not alone.

Then he noticed his neighbor coming out of the clothing store across the street. She had moved into the apartment next door just a week after Susan moved out. He'd only spoken to her briefly on the day she moved in. Of course they had shared small chit-chat in the halls and elevator like neighbors do. She was very cute, but he didn't even know if she had a boyfriend. She looked like she was barely out of college. Oh well, she probably wasn't interested in an old guy like him anyway.

As he stood there watching her cross the street to come home, Ed's head suddenly appeared over his right shoulder and he said, "What you looking at, Doc?"

This startled him so much that he spilled his soda down the front of his shirt. "Man, don't do that!" He was wiping the soda off his hand and forearm with his already-soaked shirt. "You scared the hell out of me, Ed!"

"Sorry Doc! It's a ghost sleepover. I just thought you always sensed us before. Why not here?"

Doc was lost in thought as he kept trying to wipe off the remaining soda. "You know, that's a good question." He paused before continuing. "I guess the answer would be that, in the forest, everyone was running on pure adrenaline most of the time. But back here and after a nice hot shower, I feel so very relaxed. You just caught me daydreaming. That's how you snuck up on me. I guess."

"So, who is she Doc?"

"What? Who is who?"

"The girl you were staring at crossing the street. That's who."

Martha's voice suddenly rang out from behind the two men. "What girl? Who's staring at a girl? Ed, you better not be doing what I think you are doing."

Ed turned and stepped just out of reach of her as she quickly came to a stop right by Doc. "Hey! Wasn't me, it was him, baby."

"Yes Martha, he's right. I was watching, NOT STARING AT, my neighbor as she crossed the street. Then Ed scared me out of a year of my life by popping his head around my shoulder."

Ed laughed as he added, "He spilled his soda. It was hilarious. You really missed it, babe."

She quickly pointed her finger at Ed. "Okay, buster. We obviously need to set some rules for you. Might as well do it now."

"Rules for me? What rules?"

"It's okay, Martha. It was my fault. I'm probably just a little jumpy from being so keyed up in the forest for all that time. Really. Not Ed's fault."

Ed smirked at Martha before he turned to Doc. "So she's your neighbor, huh? Maybe she saw you and she'll stop by to welcome you home!"

Doc shook his head. "I doubt it. We really have only spoken a few times in passing. I don't know her name, nor does she know mine. She probably has a boyfriend. Besides, she's never stopped by in the few months that she's lived next door. I doubt she even knows I'm back."

With his words still fresh in the air, there was a soft knock on his apartment door. Three heads spun to stare at it as if they could see through it. Then to Doc's total surprise, a sweet voice said, "Ted? Are you home, Ted?"

Martha immediately said, "Wow. I never thought in all this time to ask what your real name is, Doc."

Ed had his goofy look as he said, "Well it seems like his real name is Ted." Then Ed looked right at Doc's face and said with a smirk, "Odd how she doesn't know your name. TED!"

Doc's mouth was wide open as he shrugged at the kids.

"Yes. I'm here, just a minute please."

Martha again pointed at Ed. "And you get your shirt on, mister! NOW!"

Ed hesitated as he asked, "Why? She can't see us. DEAD, remember?"

"I don't care, Ed. It just isn't proper. And besides, I don't want my boyfriend walking around half naked in front of other women. Dead or alive!" Since he still hadn't moved, she took a step towards him and he quickly retreated to the bedroom. "Well, Doc? Aren't you going to let her in?" Then she turned and started walking towards the bedroom. "I'll keep Ed occupied so you two can be alone."

Doc slowly walked over and opened the door.

"Hi, Ted! You remember me? I'm your neighbor Wendy."

"Of course I remember you, Wendy."

In the background he heard Ed yell, "He knows your name now, Wendy! Ouch. What was that for? What? She can't hear me. Did you forget already?"

"Honestly, Ed. If you remind me one more time that we're dead. I'm going to, uh, well, I'm going to . . . well, you know."

"You're going to what? Come on Martha, say it." He started laughing as he barely got his next words out, "Go on. It's killing you, I know. But you can do it. SAY IT!"

At this point, even Martha was laughing as she choked out the words, "I'll kill you!" Then the two of them laughed so loudly that it made Doc start laughing to the point where he almost spilled his soda again. His eyes had tears in them so he wiped them with his free hand as he chuckled.

"Are you okay, Ted? Should I come back at another time? I didn't mean to interrupt you. I know you just got back, because you weren't here when I went across the street to pick up my dress. Perhaps I should let you rest."

Doc was slowly regaining his composure as he said, "No, Wendy. You aren't interrupting anything. And yes, I did just get home about an hour ago." Then he noticed her looking at his wet T-shirt. "Oh, and sorry about this. I just spilled my soda on myself a moment ago. Sorry."

"Oh. I should apologize to you for that."

Doc looked confused. "Excuse me. What are you apologizing to me for?"

"For making you spill your drink. I saw you standing in the window when I was crossing the street. I waved and then you went to wave back. I think that is when you spilled the drink. So, you see it was partly my fault it happened."

Doc heard Martha say loudly, "Invite her in, Ted! I'll control this big goof. Invite her in!"

Then Doc heard Ed say, "I'd check her fingers first. If they look like she's used them to poke people before, I'd . . . OUCH! Hey! Don't let her in, Ted! OUCH! OUCH!"

Doc was faking a coughing fit in a veiled attempt to cover his laughing. His eyes were beginning to water, so he hastily wiped them again with the back of his free hand. "Would you like to come in, Wendy?"

Again Ed was heard. "Bad move, bro! Watch her hands. Be very afraid of her, OUCH!"

"Are you sure I'm not interrupting you?"

"No, not at all. Please. Come in."

She was so very pretty. The top of her head was even with his shoulders. She smiled and shyly looked up at his face as she stepped through the door. "Do you have something in your eyes?"

"Uh, no. Well, maybe. I must have gotten some soap in them when I was showering a minute ago. It will stop here in a minute."

Martha was heard saying, "Yes, Doc. It will stop now. Ed! Please! It's not funny. You'll ruin this for him. He's our friend. Okay?"

"Okay, okay. Sorry, Doc." After a second, Ed said calmly, "See. I stopped. So put down the finger and step away, miss. Step AWAY from the finger, lady!"

Doc's senses were on high power again, and he imagined Ed diving over the bed to escape Martha's outstretched finger.

Wendy had stopped just a few feet behind Doc, and she was slowly looking around the room. She hadn't noticed that Doc was still facing the open door, his shoulders shaking ever so slightly as he tried to keep from laughing out loud.

"I like your apartment, Ted. It's very well organized. I've never seen a man's apartment this clean. If I didn't know that you had a live-in girlfriend, I'd probably have thought that you were gay." Realizing what she had said, she immediately covered her mouth with one hand and turned to face Doc.

Doc stopped laughing the moment he heard her statement. He knew she was probably turning to look in his direction. He gently shut the door before he turned to face her. His mind was processing what she had said about him having had a live-in girlfriend. Odd, he didn't remember them ever discussing that sort of topic in their very brief encounters. In fact, that was exactly why he didn't know if she had a boyfriend or not. He wondered how she found out.

"I'm so sorry, Ted. I shouldn't have said that. That was a rude thing to say and so stereotypical. Sorry."

Doc smiled as he shook his head. "Don't worry about it, Wendy. I know what you meant. As a matter of fact, it's only clean because I had just cleaned it up the day before I was called out." He shrugged. "I just haven't been home long enough to mess it up. Come back in two days and I assure you it will look like every other guy's apartment you've seen." Then his eyes bugged out as he realized what he'd said, and the implication it carried.

"Oh, I didn't mean that like it sounded. Really! Now *I'm* sorry."

She was smiling, and her eyes shone in the sunlight streaming through his bay window. The edges of her hair caught the bright light and it formed a glowing halo. Doc couldn't help but think she looked like an angel.

"Ted, I know what you mean too." She had the sweet laughter of an innocent young girl. Their eyes locked as they took each other in. Doc opened his mouth to speak, but she suddenly turned and pretended to be surveying his apartment again.

"So, what you're saying is that I should memorize this clean apartment as it is now." She twisted her shoulders just enough to look over her shoulder before she added, "In case the next time I'm here, it isn't so clean. Huh?" Again, she smiled softly before she headed towards his desk.

He followed her, stopping just behind her left shoulder. He was looking at her profile as she surveyed the scattered books and files on the desk.

"I had heard that you were really into the Civil War." She glanced up over her shoulder at his face. "I see this was true, too. Looks like you're a very serious historian, or something." She then looked down at the desk again. Though focused on her head, sudden movement in Doc's peripheral vision drew his attention to the kids' door. Ed had just poked his head out through the door and turned to smile at Doc.

"He's something all right! But I didn't know you were a historian, Doc." Then Martha's hand popped through the door and grabbed Ed's hair to quickly pull his smiling face out of sight. "Hey! Careful with the hair, lady. You want to be dating a bald dead guy?" Then both were heard laughing.

Doc realized that he was actually getting used to the kids interacting with him as he talked to Wendy. He was concerned about keeping his conversations separated between the living and the dead. But now, in these last few minutes, he saw it was going to be okay. He breathed a soft sigh of relief. But just as he was having these thoughts, Wendy suddenly turned her head towards the kids' door. She paused as if she heard something. Before Doc could say anything, she asked, "Is that door a bedroom?" She turned to look him in the face. "You have a two bedroom apartment?"

"Yes. Don't you?"

"No. I wanted one, but I just finished college a year ago and couldn't afford it. I've only been at this job for a few months. Maybe later." She had gone back to looking at his desk.

Doc was wondering if she had really just noticed the kids' door, or if she had heard or sensed something. The kids were getting more and more emotionally charged in their cutting up. Could they be getting so excited that they would be visible to a normal person—like Wendy? He recalled that morning in the forest when they all caught the kids lying naked at the crash site. They were visible to his normal sight. Oh my God! What if that's going on now. How could he get their attention to settle them down?

Wendy picked up a photo from his desk and abruptly asked him, "Where did you get this?" She had turned to face him, and had the photo held out for him to see.

"Oh. I took that the last time I was in Gettysburg. Pretty, isn't it?"

She was slowly shaking the photo as she asked, "Are you saying you were out there? You took this picture yourself?"

"Ah, yeah. Why? Have you been there? Have you been to Gettysburg?"

She stood there silently, looking at him, then at the photo.

"So you know the Tolson family well enough for them to let you out there?"

"Wait a minute. You know the Tolson family too?" She nodded. "They don't just let anyone out there. It took me two and ½ years to talk them into letting me look around out there. So you must be family. Is your last name Tolson?"

She laughed as she returned the picture to his desk. "No, my last name is Elgend. I just know them."

"Well, you must know them very well if they let you go out there."

She again was facing him. They were standing closer than before.

"You know, Ted, it is a really small world. We both know them. Their daughter and I were roommates in college for four years. I've stayed at her house a lot of times. She and I used to ride horses all around out there. That's why I recognized that photo."

Doc was thinking that he may finally have met someone that could help him get onto the adjoining property as well. What a stroke of luck this could be!

"Wendy. Take a look at the pictures in the photo album on the top shelf." She pointed at it. "Yes. That's the one. Go ahead. Let me know if you recognize any of those photos." She took it down from the shelf, but looked up to smile at him before opening it. She froze as her eyes fell upon the very first picture, then her head snapped up to face him.

"You got to be kidding me! You've been over there too? How? When? I just don't believe it."

Doc realized he must have a serious look on his face right now. He didn't want to seem too eager, or she might stop talking. So he forced an improvised smile before he answered.

"So you recognize that place, too. Have you ever been over there?"

"Absolutely. Are you kidding me? I recognize that spot because Linda and I used to rest the horses up the hill in those trees. They overlook that entire area. But it's still a long ways away. I just can't believe you were over there. I thought the man that owned that land NEVER let anyone out there. EVER! Even Linda hadn't been near that barn. How'd you talk that man into letting you go out there?"

Doc was looking down at the book in her hand as he lightly bit his lower lip. "Well, to tell the truth, I haven't been over there either. And you are absolutely right about that man not wanting anyone out there. I've talked to him twice and the first time was not fun. But he was more forceful the second time and told me never to talk to him again. He was polite, but I realized there was no way he would ever say yes."

She asked, "So how did you get that photo? Did you get somebody that works there to take it for you?"

"I thought about it and actually approached one of the ranch hands in a bar one night. But he said 'NO' the minute I brought it up, and then he left. So I did the next best thing. I bought a long-range telephoto lens for my camera. Cost me $2500, but it was worth it. Especially since it seems that I'll never get to go over there for real."

"You paid that much for a long range lens just to take a picture of an old house and barn? Why?"

He felt a little embarrassed now because he couldn't tell her the truth. "Well, I have my reasons. But it's something I don't even discuss with my friends. Sorry. I hate to be evasive, but you have to understand that there are some things I just can't share with you at the moment."

She let her gaze linger on his eyes for a little bit before she smiled. "I understand. Really I do. If you think about it, we've talked more today than we have during our meetings in the hallway, elevators and parking garage combined. So we still don't know each other all that well." Then she inched just a little closer and looked up into his eyes. "But that could be remedied if you were so inclined to do so." Then she walked over to his big bay windows.

She spoke as she stood looking out the window. "You have a beautiful view of the entire street from here. I wish I had a bay window like this." She stepped closer to the center of the windowsill and looked both ways. "Wow! You can actually see both street corners if you stand right here."

Doc had slowly walked over to within a few feet of her before he had stopped. He looked at her and thought how pretty she was. Her eyes glowed with such an innocent little girl's joy of life that he found it hard to believe she was out of college.

"I agree. I've spent a lot of time standing right where you are now. Sometimes I'll watch the street come to life in the mornings. Other times I've stood there and watched it close down late at night." He was now standing only a few inches from her shoulder. "But my favorite time is around noon on Saturday. There are so many people going from shop to shop. There are some people that come walking from blocks away. They pass right by here, only to disappear a few blocks farther away." He paused. "Yes, I like this window very much."

They both stood in silence, each looking out the window with their own thoughts. Without looking at him, she quietly asked, "How bad was it up there in the mountains? If you don't mind me asking."

He hesitated to answer too quickly. "I've seen some bad things. Actually a lot of bad things. But none of them compared to what I saw up there. You expect to see death in a war zone, but not in a beautiful setting like that valley. It seemed so unreal. The first few hours were the absolute worst. We were running around and checking for any survivors. Of course we knew, before we even arrived, that there was absolutely no way anyone could have survived that impact. But you have to have hope. Right up till you check the last body. Then when all hope is gone, you're hit with the total loss of life all at once. It was hard to breathe at times."

He paused to rub one hand over his eyes, then mouth and finally let it fall from his chin. "So many lives snuffed out in what must have been one hell of a blinding explosion. Then you look around and realize that you are standing right in the middle of it. Plus you are going to be recovering all those bodies. One at a time, over several days." He paused and looked up to see the shocked expression on her face. "Oh Wendy. I'm so very sorry. I don't know what I was thinking. I just started talking and got carried away. I'm so very sorry."

She looked out the window for a second, then down at her shoes. "I can't imagine how bad it must have been. All of the things you've seen. I probably shouldn't have asked. You just got home and all cleaned up. You're ready to relax and clear your mind. Then here I come, grilling you about those silly photos before forcing you to think about things you certainly want to forget."

She turned to face him. "I'm really sorry, Ted. I saw you, and since I hadn't seen you for a while, I just wanted to say 'hi'. Really, that was all I wanted to do." Then she paused as she turned back to face the window. Slowly her eyes fell until she was looking at the floor. "But I have to admit that I *am* curious about the whole thing up in the mountains. But I shouldn't have brought it up. Sorry." She spun around and headed for the door with her head down.

He hesitated long enough for her to almost get her hand on the doorknob before he spoke. "Wendy. Wait. Please wait." He hurried over and they stood facing each other. With his hands stuffed deep into his pajama pockets, he looked down into her eager eyes. "It's okay to be curious. It's just human nature. But you're right about me just wanting to forget about it for a while." He leaned his head back and looked at the ceiling. "Look. This will sound very odd now." He pulled one hand out of a pocket and waved it towards where they had been standing by the windows. "After all that depressing talk over there. But I would like to do something you mentioned earlier. That is, if you really would like to."

She dropped her hand from the doorknob and scooted a little closer to him. "What did I mention earlier?"

"You said I could remedy our not knowing much about each other if I were so inclined. Remember?"

She had a youthful smile on her lips. "I think I *do* remember saying something like that."

"Well, I was thinking that when I get back, maybe you'd let me take you out for dinner one night. Or have a drink somewhere around here. You know. Some place quiet so we could talk." He was glad to see that her eyes were beginning to sparkle again.

"I'd like that, Ted. I think I'd like that a lot."

"Good. So I'll knock on your door when I get back, and we'll make plans." He was smiling again.

She reached up and opened the door. As she stepped through it, she asked, "Are they sending you out again so soon? When do you have to leave?"

"Oh no, they aren't sending me anywhere. I am taking some friends to Gettysburg to poke around for a week or so. It will help us get our minds off of what we saw in the mountains."

"So these friends were up there with you in the mountains?" He nodded. "Well, you all deserve the time off. That's for sure. When do you plan on leaving?"

"Well, was going to leave day after tomorrow, but just might leave tomorrow. They gave me two weeks off starting next Monday. So why wait?"

"Well, have fun, but I'd stay away from that land owner you mentioned. It doesn't sound like he's going to help you out. But, you never know. This could be your lucky trip!" She smiled as she said, "Bye, Ted. See you when you get back." Then she turned and quickly walked over to disappear through her door.

Doc just stood there for a moment and stared at her closed door. Then he heard Ed behind him.

"So, Doc, sounds like you're locked in for a dinner date with the hot chick next door. Way to go BRO!"

Doc closed his door and turned to find Martha also standing there.

"Doc, I heard what you told Wendy about being up there at the crash site. I have to tell you that I never thought about how you guys were dealing with all that you saw up there. As I listened to what you said, I suddenly felt ashamed that we were running around, laughing and carrying on like a couple of kids at a playground. You were doing such gruesome work and we were playing pranks on you. I'm sorry."

Doc shook his head "'NO! You and Ed have nothing to feel ashamed about at all. In fact, you both helped us all get through that ordeal more than you know."

Ed had a puzzled look on his face as he asked, "Uh, how exactly did we help?"

"Look. It was a very depressing place until we met you two. We all talked about how nice it was to see you two playing and chasing each other around. Bob could only see you, but he knew that you were both laughing. Vic and I could hear you. I admit that we did talk about the irony of it all."

Martha asked, "Irony? What do you mean?"

"Well, here we were, surrounded by death everywhere. There were so many lifeless forms. It was just too much to comprehend at times. We all found ourselves craving signs of life. Then there were these two spirits that were so full of childlike joy that it brought us a real sense of peace. You actually made it bearable for us." He paused, then began again. "I know you don't know why we called you the 'kids'. Do you?"

Ed hung his head. "I do. It's because I do stupid things like a big kid all the time. Right? Martha tells me that every chance she gets."

"Ed, that's not the reason at all."

Martha and Ed looked at each other before looking back at Doc.

"We were all talking one night back at the camp. You know that Bob has kids, right?"

Both Martha and Ed nodded 'yes'.

"Anyway, Bob made a comment about how depressed he had become before he became aware of you two. Then Vic said he actually liked listening to you both goofing off and laughing all the time. Said it made him feel better, but he wasn't sure why. Then Bob said he knew why. He told us that whenever he had a bad day, he would sit outside to watch and listen to his kids. They were so full of life and didn't have a care in the world. After watching and listening to them for a while, he always felt better. Vic finally said that you two were our kids up there and we all laughed. We referred to you as 'the kids' ever since.

"So you see, you helped us get through it. We even talked about how it was a shame that the other guys didn't get a benefit from your playing around. But then one day Vic mentioned something a logger told him. He said the guy had been very depressed at first. He said that things really turned around for him because Vic, Bob and I were always happy. And we were only happy because of you two. So we were affecting the others in a good way, and it was all because of you."

Martha and Ed stood there looking at Doc. Then Martha finally said, "I would never have thought of that, but it really makes sense in a way."

Doc and Martha both noticed that Ed's attention had turned to something beyond the bay windows. It was obvious by his expression that he wanted to go to that computer store across the street, but he seemed hesitant to ask. Martha smiled at Doc and then spoke to Ed's back. "Ed? I know you want to go. So go!"

Ed quickly turned to face her. He had a look of a small boy who was not sure if it was really okay for him to do something. Then she said, "Get out of here, you big goof. Go have some fun." A huge smile spread across his face. He started to turn to move towards the windows, but she grabbed his arm. Once he was looking her in the face, she said, "Don't get into any trouble." Then she set his arm free.

"I won't! Promise!" Free to go to his computer nirvana, he ran towards the windows. To their utter amazement, he just jumped through the glass and disappeared from sight.

Martha took a short quick breath as she said "Oh!" She and Doc both stepped quickly to the windows to look down. There was Ed's head and shoulders sticking out of the top of a parked car. He was looking back up at them and simply said, "Oops! Kind of overshot my landing." He then began to run over to the computer store door. Once there, he briefly turned to wave at them before he disappeared inside.

Doc started towards the kitchen, but stopped at the tile. "Martha, I'm getting something to drink. I wish I could offer you something."

"That's sweet of you, Doc, but really not necessary." She walked towards the desk and started looking at his pictures of Gettysburg. "Ed and I never even think about food or drink anymore. We did at first, but there isn't any urge to any more. So don't worry about it or us. We are fine. You need to just go about living just as usual. We are fine."

Doc was pouring another soda as he spoke. "You may not believe it, but it's really nice to have you two here in the apartment. I was really having a hard time being here alone. Just too many memories of Susan. I had even thought about moving to another apartment, but just couldn't bring myself to do it." With a new drink in his hand, he spoke as he strolled over to stand beside Martha. "I actually love this apartment. The view, everything."

She was studying each exposed picture. "So this is where we are going?"

"Yes, that one there is the place I have been. But, this one is where I'm really interested in getting to."

"Why? What's there? Or do you even know what's there?"

"No, I don't know what is there."

She was bent over looking at the pictures but looked up to ask, "So what do you *think* might be there?"

"Well, I don't really know. All I do know is that Mr. Gruber always returns to that building. And I can't get to it to see what he's doing inside."

She finally stood up and faced Doc. "So you think that

whatever he's doing there is important? Why?"

"Something is holding him back from moving on, and I just have a hunch that the answer is inside that barn."

"Maybe he always liked being in that barn. Maybe he has some fond memories of something that happened in there. It was a long time ago, wasn't it? I don't see how you'll ever figure that out."

"Well, that is where you and Ed come in."

"We do? How?"

"Since I can't get there, I was thinking that you and Ed could wander over there to look around for me. Maybe even talk to Mr. Gruber too."

"Oh, I get it! This sounds like fun. Of course we'll do that for you, Doc. But are you sure that Mr. Gruber will talk to us? Wait a minute. Are you even sure he'll see us?"

Doc had reached down and picked up a picture from the bottom of the stack and showed it to Martha. "This is a better shot of the barn. And YES, I am very sure he will see you. He sees all the spirits of the soldiers that died there. He sees them just like I do. When he's talking to me, he looks around at them and makes comments about them all the time."

"You said he thinks you're a ghost. Right?"

"Yes. He's mentioned that several times to me. He even asked me why I don't look like the others. That means that he sees a difference between me and them. But I never have understood why he can't tell that he is a spirit. At least not until I saw you and Ed."

The expression on Martha's face changed and she hesitated before asking. "What do you mean until you saw us? Do we look different to you than those soldiers and Mr. Gruber? I don't understand."

Doc was smiling at her as he spoke. "You don't realize how special you both are. The soldiers all look slightly less clear than does Mr. Gruber. It's very obvious that he is more closely tied to the living world than are those soldiers."

"Oh, so we look like Mr. Gruber? That's cool."

Doc slowly shook his head. "Well, actually, you and Ed are easier to see than even Mr. Gruber is. You're both much more well-defined in appearance than he is."

"So you're saying that Ed and I are more tied to the living world than he is? What's so special about us?"

"Well, Martha. The soldiers are not aware of anything around them. They are obviously only seeing things as they were in the battle, when they died. But Mr. Gruber sees and interacts with me, But like the other soldiers, he mostly only see things in terms of the timeframe in which he lived. I just know it. He can tell that I'm different. Which reminds me, he is probably going to mention your clothing. He asked me once why I was dressed so oddly. So he'll probably also notice and comment about how you two are dressed as well. So you just need to be prepared to tell him that you are from a long ways off. He accepted that answer from me. He's never asked about it again. But there are still several other things that I'm hoping to get a better understanding of when we get to Gettysburg. I'm very interested is seeing how Mr. Gruber reacts when he sees you two."

"Why? What do you think is going to happen? I'm getting kind of scared now. You don't think he will try to hurt us, do you? Is he mean?"

Doc chuckled. "No, he's not mean at all. He's been very polite in every encounter I've had with him. I bet he was a very nice man when he was alive. You're going to like him. Trust me."

"Doc, I *do* trust you. Very much."

"Good. And as far as what I think will happen - I believe he'll think that you both are alive like him. So all I want you to do is talk with him. Just like you do with me. But I don't want you to give him any reason to question what year it really is. His surroundings are mostly just as they've always been. He's there on land that he's always known. The structures there are the same, too. At least I guess so. He's never mentioned anything about them looking different."

Martha noticed that Doc had yawned twice now. "Doc. You look like you are getting tired. Maybe you need to go to sleep. Get some well-deserved rest, Doc. You need it."

Doc nodded 'yes' before speaking. "You're probably right, but I just hate to go to bed and leave you sitting all alone here. I was thinking that I'd just sit with you until Ed comes back. I don't want you to be alone, Martha."

Her eyes sparkled as she heard how her new friend really cared about her being left alone. "I'll be fine, Doc. Really! I'll just sit on the windowsill and watch the people go by until Ed decides to come home. Well, I mean back to your apartment, of course." She smiled and giggled a little. "If he doesn't come back soon, I'll go over there and see what he is doing. I just want to give him a little space to do his thing alone. He's talked a lot about the computer stores he liked to visit. He's happy right now, and I'm happy for him. You know Doc? I really love him."

"I know, Martha. I also know he really loves you, too. And that's another thing that makes you two so unique."

"Why would you say that, Doc? People fall in love all the time. Don't they?"

"That's right, Martha. But think about it. You and Ed didn't fall in love while you were living. You both have fallen in love in this in-between state you are existing in. You're aware of your situation and yet you both fell in love. You're doing the same things that living people do. Me and the guys discussed this very thing on several occasions. You two seem so alive, yet you're obviously spirits. You even know you are spirits. That's just incredible by itself. I know I keep saying this, but it is because of this very thing. I've seen and interacted with ghosts for years, from childhood to the present, yet I've never known any spirits like you."

Doc put his hand over his mouth as he yawned again. "Sorry, Martha. I think I need to take your advice. Look how quickly it's getting dark outside. I'm really getting tired. You sure you'll be okay alone here?"

She looked at him for a second before responding. "I wish that I had met Ed when I was alive. But I can touch him now and feel him holding me. It may sound odd, but I just wish I could have met you while I was alive, too. It would be nice to give you a hug." Her eyes opened wide as she realized what she'd just said, and how it may have sounded. "As a friend, you understand. I mean, hug you as a friend."

Doc laughed out loud as a large smile appeared on his face. "Of course I understand, Martha!" Then his smile softened and his demeanor changed to that of a close friend. "I also wish that I could have met you both while you were alive. You both seem like such pleasant people. Living or not, I am very glad to know you both."

He headed to his bedroom. "If you need me for anything, anything at all, you come wake me up." Before he closed his bedroom door, he tilted his head slightly to one side and said, "Please make yourself at home. I mean it now, anything at all. Good night, Martha."

She stood watching the people below as they moved along the well-lit sidewalks. Some were shopping, while others were out for an evening stroll after a fine meal in one of the local restaurants. There were the single people who tend to walk faster as if they were on a mission. Then there were the couples. Some of them also moved along quickly. However, many of the young couples seemed to wander aimlessly. They were in no hurry at all and either held hands or were locked arm in arm.

She felt her chest tighten as her tears blurred her vision. She was so happy to have found Ed and finally have the one thing she always wanted in life: a boyfriend. Still, it was hard not to envy these lucky couples enjoying each other's company on such a beautiful evening. How she wished that she and Ed could have met while alive. How much indeed she wished it had been so. They could have been one of the young couples below who appeared so happy and in love as they pretended to window-shop.

Her emotions continued to tighten her chest until the last tear was squeezed out to drop upon the windowsill. With eyes closed, she began to recall those fun filled days in the forest as they laughingly chased each other through the trees. How nice it had been when Ed held her as they lay on the snowy creek bank, in their private winter retreat, not feeling the cold. She remembered that beautiful evening when she and Ed had made love in the crash circle. She so vividly recalled Ed's face as he fell asleep with his head on her exposed breasts. It was a very special feeling that they both shared as they had climaxed before falling into a deep, trance-like sleep. It had been quite a shock when the guys had gotten there early that morning and caught them both in their naked glory. Embarrassed, yes! But there in her mind, she saw only Ed's sleeping face. It was forever etched in her memory and she would forever cherish it. With her eyes still closed, she softly called his name. "Ed."

"What? Why you whispering? Did Doc go to bed already?"

Hearing his voice, she looked up and saw him standing before her. Odd, she didn't even remember sitting down on the windowsill. How long had she been sitting there? It was totally dark outside now. The room was filled with a soft, romantic light. There were shadows that danced across the walls. She glanced outside to see the wind gently moving the trees' branches in front of the streetlights. Ed stepped closer and gently placed his big hand on her shoulder. She very slowly lifted her head to once again look at the man she most assuredly loved.

"Martha? You okay, baby? I didn't mean to wake you, but you called my name and I thought you were talking to me." His face displayed both compassion and concern for the woman he loved. "Guess you were dreaming, eh? Must have been about me, right?"

She watched as his face transitioned back to his usual happy smile. Before he could blink, she had stood up and stepped tightly against his chest. Two eager arms quickly wrapped around his neck to pull his head towards hers. A split second before their lips touched, she said, "Yes. It was definitely about you, Ed."

Ed was caught up in the emotion of the long, passionate kiss. It affected him like no other kiss before it. His knees became weak, and he actually wondered if he should sit down. That's when she pulled away and took his hand to lead him to the bedroom. She had a look in her eyes that he had never seen before. It was calm, yet filled with desire. She was walking backwards and pulling him along. He matched her stride and slid his arm around her waist as they began to slip through the closed door. The soles of their shoes were the last to be drawn through it. Ed's voice was heard as he asked, "Have you been drinking?" Then came the inevitable "Ouch!" followed by giggling.

• • •

The sun had been up for several hours when Doc finally emerged from his room. He walked in a blind daze straight to the kitchen and readied the coffee with both eyes barely open. With a slight wobble, he reached into a cabinet for a cup. Once in hand, he stood motionless as he strove to focus his eyes in the bright light pouring in through those massive bay windows. The sight of two months of bills neatly stacked on his counter reminded him of two great friends that he now owed big time: Mark and Cindy Salza. Mark was a fellow EMT who Doc worked with occasionally. Cindy was his very lovely young wife who volunteered to watch Doc's apartment and pay his bills for him while he was gone. Doc examined some of the signed checks, thinking 'Cindy signs my name better than I do.'

The Salzas were also the ones who brought Doc's SUV from the Army Reserve center to the airfield so he wouldn't have to catch a ride home. They were truly his closest friends. Since the coffee was going to take a few minutes, he decided to run down to the first floor and check his mailbox. Once in the hallway, he slowed down, hoping that Wendy might emerge and they could go down together. At the elevator, he hesitated for a few seconds before accepting that he would not be seeing her on this mail run. A quick push of a button and the doors slowly closed. He glanced down at his bare feet and recalled how she always told him he was going to catch a cold running around barefooted. The smile on his face was replaced by burning eyes from the bright light streaming in, as the doors opened on the first floor. His hand was practically covering both eyes so he didn't see the figure waiting to get on. The sudden bump of someone elicited his immediate 'Sorry' even though he had no idea who it was.

"How many times do we have to discuss this running around barefoot like a kid?"

He still couldn't focus, but a huge smile erupted across his face because he knew who it was. "Morning, Wendy! I was hoping I'd bump into you before I left."

"Well Ted, now you have. I will hold the elevator if you promise to hurry."

His eyes had focused enough now and he jogged over to the panel. A flip of the wrist and his hand dove into the box for his mail, the little door slamming shut a few seconds later. She was shaking her head and staring at his bare feet as he hopped into the elevator.

"So you were hoping to see me this morning? I was hoping the same, but I overslept. Thought for sure that you were up early and gone as usual."

He laughed, "Must be something in the water. I overslept too."

"Have you decided when you're leaving for Gettysburg?"

"I think I have. I'll probably sleep, off and on, the rest of the day. That means I'll be wide-awake at midnight. So I figure I'll just drive through the night and most of the day tomorrow. I'll stop at a motel late tomorrow evening. This way, I'll be tired enough to go to sleep at a regular time. It will let me get my days and nights back in sync before I hit Gettysburg the next day."

"That's a long road trip, Ted. You don't want to push it and have an accident."

"I've driven out there twice a year for the past few years. I'm used to it. I'll be fine. Really."

They paused at her door. "Well, I'll say a prayer for you to catch that land owner in a good mood. Maybe you can check out that mystery barn you seem so interested in. Good luck and drive careful."

"I'll see you when I get back, Wendy."

He found himself standing there and staring at her closed door for a few seconds before he turned to his own door. The aroma of fresh-brewed coffee hit him the moment he entered his apartment, pulling him into the kitchen. As he closed his eyes to savor that first sip of the day, the ringing of the phone startled him.

In his hurry to answer so the kids would not be awakened, he dropped it. A voice was heard saying 'Hello? Hello?' as the phone bounced from the counter to the floor. In a feeble attempt to trap it with his foot, he not only hung up but also sent it sailing across the floor and under the kitchen table. 'Damn, damn, damn,' he muttered as he slid on his pajama knees and hit the table's metal chairs just a little too hard. With both hands, he quickly grabbed them to stop the noise. He sat for a moment and listened for any evidence that the kids may have heard him. Whoa, he thought. That was close. He slipped one foot through the chair legs and flipped the phone with his toes. He sighed, thinking how lucky he was that the kids hadn't heard him.

"What are you doing in here, Doc? Playing soccer with that phone?"

Doc looked up from the floor to see Ed standing at the tiles edge with Martha a few feet behind him on the carpet. "Oh. You heard that? Sorry."

Ed snickered as he spoke, "Are you serious? Everyone in the building heard that."

Martha moved to Ed's side. "Did you fall, Doc? Are you okay?"

"Oh no. I didn't fall."

She noticed his overturned cup and the coffee dripping over the counter's edge. "Doc! Look! I'd clean it up for you if I could, but . . . "

"Damn, damn, damn." He leapt to his feet and laid the phone on the counter's edge to pick up a towel. No sooner had he begun to mop up the coffee than the phone rang again, so he reached for it, only to have it slip out of his hand. He tried to stop its fall with a knee and then a foot. This sent it bouncing off the cabinet door and back between his feet. Of course it was once again headed for the chairs. He was determined not to have it end up under that table again, so he repeated his slide to stop it. His foot flipped it out onto the carpet as he said, "Not again you little bastard!"

So there he was, lying spread out on the kitchen floor, staring up at two ghosts who looked totally bewildered as they shook their heads in amazement. All the time, a voice from the still-spinning phone was saying, "Hello? Hello? Doc? You there, man?"

Martha leaned over the phone. "Hey that's Vic! Hello Vic! It's Martha. Doc's tied up. Can you hear me Vic? Vic?"

Doc was flat on the floor, but his head was lifted so he could see her. "Martha! He can't hear you."

"But he hears me all the time."

"Trust me on this. It doesn't work over the phone. Just like I can see you, but not in a mirror. Get it?" Then he yelled out loud, "Vic, I'll call you back in a few minutes man. Okay?"

Vic replied, "Ok Doc. I'm at home." Then a dial tone filled the air.

Still bent over the phone, Martha said, "Bye, Vic" to the dial tone.

Ed watched her do that before he looked over his shoulder at Doc. "That was a really good save there, Doc. You sure you never played soccer?"

Doc grunted "No!" before his head hit the tile floor. "Ouch."

It took Doc a few seconds to regain his composure and get to his feet. He walked over to retrieve the phone before cleaning up the coffee.

At last, he and the traveling phone sat down in a kitchen chair, his head in one hand while the other hand's thumb pushed the redial button.

"Hi, Vic. Yes, I'm okay. No, everything is okay. I just spilled my coffee and then I dropped the phone."

Martha knelt down so she could look into his face. "Tell him I said hi!" Doc nodded that he would.

"Martha says hi, too. What? Well actually I have. I plan on leaving around midnight tonight. Why? I thought this way, I wouldn't have to worry about people seeing me talking when there was nobody in the car but me. Yes, I thought that was a good idea too. You are? So when are you taking her to the airport? Really? Of course you're welcome to come along. In fact, I'd really enjoy the help driving. Plus the kids will be glad to see you. What? Bob wants to go. Are you kidding me? Of course he's welcome to come along too. I can't believe his wife is letting him come. His wife talked to your girlfriend? Oh, I see. Well that's great! We'll all be there together. This will be fun. Sure, man. I'll swing by and pick you up first, and we'll get Bob on the way out of town. That's perfect. See you around midnight. Tell Bob we should be at his place about 30 minutes later. See you then, Vic."

Doc hung up the phone and poured a fresh cup. The kids waited until he was sitting at the table, coffee in front of him. Martha asked, "Do you want us to let you be alone for a while? You seem like you're not awake yet."

"No, I'm fine. I'm just having a hard time getting going this morning. I still can't believe that I slept so long. I'm usually up around 5:00 in the morning."

Ed said, "Doc. You've been under a lot of pressure for quite a while. It was your first night back in your own bed. I'm surprised you were up before we were."

Martha slipped her arm under Ed's. "So it sounded like both Bob and Vic are coming along too. Right?"

"Yep. It's going to work out really good this way. With three of us to take turns driving, we'll be able to make really good time. It'll be safer too."

She asked, "So are you going to be able to go back to sleep after drinking that coffee?"

"I probably could the way I feel, but I thought I'd sit and watch some television for a bit. I won't last long, I know. I'll be back in bed in an hour or so."

"Well, Doc. Ed and I were thinking about going for a walk down the street. You know, just to look around. He's seen all he wants at the computer store and I want to get out for a while. Do you mind?"

Doc sat up. "I think that's a great idea. There are a lot of nice things to see around here. If you go to the right, there is a huge public park only seven blocks away. There are paths all through the trees. There must be ten different playgrounds over there. There are always lots of families with kids there. If you stay on the main path, you'll pass by two ponds. Each one is different but they both have fountains shooting water more than 20 feet in the air. At night, there are underwater lights. It's very romantic and very pretty. You'll like it."

She smiled and patted Ed's arm. "That sounds wonderful. But how will we know when to come back? Neither of us have a watch."

"Not a problem. The park closes at 10:00 on weekdays. A cop on horseback comes through the park around then to make sure everyone has left. Plus they turn off the lights in the ponds. If you come back to the street then, you'll see a big clock on a light pole in the middle of each block. You can walk around all you want and know what time it is. Now go enjoy yourselves."

The kids started making their way to the bay window. Doc watched them as Ed put one arm around her waist and she grabbed hold of his outstretched hand. Then he counted 'one, two, three' before he lifted her just enough for them both to hop through the window and drop out of sight.

Doc's curiosity got the best of him, so he sprinted over to the window and looked down. There on a busy sidewalk, with people walking all around them, were two spirits. Ed was holding her waist on both sides as she clapped her hands, jumping up and down like a little girl. She was so proud of herself. She finally hopped right up on him and wrapped both legs around his waist. They were kissing as he slowly turned her in circles.

Doc felt himself getting choked up as he watched them. He was so happy that they had found each other and were obviously very much in love. He wished he could find what they had. He eventually found himself wondering if he would even be willing to die to have it.

Once Ed had lowered her to the sidewalk, they both looked up and waved at him. He gave them a thumbs-up and pointed in the direction of the park. Once they were out of sight, he collapsed into his favorite chair to watch some TV.

Chapter 15

ROAD TRIP TO GETTYSBURG

DOC WAS WIDE-AWAKE after his shower. His bags were packed and waiting at the front door. He was actually 20 minutes ahead of schedule. As a reward, he was enjoying a fresh cup of coffee while standing in his favorite spot by the bay windows. There were only four late window shoppers meandering along the sidewalk below. It was odd that he hadn't seen the kids yet. Oh well, let them be late. They deserved some free time to act as if they were still alive. He smiled at the thought of Martha getting to walk along the street with Ed.

His mind drifted from thoughts of the kids to thoughts of his beautiful neighbor Wendy. It seemed so long since Susan had left him. Why had he been so hesitant to talk to Wendy? He had always found her very attractive, and her innocent air drove him wild. Still, he had resisted doing more than casually talking to her during their chance meetings around the building. He looked out the windows again, but saw nothing. His mind was replaying Susan's leaving, then his mobilization to the crash and meeting his new spirit friends. Then it dawned on him that it had taken all of these massive events to bring him to the point to where he was ready to ask Wendy out. The passage of time was amazing, the way it took your life in one direction or another.

His senses picked up the faint sound of the kids talking. His impulse was to look out the windows and look both ways, but they were nowhere to be seen. Then it dawned on him that they were in the hallway. He turned to greet them as they strolled right through the closed door. They were locked arm in arm and looked incredibly happy. He took his last sip of coffee just as the kids came to a complete stop just a few feet from him.

Martha said, "Doc. You look rested. Are we late?"

"Nope! You're actually a bit early. Looks like you both had fun."

Martha leaned her head on Ed's shoulder and smiled. "See you have another cup of coffee."

Ed couldn't resist. "So, Doc? Have you been kicking the phone around any more? Like practicing?"

Doc grinned at Ed. "Very funny, dude."

Martha asked, "Are you packed and ready?"

Doc nodded in the direction of his bags.

The kids glanced at them, then Ed excitedly said, "Oh no! Martha, we still have to pack!"

"That's right, Ed. Sorry Doc, it will just take us a second." Then the kids both started giggling and made faces at each other.

"Ok, you two lovebirds. I think we need to get going." He rinsed out the coffee cup in the kitchen sink and looked around the apartment to make sure the lights were all turned off before he picked up his bags. Once they were in the hallway, he intentionally slammed the door hard enough to shake the wall. He was trying to nonchalantly peek at Wendy's door.

Martha said, "That was a little loud. Are you in a hurry now, Doc?"

Ed had noticed where Doc was looking. "Or are you just trying to wake up your neighbors? Like Wendy?"

He coughed before he turned and walked quickly towards the elevator. "Come on. We have a long trip ahead of us."

Doc was not talking, and the kids were still holding on to each other as they had been all day. Ed suggested they get into the very back seat and leave the front ones for Bob and Vic. It took only a minute to exit the parking garage and pull into the desolate street.

The kids looked from side to side as they zipped past the neighborhood shops. Martha again laid her head on Ed's big shoulder. "I had a wonderful time today, Ed. I wish it could have lasted forever."

"Me too, baby. It was such a beautiful day out. I feel so relaxed. I feel, uh, well . . . almost normal."

Martha looked at Doc's reflection in the rear view mirror. "Thanks, Doc. That park was lovely. You are so lucky to live in such a beautiful place."

"I knew you'd like it. Susan and I used to go there all the time. Well, at first we did."

Nothing else was said all the way to Vic's place. He was standing outside waiting for them when they pulled up. Doc pushed a button and the SUV's back door lifted automatically so Vic could load his bags in the back. As the door lowered, Vic saw Doc pointing to the front passenger seat. A second later, he was buckled up as Doc drove away.

Vic nodded at Doc, but spoke over his shoulder, "Hi Martha, Ed. How was Doc's apartment?"

Ed let Martha do the talking all the way to Bob's house. They saw two figures on a porch halfway down the block. It was Bob and his wife, saying goodbye. With one final, quick kiss, he picked up his bag and loaded it next to Vic's. He waved at the kids in the back as he opened the rear passenger-side door. "Hi, guys! Martha. Ed." Just as before, Doc accelerated from the curb. Bob waved one final time to his wife and then snapped his seat belt closed.

Vic commented, "So we're off on a road trip to Gettysburg."

The next few hours were full of friendly chatter about a myriad of topics. Bob filled everyone in on his family's activities. Martha listened intently to all his talk about his kids. She never said anything, but Ed could tell that she was sad at one point, and was probably thinking how nice it could have been to have kids of their own. He knew he was right when she suddenly grabbed his arm before closing her eyes and leaning against his shoulder. He found it odd that he again felt sad because Martha was obviously sad. He hated it when she got this way, so he did the 'Ed' thing and said something stupid that made all the men laugh. Of course, Bob kept asking Vic what was so funny, which was always good for an extra round of laughing. As always, Vic finally told Bob and he laughed too.

Then Vic took his turn talking about everything his girlfriend and he had done, and how good it felt to be home. It was all light-hearted conversation until he admitted that he had a terrible dream last night. He had woken up in a cold sweat, and later, his girlfriend found him sitting in the dark. It took her a while to talk him into coming back to bed. Bob asked what the dream was about, but all Vic would say was that he was glad they were driving to Gettysburg. Everyone in the car realized that the dream must have been about the crash site. This triggered a long period of silence, with everyone lost in their own thoughts as they looked out the windows.

Doc noticed the lapse in the conversation, so he asked Martha to tell everyone about her day in the park with Ed. He couldn't see her face, but he knew she was smiling as she spent almost an hour telling them about it. Vic was keeping Bob informed at selected intervals so he knew what she was saying. After she had finished, she too fell quiet.

The silence didn't last long before Ed started telling the guys about Doc's love life and his crush on his neighbor Wendy. It didn't matter that he was making most of it up, because what he was saying was so funny. There were several times that the male laughter became incredibly loud and Martha had to get them to settle down. Ed only waited a minute before he switched topics, telling them about Doc's soccer abilities with a phone. This again led to some hilarity that even Martha couldn't stop. She realized that the male hormones in the car were beyond her control, and simply chose to let them die down by itself. The car full of friends finally fell silent and there wasn't a dry eye in the car. Each one, living or dead, had eventually wiped their eyes from having laughed so hard.

Then came the inevitable need for fuel and a pit stop, so everyone could stretch their legs. With all eyes on the exits, one was targeted. Doc followed the white line off the main highway to the access road. As they arrived at the gas station, they realized there was a line of vehicles waiting for every pump. So Doc took the number three spot on a pump by the side of the building. It was the typical 'Gas and Snack' convenience store that now dot the highways. Doc suggested they all get out and walk around, since he was the only one that needed to stay in the vehicle, but they all stayed as well.

Martha looked around. "This place is out in the middle of nowhere. It just looks scary here. I'd never be able to work in this place. I'd just be too afraid that it would get robbed. In fact, I'm kind of scared, even though I'm here with four big guys who would protect me." She smiled at them all.

The passenger side of the SUV was facing the building. Bob's attention was on two young men who were loitering just at the edge of the store windows. He was squinting because he had a hard time focusing on the two. "Hey, guys. Do those two dudes by the corner of the building look like they're up to no good to you?"

Vic immediately said, "What guys by the corner? The far corner?"

Doc said, "No, he meant this corner, Vic. You can't see them because they are spirits."

Ed chimed in. "Look Martha, ghosts! Now you have a real reason to be afraid. WOOOOOOOOO!" Of course, she slapped his arm.

Bob commented, "That explains it. At first, I just thought I couldn't see them clearly because of the poor lighting over there. But I can tell you're right now that you mention it. Wow!" He looked at Doc. "Am I going to start seeing ghosts everywhere now? I don't know if I'm going to like this at all." Then he turned to face the kids. "Sorry. I didn't mean you." He knew they understand because both of them nodded that it was okay.

Vic rolled down his window and leaned his head out a bit. "They're talking about the guy behind the counter being alone. But I see several people in there, and it's a woman behind the counter."

Doc spoke up. "Ok. Here's what's going on and what's probably about to happen. They are spirits and are stuck here at this place. They are reliving a traumatic event in which they were probably killed. They see the guy that was here on the real night this happened. However, since we don't see that guy's spirit, I would say that he lived or died later at the hospital. But from their perspective, they see him. They are like so many ghosts that met a very sudden and violent end. They get stuck in an endless rerun of the events that led to their death."

Martha said, "You mean they're doomed to repeat this over and over forever? How dreadful!" She sat up with her elbows on her knees, holding her hands over both sides of her face as she watched them.

Doc continued, "I'm afraid so, Martha. I've seen this a thousand times since I was a kid. Anyway. You're going to find this very interesting. When they go in there, you have to remember that we'll only see half of what happened that night. They won't see those people that are really in the store at all."

Vic spoke. "Damn it. I wish I could see what you all are seeing. I know what you must feel like now, Bob. Just getting half of what's going on all the time." He totally shocked everyone as he suddenly released his seat belt, opened the door and got out.

After shutting it, he talked to them through the window. "I can only hear them talking, so I'm going inside to listen to them when they come in." He quickly walked towards the building.

Martha screamed out the window at him. "Vic. No! Come back, Vic. Come back!" Then she turned to Doc. "You have to make him get back in the car, Doc. I don't want him to get hurt. Get him back in the car! Please, Doc."

She was obviously very upset at the thought of her friend walking into this mess. Ed wrapped his arm around her shoulders and pulled her tight against his chest. "It's okay, baby. Vic will be okay. Promise! You have to remember those two guys are just ghosts. Like you and I. They can no more hurt him than we could. Shhhhhh. Okay?"

Bob couldn't hear how upset Martha was. He was fixated on Vic walking towards the building. Even though he knew the two guys were just ghosts, he instinctively placed his hand on the door handle. Then he released his seat belt as his friend passed by the two ghosts at the corner. Vic walked into the store and pretended to be looking at the candy rack just opposite the cash register.

Doc said, "Ed's right, Martha. Vic is in no danger at all. He'll be fine."

Then Bob blurted out, "Oh shit! Look, they have guns. Both of them! And there they go."

Martha again started screaming. "Doc! They have guns! Do something! Ed!"

Ed had a hard time holding her still.

The two spirits rushed into the store and passed right through the first few people standing in line. They stopped a few feet from the counter and appeared to be pointing their guns at the woman behind the cash register. Evidently, Vic heard Martha screaming and he took a few steps towards the door. This put him right in front of one of the gunmen just as he fired his pistol. Everyone in the car saw the puff of ghostly smoke from the barrel and then saw Vic disappear as if he had fallen to the floor. Martha Immediately started screaming again, louder than anyone thought possible. Doc and Ed were both wide-eyed at what they had just seen.

Bob reacted by yanking the door handle up, a split second later he was in an all-out run into the store. Doc's expression indicated that he wasn't really sure what had happened either. The shooter's shirt turned red in the middle of his chest as he flew backwards and disappeared through a snack rack. The other gunman fired his pistol twice. Then he dropped his pistol and grabbed his right thigh. He held his other hand up and started backing out the door. He walked backwards right through the same three people that he had passed through while entering. He stopped after stepping onto the asphalt and he raised both hands straight up. He was still holding that right leg a little off the ground, balancing on the tip of his shoe. Then he doubled over as both hands grabbed at his chest. The back of his shirt turned red in two spots before he fell down.

Bob hopped over the ghost on the ground and yanked the door open wide before rushing inside. Everyone in line froze and looked at Bob due to his dramatic entrance. That's when Bob saw Vic on one knee.

Vic was picking up the change that he had dropped on the floor a moment ago. Even Vic was surprised at Bob rushing in as if in a panic. He looked at Bob and simply asked, "What?"

Bob now realized that he'd made a very big scene and was being stared at by everyone. All he could think to say was, "Men's room!"

Vic, everyone in line and even the woman at the cash register all pointed to the back of the store. They said in unison, "Back there!"

Martha was still screaming, her hands over her face.

By now, Doc was entirely confused by what he'd seen. When everyone pointed to the rear of the store, Bob took off running again. Doc mumbled out loud to himself, "Ok. I'm really confused. Where the hell are you going now, Bob?"

At this moment, Vic came back into view as he stood up. He leaned around a rack to watch Bob. Again, Doc talked out loud to himself.

"Ok! That's better. Welcome back, Vic!"

Hearing Doc say Vic's name, Martha immediately sat up and looked inside the store. Her eyes were so teary she couldn't see Vic clearly. Again, she let go of a

Blood-curdling scream. "Oh no! Vic is a ghost now! NO! NO! He can't be dead! I told you not to go, Vic! No!"

Ed took his eyes off her long enough to look into the store. He saw Vic clearly and didn't understand what she was talking about. He looked at her, then Vic, then back at her. That's when he noticed that her eyes were completely covered with tears.

"Baby. Shhhhh. Vic is fine. Wipe your eyes and look again. He's fine. Shhhhh, baby Come on, Martha. Calm down and look."

She wiped her eyes and looked at Vic. He was paying for his candy. With that done, he slowly walked back out to the car. As they watched Vic cross the parking lot to the SUV, Ed said, "Look. The dead ghost is gone."

Vic was almost to the door when he stopped. The car in front of Doc was driving away. Doc moved up to the pump and got out. Vic walked around to Doc's side of the SUV to talk to him.

"What the hell was up with Bob? He came busting into the place as if he was going to rob it. Scared the HELL out of everyone! Is he sick or something?"

Doc was stepping around Vic as he hurried to get the pump's nozzle into the SUV. He didn't answer Vic. Instead, he picked up the squeegee and headed for the windshield. That was when Martha leaned against the window and started talking very loudly.

"We love you, Vic. So glad you are all right! Very glad you are okay, Vic!"

Vic took a bite of his candy bar as he leaned down so he could see what the kids were doing. Confused by what Martha had said, he pointed the remains of his candy bar at Doc's SUV before he spoke.

"What was all that about? Did I miss something when I was inside?"

Doc chuckled as he finished cleaning the windows. There was nothing left to do but wait for the pump to shut off, so he leaned against the side of the vehicle and ran his hands through his hair. "Can't talk here. Too many people around. I'll tell you when we get back on the road."

Vic nodded and leaned back against the pump. "I thought I'd eat this candy out here. It just doesn't seem right eating stuff in front of the kids when they can't have any. I know. I know. I'm just being weird, right?"

Doc nodded that he understood what Vic felt. He stepped back and leaned against the other side of the pump. His arms were crossed and his eyes were fixed inside the store. "You know, if Bob doesn't come out by the time the pump shuts off, one of us will have to go get him." Both men stood silently as they watched for any sign of Bob inside the store. Just as the pump shut off, Bob walked out. He had waited as long as he could so it would appear that he just really needed to go to the men's room.

The click of the pump shutting off got the two men moving. Vic headed around to the other side of the car and got in. Doc barely had the gas cap door shut before Bob opened his door to get in. The moment everyone's seat belts were secure, Doc accelerated out of the parking lot and back onto the highway.

Martha again told Vic she was so very glad he wasn't hurt. Doc began to fill Vic in on what all transpired from their point of view in the car. After he heard the entire story, Vic spoke to the kids over his shoulder. "I'm sorry I upset you, Martha. It wasn't my intention. I just wanted to hear what was going on. I wouldn't have gone in if I had of known what it would put you through. Really sorry, Martha."

"That's okay, Vic. I know you didn't do it on purpose, silly. I am just so very thankful that you are okay. I was so worried about you. You are my friend. You all are our friends. And we love you. You are being so nice to us and trying to help us." Then she leaned forward even though she knew Vic couldn't see her. "Just don't do that ever again, mister. If I wasn't already dead, you'd have scared me to death!" She started to nervously giggle at what she had just said.

Ed commented, "Well you really had me worried, babe."

She smiled and said, "You worry about me because you love me. Don't you?"

Ed got his goofy smile back as he quickly replied.

"Well actually, it dawned on me that all of your screaming might draw the attention of those two ghosts with the guns. You see, I still have my wallet in my pants. So they are robbers and I am thinking, damn, I have GHOST MONEY!"

Vic was the first to laugh, and the entire vehicle quickly erupted into deafening laughter. Ed's joke was the perfect catalyst for them all to release their intense emotions of the past few minutes. It took several minutes for the car to finally fall silent. Each individual was replaying the gas station scene over and over in their minds.

Martha broke the silence with a comment. "I know that those two guys were doing wrong by robbing that store, but I can't help feeling sorry for the guy that was killed in the parking lot. It just didn't seem right somehow."

Vic said, "Who was killed in the parking lot? What didn't seem right?"

Bob told Vic, "The guy that fired first was killed inside. The other guy was hit in the leg and dropped his gun. It looked like he put up his hands and backed out the door. He had both hands high in the air when he was shot twice in the chest."

Ed said, "I know what you mean baby, but they shot at that guy behind the counter. And as far as we know, he was hit and bleeding. You don't know if he thought he was dying or what. I'm not saying it was right, but I could understand why he shot that guy."

She said, "But he had his hands up. He didn't even have a gun any more. Remember?"

Bob spoke up. "Well it could have just been adrenaline and the heat of the moment. In combat, I've seen guys still shooting dead guys. They'd empty their entire clip of ammo before they'd stop. Right, Doc?"

Doc nodded. "Yep, I've seen that too. But I think I agree with Martha. That guy did have his hands straight up in the air. I don't think I'd have been able to do it. Not like that."

Nothing else was said for a while. Just like with everything else in life, when you have a group of people, there will be differing opinions. They were all good people and all good friends. Their silence was their way of agreeing to disagree.

Eventually, everyone except Doc was asleep as the car sped through the night. Doc was amazed how quickly they had all nodded off. He felt sure it was due to their recovering from the intense scene at the gas station. Or, perhaps it was just the early morning hours taking a toll on everyone. It didn't really matter since he was wide-awake and enjoyed the silence. He loved being on the road at night, particularly when he was headed to his dream location, Gettysburg. He relived every encounter he had ever had with the spirits there. He especially liked thinking about the possibility of helping Mr. Gruber, since he now had Ed and Martha to help. He intentionally let the gas gauge go much lower than he usually would have. Everyone was sleeping so soundly that he didn't want to wake them by stopping again for gas. Finally, they all were awakened by the early morning sunlight that came in through the windows.

"Morning," was the comment of each passenger as they opened their eyes and began to stretch. Doc started tapping on his GPS unit to find the nearest gas station. Once they had arrived, Bob and Vic went inside to the men's room. Martha and Ed took the opportunity to walk around the parking lot while Doc filled up. With everything done, he started walking towards the men's room himself. Vic and Bob met him at the store entrance.

"Hey, Doc. Why don't you let one of us drive for a while? You get in the back and get some shuteye."

Doc took a deep breath. "Sounds good." He tossed the keys towards Bob, but Vic snatched them out of the air. "Me first!"

Vic had the SUV pulled up by the store's front door when Doc came out. The kids had freed up the back bench seat by moving up to the two middle seats. Martha gladly hopped into Ed's lap when Doc opened the side door. Once he closed it behind him, he slipped into the very back seat. Ed acted as if he wasn't going to let her get out of his lap, but she wiggled free and took her place in the other seat. Vic commented, "I have this same GPS unit."

A few moments later, the car was up to speed on the highway

and Doc was asleep in the back. His last words had been, "Seriously. Play the radio. It will not bother me in the least. Let Ed and Martha listen to whatever they want. All of you talk and have a good time. Road trips are supposed to be fun. So have some." Then he closed his eyes and was out.

Vic and Bob were amazed at the affect the music was having on the kids. Martha was practically dancing in her seat half the time. As always, Ed would periodically say something so hilarious that they would all laugh for a while. Doc never moved at all. They finally lost the radio station that had been playing dance music, and all they could find to replace it was a smooth jazz station. The mood in the car switched to a more mellow atmosphere. That was when Ed saw a sign.

"Wow. We are only 45 miles from where I used to live. It's odd, I never came into the area from this direction. I don't recognize anything."

Martha asked Vic, "Hey. Let's go by where Ed lived. I want to see it. Okay?"

Ed started shaking his head. "No, No let's don't. There isn't anything to see there. Nah, let's just keep driving. Besides we'll lose two hours or more if we do that."

Once Vic filled Bob in on what Martha wanted to do, Bob said, "Sounds good to me. I don't think Doc will mind."

Vic commented, "It's really not that far. We have all week or even more if we want. Are you sure you don't want to go, Ed?"

Martha looked at Ed and became very quiet. "Oh, I'm sorry, Ed. If you don't want to go by there, I think I understand. I wasn't thinking baby. I just thought it would be fun to see where you lived."

Ed chuckled a little. "No, it isn't anything like that, Martha. It won't bother me to go there. It's just that there really isn't anything to see. It's not as pretty as where Doc lives. But if everyone wants to go by, sure. Let's go."

Though Doc was still lying down and out of sight, his voice was clearly heard. "Good. We're all in agreement. Let's go see Ed's old stomping grounds. We all need to get out and walk around anyway. It'll be fun. Vic knows how to put your address into the GPS, so no problem. I'm just going to close my eyes until we get there."

Martha was visibly excited about visiting Ed's home town. Ed began describing the area. Before they knew it, they were stopping in front of his building.

Ed just stepped right through the door and onto the sidewalk before Vic had even put the car in Park. Martha did the same and held his hand while they waited for the others to get out. Ed commented, "I never noticed that there were parking spots right here in front of the building. But then again, I didn't have a car."

Vic locked the SUV and tossed the keys in Doc's direction, but Bob intercepted them in midair. "Nope! I'm next. Sorry, Doc, but you drove all night. I know you're tired because you didn't even wake up when we stopped to get gas that last time."

Doc just mumbled as he stretched and rubbed his eyes. "I feel fine. Just don't drive like you do when I ride with you. You'll scare the hell out of everyone."

It was an old three-story building with stairs instead of an elevator. Ed led them to the second floor. They followed him down the hall to an open door and a strong smell of fresh paint. Ed pointed inside. "Well, this is it. But it looks like somebody took everything." They all stepped inside the empty apartment, but nobody was there. Ed commented, "Looks like the workmen are on a break."

Martha smiled and patted Ed on his belly. "Sorry, hon. I know you wanted to see your old stuff. I would."

"You know, I thought that too when we first decided to come here. But not now." Ed pulled her hand up to his lips and kissed it. "I have you now. Nothing else matters anymore. All I need is you."

She quickly pulled him close and kissed him on the mouth before she said, "Don't you ever forget that, either mister. EVER!"

The three men had started looking around. It was a good-sized, two-bedroom apartment. Bob said, "Wow, Ed. You had a lot of room here. Nice place."

Suddenly Ed released Martha's hand and walked over to where Doc was standing. He turned around to look at the open door then turned back and pointed down at the doorframe.

"Quick Doc. Push that piece of the baseboard. Do it kind of hard, like you were pushing a button to get it to pop out."

Doc knelt down and did it. The piece of molding popped off then fell to the floor. There was an old cookie tin stuffed into the wall. Everyone heard footsteps coming down the hall towards them. Doc grabbed the tin box and quickly put the molding back in place. He barely had enough time to stand back up before an old man walked in through the open door.

"What are you three doing in here? Who are you? What do you want?"

Ed and Martha moved behind Doc, and Ed whispered into Doc's ear. "Don't worry, Doc. I'll tell you whatever he asks about."

Then Doc stepped towards the old guy. "Well sir. I'm Ted and I came by to see my friend Ed. Did he move? I don't remember him saying anything about moving."

The old man's head dipped a little as he now believed that Ted didn't know yet what had happened to Ed. "Son, I am so sorry to tell you this. But Ed was killed in a plane crash a few months ago. I'm really sorry."

Doc put on a very convincing act as he closed his eyes for a second, then stared at the old man. "What do you mean he was killed? What plane? Are you sure?"

The old man stepped closer and took Ted's hand. "I'm sorry, son. I didn't mean to just blurt it out like that. I just didn't know how to tell you. I'm sorry."

Ted slipped his hand free from the old man and patted him on the shoulder before he turned to walk towards the windows. He stood there for a second and started talking while he looked out the window. "Dead? I just can't believe it. I knew he hadn't been on his computer for quite a while. But DEAD? Wow! Last time I talked to him, he was so excited about going to a convention somewhere." Then he snapped his fingers and spun around quickly to face the old man again. "That's right. He was going to a gaming convention but I couldn't go. I forgot all about that. My company sent me out of town. Man, I just can't believe it."

Doc stepped a little closer to the old guy and showed him the old tin box in his hand. "I found this at a flea market when I was on the road. I knew he had one just like it. He always said he'd like to have another one, so I bought it for him. We were driving by here on our way to Gettysburg and I thought I'd stop by to surprise him with it."

The old man was looking closely at the tin box. "You know, son? I remember seeing a box just like that on his desk once. You must have known him well. Do you know how to get in touch with any of his next of kin? I can't find anyone. I stored all his belongings in the basement until they could come get it."

Doc shook his head. "Well, he was an only child. His parents are gone and he always told me that he had no family left on either side."

"Well I don't know what I'm going to do with all of that stuff then. I guess I'll just leave it down there until I figure out what to do with it."

"Well sir. I know that Ed had told me that if anything ever happened to him, he wanted all of his stuff to go to some children's shelter around here. That's all I can tell you."

The old man smiled as he said, "I remember him doing a lot of things for those kids down there. If you're sure he has no family, then I think I'll honor his wishes."

Doc said, "I think he'd like that, sir. Yes, he would like that a lot. I'm sure of it. Well. We'd better be getting back on the road. We have a long drive still. It was nice to meet you, sir." They shook hands and he started to walk out the door.

The old man said, "Son. Since you were his friend, I'll let you in the basement if you want to look around and take something to remember him by. I think he would like that, too."

They followed him to the basement. He unlocked it and turned on the light for them. "Now you boys make sure that you pull the door shut when you leave. It will lock by itself. Take all the time you need, no hurry."

Ed quickly whispered something else in Doc's ear. "Sir, do you remember seeing a wooden box about this big with a big American flag painted on the top of it?"

The old guy thought while he looked around the room then he started walking over to the corner. "Yes I do. I think I put it over here. YES! Here it is. Is this what you want to take, son?"

"No sir. But I want to show you something." Doc turned it around and pushed on the back panel. A secret drawer popped out. He reached in and pulled out a huge stash of hundred dollar bills. "Sir, would you do me a favor? If Ed owed anything on his apartment, you can take it out of this. Then give half of the rest of it to the old lady on the other end of Ed's floor. I think he said her name was Wanda. He always spoke of how nice she was. He would want her to have it. Tell her he left it to her for that trip she always wanted to go on. Then take the other half and give it to the shelter, too. Would you mind doing that, sir?"

The old man had tears in his eyes and sounded a little choked up as he spoke. "Yes. I can do that, son. I know Ed watched out for her. It will do her good to finally go on that trip. I always liked Ed. He was a good man, that friend of yours, and so are you, son. Drive safely on your trip. Now, if you will excuse me, I have to go find those painters I hired. They just disappear whenever they want to." Then he turned and walked away.

They walked around looking at all of Ed's stuff. He told them about everything they picked up. After almost an hour, the three men had each picked out something of Ed's to keep for sentimental reasons. Each selected item came with a personalized narration of what it was, where it came from and what Ed thought about it. These would always be cherished items from a very unique friend.

Once back in the car, they quickly placed their newly-acquired treasures securely in the back of the car. As Bob pulled away from the curb, Doc reminded him not to drive as he usually did.

The kids offered to let Vic stretch out in the very back, but he said he would rather sit up in one of the captain seats instead. Martha and Ed made their way to the back seat. She was holding Ed's hand with her head leaning on his shoulder as usual. "I'm glad we came here. I think I love you even more now."

Ed asked, "Why?"

"You never told me you used to do things for the poor kids in your neighborhood. I think that is so sweet. And you gave all your stuff to the shelter that helps them. And giving that money to that lady, I just wanted to cry when you told Doc to do that. I am so proud of you, Ed. You're a good man. And you're my man. Don't forget that, mister."

Doc looked back at Ed. "You *are* a good man, Ed. It is a real honor to know somebody like you. I mean it, man." Vic and Bob both echoed Doc's remarks.

Vic asked, "If you don't mind me asking, Ed - any idea how much money was there?"

"Well, the last time I counted it, there was over $11,000.00."

Martha hugged him even tighter. "You guys hear that? My guy is a very good man."

A few blocks farther, Ed pointed out the children's shelter as they passed by it. Doc noticed that Ed was smiling as he saw some of the children playing just outside the shelter door. Then Martha reached up and pulled Ed's face downward for a kiss. That was when Doc looked back towards the front of the car.

Bob drove for most of the day, but during the second fuel stop, Doc insisted that he drive again. Ed had taken it upon himself to periodically report what time the GPS unit was predicting their arrival at Gettysburg.

Ed suddenly announced, "At the sound of the tone, the official GPS arrival time to Gettysburg is, drumroll please . . . " Martha started making the drum sounds. "That's right, everyone. We will be arriving at our chosen destination at exactly 3:00 in the morning." Then he smiled and leaned his head against Martha's head and the two of them would scream out "TONE!"

Though the kids had been doing this all day, the men could not help but laugh each time they did it. It was obvious that the kids were becoming increasingly excited about visiting Gettysburg as they drew closer to their destination. Vic and Bob were smiling as they watched the kids bouncing in their seats while repeating, "Comb your hair. We're almost there."

Doc, on the other hand, realized that they were still six hours away. He did some quick math in his head and then interrupted the kids' jovial singing.

"Hey everyone, listen up a minute." He paused until it was quiet. "I'm thinking that we should stop for the night. If we drive on, we'll just get a room and be too tired to do anything tomorrow during the day. So, I think we should get some rooms fairly soon and a good night's rest. Then we can get up early, eat breakfast and be there by 2:00 p.m. That's a perfect time to find a hotel and check in. I could start setting some things up that we need in place before we tackle the whole issue of Mr. Gruber. Then we could actually do some sightseeing. What do you think?" Everyone agreed.

Bob spoke up. "What do you think about getting two rooms? We could get one single room with two full size beds. Doc, you and Vic can have the beds. I'll sleep on the floor. Just let me swipe a bedspread and a pillow from one of your beds. I'll be fine. This way, the kids can have their own room and some privacy. We might even save some money with just getting a single room. OK?"

Doc and Vic were already shaking their heads in agreement when Martha said, "That is so sweet of you guys, but you don't have to do that. Ed and I can walk around all night. We'll be fine."

Vic replied, "No, that's not good for me. I wouldn't be able to sleep with you both stuck outside. You are our friends and you need your own room. I agree with Bob. But, I'll sleep on the floor, Bob. You take the bed."

Ed started laughing and kept on till everyone stopped talking. "First of all, Martha had been telling me all day she was a little scared about walking around Gettysburg because of all the ghosts." He turned to look at her before he said, "So I know you don't want to walk around all night. Do you?" She lost her smile and got that afraid, little-girl look on her face. She glanced towards the men as she shrugged and reluctantly said "No." Then Ed gave her a little kiss before continuing. "Look, guys. Martha is right. That is a very nice gesture but not necessary. I think it's time for you to look inside the tin box, Doc."

Doc had placed the tin box in the glove compartment so he motioned for Vic to get it out. Vic put it in his lap and opened it. He sat there staring at it and then said, "Damn."

Hearing Vic curse, Bob turned to look at Martha and said, "Aren't you going to get onto him for saying that?" She just looked at him and again shrugged her shoulders. Bob's mouth fell open before he said, "That's just not fair. You always get after me when I let a curse word slip." He turned back around and faced the front as he softly mumbled like a little boy, "That is just not fair. The tall guys always get the breaks." With his back to her, he didn't see that she was talking to him. "I still love you, Bob. And Vic is going to apologize for saying it. Aren't you, Vic?"

Vic quickly said, "Sorry, Martha," but he never took his eyes off the open tin box.

Hearing Vic's apology, Bob again softly mumbled. "That doesn't count. You only said it because I brought it up. She didn't make you apologize like she does me. It's just not fair."

Doc rolled his eyes and chuckled. "Well I think I'm right about everyone needing to get a good night's rest. It's beginning to sound like grade school in here." Everyone laughed, even Bob. But he couldn't help himself as he repeated, "Well, it still isn't fair."

Doc glanced over at the tin as he asked, "Is that money?" Vic nodded 'yes' as he picked up a handful of hundred dollar bills to show him.

Ed started laughing again. "I was wondering if anyone was ever going to ask me what was in that tin but nobody ever did. Yes, it's money. And it's to pay for this trip and something else."

Vic chuckled before he spoke, "I'd say that there is enough cash in here to pay for this trip and one hell of a 'SOMETHING ELSE'! How much is in here? It looks like a lot."

Ed smiled at Martha and she nodded at him. "You are doing this trip to help us and our fellow ghost, Mr. Gruber. So I want to finance the entire venture. There is enough in there for all the rooms for the week, your gas, and all your food. Plus the 'something special'. Okay?"

The men were stunned by Ed's generosity. They all hesitated while looking back and forth at each other. Then Doc said, "It's your money, Ed. Thanks, man!"

Vic was still looking at the money. "But there is way more than we will need for all of that. What's the rest for?"

Ed nodded at Martha and she began to explain. "At the last gas station, Ed told me what was in the box. He wanted to pay for the trip but he also wanted to do something very special for the three of you. I had this idea and Ed liked it. So, please think about it seriously. Don't decide anything for a few days. Okay?"

She looked at each man until she saw each head nod 'yes'.

"Good. Now Ed says that there is over $25,000 in that tin. Here's what we want you to do with whatever is left over after this trip. You all are being so nice by wanting to help us and Mr. Gruber. So, we thought you might be interested in helping other ghosts too. That extra money is for the three of you to start working together to do just that. We thought you could form some type of a ghost rescue society. We think it would just be the three of you. Of course, you can bring in other people that you find with similar abilities as yours. The bottom line is that the money is for the three of you to use to help other stranded spirits. What do you think? No WAIT! I didn't mean to ask you that. I, uh we, really want you to think about it for a few days. Please talk it over before you decide."

Once Vic filled Bob in on what the kids were suggesting, the three men fell silent. Each man was deep in thought about this new and very intriguing possibility. Vic suddenly said, "But we haven't helped anyone yet. What if we can't help you or Mr. Gruber?"

Ed fired back, "But you have helped us. Just by talking to us and being with us while we work through all this." Ed waved his hand around. "Two months ago, we died. It has been a hard adjustment, but look at us. Here we are with you guys on a road trip. How cool is this? We are sightseeing with friends and having a blast. Plus, we possibly are going to help another stranded spirit in the process. Yes, you all have done a lot for us. Earlier today after we left my old apartment, you said it was an honor to know me. It's actually our honor to know all of you."

Martha leaned forward. "And we mean that very much."

There was silence again. Eventually Bob said, "I like the idea personally. I'm in."

Vic and Doc answered as one. "Me too!"

Martha let out that little girl squeal as she clapped her hands a few times. Then she fell backwards in the seat to look up into Ed's smiling face. "I told you they'd like it!" Bob and Doc thought that she looked so very cute as she beamed with self-confidence.

Everyone was excited about this new venture. The happy atmosphere turned into a search for the right motel. Once they were checked in, each went to the door of their own room. They had four rooms next to each other. Just as everyone opened their door, Martha asked Doc if he would mind coming into their room to turn on the radio. He did, and the kids settled on an FM channel that played nothing but old songs.

They all met in the hallway at 6:00 the next morning as planned. They piled back in the car and went in search of a diner that the desk clerk had told them about. It was a landmark around these parts and had been in business for over 80 years.

It was off-season and a weekday morning, so the diner's parking lot was virtually empty. They found a parking spot by the front door. The men were out of the vehicle quickly, but then they all pretended to stretch their legs to give the kids time to get out. In his usual fashion, Ed just stepped right through the side of the car but Martha insisted on a more ladylike exit. Inside, they were greeted by a smiling waitress who led them towards a table. Vic had pointed before he asked for the very large circular booth back in the corner. Martha politely thanked him for thinking about her and Ed. With their order taken and fresh coffee delivered, the conversation began. There were only a few people there. Several truckers were sitting in swivel chairs along the old-style counter.

Martha and Ed were inspecting the antique knick-knacks everywhere. Bob was sipping his coffee and watched an older waitress who was standing just behind the cash register. It was early, and he still wasn't awake. She was smiling at the truckers and appeared to be talking to them. After a few more sips, he began to notice that the men never looked up to answer her. Then it hit him. He didn't hear her talking.

The early morning sunlight illuminated the stacks of red plastic drinking glasses on the counter behind her. That's when he finally noticed that the glasses were behind her, yet visible right through her. He looked over at Doc and coughed to get his attention. When Doc looked at him, Bob nodded his head in her direction and said quietly, "Behind the register."

Doc glanced over and nodded that he saw her too. Vic looked over and then commented, "Well, I hear a woman, but I don't see her." Then his eyes widened. "Another one?"

Martha and Ed commented at the same time, "I see her too."

She must have heard them, because her attention was instantly drawn to their table. She stared at them as if she wasn't sure of something. Then she walked right through the counter and came up to their table. She was looking directly at Ed and Martha as she stood there with a quizzical look on her face.

"Can you two see me?" was all she asked.

Martha and Ed looked at each other, then back at her. Martha crouched a little lower in her seat like a child who thought she was in trouble. In a slightly shaky voice, she answered her. "Yes ma'am. We see you."

"Do these others see me too?"

Vic realized she was looking at him, as everyone else was as well. "Well, ma'am. Everyone here sees you but me. I can only hear you."

She softly said, "I'm sorry, sir. I didn't realize you were blind. Forgive me." Then she hesitated before looking back at Martha. "You look different from the others at this table. Where are you from, young lady?"

Martha looked scared as she scooted closer to Ed and slipped her hands around his arm. She laid her head on his shoulder but neither one of them took their eyes off the woman or answered her question. Bob didn't hear what was being said, but he noticed Martha's fear. His protective instincts kicked in. "Hey lady, you're scaring her."

The woman reacted by immediately staring down at Bob. Her eyes danced all over his face as if she was studying him for some reason. Bob's reaction was suddenly that of a little boy. His eyes bugged out and he quickly looked at everyone around the table before he looked back at the woman.

Everyone at the table was staring at her, waiting for her to continue. To their surprise, her demeanor softened dramatically. She smiled and said, "I'm sorry, sweetie. I don't know what came over me."

Then she blinked her eyes a few times before she looked back at the cook and a waitress, who were standing and talking by the door to the kitchen. She was still looking at them as she said, "You know? I don't remember hiring them." Then she turned back to face the table and smiled at everyone. "It's been one of those mornings. I guess I'm still not awake. Forgive me, young lady. Have ya'll ordered yet?"

Though she was still focused on just Ed and Martha, everyone except for Bob started nodding their heads 'yes'. The Lady said, "Well, good. I'll just go check on your order." She began to leave but stopped. Then she slowly turned back to face them yet again. "I really don't mean to scare you or offend you in any way. But I just have to ask you something. I know this is going to sound crazy but, well, here goes. You two seem kind of familiar. Have we met before?"

Ed looked at Doc before he spoke. "Ma'am, we've never met. But there *is* a reason you're focusing on the two of us. Are you sure you want to know why?"

The woman smiled ever so lightly. "Well, why wouldn't I want to know. Uh, but know what?"

Martha's confidence surged as she pulled away from Ed's shoulder. She leaned over the table towards the woman. "You're like us."

The woman's expression turned serious. "I don't understand. What do you mean like you?"

This was where Martha's confidence faded. She looked over to Doc for some help. The lady followed Martha's lead and looked at Doc too. Bob coughed to get Doc's attention. He then nodded at a picture on the wall and said, "Behind you, Doc."

Hearing Bob, the lady looked right at him and he immediately smiled like a kid caught with his hand in the cookie jar. Doc glanced over his shoulder and saw it was a portrait of the woman. There was a gold plate at the bottom of the picture with an inscription. It said, 'Miss Wheaton. The last of the founding family'. The dates of her birth and death were printed below those words.

Doc uttered "Uh-huh." Everyone looked at him. When the woman saw what he was looking at, she said, "That's me." She smiled. Doc looked up at her and calmly said, "Yes ma'am, it is you. Did you notice the inscription at the bottom of the picture?" She looked back at it and read what was printed. All expression left her face and she froze.

After the woman had stood there without speaking, Martha asked softly, "Miss Wheaton? Are you okay, ma'am?"

The woman looked back at Martha and said, "That's very weird. Who would put something like that up in my store?" Then she turned around to look at the cook and waitress again before she added, "I don't know who those two are, but I'll bet they have something to do with this."

Doc spoke very softly. "Miss Wheaton. Please, look at me."

The woman slowly turned and looked down at him without saying a word.

"Ma'am. They didn't put that there. They just work here. I know you can tell there is a difference between these two kids and the three of us. The kids are, in fact, like you. That is why you came over when you saw them. Think about it. You know I'm right."

She slowly nodded her head as she stared at Doc. Then she looked at the picture again for just a moment. Her eyes teared up and she lifted one hand to cover her mouth as she said, "Oh my God. Then I'm . . . I'm . . . " She suddenly turned to the kids and said, "Oh sweetie, I'm so sorry for the two of you. I'm an old lady but you two look so young. I am so very sorry for you both."

Martha had tears in her eyes now as did everyone else at the table, even Doc. Martha said, "We're fine, Miss Wheaton. Really, we are. And you will be too." She looked at the three men before she continued, "These are our friends Doc, Bob and Vic. They are helping us cope with our situation."

The woman interrupted Martha. "Is it because you don't have any money, dear?"

Vic couldn't keep from laughing as he looked at Ed. "Well, *he* has a lot of money."

Martha glanced at Vic, then Bob. He immediately looked away, only to find the woman staring down at him. He lost his smile and once again displayed the look of a boy that just got in trouble, especially when she pointed at him. He didn't hear her ask who he was, but he saw her mouth moving.

Doc drew the woman's attention again. "Miss Wheaton? Please. What is it that you really want to ask?"

She looked around the table and settled on Doc's face. "I, uh, don't really know. This is all so, so, odd to me. I know that . . . well, I guess I know that I'm not really alive." She glanced back up at the picture, "Am I?"

Doc answered. "No Ma'am. I'm afraid you are not."

"So is this heaven?"

He shook his head 'no'. "I'm afraid not, ma'am. You never left here."

She looked around the room, then back at Doc. "I just love it here. My family opened this restaurant before I was born. I grew up playing out back. Then I started helping out as I grew older. But I don't understand why I'm still here. What's wrong with me? Oh my GOD! Was I such a bad person that I can't go to heaven?"

Doc spoke up quickly. "No, that's not it at all."

She spoke through teary eyes and with a choked up voice, "Are you sure? How do you know?"

Doc again consoled her. "You are here because you want to be. It's that simple."

"Because I want to? I don't understand."

Doc smiled up at her. "Let me ask you a question, ma'am. What is your biggest fear? Don't think about it. Just say what first comes to mind."

The woman didn't hesitate at all. "That this place would close down! It was my parents' dream to own a business. It was my family's whole life. In fact, it was my whole life ever since they passed away. This place is why I never got married. Never had a family of my own. It was my whole life."

Doc pointed over his shoulder at the picture. "Miss Wheaton. The date of your death was ten years ago. I only point that out so that you know this place didn't close down. Obviously somebody took it over. It seems to be flourishing very nicely, if you look around."

She did. "I don't remember that counter wrapping around this end like that. And there seems to be a lot of extra booths along this wall. Odd, I hadn't noticed that before." Then she looked outside. "And the parking lot is really a lot bigger. And where did those trees come from?"

That was the last thing she said. She suddenly became very focused on the trees at the edge of the parking lot. After a moment, she floated right past the kids and out into the parking lot. Everyone turned to watch her drift over to the trees and stop.

Martha grabbed Ed's arm, "I'm scared. It's going to happen again. Isn't it, Ed?"

Vic asked, "What's going on? What's going to happen?" He looked at Bob. "Come on, buddy. I always fill you in on what's being said. So give it up. What is happening?"

Bob pointed to the trees. "She floated out there to the trees and is just staying there. I don't have a clue what Martha is talking about."

Ed spoke up. "She is about to be taken. Same thing happened the first night at our crash site. All the other spirits drifted out to the tree line and just stayed there until this big flash of light took them."

Everyone was stretching their necks to watch the woman by the tree. Even Vic looked but he saw only trees. "Damn it! This isn't fair. I can't see anything."

Bob looked at Vic, then Martha before he said, "You see what I mean. I'll tell you what isn't fair."

Doc said, "Not now, Bob. I want to see what happens. Ed, how long did they stand there before the light came?"

Ed didn't have time to answer. There was a blinding light so intense that it was easily seen in the bright morning sunshine. The woman was gone. Everyone except Bob heard a loud whooshing sound that accompanied the light.

Vic said, "What was that sound?"

That's when the waitress's voice was heard behind them. "What are ya'll looking at?"

They all turned around. The young waitress was standing there. Bob studied her for a moment before he slowly reached out and poked her arm with his finger. She looked down at him. "Are you okay, mister?"

Bob realized that she was real. "Uh, just checking."

She smirked. "I see you've been talking to that idiot at the hotel who tells visitors about ghosts here at the restaurant. Didn't he? Well, I assure you I'm real. And your order is REALLY almost done. Do you want some more coffee?"

Doc was the first to regain his composure. "Yes ma'am. Please?"

She filled all the cups and left.

Vic was still curious. "What happened? What was that sound?"

Doc ran one hand through his hair and then rubbed the back of his head before he spoke. "That was a new one for me. There was a blinding light and then the whooshing sound. She was taken away by that light."

The waitress was on her way with their food, so Doc suggested that the conversation be put on hold until they got back on the road. They all agreed. The food was hot and very good. The kids excused themselves to walk around the parking lot while the men finished their meals. Neither Ed nor Martha wanted to go anywhere near the trees where the woman had disappeared. Eventually the men emerged and they all piled into the car for the last leg of the trip.

As they pulled out of the parking lot, Ed proclaimed, "Gettysburg, here we COME!"

Chapter 16

A GHOST IN A BARN

AFTER THEY LEFT the diner, there was a lengthy silence. Everyone seemed content to listen to the radio, but this was a subterfuge. All were occupied by their individual thoughts of what had happened.

Martha had her arm linked under one of Ed's arms and was holding his hand. She leaned against his shoulder as usual, her other hand making slow, small circles on his chest. Vic and Bob both stared into nothingness. Doc was relieved that his driving duties required his full attention, leaving him no time to ponder what they had witnessed happen to Miss Wheaton. Only Ed had fully accepted what had happened to the nice lady at the diner. He looked at the passing scenery with his usual childlike interest, smiling except for when he noticed Martha's blank expression. A quick glance at the men, then he would return to sight-seeing.

Eventually, Martha pulled them into a conversation about Miss Wheaton. "You know, I keep wondering about the light that took Miss Wheaton. It was so very white and bright. We all saw it."

Vic corrected her. "I didn't see it! I wanted to. I just felt left out of the whole thing."

Bob rolled his eyes. "You finally understand how I feel when I don't hear what the rest of you do."

Doc commented, "I couldn't believe how bright the light appeared in the morning sun as well. That was some crazy bright light. What you thinking about it, Martha?"

"Well, I keep hoping that since it was so white, it must have taken her to a good place. Right?" Her eyes were focused on Doc's reflection in the rearview mirror. When he didn't answer, she asked again. "Doc, don't you think the fact that the light was so bright white it must mean she was taken, uh, you know, to heaven?"

Doc cleared his throat and glanced out his window as if he were checking the rear view mirror, but he was stalling. He just didn't know what to say. After he had hesitated as long as he could, he spoke.

"Martha. I think it's sweet that you hope that for her. You're a very good person for it. I hope that you are right and I'll bet everyone in the car hopes the same thing. But the truth is that I just don't know. That was the first time I've ever experienced that particular event. I don't have anything to compare it to. It could only be compared to witnessing a bad person when they are taken. And personally, I don't want to see that."

Ed looked down at Martha and felt her concern for what happened to Miss Wheaton. It was one of those moments when his heart hurt because she was hurting. He tried to comfort her.

"Well, I think that is exactly what the white light signifies. I do!"

His comment caused her to raise her head and look into his face as she eagerly asked, "You do? You really think so? But why?"

Though he had only meant to comfort her by agreeing with her, it never dawned on him that she might ask him why. He now took Doc's lead and looked out the window for a moment to stall as he came up with an answer. Then it hit him. He looked at her and answered as if he was positive he was right.

"It's simple. Remember that first night at the crash site?" He paused to give her time to reflect. "Well, every one of those spirits were taken by that same bright light. None of those people were killed because they were bad. They, uh, we all died in a tragic accident. I know neither you nor I talked to everyone else on the plane. But I also know that I made eye contact with each one of them. They were all smiling and laughing. That plane was full of good people. And every one of them was taken by that bright white light. Yep! I know I'm right. I do!" Then he smiled at her and waited for her reaction.

She still had a blank expression on her face as she was processing everything he'd said. Just when he started to think that she doubted him, she smiled and raised up to kiss him on the lips. Then she slowly slid her head back to rest it once more on his shoulder. As she started making those small, slow circles again on his chest, she spoke.

"That does make sense. I like that answer. It makes me feel better. Thank you, Ed." She eventually closed her eyes to drift off to that place they went to when they looked like they were asleep. Ed was happy to see she still had a small smile on her lips. He took one last look around and gently lowered his head until his cheek rested on top of her head. His eyes blinked a few times, then slowly closed as he joined her.

Bob glanced back at the kids. "They're asleep. They look so peaceful together when they do that. It's almost like we have two angels riding in the back." Then he turned back around and yawned. With their stomachs full and little to do, Bob and Vic soon fell asleep as well.

Seeing that everyone was asleep, Doc was free to plan his moves once they got to Gettysburg. Peaceful silence ruled the car as the next four hours flew by. Doc had waited as long as he could before being forced to stop for fuel. The moment the SUV stopped next to the pump, everyone began to stir. Doc started refueling while the guys both headed to the men's room. Ed stepped through the side of the car and this time pulled Martha out with him. She immediately slapped his shoulder. "You know I don't like doing that." Then she turned to say, "Doc? We're going to stroll around a bit, okay?"

Doc couldn't answer her because there was a woman standing just on the other side of his pump. He looked at her and said, "Morning ma'am." Martha smiled at him. "You're so polite, Doc." Then she and Ed wandered off hand in hand.

The men came back out just as Doc was putting the pump nozzle away. Bob said, "Hey, Doc. Let me get the windows while you hit the men's room." Doc graciously accepted and ran off towards the building.

A few minutes later, Doc returned to a car full of travelers who were eager to get to Gettysburg. They were barely back on the highway when Bob commented. "The GPS says we have another two hours and 20 minutes. So what shall we talk about now?"

Doc spoke up. "Well it may say that on the GPS, but we are going to be at our hotel in about 45 minutes. I called and made reservations last night from the motel. So, we already have rooms waiting."

Vic asked, "So the GPS is wrong by that much? I thought they were more accurate than that."

Doc replied, "They are very accurate, but it's plotting time to the city center of Gettysburg, not a specific address. Our hotel is on this side of town. I like to stay there because the price is right and it's a very nice place, too. But the main reason I like it so much is that it's equal distance from the main battlefields and the farm where Mr. Gruber is."

Bob asked, "So what's our agenda, Doc? Are we going to the farm first?"

"Well, I thought we could check in and drop our stuff in our rooms first. I don't want to just show up at the farm and ask if we can look around. No, I thought I'd call a few people I know around town and ask if they have seen any of the family members this morning. If they have, then we can just accidentally bump into them."

Bob was nodding in agreement, but it was Vic that spoke. "You never cease to amaze me with your craftiness, Doc."

The rest of the trip to the hotel was filled with the kids' comments about the old buildings and scenery they were passing. They arrived and checked in. Doc was the last one back to the car after making his phone calls. They all piled back into the car and headed to a shopping area where someone had seen the land owner's daughter.

Once there, they began their search for a suggested shop that she frequented. Fate wasn't on their side this time, as she was nowhere to be seen. After walking around for almost an hour, Bob spied what appeared to be a very nice restaurant and asked if anyone else was hungry. Vic and Doc agreed that it was definitely time to eat. Ed and Martha had noticed an old town park across the street so they said they would hang out there while the men ate.

The three visitors were quickly ushered to a table by a huge, natural rock fireplace. An elderly woman walked up to them just moments after they sat down.

"I know you three. I saw you on the TV news this morning. I just wanted to say how proud your parents must be of your work at that plane crash in the mountains." She leaned down and placed her hand on Vic's shoulder. "That was such a sad story of all those people that died there. I can't imagine what you must have seen." Then she turned and walked away with her husband.

The men all looked at each other before Vic said, "Did she just say she saw us on TV?"

Doc looked around and noticed there were several people at other tables who were also looking at them. "Well, it looks like lots of people watch the same station around here. It has to be that reporter and camera crew that came to the crash site. Remember?" The others nodded. "This is not good. I would have rather been a little more discreet about our presence."

Bob watched the old lady talk to the restaurant hostess and point to them as she checked out. The moment the woman left, the hostess pulled out her cell phone and began texting. She was looking right at their table. "I don't know, Doc. I grew up in a small town. When a stranger came to town, everyone knew about it very quickly and where they were, too. So this could work to our advantage. You said you wanted to find this farmer's daughter. Well sir, I have a feeling she just might find you first."

Their conversation moved to other subjects. Doc shared historical information about this old restaurant and other local shops. The food was good and filling. For an hour, the men enjoyed a peaceful time. The conversation eventually moved on to what men usually talk about . . . women. Doc was telling them how beautiful the farmer's daughter was at the exact second she entered the restaurant. She walked right up to the hostess who pointed them out. Doc waved at her, then stood up as she approached their table. He introduced Linda Tolson to the other two as she sat to talk with them.

"Wow, I'm so excited to see you, Ted! And both of you gentlemen as well. Did you know that there was a documentary show this very morning about that awful plane crash? I couldn't believe it when I saw you on my TV. And now here you are. Isn't this just so phenomenal? It's like I was destined to see you today."

With a badly hidden smirk, Bob spoke up. "It's such a coincidence, isn't it? What were the chances that we'd run into her?"

Vic choked as he started to laugh at Bob's wisecrack. "Sorry, ma'am. I haven't had food this good in a long time. Guess I need to slow down."

Even Doc realized now that she was more beautiful than he had described. Odd that he had never noticed before, he thought to himself.

"Linda, it's good to see you again."

"Were you even going to come see me, Ted? By the way, why is he calling you Doc? You never told us that you were a doctor. You little rascal, you!"

"No, no, I'm not a doctor. I'm an EMT in the civilian world and a medic in my military life. They just always call me Doc. Don't pay any attention to them."

"Oh, I bet Mom and Dad will be interested in hearing all this new stuff about you. We just thought you were a very serious Civil War historian. You know, with all the knowledge you have of the area. I can't begin to tell you how much you impressed my father with what you know about everything."

"How are your mom and dad these days? Fine, I hope. Maybe I'll get to see them while I'm here." He was playing it cool in hopes she would invite them out to the farm.

"Well, you just missed them. We all ate at the club and then they went home while I looked for a gown to wear to the ball next week. I don't really want to go, but you know my parents. They're so old-fashioned about the town's historical functions." She looked at the other two men. "They always remind me how important it is for us to keep the old ways alive. I used to love the dances when I was younger, but I've been doing it all my life now. It's really getting boring. I'm never going to find a husband dressed like I'm stuck a hundred years in the past."

Vic smiled. "If you don't mind me saying, Miss, I'm sure every guy there fights for a chance to dance with you."

Her eyes lit up and it was obvious that she was checking to see if Vic was wearing a wedding band. Seeing his finger was bare, she leaned towards Doc. "Is he, uh . . . "

"Sorry Linda, they both are taken. He just hasn't finalized it like old Bob there." Doc pointed at Bob, who smiled and said, "I'm the luckiest man in the world. And, you don't want Vic here. He's got secrets!"

Vic's eyes widened as he glared at Bob. Then she said, "Hmm. Big, strong, handsome and has secrets. Intriguing. Too bad you're taken."

Vic's glare changed to a cocky smirk as he said, "Hear that, BOB? One of us is handsome, and it ain't you."

Doc smiled at Linda and chuckled before he said, "Please don't get those two started. I have to spend the rest of the day with them. You have no idea how they dig at each other."

Linda smiled at Bob and said, "Well for the record. I think all three of you are very handsome."

Vic quickly interjected, "But only one of us is tall!" This time, Bob glared at Vic, who was a good three inches taller than him.

Linda laughed politely before saying to Doc, "I see what you mean. But they *are* cute!"

Hearing this, Bob and Vic leaned back in their chairs before beaming exaggerated smiles directly in Doc's direction. He then leaned back in his own chair, ran his hand through his hair and sighed. "Linda! You're not helping."

"Well, anyway Ted. I'm supposed to invite all three of you out to the house. Mom and Dad want to see you all. Will you have time? Please say yes."

Doc looked around the table before he answered. "Well, we really didn't have anything planned for today or tomorrow. Sure. We'd love to come out. Just tell us when."

"Great! Then why don't you just follow me out there now. If you're through with dinner, that is."

The two were nodding that they were finished, so Doc agreed. He told her he remembered the way and would meet her at the house.

As they stood to leave, Linda stepped up to Doc and kissed

him on the cheek as she whispered in his ear, "You're the cutest. You know I've always thought that." Then she waved goodbye to the others and made an unforgettable exit.

Once outside, the kids saw them and came running across the street. Martha stopped to let a car go by, but Ed pulled one of his unexpected stunts. He ran out in front of the car and stopped to face it while flexing his arm muscles. Of course Martha put her hand to her mouth and yelped 'Oh!' as the car passed right though him. Then he saw her raise that finger to poke him, so he ran for safety on the other side of the guys. Ed kept running in the opposite direction from her while using the men as an obstacle. Finally, Ed let her catch him. She decided to forgo the usual poke, and took his hand before they playfully followed behind the guys.

The drive to the farmhouse was beautifully scenic. Doc shared as many historical facts about the route as he could. Only once was he interrupted, when Martha asked if he were sure it was okay for her and Ed to come into the house. Ed gently reminded her that they wouldn't even know they were there.

As the car pulled into the circular driveway, they saw Linda and her parents emerge from the house, standing on the steps of a massive, colonial style porch. The parents greeted them graciously, which left the men feeling rather special as they entered the house.

Ed told Martha, "See. That's southern hospitality and these are very nice people. If we were alive, they'd have invited us right in too."

"Yeah, but we aren't alive. How do you think they'd act if they knew two strange ghosts were just inviting themselves in?"

"Well, if you are afraid you're going to offend them. Just don't eat the cookies!" Once he said that, he took off running past the group and into the house to look around.

Seeing Ed speed by, Bob glanced back at Martha. She had that little girl smile on her face. She walked behind the group all the way into the parlor before she heard Ed yelling, "Hey Martha! You gotta see this!" Doc snuck a peek back at her and winked. Since she felt she was cleared to go, she took off after Ed.

It was an expansive room with many large windows that let in a lot of light. The furniture was all elegant dark mahogany and tapestried upholstery; the kind one would expect to find in a colonial home of the past. The parents motioned for the men to take their choice of several high backed chairs. They were arranged in a semi-circle, facing a huge ornate couch. The men waited until Linda and her mother had sat down on both ends. However, the father stood and motioned for the men to be seated as he said, "Gentlemen, please."

Mr. Tolson didn't speak until he was seated between his wife and daughter.

"So, Ted. Linda tells us that there is a lot that we still don't know about you."

"Well sir. I apologize for not mentioning it. I assure you that it was not intentional on my part. It just never occurred to me to talk about my past, and what I do for a living."

Mrs. Tolson smiled before she spoke. "We know that, Ted. Don't let this old stuffed shirt get to you. He just likes to do that to people. Haven't you learned that by now?"

Linda patted her father's forearm lightly. "Dad, please don't make our new guests nervous. They are all here on holiday."

Mr. Tolson's demeanor softened. "She's right. I do apologize." He pointed around the room. "In these surroundings, it's sometimes hard not to take on a certain type of air. Forgive me, gentlemen."

Vic spoke up. "I totally understand what you mean, sir. You have some very beautiful vintage pieces in here." He pointed to a huge mirror with gorgeous, intricate carvings all around the frame. "Is that a Hugo Lonitz?"

Both parents looked at each other, eyebrows raised. "Yes it is, young man. I'm impressed that you recognize his work."

Bob and Doc were staring at Vic with equally surprised looks. "My girlfriend Glenda's parents are antique dealers. We've been together for over four years, so I've been to their house many times. I get a guided tour every time I go there. They're always so eager to show us their newest acquisitions. I guess it rubbed off a little." He smiled.

Linda's mother asked, "So you all came here on holiday?"

Doc spoke. "Yes ma'am. I always find it so relaxing here. It's peaceful, for me. When I mentioned that I was coming here to relax and unwind a little, they asked to tag along. Considering that the three of us have just spent two very intense months together, it seemed like a good idea."

Mr. Tolson commented, "I can't imagine how much you young men must need just that. So, if there is anything we can do to help you relax, please just ask."

To Bob and Vic's amazement, Doc replied, "Well, we appreciate that, sir. But we didn't come here to intrude. Thank you for offering."

The mother leaned closer to her husband and placed her hand on his. "Darling, Ted has always found the back pastures to be very beautiful. Why can't he show his friends around out there?"

Bob spoke up. "Mam. I, well we, really appreciate the offer but as Doc said. We don't want to intrude at all. You are obviously very nice folks. There is so much to see around the regular tourist area, I'm sure we'll enjoy it."

Mr. Tolson sat up straight. "Yes, there are a lot of very interesting things to be seen in town. But Son, there are things on our land that are just as interesting and few have ever seen them. So, I agree with my lovely wife." He patted her hand. "I think it would do you all some real good to just go wander around the pastures." Then he pointed at Ed. "And you have one of the most knowledgeable historians for a friend. I have no doubt that he'll keep your attention with all his stories. Why, he knows more about what has happened on our land than we do."

Doc chuckled. "Well, I don't know if that is exactly true, sir. Every time you and I have gone out there, I've learned from you as well. I would love to show my friends around. Would now be too soon to start?"

"Not at all! That was the first thing I liked about you, Ted. You didn't waste time getting out there to look around. So it is settled. You young men are going to spend some time out on our land.

"Sylvia and I are going out of town in a few hours. I will call now and tell our foreman that you and your friends will be coming by. Ted, you can use the entrance by the foreman's cabin. And of course, the horses are available to you as well. Please come as often as you like, and stay as long as you wish." He then looked at his daughter. "When are you going to see your friend?"

"There's been a slight change in plans. I'm picking her up at the airport later this evening, and we are driving over to see some mutual friends in Hanover. But like you said, Dad, Ted knows his way around here. They'll be fine."

Mr. Tolson started to rise and the three men quickly stood. "I must apologize, gentlemen. My wife and I have to get ready. It has been a pleasure meeting you all." He then looked at Vic and said, "I'd especially like to chat about antiques sometime with you son, should we get a chance once we return."

"I'd be very happy to do that, sir."

The father took his wife's hand and helped her to her feet. She smiled and bid them farewell. The father nodded and simply said, "Gentlemen."

Linda walked the visitors back to Doc's SUV. She gave Bob and Vic both a big hug, but saved Ted for last, and again whispered in his ear. "I hope you're here tomorrow when I get back. I might just have a surprise for you." Doc's smile showed he wasn't expecting that. Bob had opened the car door and then stepped away as if he was taking one last look around. The kids quickly climbed into the back seat, then Bob got in. Doc slowly pulled away on the gravel drive.

It was a 20-minute drive to the foreman's cabin. Ed dominated the entire conversation by talking about all the things he had seen around the big house. He had eventually found Linda's room, and Martha had caught him looking around in her closet. She had chased him out, but according to Ed, she was in there for quite a while before coming out. With this revelation now exposed, she blushed before explaining "Well! She had a lot of very beautiful gowns in there. I had never seen so many in one spot before. It was like a dress shop in there!" Then she giggled, before covering her face with her hands and bending over until they were in her lap.

The foreman was just saddling the last of the three horses as they drove up. Bob suddenly seemed nervous as he looked at Vic before he asked, "Am I the only one of us that has never ridden a horse?"

Vic smiled. "I used to ride a horse every Saturday afternoon."

Fearing that he'd be embarrassed by not knowing how to ride, he asked "Every Saturday?"

Vic chuckled as he said, "Yep. Until the damn thing broke and the grocery store replaced it with a rocket ship!"

Bob glared at Vic as the kids broke out laughing. Doc looked away, but his shoulders shook slightly, giving away the fact that he too was laughing.

The moment Vic opened his door, Martha grabbed Ed's arm and said, "Oh no you don't, mister! You're going to get out like a normal person this time."

He had that childish grin as he said, "Normal person? Da, DEAD!"

As she raised that finger of hers, all the guys hurried to get out before she struck. Each man still had one leg inside when Ed said, "OUCH! Okay, okay! Ladies first." As soon as she had let go of his arm, he jumped right out through the side of the car. Once outside, he ran off towards the horses. "Fooled ya! Bet you can't catch me!"

"Hello, Mr. Ted! We haven't seen you around here for a while. It's good to see you, sir." The two men shook hands. "Didn't know if your two friends knew how to ride, so I saddled up these two. They are the ones we put kids on and will follow yours wherever you go. They're good animals, these two."

Then came a real dilemma. Vic looked at Doc as he nodded at the kids. Ed said, "Doc, you take Martha with you and I'll ride with one of the guys." Hearing this, Doc quickly mounted his horse as Ed helped Martha get on the back. Surprisingly enough, Martha was able to balance very easily as she appeared to have her hands on Doc's shoulders. Though he felt a strange tingling sensation on his shoulders, Doc didn't let on.

Turned out that Vic really could ride. He mounted his horse like a cowboy, took the reins and began walking the animal around the rest of them. "Yep! Looks like all those quarters really paid off. It feels about the same, but I'm up higher."

The foreman had just helped Bob into the saddle when Ed walked right past the horse's head on his way over to Vic. To Doc's amazement, Bob's steed watched Ed's every movement, and snorted as she tried to back away from Ed. The foreman quickly patted the mare's neck. "Whoa Betsy! Settle down, girl." By this time, Ed had scurried over and jumped up behind Vic. Bob looked as if he was going to have a heart attack, but his horse settled down immediately now that Ed was not close to her. "She'll be okay now, young man. Just hold these loosely in your hands and she'll follow the other two animals wherever they go. You'll be okay. Just remember to mount from the left side every time. Pat her neck every now and then. She likes that. You two will be fine."

They all waved at the foreman as each animal fell in line behind Doc's. There wasn't any talking until they had cleared the first hill and the foreman was out of sight. Doc constantly assured Bob he was doing just fine during the entire 40-minute ride. He brought them to a fence line between the Tolsons' land, and the land where Mr. Gruber hung out most of the time. They all dismounted and started walking uphill along the fence towards a big group of trees. Ed ran up to hold hands with Martha, and they walked along with Doc. They were within a hundred yards of the trees when Doc stopped and wrapped his horse's reins on a fence post. Vic did the same and quickly helped Bob tether his own horse. Then they walked up to join Doc and the kids.

Doc pointed over the fence at a small red and white barn. "That's the barn I always see Mr. Gruber going in and out of. He also walks up to those trees on the hill. That is where I've always been able to talk to him." Doc was looking all around. "But he must be back in his barn. I don't see him anywhere. He'll be dressed in a white shirt with an old straw hat. He'll look like a farmer, not a soldier. Do you see him anywhere, Bob?"

When Bob didn't answer, everyone looked at him. It is obvious that he was seeing things all around them. He kept looking towards different spots and squinting as if he was focusing on something far away. Finally, Bob started talking while he kept glancing around the meadow.

"I don't see anyone dressed like that, but I do see a lot of soldiers moving all around us. They appear and disappear. They're everywhere!"

Martha had also started noticing the soldier spirits everywhere. She grabbed Ed's hand as she shoved herself firmly up against him. He had been looking around too, but looked down at her when she did that. "It's okay, babe. We talked about this, remember? Those spirits don't see us at all. Like Doc said, they are seeing things the way it was before they died." He rubbed her hand. "It's okay."

Doc stepped over to Bob. "I'm sorry, I forgot to warn you. There were several large skirmishes all around here. You're going to be seeing soldiers' spirits everywhere out here. Then it will stop for a while, and start back up later. You'll get used to it. I did."

Doc glanced at Vic. "How are you doing? I know you can't see anything, but you may hear things. I usually do. I've heard screams, yelling, lots of gunshots and an occasional cannon or two."

Vic nodded. "I'm way ahead of you, Doc. I was hearing that before we got to the fence. I'm good."

Doc stepped back over to the fence by the kids. "Ok. How you doing, Martha? Ready to go meet Mr. Gruber?"

She had no expression on her face. "Aren't we all going?"

"Well, no. We can't go over the fence. I promised Mr. Tolson I would honor his neighbor's property line. So it will just be you and Ed. But you'll be fine. Mr. Gruber is a very nice man. I just wish I could be there to hear what and how he talks with you. So, Ed, I want you to pay attention to all the little details of what he does. What he looks at the most, where he stands, what he's doing, every little thing. Plus, you have to remember exactly what he says. You two are going to be my eyes and ears over there. I know you can do it. Now, I'll bet he is inside that little barn. So just go look in it first."

Ed asked, "What about that big house farther over there?"

"Well, if you don't find him in the barn, you could check in the house. I've seen him go in that direction. But never actually saw him go into the house before. Doesn't mean he doesn't go in there, just means I haven't seen him go there."

"We'll be fine, Doc. Come on, Martha. Let's go meet a ghost in a barn."

Martha patted Ed's arm. "You mean meet Mr. Gruber."

They both walked right through the fence and leisurely strolled over to the little barn. Ed started to walk right through the barn door, but Martha stopped him. "Wait a minute, Ed. Should we knock or something? It just seems wrong to walk right on in without letting him know we are coming."

"Well, I doubt that we can knock, but I'll try." He tried to knock, but his hand passed right through the wood. "Yep. Just what I thought would happen. Come on Martha, let's go in and see if he's here."

She still had a fast grip on Ed's hand as she covered her eyes with her other hand. "Ok. I'm ready. Take me in."

Ed pulled her along through the wall and into the dim light inside the barn. As their eyes were adjusting to the low light, their sense of smell was on overload. The air was full of a sweet smoky smell. She said, "It smells like there was a big fire in here."

Ed sniffs a few times then said, "No, that would be BBQ that you are smelling." He sniffed several more times and then proudly announced, "This was a smoke house!"

Their eyes had finally adjusted and they both slowly looked around. Martha suddenly pointed. "There he is. He looks just like Doc described him. How cute!"

There was a stone structure right in the middle of the barn. It appeared to be a six-foot long, four-foot high fire pit made entirely from stones. It had a big opening on the top of one end, and there was a heavy metal grate over the opening. The spirit was lying down on top at the other end of it. His head was close to the grate and his legs were dangling down over the end of the pit. Martha hadn't let go of Ed's hand, and his curiosity was causing him to pull her along.

"Is he asleep, Ed?"

"Looks like it. I wonder why he is lying on that thing. Maybe he did it as a child or something?"

The man suddenly opened his eyes and sat up. He just stared at them for a few minutes. "Who are you two? What are you doing in here?"

"I'm Ed and this is Martha. Are you Mr. Gruber?"

Hearing his name, the man pulled his head backwards as his eyes widened. "How do you know my name? What do you want?"

"Well sir, we came to talk to you."

He looked at Martha, "You look scared, young lady. Are you okay?"

"It's dark in here, and she's afraid of you, sir."

The man's face slowly took on a gentle smile. "Oh I'm sorry, young lady. I didn't mean to scare you."

Martha realized now that he was a nice man just like Doc said. "That's okay, sir. I'm not afraid anymore. I'm sorry we just walked in on you." She looked around before she continued.

"You must like it in here. You were asleep when we first came in. Sorry if we woke you up."

He looked confused as he talked. "I don't really know why I come in here. It just seems that I'm supposed to be here. I can't explain it, but I feel like I belong here for some reason."

Ed spoke up, "Well if I built a barn like this, I'd come out here all the time."

The man looked around as if he didn't know where he was. "I didn't build this. In fact, I don't know who did. This is the very spot where I built my first cabin for me and my wife. It wasn't much bigger than this." He smiled as he looked down at the ground. It is obvious that he was reliving those days in his old cabin. "We spent five winters in that little cabin while I built her a proper house. We kept the cabin in great shape in hopes that one of our children would live in it one day. But that damn war came along and a cannon blew it to pieces. All that was left standing was the fireplace and part of the chimney. I wanted to rebuild the cabin around it. Sadly, it started tilting and I just knew it was going to fall over one day. I do remember trying to shore it up to keep it from falling." He put his hand on top of the stone pit. "But I see it fell over anyway." He stood there feeling of the stones with both his hands. "I built this thing with my own two hands, stone by stone. It took me two weeks of back-breaking work to get it done."

Martha said, "Maybe that is why you like it here."

He now stood at one end of the stone structure. "This thing must have just lain over on the ground one day. Look what somebody did. The chimney was very tall. The top part must have broken off in the fall. It looks to me like they used the stones to close in the two ends."

Ed now stood at one end and looked down the length of it. "Wow, I see what you're talking about. This opening here was the fireplace opening when it was standing up. It's on top now because the fireplace just fell backwards. This must have been the bottom. I think you're right, sir. It looks like they closed in this end of it with stones and then put that metal grate over the opening. They must have done the same thing on the top part where you're standing. They just turned your fireplace and chimney into a big fire pit."

Martha got excited and spoke. "Oh, and I bet I know why you don't recognize this barn. The new family came along and fixed up your old fireplace into a pit. Then they built this little barn around it to make a smoke house. That's why you don't remember it. You must have already been, uh . . . " She realized that she was about to say 'already dead', but didn't want to shock him.

"What new family, young lady? Are you saying your family built this on my land without my permission?"

"Oh, no sir! Ed and I are not from here. We just got here today."

The man thought a bit about what she had said while he walked to the front of the barn. The kids followed along behind him.

Ed asked, "Sir, have you ever seen anyone in this barn before?"

Mr. Gruber thought for a few moments, then nodded. "I do remember some people that came in here and hung meat on the hooks before starting the fires. I thought they must work here, so I never said anything to them."

Ed looked around and asked, "What hooks?"

The spirit pointed up at the framework of boards that ran from one end of the barn's ceiling to the other. Seeing they were gone, he took off his hat and scratched his bald head. "Well, that is odd. Those boards used to have big metal hooks every two feet or so. When did they take them down?"

Marta asked, "So did anyone else ever come in here? Before us?"

Mr. Gruber again thought for a moment before he answered, "No. Not that I remember." Then he snapped his fingers and said, "Wait a minute. I do remember a man with his daughter coming in here once. I heard him telling her that he was thinking of tearing down the barn. I don't really know who built this barn, but it is on my land. He had no right to tear down anything, so I chased them both out of here."

Ed quickly asked, "Are you saying they saw you?"

The spirit had a stern look on his face as he stared at Ed. "Of course they saw me! Why wouldn't they?" Then he turned to Martha. "Is there something wrong with him?" He nodded at

Ed. "I don't mean to be rude, miss, but is he okay?"

Martha grinned up at Ed. "Well sometimes Ed here is a little hard to take. But no sir, there isn't anything wrong with him." She rolled her eyes at Ed before she focused back on Mr. Gruber. "So did the man or girl say anything to you?"

"Well, not in here they didn't. They knew I meant business, so they skedaddled. It was outside that I realized the little girl was nervous. It made me feel very bad about how I had treated them. That's when I saw her standing behind her dad, and heard her tell him she was scared." Mr. Gruber's face showed his regret. "It broke my heart to hear that cute little girl tell her daddy that. I was just ashamed of how I had acted. That's when the man told me that he was sorry he had intruded upon me. He seemed very sincere. So I believed him when he said that he would make sure that nobody would ever bother me in here again, and he gave me his word. Then I apologized to him for scaring his little girl. He was an honorable man. I have never seen him out here since that day."

The kids followed him as they all walked right through the door and out into the sunlight. He led them a few feet away from the barn, stopped and pointed at the big house. "What you just said about another family makes sense now. You see that house? I built that for my family. But I only built that half of it. I've been wondering who would have the nerve to come along and build onto somebody else's house like that. I went in there once, to find out who they were and what they were doing in my house." His face lost all expression before he looked at the ground. "But I don't go in there anymore. Just can't."

Ed asked, "Why can't you?"

Mr. Gruber looked around slowly then spoke. "I saw a woman one day. All I wanted to do was ask her some questions. She started screaming and went hysterical. Then that same little girl I scared in the barn came running in yelling 'Momma'. She looked at me and said 'My daddy promised you that nobody would ever come in your barn again. He's kept his promise. You said you were sorry for scaring me, and now here you are scaring my momma. Why?"

The spirit glanced back at the barn then back at the kids. "Well, it just broke my heart again when she said that to me. I didn't mean to scare her momma. Honest. I just wanted to ask her some questions." Then he appeared to wipe his eyes. "So I haven't been back in there again. Besides, I believe that I belong in that barn. It just seems right for me to be there." Then he took one last look at the kids before he turned to walk back into the barn.

Martha had tears in her eyes now. "Mr. Gruber!" He turned to look at her. "I don't think you are scary, either. You're a good man. Honest."

He lifted his head up high and stood tall again. His smile was that of a loving grandparent as he nodded at her before he disappeared through the barn door.

Ed asked, "Martha? Should we follow him and see what he does?"

"Maybe later Ed. Look." She pointed back towards the fence. "Doc's waving at us to come back. Let's go."

As the kids playfully chased each other back towards the fence, Doc motioned for them to meet in the trees at the top of the hill. Ed quickly flicked one of her ears and yelled, "Last one to the trees is a dead man. Or woman!" It was obvious to the men that he slowed down to let her get close enough to catch him before he reached the trees. She passed by him and touched the first tree. As she clapped her hands while she jumped up and down, Ed wrapped his big arms around her before jumping too.

The men tied up the horses again and they all sat in the shade on the cool green grass.

Doc eagerly asked, "So what did you see? Was he there in the barn? Come on, out with it!"

Ed chuckled just a little bit. "Whoa there, Doc. Chill!"

Martha told the entire story exactly as it had happened. Doc only interrupted once to ask if Mr. Gruber really said he belonged in the barn. All three men were mesmerized by Martha's report. There was total silence once she was done. Vic was still finishing the story for Bob, when Doc leaned back against a tree and started rubbing his hair with both hands.

"This is just amazing, but I don't know what to make of it. It is obvious that something is holding him there. Even he said he felt like he was supposed to be there, yet he admits he didn't build the barn or even know who did. The only connection seems to be that his first cabin was on that spot and the old chimney is still there. But that just doesn't make any sense. I don't see how he could have that strong of a connection to either one. It just doesn't make any sense to me."

Vic pointed to a lone rider coming straight for them. "Doc, looks like Linda is coming out to check on us."

Bob immediately interjected, "Not us. Just Doc!" As the rider got closer, he added, "That's not Linda. Who's she?"

Ed spoke up, "Hey! It's Wendy."

Vic quickly asked, "Who's Wendy?"

Martha said, "She lives next door to Doc. Remember? I told you all about her on the trip here."

She rode up and stopped right in front of them. "Hi, Ted! Bet you didn't expect to see me out here."

She dismounted and tied up her horse. Doc stood and walked over to her. "Well, no. We all thought it was Linda until you got closer."

Wendy followed Doc back to his tree and sat down right beside where he had been sitting. After Doc had reclaimed his spot in front of the tree, she spoke again. "Well, we both would have been here, but she latched onto a young doctor she met at the airport before I landed. They just dropped me off at her house and said you'd be out here." She turned to Vic and Bob. "So has Ted been telling you all the history of this place? Linda's dad says he's a walking Civil War encyclopedia."

Doc asked, "How did you know we would be here?"

She laughed. "Easy. This is the best view of that barn you took the picture of. I'm still not sure why you are so fascinated with it. It's just a barn. I don't think anyone is ever allowed near it."

Doc asked, "How much do you really know about the man that owns that land?"

"Well, enough to know that he isn't going to let you near it. I can tell you that right now."

Doc thought for a few moments. "Wendy, I know we barely know each other but I have to ask you a rather odd question. Have you ever heard anyone talk about seeing spirits or ghosts out here?"

She got a very strange look on her face as she sat and stared at him. "A ghost? Really? Now you are sounding like most of the tourists that come here secretly hoping to see a ghost. But if you are asking me if I know anyone over there that has seen a ghost, well . . . I'd have to suggest you ask them."

Vic asked, "Do you or Linda know the daughter of the man that owns that land?"

She looked at Vic, "He doesn't have a daughter. He just lived there with his wife until she died a few years back. What made you think he had a daughter?"

Doc cut in. "I'm going to go out on a limb here. You're going to find out sooner or later anyway. I have a real interest in ghosts. That's a big part of why I come to Gettysburg. Plus, you see, we heard a story about him and his daughter encountering a ghost in that barn."

Everyone noticed that Wendy's complexion suddenly lost all of its color, as if she had just seen a ghost. "Uh, well, that's just crazy, Ted. Surely you don't believe in that stuff."

Doc noticed that she had begun to fidget and wouldn't make eye contact. He'd seen similar reactions from lots of people that have had encounters with spirits. It's like they're still in denial about what they saw, and they would get very nervous when people asked them about it. He knew she was hiding something. "Wendy. I didn't mean to make you nervous. We're not crazy. We are just interested in someone."

She looked at each man, then back at Ted. "Who are you interested in? Do you have a name? If I don't know them, Linda probably does. She knows everyone in these parts. Especially if it's a he, and he is an eligible bachelor."

Doc hesitated but went for it anyway. "Does the name Gruber mean anything to you?"

Her mouth fell open and she leaned back for a few seconds, then sat up. "You got that name from a land deed or something like that, right? Didn't you? Tell me the truth, Ted."

He knew he was onto something with her now. "No. In fact, I think that Mr. Gruber's spirit is hanging around that barn. I think you know it, too. Why is that?"

Though the group didn't think her skin could get any whiter, it had lightened up another few shades. She had absolutely no expression of any kind on her face and her eyes were motionless. "Uh. No. That would be, or I mean, I'd be or sound crazy to admit that to anyone. That's just nuts, Ted."

Doc leaned towards her with as gentle of a look as he could muster. "Wendy. I'm not trying to put you on the spot. But you know something that I need to know. I don't want to embarrass anyone. In fact, I just want to help. Truly help everyone concerned."

She now had a quizzical look. "Help? How? And who exactly are you wanting to help?"

"I suspect that the people that live over there are seeing ghosts. Mainly Mr. Gruber. I want to find out what is keeping Mr. Gruber around that barn. If I figure it out, then we'll have a chance to fix it so he will move on. And that would benefit everyone concerned. Wouldn't it?"

She shook her head. "I am still having a hard time believing that you have talked to a ghost and found all this out. It just seems too farfetched for me."

Doc immediately said, "I just need to talk to Mr. Parkland. I can convince him that what I'm saying is true."

She laughed. "Ha! I don't know how you'd ever convince that man that a ghost told you anything. What could you possibly tell him?"

Doc said, "Ok. I'll tell you. I would tell him that I know he promised Mr. Gruber that nobody would ever intrude upon him again. And that Mr. Gruber apologized for scaring his little girl." He could see in her frozen face that he had struck a nerve. "Oh, and one more thing. I'd tell him I know that his wife saw Mr. Gruber one day in the house and she went nuts. Their daughter came running in and yelled at him to stop scaring her momma."

She covered her face with both hands and took several deep breaths. Doc could tell by her actions that she had heard these stories before. He didn't know who had shared them with her, but she definitely knew what he was talking about.

Finally she looked at him again. "Let's just say I don't find what you are saying to be all that, well . . . unbelievable? Just exactly what are you wanting me to do?"

"I need you to convince that land owner to talk to me. I'll take it from there. Maybe you can convince Linda to help me. She's bound to be able to get him to talk to me. What do you say? Will you help us?"

She shook her head. "Linda is not going to get you anywhere. If anyone is going to be able to get him to talk to you it will be his niece."

Doc was visibly excited now. "Great! Do you know her? Think you can get her to talk to me?"

Wendy was still shaking her head as she spoke. "Well, I'm not sure it will work, but I'll talk to him for you. Just don't get your hopes up."

Bob smiled as he said, "You mean you'll talk to her for us. Sorry, I hate to correct people, but I'm a teacher and it's a habit. Sorry."

Doc was still very excited. "So when can we talk to her?"

She smiled. "Well. You *are* talking to her." They all fell silent. "Yep, I'm his niece."

Chapter 17

A SECOND CHANCE FOR EVERYONE

EVERYONE WAS STUNNED by the revelation that Wendy was the landowner's niece. Doc was shaking his head.

"But your last name is Elgend. His last name is Parkwood. So that means . . . ?"

She cut him off. "It means that my mother was his sister. My parents were both killed in a car accident when I was ten years old. My uncle and his wife raised me as their own, right here. My aunt couldn't have children, so they treated me as their own daughter. It was a win-win for everyone. But I'm still not sure he'll talk to you. He has some very strong feelings about this whole thing. But I'll still take you over there. When do you want to go?"

Before anyone realized what had happened, Doc stood up and started walking towards the horses. Wendy called out to him. "No need to saddle up. It's a short walk to a gate between the two properties." She was pointing down the back of the hill at another small grove of trees. They were nestled up against the fence just a little farther to their left. With all the horses in tow, they slowly walked down into a little valley.

Doc was looking around as he spoke. "I've never been down here because the best view of the barn was from up there. So there's a gate down here?"

"Yes, this is how I'd ride over and visit Linda when we were kids. It's also how I slipped around you without you seeing me. I rode around the hill behind you, so it would look like I was coming from Linda's house. I didn't want you to . . . well, you know."

They all went through the secluded gate and emerged from the ravine just a hundred yards from the barn. They were almost to the back door of the big house when her uncle appeared. He walked over to meet them halfway. After sharing a gentle hug from her uncle, Wendy introduced them all. Then the uncle invited them all into the house for some lemonade.

Wendy took his hand and spoke softly.

"Uncle Thomas. I have something to ask you. Please, please don't get mad until you hear me out."

He had a concerned look yet a loving smile as he said, "Wendy, I could never be angry at you. Surely you know that by now, dear."

"Ok. I'll expect you to honor what you just said. So, here goes." She cleared her throat as she quickly glanced at Ted. "Doc here wants to help us."

"Do what, hon? Help us do what?"

She hesitated just a little longer and took one last big breath. "Ok. Here it is.

"He knows about Mr. Gruber and the barn. He knows what happened that day we went in there. I don't know how he knows, but he knows. I still can't believe it myself, but he does know. He described it perfectly."

Her uncle's face had lost all expression, but was still calm. He slowly looked at Wendy, then at Doc. There was an awkward pause before he spoke.

"I see. Well, gentlemen. I'm afraid I'll be asking you to leave my land. Now!"

Vic and Bob had already turned to go, when Doc looked at Wendy and said. "So it was you that Mr. Gruber scared that day." He looked directly at her uncle. "The day you promised him that nobody would ever intrude on him in that barn again."

Both Wendy and her uncle looked at Doc, amazed.

Wendy asked, "How do you know that, Ted? How? Tell me right now and tell me the truth. How?"

Ted looked around at the others and he noticed that Martha was behind Bob, and Ed was missing. "Ok. I'll be honest with you both. I sent some friends into the barn about two hours ago to talk to him. They then came back over to the trees and told us what was said. We were there talking when Wendy showed up. That's how I know."

The uncle immediately looked at Vic and Bob. "You two had the nerve to come onto my land and go into that barn without permission. If I'd have seen you, I'd have shot you. You understand me gentlemen?"

Bob and Vic were shaking their heads as they said in chorus, "But it wasn't us!"

Wendy looked at Doc. "Wait a minute. If it wasn't those two, where did the other two go? I didn't pass anyone as I circled you in the trees."

The uncle said, "I want to talk to these two friends of yours, young man. And I mean right now. Where are they?"

Bob said, "Doc. Uh, why don't me and Vic just go back to the trees." He looked at the uncle and quickly added "With your permission of course, sir."

"You two young men just stay right where you are." The uncle then looked at Doc again. "Young man, I expect you to produce these other two friends and right now. Where are they?"

Doc coughed, then chuckled as he looked down at the ground.

"You find this funny, young man?"

Doc shook his head and coughed again before he spoke. "No sir. I assure you I don't mean any disrespect, but what you are asking me to do is only going to complicate the situation even more. You won't believe my explanation and I'm not sure I can convince you I'm telling you the truth."

Before her uncle could respond, Wendy said, "Ted. Why wouldn't we believe you? What is making you cover for these two friends? Do we know them?"

"No, you don't know them. Okay. Okay." He took a deep breath. "One of them is standing right behind Bob. Right there. But the other one seems to have wandered off like he always does." He then took a quick look around.

Wendy was looking behind Bob. "There's nobody behind Bob. Please don't make me look like a fool in front of my uncle. Ted?"

Suddenly, Ed came running around the corner of the house. "Doc! Doc! You're going to want to see this. Come on, Doc! Now!"

Vic turned towards Ed's voice but Doc and Bob both saw how excited Ed was.

Doc asked Ed, "What? What do I need to see now?"

Wendy and her uncle looked at each other, then back at Doc.

Ed said, "Come on, Doc. All of you need to see this graveyard over here. Come on!"

"What graveyard? Where?"

Again Wendy and her uncle looked at each other before the uncle asked, "Who are you talking to, and how do you know about that graveyard? It can't be seen from anywhere because of all the trees around it. Have these friends of yours gone over there too? Damn it, they have no right to be looking around my land!"

Doc looked at him. "Sir. Please. I'm just going to blurt this out, so forgive me. The three of us—Bob, Vic and myself - worked on recovering a plane crash up in the mountains for two months. We met two young people there. They are rather unique, to say the least. They were on the plane that went down."

Wendy immediately said, "But nobody survived that crash. They said so on the news. Why would that be kept secret from the news media? WHY?"

Again Doc spoke quickly. "Look. Nobody survived that plane crash. Neither did our two new friends." Doc paused as he noticed the confusion on Wendy and her uncles faces. "Now do you understand? They are the ones that went into the barn to talk to Mr. Gruber. That's why I can't really produce them for you. But now that I think about it, I can prove to you they exist, and that they're here with us right now."

The uncle had closed his eyes and was just standing there. Then he looked up. "Son, if you are scamming us in any way, I will get my rifle and give you 10 seconds to get off my land. Do I make myself clear?"

Bob raised his hand as if he were a kid in school. "Uh. There is really no need for Vic and I to be around for the rest of this discussion. So why don't we just walk back, you know, to the trees and get off your land, sir?"

Doc, Wendy and her uncle all said at the same time, "NO!"

Vic mumbled, "Okay. No problem. We'll just stay and help out."

Doc looked at the uncle and held up one hand. "Bear with me, sir." Then he looked at Ed. "Ed. Just tell me what it is you want me to see. I need you to help me out Ed before this good man shoots us all."

Ed looked at Wendy's uncle, then back at Doc. "Okay, Doc. Listen up. The old graveyard is full of the Gruber ancestors. Almost all of the headstones say 'Rest In Peace' at the top of the stone. But not Mr. Gruber's stone. It says, 'Rest In Peace Wherever You Are'. Got it, Doc? Wherever You Are."

Doc turned to the uncle and told him what Ed just said. The uncle looked at Wendy. She said, "Don't look at me. I never noticed that."

Before the uncle could respond, Doc snapped his fingers. "That's it. Good job, Ed!" Doc turned to the uncle. "Don't you see, sir? That's why Mr. Gruber is hanging out in the barn. He said it himself. He told the kids that he felt like he was supposed to be in the barn. It was like he belonged there. It all makes sense now."

The uncle interrupted. "You have kids out here, too? Damn it, son. How many people, and, or, spirits did you bring with you? Sounds like a small army!"

"Well, sir. We call the two spirits we picked up in the mountains 'the kids' because, well . . . it's a long story, sir." He paused for a second. "Anyway, I know exactly how we can help Mr. Gruber move on. It will also mean you won't see him at all around the barn. This has to be it!"

Everyone stared at Doc as Wendy asked, "What are you talking about? What makes sense? Ted, *you* aren't making any sense!"

"Ok. Look, everyone. Mr. Gruber told the kids that he was going to shore up that leaning chimney so it wouldn't fall. He also acted like he didn't know when it actually fell over. Get it?" He looked around and realized they still didn't understand. "The chimney fell on him! That *has* to be what happened. That explains the words on the top of his headstone, and why he hangs out at the barn. Understand?"

Bob looked at Vic, Wendy looked at her uncle and Martha watched Ed running off around the house again. She rolled her eyes and took off after him. Doc saw them leaving and shook his head.

To Wendy's complete amazement, her uncle said, "Okay, young man. I am not saying I believe any of this. But! I don't see how you could possibly know about what I promised Mr. Gruber. So, and I can't believe I'm saying this, what exactly are you proposing to do now?"

Doc seemed to relax a little as he looked at the barn. "I want to send the kids in to talk to Mr. Gruber again. I want them to convince him that we just want to help him, so he'll let us all come in. What do you say, sir?"

Hearing this, Wendy moved behind her uncle just as she had on that fateful day they first met Mr. Gruber.

"Okay, young man. But mark my words. Unless your two friends convince Mr. Gruber to come out and release me from my promise, NOBODY goes in there. NOBODY!" Then he shook his head before he added, "Okay, make that NOBODY that's alive. That means none of us. Understand?"

Doc nodded in agreement. "Good! Now all we have to do is find the kids."

Bob immediately said, "Vic and I will go get them. I saw them run around the side of the house that way." Relieved to put distance between themselves and Wendy's uncle, they took off in search of the kids.

The uncle reached around behind him and pulled Wendy to his side. "Don't be scared, Wendy. It's all going to be fine. Besides, I didn't think you were scared of Mr. Gruber since that day you yelled at him in the house."

She almost seemed embarrassed. "I don't understand why I'm feeling like this now. That day in the house, I was just so mad that he scared Mom and made her cry. I didn't even realize that I was yelling at him till he was gone. But standing here, in this very spot where you made that promise . . . Well, I guess I just felt like that same little scared girl all over again. But I'm better now, Dad. Really."

The sound of the two men running back prompted the uncle to repeat his terms to Doc. "Remember, son. If Mr. Gruber doesn't come out, nobody goes in. Understand?"

"Yessir!" He looked at the kids. "I need you both to go in and convince Mr. Gruber to come out and release Mr. Parkwood here from his promise. You have to get him to come out."

Martha said, "We will, Doc. Come on Ed." They disappeared through the doors. Not sure if or how long it would take, everyone quietly waited. There was a sudden gasp as Wendy and the uncle both saw Mr. Gruber walk out through the door.

The spirit walked right up and stopped in front of them. "Sir, I appreciate you having kept your word, but I release you from it now." He then looked at Doc. "It's you! I haven't seen you for a while, son. It's good to see you again." He then walked towards the doors as he called out to everyone, "Please, come. Everyone. Come on in."

Vic, Bob and Doc all eagerly walked right over to open the door before looking back. Wendy and her uncle hesitated before entering. Once inside, they all gathered around the smoke pit.

Doc spoke. "Mr. Gruber? Do you remember anything at all about the day this thing fell over?"

"I didn't at first, but your friends here helped me remember more about that day. I was propping up the back of the chimney with some logs when they started firing those damn cannons again. I was almost done when I noticed my old hand axe was laying right there at the base of the fireplace. Seems like I walked over and bent down to pick it up. That's when a cannon ball hit the tree that used to be right there." He stopped talking and closed his eyes. "Oh my God. I remember now. The ground shook so hard from that blast, that the logs all feel down. I tried to stand up to run, but everything went black. Odd, but I don't remember anything else. Huh. Sorry."

Doc said, "Mr. Gruber. How would you like to rejoin your entire family, sir?"

He smiled wide as he said, "Son, I'd like that very much. Very much indeed. Do you know where they are? I haven't seen them for so very long. Do they still live around here?"

Doc turned to the uncle. "I'm not sure where yet, but we are going to need some shovels. With your permission of course, sir."

Again, Bob and Vic volunteered to go get them. The uncle took them outside and pointed them towards a shed. He explained where several were and the men bolted in that direction. When he turned to go back into the barn, he found Doc was standing there. He asked Doc, "Son, why did he ask you if his family still lived around here? I don't understand."

"Well ,sir. I'm afraid that he doesn't even realize that he's dead. That's why he'll have no emotion about us pulling bones out from under that pit. He won't realize whose bones they are. As hard as it is to believe, he thinks we're the ghosts. He has no concept of how much time has gone by, nor does he question why he's out here."

A few minutes later, Bob and Vic returned with shovels. Vic asked Doc, "So where do we dig first?"

Ed had walked over to the pit and said, "Doc. Let me find out where he is." Then he got down on his hands and knees about four feet from what had been the bottom of the fireplace. Martha asked, "What are you going to do, Ed? Oh, please be careful." He said nothing, but grinned at her before turning and plunging his head into the ground at the edge of the stones. He was apparently moving his head and shoulders from side to side as he inched forward into the stones. Eventually, only his ankles and shoes were sticking out. Then they were sucked into the stones.

In a few seconds, he popped out of the top of the pit and was visible from the waist up.

"Found him Doc! He's right here. You guys need to dig right there. He's practically right on the surface, and just a foot or so in from the edge of the stones. I'd dig down about three or four inches so you don't break any of the bones."

After Doc explained that Ed had located Mr. Gruber's bones, the uncle stepped closer to oversee the digging. Wendy glanced up at Doc before she moved closer. Never breaking eye contact with him, she lifted his arm and wrapped it around her waist as she pressed against his side. They stood and watched the men dig.

Bob called out, "I found one!"

Vic said, "Be careful with it. Looks like it's been crushed really bad. Don't want it to crumble now."

The uncle looked around and pointed to an old wooden box in the corner of the barn, "Ted, we can use that to put the bones in." Doc hurried to retrieve it. Once Bob took it, Doc stepped back besides Wendy and she did the same thing she had done before.

Eventually the digging stopped as they thought they had located all the bones. The uncle looked at Doc and asked, "Well, you seem to know what to do. What now son?"

"With your permission sir, we need to bury the bones in that cemetery with the rest of his family."

"That makes sense, but we'll need to get a coffin, right?"

"No sir. All the coffins that were there in the cemetery have long turned to dust. We just need to put his remains in the ground and cover them up."

The uncle hesitated. "I'm not sure that's right. It just seems wrong somehow."

Doc tried to explain. "Sir, a coffin is a ritual that man uses. Mr. Gruber is in spirit form. It's like a twilight existence. He's neither here with the living nor there with the dead. We need to do this so he will be free to move on. Do you want him to remain in this limbo for eternity?"

"No. I do not. You're right, young man. We'll do it your way. I see now."

Bob gently picked up the box of bones and they all slowly moved towards the barn door. Ed stopped them all in their tracks. "Doc? Look." He pointed towards Mr. Gruber, who was still standing by the pit. He was looking at them as if he wanted to follow, but he also appeared confused. "What's wrong with him, Doc? Why isn't he coming with us?"

Doc thought for a moment. "It can only be one thing. We didn't get all the bones." It was odd to see how Mr. Gruber relaxed as the box of bones got closer to the pit. It took Ed a few minutes, but he found two more bones and pointed them out to Bob. With the last bone in the box, Mr. Gruber happily walked along beside the kids as everyone headed towards the graveyard.

Doc motioned to Ed to come up alongside him, "You and Martha keep him busy and where he can't read the headstones. I don't want him getting upset." Ed nodded that he understood.

Martha and Ed stopped by the trees that surrounded the graveyard and asked Mr. Gruber to tell them how he built that big house by hand. He immediately began to explain in detail, obviously very proud of his achievement.

Bob and Vic began digging a hole about four feet deep right in front of Mr. Gruber's tombstone. The uncle turned to Doc. "I heard Mr. Gruber say he was glad to see you again. If you never came on my land before, how did you ever meet him?"

"Well sir, I found him up on the hill in those trees one day. I actually talked to him several times up there. He always seemed to be looking for something, but he would never tell me what it was."

"Well son. I think I have the answer to that. His youngest boy fell out of a tree up there, broke his neck and died on the spot. Mr. Gruber insisted that the boy be buried right there. But his wife never liked him being that far from the house. So when Mr. Gruber disappeared, she had her other sons build this family grave yard close to the house. Then she had the boy's remains moved here, so she wouldn't have to go so far to talk to him. I have an old Gruber diary in the house. It tells all about it."

With the hole finished, Bob and Vic began gently stacking the old bones in the ground. Once they were all in the hole, they looked at Doc. The uncle asked Doc, "What is going to happen now, son? Have you ever done this type of thing before?"

Doc chuckled softly, "Well, not exactly sir. But I can tell you what I think is going to happen. Mr. Gruber is going to leave us. I'm not sure if you and Wendy will see it, but you may since you both see him now. If you do, it will be the most amazing thing you have ever seen in your life."

The uncle now chuckled. "Son, I've spent the entire afternoon looking at the spirit of a man that died a century and a half ago. I thought *that* was the most amazing thing I'd ever seen in my life. I can hardly wait to see what you're talking about!"

Doc motioned for the guys to start covering up the bones, then he yelled at the kids to bring Mr. Gruber over. The three spirits came strolling up. Mr. Gruber was smiling as he continued to explain how he built the house. When the last shovel full of dirt was tossed on the hole, they patted it down softly.

Mr. Gruber suddenly stopped talking and lost all expression in his face. His head turned and he focused for the first time on the hole where his bones had been placed. Without hesitation, he walked over and stood in front of his gravestone. His head movements indicated that he was reading all the other gravestones. Once done, he stepped forward and touched his own stone. Then he stepped backward onto the freshly-filled hole before he turned around to face everyone. He smiled and said quietly, "Thank you all for helping me go home to my family." Then he closed his eyes and tilted his head back as if he was looking towards heaven.

His body was engulfed in a blinding white light and there was an extremely loud whooshing sound heard by everyone except Bob. The light only lasted for a second or two, and was gone as fast as it appeared. Doc didn't have to ask if Wendy and her uncle had seen the light, because they were blinking like everyone else.

The uncle immediately bowed his head and spoke out loud.

"Dear Lord, thank you for taking Mr. Gruber to once again be with his family. Though I only knew him a very short time, I found him to be a gentle man of faith. He endured a long separation from those he loved, and he did it with selfless dignity. He was a very good man. Amen."

Bob and Vic both sounded choked up as they said, "We'll just be putting these tools back where we found them, sir."

Wendy gave her uncle a kiss on his cheek, then spoke through tears as she said, "That was beautiful, Daddy. It was just perfect."

Doc put both hands over his face and breathed a sigh of relief before clapping them together. "So it's done. YES!"

Bob and Vic were smiling as they ran back. The uncle asked Doc, "Are your two spirit friends still here, young man? And if they are, I'd like to know their names please."

Doc nodded, "Yes sir. They're both standing just to the left of Bob there. Martha is closest to Bob and she's holding Ed's hand."

He looked at Wendy first then to where Doc pointed. "Ed and Martha, I would like to express my appreciation to you both for what you've done here today. I think that it is very admirable of you to help Mr. Gruber like you have. I just wish that there was some way that we could help you. I don't know if this is the kind of place where you would consider staying, but you're both very welcome to do just that. This is my home and I guess what I'm trying to say is that it can be yours too. I hope you will consider it. Oh, and I really hope that someday I'll get to actually see you both. It would be my honor to do so. Thank you both again."

Doc was watching the kids and nodded as they talked. Then he turned to the uncle. "Sir, they both want you to know how humbling it is to have such a gracious offer from a man such as you. The offer to stay here is appreciated and very kind. But they want you to know this. They are more impressed with the fact that you addressed them by their names while acting like you could see them. They realize how difficult it must have been for you to do that. It just proves that you are a man of true character. They would like to come by now and then, just so they could look in on you. Oh, and Ed says he can't believe you are inviting two more ghosts to come live here, with all the ones that are already here. Ed's a joker, sir. He always makes us all laugh. It's just his way."

The uncle smiled and said, "I'd like for them to drop by whenever they want. For my part, you're both friends that I will always long to see."

Vic said, "Bob has expressed a desire to enhance his riding skills. So the kids and I are going to help him get some extra saddle time. If you folks will excuse us, we are going to be riding around the hill for a while."

Bob added, "Doc, this could take a while. So feel free to chat with Wendy and her uncle for as long as you want. Just keep an ear open in case I fall off that big animal and break something."

The uncle stepped over and shook both men's hands. "You both are also very welcome at my home any time you are in Gettysburg, gentlemen. Any time at all."

Bob and Vic headed towards the horses as the uncle asked Doc, "Would you like that lemonade now, young man? I have about a million questions to ask you about ghosts."

"Sounds good, sir. I'll be happy to tell you what I know. Just don't expect me to prove it!"

They all laughed as they left the graveyard. Wendy was holding one of her uncle's hands as they walk. She motioned for Doc to take her other hand, and they headed back to the house.

• • •

With Doc educating Wendy and her uncle on ghosts, the others were in the ravine and passing through the gate. Vic and his horse were the last ones through the gate, so he pulled it hard to make sure the latch caught. The sound was still vibrating through the metal frame as he turned to follow the others. But he was stopped by the sight of Bob and the kids standing in front of a man dressed in an immaculate white robe. He almost appeared to have a glow about him.

He looked right at the kids. "You know, I came here to collect Mr. Gruber and here you two are. I've been looking for both of you."

Vic walked up beside Bob and stopped. Neither one ever took their eyes off the robed man. Though they spoke at the same time, they said different things. Bob said, "I can hear him!" while Vic said, "I can see him!"

The kids both looked at the men then back at the robed man. He looked at the men and said, "What? You can see and hear me? No you can't."

Bob and Vic simply nodded 'Yes' in unison. Combined with their blank expressions, they resembled two bobble head dolls.

Martha asked, "Vic, you can see him? Really?"

Ed asked, "Bob, you really hear this guy?"

Bob and Vic continue to mimic bobble heads as they turned towards the kids.

The robed man glared at the kids. "Wait a minute! Are you two talking to those two? No, no, no! You can't be talking to the living. Are you crazy! This is just unacceptable, people!"

Bob saw that Martha had stepped behind Ed, so he took a step towards the robed man. "Hey, buddy! You watch how you talk to our friends."

Vic stepped up to Bob's side. "You have no right to scare her like that, mister."

Having the two men step towards him in such a threatening manner caused him to react. He suddenly glowed with a great white intensity that shocked both the men and the kids. Bob quickly took a step back behind Vic and patted him on the shoulder. "Looks like you pissed him off there, Vic."

Vic immediately looked back at Bob. "Me? You're the one that bolted towards him. Why, he probably thought you were going to hit him."

The robed guy rolled his eyes as he stared at the two men. "Hey! Hush. Both of you! Not another word. I mean it now. Shhhhhh!"

Both men stared, wide-eyed. Though neither of them took their eyes off him, they both were compelled to say one more thing.

Vic said, "See what you've done now? We've been shushed by a ghost. You are always getting me in trouble. You happy now?"

Bob replied, "Me? You're bigger than me, buddy. He was probably scared that you were going to step on him with those humongous boots of yours. Can you blame him for overreacting?"

Ed couldn't help himself and laughed as he said, "I guess both of you are in time out! HA!"

The robed man now glowed even brighter, and his size grew until he was a few feet taller than all of them. Seeing that they had finally stopped talking, he slowly returned to the size of a normal man and the glow faded away. He didn't say anything at first, but just looked at the men then turned to the kids, saying nothing.

Ed stepped behind Martha. "I don't think he'll hit a girl. At least I hope not!"

The robed man shook his head before looking towards the sky. "Why me? Why? I was having SUCH a good day. Three sudden expires and a long time stranded spirit. All successfully brought home. I was on my way to a record." He then stretched out his arms and again looked skyward. "And now this? Spirits consorting with the living. Really?"

He dropped his arms to his side and they made a loud pop. Then he pointed at Ed. "I would never HIT anyone. Can't you see what I am? I'm here to help you both. Not hurt you at all." Then he looked at Martha while he pointed at the men. "Are those two always like that?" Then he held both hands out to stop her from answering. "NO! Don't answer that. I'm afraid to know the answer." Finally, he looked at the men. "Now look, gentlemen. I am not sure what is going on here, so PLEASE don't interrupt me again. OK?"

Bob and Vic were again doing their bobble head act.

He waited a moment to be sure they were going to remain silent, then he turned to the kids. "Ok, look. I don't know why you left the area where you died, but you did. So, let's just skip that question altogether. What's done is done. Moving on. What possessed you to come here to Gettysburg? Surely you knew we were looking for you. And you come to the one place on earth that has more marooned spirits per square inch than anywhere else! Did you just want to make my job even harder?" Again he held his hands out towards the kids. "NO! Don't answer that either. Never mind. It's okay. I think."

Ed was still standing behind Martha as he held up one hand like a kid in school. She saw his hand go up and she spun around to shove him in front of her. They were playfully struggling to be the back person when they heard the robed guy.

"Excuse me! Can you two stop playing around?" He looked at them, then the men, and then back at them while he again pointed at the men. "I can see that those two guys' behavior is rubbing off on you two. See what happens when you hang out with the living?"

The robed man noticed that Ed still had his hand up before asking, "WHAT?"

Ed slowly said, "Well We didn't have any instructions telling us what to do and not do. So it's kind of your fault if we broke any rules. Don't you think?"

Martha then added, "That's right, mister. How could we know what to do? And these guys are just trying to help us. They are our friends, and I don't know what we'd have done without them."

The robed man's demeanor softened considerably as he studied the kids. "You both are rather unique. I have never encountered any like you. You're unusually articulate. You also seem to be spatially aware of both time and your situation. Hmm. Interesting. There is definitely more going on here that I'm not yet aware of. I'll need to check in and . . . "

He was interrupted by Doc's booming voice asking, "What's going on here?" Everyone turned to face him. Since nobody answered, Doc asked again. "What are ya'll doing?"

The men and the kids silently began nodding their heads in the direction of the robed man. Doc watched for a moment. "What's wrong with all your necks?" Then he smiled and added, "Oh no you don't! I don't know what you're up to, but I'm not falling for it this time! Nope. Not going to do it!"

Bob said, "Doc! Over there!" and he nodded again in the direction of the robed man.

Doc looked around with a quizzical expression before he raised one eyebrow. "What? Over where?"

Ed said, "Wow. Doc doesn't see him."

Martha said, "He has to see him. He sees all of us. Don't you, Doc?"

Again, Doc asked, "See who? Where?"

The men joined the kids as they all tried to hide the fact that they were all pointing towards the robed man. Doc looked again, but they all now realized that he really didn't see the man.

Bob said, "Doc. There is a new guy in a really white robe standing right there. I don't know why you can't see him, but Vic does. And believe it or not, I can hear him."

Doc's confused look gave way to a huge smile as he began laughing. "I get it now. You all want me to think there is a ghost that I can't see or hear. Good one, but I'm not biting."

The robed guy said, "Ok. That's the second time someone has referred to me as a ghost. I'm not a GHOST! I'm an angel. Get it? ANGEL!"

Vic said, "Wow, so he's an angel."

Bob said, "Vic, that means you made an angel mad. That can't be good."

Vic glared at Bob. "Me? You're the one that charged at him and made him glow like the sun! Scared the hell out of me and the kids. You really should apologize to Martha."

Ed was still looking at the robed man as he calmly commented, "An angel. Huh. Who knew?"

Doc asked again, "Who are you talking about?"

The men and the kids pointed and said together, "The new guy!"

"And the new guy is an angel? Right?" asked Doc.

Bob glanced quickly at the man before he said, "Well, he says he is. Who knows?"

The robed man looked at the kids and asked, "Since you know this guy's name, I assume you hang out with him too. But if he doesn't see spirits, then why?"

Martha said, "He can see and hear spirits. I don't know why he can't see or hear you."

The new guy smiled and said, "That's because I'm not a ghost. I'm an angel. There's a big difference."

Ed said, "Enlighten us."

The angel said, "It's simple. Your friend has a gift for seeing the spirits of those that have passed from this plane of existence. But I'm an angel. I didn't live in this plane so therefore I didn't pass from it. That's why he can't see me."

Bob and Vic looked at each other quickly before Vic asked, "But we can hear and see the kids, the ghosts that are all around this place, and you too. Explain that."

The angel was shaking his head. "I can't. Like I started to say when this Doc guy walked up, there's something going on here that I just don't know about yet. I need to check in and find out what I'm supposed to do and how I'm to handle this." He then closed his eyes and bowed his head. He took on a soft white glow that caused everyone to feel very calm and peaceful. Then the glow faded quickly and he opened his eyes. "Okay. I understand now. At least I *think* I do."

He turned again to look at the kids. "I'm here to offer you both a second chance at life. But before I do, I must offer these men something." He turned towards Bob and Vic. "You will have to explain this to your friend Ted, or as you call him, Doc. It seems that I am to work with the three of you from time to time going forward from today. You each have special gifts, but your real strength will come from working together. So remember that. It was a very impressive thing that you did by helping Mr. Gruber to pass over for me to take him home. Your work did not go unnoticed." He looked upwards to illustrate who had noticed. "So, it is hoped that the three of you will continue to collectively help spirits that are stuck like Mr. Gruber. It is totally up to you three to decide if you want to do this, or not. But if you choose to continue, then I will be available to help. Not at your beck and call, just as needed."

Bob asked, "And who decides when you're needed?"

The angel again looked upwards. "Who do you think? Now, please explain all this to Doc, or Ted, to him." He then turned to the kids.

"Ok, now it's your turn. I've never been involved with what I'm about to convey to you. I've heard about it, but this is my first time. So here goes." He looked over at the men just as they finished bringing Doc up to speed. Then he continued. "You are both being given a second chance as I said. That means that you are being allowed to go back and live a life again."

He watched the kids as they both looked at each other, then wrapped their arms around each another. Martha laid her head on Ed's chest but kept her eyes on the angel. Ed lowered his head until his cheek was resting on top of her head. He too was looking intently at the angel. Ed was the first to speak.

"I lived a life alone. It wasn't until after my death that I found what I had wanted in life. If we let you send us back to the living, can you promise that we will be together in this new life?"

The angel paused before speaking. "I'm afraid not, son. There are never any guarantees in life. Free will. You know that."

Ed continued, "I can't speak for her, but I'd rather stay together in this existence than go back and risk not finding her there." He lifted her head with his finger and looked into her eyes. "I mean it, Martha. I want you so much. I want to be with you so much. I can't stand the thought of not being with you. Not now that I've had this time with you. It's not life as we knew it before, but it's not bad. I feel you and you feel me. We don't want for anything, we're never cold or hungry. It's not bad this way. And we're together. But I will do whatever you want, babe. If you want to go back, then I go where you go. And if we do go back, I can promise you that I will NEVER stop looking for you. NEVER!"

She had tears in her eyes as she gently kissed his lips. Then she turned to the angel. "I just can't lose him, either. He's what I always wanted. I just don't know what to do. You're an angel. Please help us decide what to do."

All three men had tears rolling down their cheeks as well. Even the angel was visibly shaken by the emotions in the air. "I can't make this decision for you. You have to decide on your own. I'm sorry."

As Bob filled Doc in on what the angel said, Doc spoke up. "Excuse me sir. If they stay here in this existence, will they go on as they are now?"

The angel looked at Doc and smiled. "Your friend has raised a very good point." He turned to the kids. "I couldn't volunteer this, rules you know. But since the subject has been brought up on your behalf by your good friend Doc, I can tell you. The answer is no. Things will not stay the same.

"As time goes on, you will become more closely aligned with the lifeless souls that you see around this place. Maybe not wandering around as aimlessly as they are, but you will change. You will not feel each other after a while. You will slowly become less articulate and animated. I can tell that you are very deeply in love, but it is hard to know what will fade in time for either of you."

Martha stood on her tiptoes so she could whisper in Ed's ear. Then he said, "I agree. We have to go back."

They looked at the men. Martha said, "We both love all three of you more than you will ever know. I . . . WE are so very glad that we met each of you. You are our friends now and forever." Then they stepped hand-in-hand in front of the angel. "As my love Ed here likes to say, LET'S DO THIS!"

The angel smiled before raising both arms wide and looking towards the sky. As he stood there he began to glow again. Then a large oval of light appeared to his left. It was the size of a door and the light was swirling like water inside that oval shape. He lowered his arms and held out his hand to Martha, "You first miss, and then Ed."

They stepped closer to the oval of light and he motioned for her to step into it. She turned to look at Ed. He said, "I love you, Martha and I will never quit until I find you. NEVER!"

With tears in her eyes and her lips slightly quivering, she stepped into the light. At the last moment before she disappeared, she looked back over her shoulder at Ed.

"Please find me."

Chapter 18

BIRTH OF 6 FRIENDS

SIX NEW FATHERS silently stared through the nursery glass at the new additions to their families. Each was lost in his own thoughts of how the new little being on the other side of the glass would grow up and turn into the most wonderful young person. They were standing within feet of each other, yet none of them were remotely aware that another new father was nearby. So intense were the visions of what life held for their offspring, that they all stood motionless as they smiled uncontrollably at the newborn babies.

Three of the men were envisioning tiny little pink dresses, dolls and a lovely little baby girl that would surely be the light of their lives. Next to their wives, each man already knew that they were looking upon one more female that would dominate the rest of their lives and they were absolutely okay with it. In fact, they could already see themselves trying to be a strong and firm father, only to crumble when their little girl said, "Oh PLEASE, daddy." No man, nor beast, would ever hurt their little girl. Not as long as they had breath and strength to protect them, NEVER.

Likewise, the other three men saw baseballs, footballs and heard the roar of the crowds that would surely be cheering for their sons' eventual athletic achievements. Undoubtedly, there would also be a steady stream of beautiful girls coming over to shyly ask if their son was home. No man would have ever had as great a son as theirs would be. They could see the day when they would happily pass leadership of their family fortunes over to the young man that would spring from this squirming miniature human. Just like the fathers with daughters, each of these men also felt very protective of their sons. But there was an instinctive feeling of a father for a son. Yes, a feeling that his son would eventually be able to defend himself as well as others. Each father would come to his child's aid when the odds were overwhelming or unfair. But in most conflicts, they would be driven to let their sons fight their own battles.

Yet there were many similarities in the futures that each man foresaw for his own child. They were sure that they would grow to be ethical adults and respected for it. Many would ask for help, and be given it by the adult versions of these newly born babies. The world would definitely be a better place now that their child was here to help out.

However, the birth of six friends would not go unnoticed by a world already full of so many people with so many agendas. Each developing child would be affected by both negative and positive events directly related to others. These were things that were out of anyone's control, even the most diligent and protective parent. Yes, the world was also a parent of sorts. It introduced so many conflicting ideas and beliefs into the development of each person. No one should ever be surprised that so many different types of individuals co-exist in their town, their country, or on their planet.

Eventually, one man broke the reverent silence. "That one's mine. Which one is yours?" Then a bonding of six men happened. The conversation revealed that the six of them lived within two blocks of each other—a rare coincidence, even in a town as small as their own. An immediate friendship emerged from this new revelation. Soon this bond would spread to include each man's wife. These six new mothers would also bond as women do. Each would coo over and playfully tickle the other's children, just as they did their own. These six families would forever be bound by friendship. And so would these six special children from sharing a common birth date.

Time passed quickly and there had been many backyard cookouts as the six families silently celebrated their common link. As their children grew, there were two that always migrated to one another. They happily played with the others too, but this boy and girl were actually observed crawling towards each other on numerous occasions. They learned to sit up together and were often seen holding each other in cute little bear hugs. Then, as the children began to learn to walk, these two were observed holding hands at they waddled a few steps together before flopping down on their diapered bottoms. To the amazement of the parents and on more than one occasion, the boy would ultimately regain his stance before he labored to help the little girl stand. A few more steps and down they would go again, only to laugh and roll around on the floor. From the two mother's point of view, they assumed that the little boy was laughing because the little girl would tickle him. However, they failed to notice what she was really doing. She would subtly poke him, and he would stare at her while she laughed uncontrollably. Their mothers viewed this as absolutely adorable. It was a common belief among the group that "those two are destined to be together."

The six youths progressed as inseparable friends from kindergarten up until they started high school. There, extracurricular activities pulled them into new groups of teenagers with similar interests. Though they all still honored the earliest childhood memories of each other, many new high school acquaintances began to dominate more and more of their time. They slowly began to follow their own paths as all young people do during their high school years. And, as is the case with almost all students, their senior year was the culmination of their high school experiences.

Two of the girls were on the drill team that performed at sporting events during half times, while the other one was a cheerleader.

Maggie Rathburn and Misty Artham endured the pressure of holding flags that rippled in the wind at these games, while Mary Thacker had to remain bubbly and bouncy in her cheerleader role. She was naturally sought after by the majority of the high school males. Though she was blonde, beautiful, flirty and very popular, Mary was friendly to everyone she met.

Misty was a brunette with a captivating smile that she showed to everyone. She was known to be quirky by both students and staff at the school. The apparent haphazardness, with which she did things, obscured the fact that she was the smartest of the three. She could easily be cast as the absent-minded professor type, if it were not for her truly beautiful dark eyes that danced with mischief at a moment's notice.

Maggie had black hair that shone in the light. Her porcelain complexion was the envy of every adult woman who saw her. This contradiction of dark hair and beautiful white skin always drew attention to Maggie, who was known by all as the friendliest person in school.

All three of the boys played baseball, but only two played football.

Ethan Drydon was one of the football team's best receivers, and the main backup pitcher for the baseball team. He was tall, blonde and considered very handsome by many of the cool girls in school. Even though he was extremely popular, he never belittled any student, and had been known to side with the non-popular kids against the popular ones. He did not like bullies of any kind.

Franklin Ekheart had never been interested in playing football, but he absolutely loved playing baseball. He was the starting right fielder and a very reliable relief pitcher. He was average height with wavy black hair, and had always been Ethan's best friend.

Emit Daniels was the starting second baseman for the baseball team. He also played football for the school, and was a second string fullback as well as a second string receiver. His ruggedly handsome appearance was enhanced by a strong jawline. His brown eyes were often slightly hidden by his disheveled sandy brown hair. There was always a mischievous smile on his face, which earned him the nickname of the Joker.

Six close friends from birth had now morphed into six self-sufficient individuals with all the differences and individual traits formed by their varying experiences. Still, there were two souls in this group that harbored a growing desire for one another. Though that desire had been obvious from birth, it had slowly become undetectable by first the parents, then the two individuals themselves. All that remained was a constant feeling that they should be looking for someone. It haunted them like a dream that stayed with in one's mind for hours after awakening. They didn't see a face, hear a voice or remember a meeting. Yet not a day went by without both of them closing their eyes and hoping for some cosmic enlightenment as to where their beloved other half was. They felt them close, and this feeling was about to burst from their thoughts into the daylight of their lives.

The six families had always planned on having a celebratory cookout just before their children's graduation from high school. It was during this symbolic get-together that the six friends decided that they should all go on a joint camping trip a few weeks after graduation. With no parents as chaperones, they could share their first taste of adult freedom just as they had shared their entry into life.

So was decided a fateful camping trip to Cantor Basin.

Chapter 19

A CAMPING TRIP

A BLUE SUV towed a trailer filled with food and camping supplies as it left a trail of music along the highway. With windows down and the stereo blasting, the six joyous occupants were laughing loudly as they enjoyed their first experience with adult freedom. The atmosphere had been this way the entire trip. As it rounded a turn, there was a small, unmanned park ranger shed at the edge of the road with brochures for the taking. A quick stop and grab only took seconds.

Since Ethan was driving, he immediately handed the brochures to his navigator. "Here you go, Frank. Just don't get us lost this time." Misty called out from the very back, "Then don't give it to Frank!" Then Misty's back seat partner added, "We only have food for a week. We're all going to DIE!"

As the laughter subsided, Frank looked over his shoulder towards the back seat. "Good one, Emit! But no need to worry. There's only one road that goes straight up the middle of the valley."

Mary and Maggie were sitting in the second row seats. They grinned at each other before Maggie snatched the brochure from Frank and found the map. "Well, everyone. Frank can read this map. The road *does* go straight up the middle."

Emit was looking over Maggie's shoulder as he commented, "Yeah, but that map only has one road on it!" He fell back into his seat and leaned over on Misty's shoulder as he rolled his eyes at her. "The last map had lots of roads to pick from and we all know what happened then. Don't we?" The collective group screamed out, "WE GOT LOST!"

Even Ethan was laughing as he glanced over at Frank, who said, "It's not funny. I told you I didn't like maps." Then he looked out the window at the beautiful scenery flying by. The laughter was quickly drowned out by the thumping bass of the next song on the CD player.

Maggie said, "Turn down the music for a minute. Okay, we need to start looking for a bridge. The memorial is not far past it, and it looks like the campsites start right around there. So we're going to have to pick where we want to set up camp."

Mary shook her head. "I'm telling you, I don't want to camp to close to that memorial. It's just too creepy! All those people died there."

Emit pushed the back of Mary's seat with his hand to get her attention. "What's the matter, Mary? Afraid you're going to see a ghost?"

Mary immediately turned to snap at him, "Hey, don't do that. And for your information, mister, ghosts are real. I know."

Emit snickered. "Oh, please don't tell us about your aunt again. It always gives me nightmares." He tried to lay his head on Misty's chest, but she grabbed both of his ears and pushed him away. "Hey. What do you think you're doing?"

"I'm scared, Misty. I just want you to hold me for a minute."

Maggie was watching and said, "He's just being a guy, Misty. I knew we should have made him sit in front with Ethan."

Misty looked confused. "What does that mean, Maggie?"

Mary rolled her eyes at Maggie before turning to address Misty. "He's just trying to get a feel of your boobs, dummy!"

Misty's eyes widened, then her lips tightened. "Well, then. Since we are friends, I should be able to feel his too!" Having said that, she quickly reached over and pinched one of his nipples as hard as she could. Emit immediately started yelling and pulled her hand off, but not until she had gotten her point across.

"Ouch! That hurt. Damn it, I was just playing around."

Misty smiled sweetly. "So was I."

Mary, who had witnessed this entire scene, said, "Hmm. I have to remember that little maneuver." She held up one hand high and Misty slapped it loudly. Maggie nodded at Misty. "Go, girl!"

Frank turned back towards the road ahead. He muttered, "This is going to be a disaster."

Ethan was looking at Emit in the rear view mirror. "I'm warning you, man. If these girls hurt you, I'm not driving you to the hospital."

Emit looked over at Misty with his irresistible smile. "I was just kidding around, you know. But, sorry!"

She leaned over on his shoulder and softly patted his still stinging nipple. Then she looked up into his eyes and said, "I know. But you need to remember that we are your friends. Not your harem!"

His chuckling caused her head to shake as he said, "Friends. Got it!"

Mary pointed ahead and sang out, "There's the bridge!"

All heads looked forward except for Maggie's. She was looking at the map again. "Okay. It says here that the memorial is ten minutes up the road on the right. There is a small parking lot there."

Ethan said, "Well, it's going to be getting dark in a few hours. So we need to go on and pick out a campsite. It's summer, but I read that the temperatures at night are still down around 60 degrees until next month. We have a lot to get done before it gets dark."

Mary commented, "I still don't know why we had to come so soon. We should have waited until then. It'd be warmer."

Misty said, "Yes, and there would be crowds of campers then too. This is so much better. I'd rather wear a coat than have to listen to all those strangers moving around in the night."

Mary again commented, "All I'm saying is that my bottom and legs get cold easily. At least when I'm cheering in that skimpy little outfit at your games, I'm warm from jumping up and down."

Emit finally spoke up. "Well." He noticed that the other two girls were glaring at him. "What?" He looked at them for a moment then continued, "All I was going to say is that I don't feel anything where Misty pinched me. So all Mary has to do is let me pinch her on her legs and . . . " He stopped again because now Mary had turned and glared at him.

Frank said, "You have to drive faster, man. We really need to get him out of the back before the girls kill him."

Everyone except for Mary looked at the memorial parking lot as they passed by. Then began the process of agreeing on how far was far enough from the crash site for Mary.

Misty was pointing out the window. "Oh, look over there. That spot looks pretty."

Ethan was now watching Mary in the rearview mirror. "I don't know. We can come back to it if we can't find a better one."

Then Emit pointed out the other side of the car at a secluded spot nestled back into the trees. A quick glance in the rearview mirror told Ethan they needed to go a little farther, and probably pick a site on the opposite side of the road from where the memorial was.

Maggie had been looking at the map again. "Hey guys. There should be a permanent bathhouse and restrooms up here on the left somewhere. It shows several campsites all around it."

Mary immediately said, "I think that sounds perfect." She was the first one to see them and said, "There they are. Oh, any one of these will do." She turned to look at the other two girls. Misty and Maggie were looking out the windows as they both nodded in agreement.

Ethan pulled off the paved road, tires crunching the gravel. Emit suddenly pointed. "Look. That one there! Isn't that a stack of firewood over by that pit?"

Frank seemed excited as well. "What luck! That's enough to get us through the night easy."

Ethan slowed to a stop and killed the engine. "This is very good. We can just concentrate on getting the camp all set up and start cooking. I like it."

The little band of friends quickly began to set up a functional yet comfortable camp. Their families had been camping together for as long as they could remember, so they slipped into a well-rehearsed routine. Soon the two large tents were up and the decision was made as to which one was for the girls.

Of course, this decision was made by the girls. With that established, each tent was quickly filled with inflatable mattresses, sleeping bags and personal belongings. Thanks to the hard work of a previous camper, there was a large fire burning before the trailer was even empty. Ethan and Emit had snatched a large wooden picnic table from a nearby campsite. They strategically placed it as close to the fire as possible. Then a large tarp was stretched over four poles to shield the table from both rain and sun.

The final touch was to place the six folding chairs around the other side of the fire. The boys set up their chairs in seconds, but the girls took several minutes, due to each one agonizing over the position of her chair. The boys had witnessed this ritual on too many occasions and simply ignored it. Only the cooler with the drinks was carried to the table, while the one with the food was left in the rear of the SUV. No need to attract any unwanted guests. At last, the boys set up four large poles about the camp and began readying four kerosene lamps. Each lamp was hung from a pole and ready to be lit when darkness fell.

Once the girls had agreed on the menu for the night, the boys were informed that they were having hot dogs. There was a collective expression of 'Great! How long?' At this point, they were kicked out of the kitchen and withdrew to the safety of the other side of the fire. Then the inevitable male horseplay started with an occasional comment from the girls.

Soon they were sitting around the table and enjoying the usual campsite chatter. Each one of the six had taken note of how well they had done as a group, especially since there was no adult supervision. The evening was filled with laughter and an occasional foot race around the table as one chased another.

It had been an entertaining evening, but the activities of the long day soon sent the tired young people to their tents.

• • •

The smell of morning coffee was courtesy of Frank. He was first to wake, and had emerged from the tent to brew it. Mary soon joined him and they worked together to add the smells of breakfast to the air. The assortment of heavenly aromas compelled the others to join in the crisp morning air. There was a calm morning conversation around the fire as they all observed the sunrise. Each friend would occasionally sigh as they recalled memories of past camping trips.

Misty sat staring into the fire as she spoke. "It's so hard to believe that we have graduated already. Wow, 12 years went by so fast."

Emit looked at her in disbelief, "Not fast enough for me. I don't think I could have sat through another hour of listening to Mr. Trupin talk about history!"

Maggie sounded very sad. "I still can't believe we're all going to different colleges. It won't be the same, not seeing each of you every day."

Ethan tried to lighten the mood. "That's why we have to make this a very memorable trip. It's our first one without our parents. In fact, we could all agree to do this every year as a type of reunion."

Misty suddenly got excited. "Yeah, that sounds great. I can just see us when we're all married and bringing our families together here. Wouldn't that be neat?"

Emit immediately said, "Whoa there, Misty! What have you been drinking? I plan on doing a lot of living before I settle down. If I *ever* settle down."

Mary spoke slowly as she stared into the dancing flames. "It's hard to believe it's all over. High school, I mean. I know it sounds conceited, but what if I'm not as popular in college?" Then she looked around at her lifelong friends. "I've always had you guys to hang out with. I know we kinda went our own ways in high school, but you were always there and I knew it. I won't have that anymore. I'll be alone in a strange new town. I'm not sure I can do this."

Frank realized she was visibly troubled by this new revelation. "Don't worry, Mary. You're very beautiful and friendly. They're not the only reasons you're so popular, but it will attract people to you no matter where you are. They'll see you like we see you, and you'll have plenty of friends in no time."

Maggie reached over and patted Mary's leg. "We're all only a cell phone away, baby. You can call anyone of us at any time." She looked around at the others before she asked, "Right, guys?" There was a collective 'YES'.

Mary looked around the circle of friends and smiled. "Thanks. I'll be doing that for sure."

Ethan stood up and began turning off the lamps before he jogged over to the car. A few seconds later, a small green football hit the back of Frank's chair and almost bounced into the fire. They all heard Ethan call out, "Come on, you deadbeats. Let's play tag like we used to when we were little." Misty had retrieved the ball and was already in hot pursuit of her victim. The others quickly followed.

The canyon walls echoed their laughter as they chased each other around the open field for over an hour. Finally the boys acted as if they were as tired as the girls, and everyone returned to clean up the camp. With the least popular tasks all finished, they hopped back in the car to go explore the plane crash memorial back down the road.

Maggie was looking at the brochure again. "There's a path from the parking lot to the crash site. Looks like a big circular walkway goes all around the center of the site." She was about to say something, but stopped when Ethan pulled into the parking lot and skidded to a stop on the gravel.

Once out of the car, the boys all walked too fast for the girls to keep up. They stopped at a huge stone with a plaque on top of it and waited for the girls. Misty immediately began reading out loud. It described the event and listed the names of everyone who had helped with the recovery and cleanup. Then they started the long walk to the actual site. The pathway led to a large circular path just like the brochure had showed. There was another large plaque where this path joined the circular one. They stopped and again Misty began to read out loud. It told the date and the number of people that lost their lives here in the crash. Each passenger's name was printed in the middle of the large metal plaque. Misty skipped the names and continued to read what was etched into the bottom of the plaque.

"All except 14 passengers were accounted for. These individuals' bodies were never recovered. In the center of the circle before you is a shiny spot that looks like melted glass. It is actually the top of a now solid mass of metal, plastic and sand that simultaneously melted together. The impact crater had filled with massive amounts of burning jet fuel, producing the necessary extreme heat that effectively combined all the substances. It is assumed that the missing bodies are also represented in this mass.

"An estimate puts the weight of this mass at over 6,000 pounds, making it impossible to move by the helicopters of the day. Although the mass could have been removed later by truck, it was determined to be impossible to extract any of the 14 passengers' remains from the mass. The families of those passengers agreed to leave the mass here as a memorial to their loved ones.

"As you walk around the circle, you will see 14 small plaques. They are the names of those that never left this valley."

Frank was the first to realize that Mary looked like she was going to faint, and was slowly stepping backwards. He touched Misty's arm and nodded towards Mary. The girls quickly took her by each arm and walked her to a nearby bench.

"What's wrong, Mary?" Maggie asked.

"I can't believe those poor people are still here. It just seems wrong to leave them here like this. I don't think I can be here."

Misty sat down beside her and held her hand. "Mary. Listen to me, Mary. You've been to graveyards before. This is no different. But here, you don't know anyone. You don't know these people."

Eyes closed, Mary was rubbing her forehead with one hand. "It doesn't feel right here. What if I *did* know one of them?"

Misty said, "Hon, you couldn't possibly have known any of these people. None of us were even born yet when this plane crashed. Remember the date? It crashed more than two months before any of us were even born."

Mary slowly opened her eyes. "Well, it still feels strange to be here. I want to go back to the car."

Misty stood up. "Come on, Mary. I'll go back with you."

The guys watched the two girls disappear down the path then they turned to look at Maggie. "Don't worry about me, boys. I feel fine." She started walking towards the first plaque. Emit bumped Ethan hard with his shoulder before running on around the circle. As Ethan took up the pursuit, Frank joined Maggie at the first plaque. They both watched the two boys jump from the path and take off into the trees.

Frank spoke up. "I'm really worried about Mary. I've never seen her act like that before."

"I have. She got all freaked out at the graveyard after her grandmother's funeral. You guys weren't there."

"I don't like to go to funerals. So she did this same thing, then? At least that means it wasn't just being here that made her act like that." He seemed almost relieved.

"I didn't say she was as bad as today. Even for her, today is very weird."

The two of them slowly walked around the circle and read every name. Just as they reached the front of the circle again, the two boys came running out of the woods and raced right past them. Maggie shook her head. "Look at them. Not a care in the world, even though a lifelong friend is having a major meltdown out in the car. But they'd be *so* interested if she was in her cheerleading outfit."

Frank added, "Or her bikini!"

Maggie rolled her eyes at him and nudged him with her shoulder. "Guys!"

Back at the car, Misty had persuaded Mary to smile. Ethan and Emit came to a complete halt just a few feet from where the two girls were leaning against the back of the SUV.

Mary smiled over her shoulder at them. "I'm better now, thanks to Misty. Are we leaving now?"

Ethan nodded as he opened the driver's door. Emit got in the front passenger seat and buckled up. Seeing Maggie and Frank coming down the path, Misty helped Mary into the very back seat. Emit told the group that they were all going to the north end of the canyon where all the rock climbers go. Ethan added that there might still be a waterfall on the rock face from the last of the melting snow tops. The girls liked that possibility.

Several playful hours were spent looking around the north end of the canyon. Eventually, the growling of their stomachs made them retreat to the camp and cook. When night fell, they all eagerly crawled into their sleeping bags. It had been a very active and somewhat emotional day.

It was almost 2:00 in the morning when one girl awoke covered in sweat. She sat up and looked around before softly unzipping her bag. She just had to get out, yes, out of the bag and the tent. It had been such a vivid dream that she could hardly breathe. The cold, crisp mountain air felt very good on her face. With each passing moment, she seemed to breathe a little easier. She rubbed her eyes as if trying to erase the dream.

Meanwhile, in the boys' tent, Ethan had been awakened by sounds coming from the direction of the girls' tent. He lay there trying to decide if it was worth investigating. Just as he was deciding to go back to sleep, he heard the loud snap of a limb breaking. This sparked him to action. He was out of his bag and then the tent in seconds. As he rounded the front of the girl's tent, he saw Maggie standing just outside the tent opening. She was looking towards the trees.

"What's going on, Mag?"

She seemed confused as she looked back inside the tent. "Mary's gone. Did you hear that big pop?"

"Yes. That's why I came over. Are you okay? You don't look awake. Are you sure Mary isn't just snuggled down in her bag?"

She leaned in and stepped on Mary's bag. "No, she isn't in here."

Ethan was very concerned now. "I better go find her. Any idea where the sound came from?"

She pointed and he ran off in search of the missing girl. The moonlight was so bright that it might as well have been daytime. With the excellent visibility, he was able to run at a good pace while avoiding branches and hopping over fallen tree trunks. After a few minutes he stopped to listen. In the quiet of the night, he could just make out the sound of somebody softly crying. Finally he saw a human shape a few yards off to his right, and he hurried towards it.

Mary was sitting on a huge fallen log and she was crying. He ran up and stopped right in front of her. "Are you okay? Mary! Are you?"

She cut him off in mid-sentence. "Go away! I don't want you here. Go back and just leave me alone." Then she threw her legs around on the other side of log so her back was facing him as she repeated, "Just go away. Please leave me alone."

He didn't know what to do. As he started to turn and leave, he realized that he couldn't leave her out here alone. Not like this. He returned and sat about two feet away from her.

"Mary. I'm just going to sit here and not say a word. Promise!"

"I told you to leave me alone. Don't you understand what that means?"

He was not sure what he should say. "What I understand is that my friend is crying alone in the middle of the night out here in the woods. I don't know why, and you don't have to tell me. But I'm not leaving you out here all alone."

She turned and looked at him through tear-filled eyes. "Why not? I just want to be like everyone else. I don't want to be unique. I just want to live."

He was confused by her last statement. "What?" He hesitated to see if she would say anything else. She was looking around as if she had said something she didn't want anyone to hear. "Mary, what are you talking about?"

She closed her eyes before she covered her face with her hands. After a few seconds, she looked at him. "I don't know what got into me." She sat up straight and held her hands on the sides of her face. "I . . . just feel so very tired all of a sudden. Maybe you're right. I need to go back to bed."

"That's a good idea, Mary. Come on." She slowly stood and he wrapped a strong arm around her as they began the walk back to camp. A few steps later, she said, "Please don't tell anyone what I said. Okay?"

Frank and Emit came running up. Emit said, "Hey! What the hell is going on? Is she okay?"

Ethan said, "Yeah, she's fine. She just went for a walk. That's all."

Frank's voice conveyed his confusion. "A walk? From the way Maggie yelled at us to go find her, I thought a bear had taken her off or something." He and Emit turned around to lead the way back. Mary waited till the two boys were far enough ahead not to hear her whisper "Thank you."

Once everyone was back at camp, Misty and Maggie quickly hustled Mary back to bed. The guys stood and talked by the fire for about ten minutes before turning in. Mary's wandering off into the woods had been an adrenaline-filled event, yet each boy quickly fell back to sleep.

It was only an hour later that one of the boys woke up in a cold sweat. His dream had been extremely vivid as well. He lay still, looking up until his eyes could finally focus on the tent top. Eventually the urge to go outside was just too much, so he slipped out of his sleeping bag, headed across the road and into the trees. He was walking rather fast, like he had purpose and knew where he was going.

Eventually, he reached a small stream. Without hesitation, he turned left and followed the creek upstream. After walking another twenty yards, he spotted movement in the trees off to his left. It appeared to be a man and a woman. They were holding hands as they walked towards the creek just in front of him. He stopped and stood motionless next to a tree. In the bright moonlight, he didn't know why they didn't see him as clearly as he saw them.

Suddenly the girl poked the guy with her finger. He released her hand and seemed to taunt her in an effort to get her to chase him. This was when the boy realized that he didn't really hear anything. But how could that be? He pinched himself hard to see if he was dreaming. But the pain was real and he grunted loudly from it. A quick glance up at the couple confirmed they didn't hear him either. What was going on here? He's not asleep, and these two people weren't making a sound. Nor did they hear him. If he didn't know better, he'd swear they were ghosts.

As he was wondering if he was going crazy, the two people slipped into a passionate lover's kiss. In just seconds, they were pulling off clothing as quickly as they could. Once undressed, they lay down on the lush green forest floor just two feet from the bubbling brook. He watched as they made love for several minutes. It was then that his focus turned strictly to the girl. Her face and her body seemed somehow familiar. Slowly he found himself yearning to be the one holding her and kissing her. A thought flashed into his mind that she belonged to him! But how could that be? She was obviously older than him, yet he felt that he was her equal in age if not older.

Just when he thought it couldn't get any weirder, the two people began to fade into nothingness. He was left staring at only the grass where they had been. He looked all around, not for them, but to see if anyone saw him staring at nothing. He shook his head hard and decided he needed to get back to camp for the sake of his sanity.

As he walked back, a light mist formed on his right. There, in that mist, were two soldiers walking with a man dressed like a lumberjack. The boy stopped and watched an apparent joke being played upon the three ghostly figures. Out of nowhere, the two lovebirds from the creek ran up behind the men and apparently yelled 'BOO' at them. Though he didn't hear it, he saw the reactions of two of the men who apparently did hear it. They jumped before facing the third man. The boy realized they were blaming the man, but then that man pointed behind the other two men at the two lovers as they laughed. Then all the ghostly figures vanished and the mist evaporated as quickly as it had formed.

Again, the boy looked around to make sure that nobody was watching him lose his mind. But it had all seemed so real. After a few moments, he had a more urgent desire to get back to camp. He hoped there would not be any encores from the ghostly actors.

To his complete disbelief, the mist formed on his left this time. Even though he wanted to start running for camp at this point, he felt compelled to stand and watch the eerie movie playing for him. The three men were back, but dressed in civilian clothes as they searched a storage room. They each moved about separately in an apparent quest to find an item that meant something to each of them alone. Many items were picked up, closely inspected and then replaced. One by one, the men made their selection until all three seem satisfied with what they now held. The boy clearly saw each item that the men chose but he didn't understand the significance of the items. As with the last spooky video, the characters all vanished before his eyes, and then so did the mist.

Before he could step forward, an oval of mist the size of a door appeared before him. He froze and he wondered if there was anything that could force him to step into it. Off to his right appeared that woman, *his* woman. She stepped up and into the swirling mist as it began to consume her. All he could now see was her face and the shoulder that she was looking back over at him. They were now face to face and he stared directly into her eyes. All of the visions had been silent up until now. As the edges of her began to fade into the mist, he clearly heard her sweet voice say "Please find me," as her lip quivered ever so slightly. His heart broke and he felt he couldn't stay here without her. He rushed towards the mist, but it vanished and deprived him of the one he now knew that he loved. She was gone.

At this point, the boy didn't care if anyone was there in the woods to witness his obvious mental breakdown. He just didn't care at all. Nor did he feel like running back to camp any more. He felt helpless to stop any other visions from appearing in front him. So he accepted his fate and slowly walked towards the camp, fully expecting to see more haunting visions in the mist. In fact, he now found he hoped for another vision, as long as it contained her. Yes, he wanted to see her again so badly that his very soul was shaking from anticipation. But the mist didn't return and he soon found himself back in camp.

Before entering his tent, he looked back over his shoulder for a moment. Then he raised his cupped hands to his face as he slowly breathed in and out several times. With one last look over his shoulder, he quietly slipped back into the tent and his bag. His movements were as that of an accomplished thief in the night. Not a sound had he made.

• • •

The smell of coffee and bacon yanked the youths from their deep sleep. Each one frantically kicked themselves out of their sleeping bags. Eager feet were hastily jammed into assorted footwear, but only four friends emerged to find that Mary was the one responsible for breakfast this morning. The scrambled eggs were in a big bowl on the picnic table and she was carrying a large pan of bacon. "It's about time you sleepy heads all got up! Everything's on the table except the coffee, of course. That you get yourself."

Ethan and Misty both spoke at the same time. "Smells good!"

Maggie looked at Ethan, then Frank. "Where's Emit?"

Frank said, "I nudged him twice. He growled at me and said he'd be up in a minute. I guess he didn't sleep well."

Misty had now walked up to Mary. "How do you feel this morning? Better?"

Mary's smile was proof that her usual bubbly self had returned. "I feel absolutely GREAT!"

Everyone was halfway through eating before Emit emerged from the tent, grabbed some coffee and found a spot at the table. Misty told him, "There's not much left, sleepy head. You should have gotten up with the rest of us."

He looked at her for several seconds as if he was studying her face for some reason. "That's okay. I'm really not that hungry right now, anyway." He then sat there staring at his cup between sips.

Everyone had noticed Emit's withdrawn mood. It seemed like he was either not fully awake, or he was concentrating very hard on solving some mysterious problem. Ethan finally asked, "You okay, man? You look like you're out of it."

Emit's focus never left his cup. "Oh, just thinking."

While they sipped their coffee, they watched Emit finally eat the bacon they had saved for him.

Eventually, Ethan spoke. "Well. I'm thinking that we should pack up and head to our next camping site. We've seen all the things we planned on seeing here in this valley."

This comment triggered something in Emit and he looked around at the group. "Leave? Now? What's the rush?"

Mary was also looking at Ethan. "Yeah! We just got here. It's only been two nights."

Misty answered before Ethan could. "Wait a minute, Mary. You didn't want to come to this valley to start with. Then you got shook up at the memorial, not to mention what happened last night. Why, I'd think you would be the first one ready to leave."

Mary smiled at her. "That's all behind me now." She looked around before she continued. "I kind of like it here now. I don't know why, but it feels, well, really like being home."

Maggie and Misty glanced at each other before Maggie asked, "So what do you want to do today, Mary?"

She didn't hesitate. "I was thinking that we should go find that creek and walk along it for a while. What do you say?"

Misty asked, "Where is the creek?"

"That way," Emit grumbled, as he pointed in its direction.

Maggie asked, "Where'd I put the map?"

Frank spotted it, leaned over and pulled it out from under Emit's plate. Once he handed it to Maggie, she unfolded it before saying, "Emit is right. It's that way."

With the precision of seasoned campers, everything was picked up, the dishes were cleaned, and the condiments put back in the SUV. Then everyone started walking in search of the creek. All except for Emit, who sat back down. Noticing this, Maggie asked, "Aren't you coming with us?" Everyone stopped walking and looked back at him. He waved them on. "No. You go have fun. I've seen creeks before. Besides, I'm still tired. I'll probably lie back down. Get out of here and go have a good time."

Everyone accepted Emit wanting to stay, except for Misty. She was the only one that kept looking back every now and then. They all made their way towards the trees on the other side of the road. Mary took point once they entered the trees and everyone else fell in behind her. There was a lot of friendly banter with some directed at Mary, but she offered no comment. When she came to the creek, she didn't hesitate as she turned to her left and walked along the water's edge. After about twenty yards, she suddenly stopped. There before them was a lush green patch of grass that rolled right over the creek bank.

Maggie and Misty stepped up beside Mary to survey the beautiful spot while they nodded their heads. Misty was the one that commented, "Nice!" All three girls sat down right in the middle of the lush patch of grass. One by one, they each lay back and enjoyed the best bed that nature had to offer.

As they were lying there, a boy was watching closely. He was focused only on one of the three girls. It was impossible for him to take his eyes off of her, and he didn't even notice the other two. He had been sneaking peeks of her for as long as they had been friends. He didn't know why, but she had always been his greatest interest of the three girls. His desire for her had been growing for the last few years. Here, surrounded by all the beauty that nature had bestowed upon this small slice of heaven, he now knew that she was meant to be his. But how does he tell her?

One of the girls casually glanced around and noticed this boy. He was apparently looking directly at Mary. It was her belief that all the guys were drawn to watch Mary. Oh, how she wished it was her that he was watching. But her gaze had spooked him, and it was obvious that he didn't like having been discovered.

It took some serious prodding to get the three girls back on their feet. They really liked this spot. Eventually the small band of friends was on its way back to camp. The air was full of joyous revelry as they made their way out of the trees and across the open field towards the tents. Misty was the first one to reach the camp. Not seeing Emit anywhere, she went straight to the boys' tent and looked inside. He was not there. As the others strolled into camp, she was actively scanning the tree line in the direction of the bathrooms. She was wondering if he could be there when she heard someone coming out of the trees behind her. A quick glance proved that it was Emit with his arms full of firewood. He walked up and dumped the wood on top of the little pile they still had left.

"I wasn't sure if we were staying tonight or not. Isn't it several hours from here to the lake campsites? If we don't stay, we can just leave it for the next campers."

Ethan looked up at the sky then down at his watch. "You know, Emit has a good point. We can't possibly break camp and drive to the lake site before nightfall. I don't know about the rest of you, but I'd rather spend one more night here and just leave early in the morning. What do you all think?"

Frank and the girls were looking at each other as they nodded in agreement.

Ethan continued. "Good. I hate setting up camp in the dark." He slowly looked around before he added "I kinda like it here, anyway."

Frank said he would start the fire back up and got to it. Emit turned back towards the trees and spoke over his shoulder as he started walking away. "I'll bring in some more wood. We're going to need a lot more than that to get through the night, and then breakfast in the morning."

Misty quickly jogged after him. "Wait up. I'll help you."

As she ran up behind him, there was a friendly slap on his backside followed by her disappearing off into the woods. Emit gleefully gave chase. Once they were out of earshot and sight of the others, she slowed down for him to get beside her. A few steps later, she spoke.

"I'm confused. You didn't want to go over there with us, but I saw you in the trees. What's up with you?"

He looked down as he walked beside her. "I don't know. I had a strange night last night and I've been in a really funky mood all day. Did you tell anyone you saw me?"

"No. Of course not. I doubt anyone else saw you. Nobody mentioned it. What do you mean, a strange night last night?"

"You wouldn't understand. It's nothing anyway."

She reached over and locked her arm around his before looking up into his face as they walked along. "It must be something or you wouldn't have thought about it all day. And why wouldn't I understand? I'm not stupid, you know."

"I didn't mean it like that and you know it. You're the smartest one of us all. Everyone knows it. I just don't want to talk about it."

She stopped walking, but held onto his arm to make him stop and face her. "Look. I know you have been thinking about Mary. I also know you were over there watching her from the trees by the creek. Why don't you just tell her how you feel? What are you afraid of?"

"I'm not afraid of anything."

"So tell her?"

He looked at her for a second, then pulled free of her arm and turned to continue walking. She just stood there watching him walk away until he stopped and looked back at her. "Well? I thought you were going to help me?"

Her blank stare slowly changed to a smile again and she skipped over to take his arm. "I'm sorry, Emit. It's none of my business. Sorry."

"You don't have to be sorry, Misty. I don't mean to be rude. We've been friends all our lives. You know me better than anyone. So you have to know that I'm just not like all the rest of you. I've always been more moody. I just can't help it sometimes. I get these strange thoughts in my head and just can't get rid of them. But I don't mean to take it out on you. Especially not you." They walked for a few minutes without speaking then he continued. "And for your information, I wasn't watching Mary."

"Sure you were." She smiled at him, but he shook his head as he pointed to a lot of scattered wood just ahead. They silently gathered as much wood as they could carry. There was nothing said at all on the return trip. She was seriously curious about what was going on with her friend.

Frank had built a textbook fire that was already rendering some seriously red-hot coals. Ethan had pulled all of the necessary items from the car and placed them on the table. Maggie and Mary had hamburger patties on the cast iron griddle. Supper was ready shortly before Misty and Emit returned with their final load of wood.

The six friends spent another peaceful time around the fire as they talked about various plans each one had for the future. Again, their seasoned camping skills were called upon to quickly clean up after eating. The dropping temperature led them all to head for the tents, and another night snuggled inside their sleeping bags. As the night before, one boy and one girl again had a very disturbing dream, complete with scenes from inside a plane destined to crash in the mountains. They both woke in a sweat and shared ghastly, vivid images that made it hard for them to breathe.

Emit laid motionless in his bag as he heard the steady breathing from his two closest friends. His mind was on overload and he couldn't get back to sleep. The sudden sound of movement outside caused him to lift up the bottom edge of the tent flap to see who it was. He saw Mary standing just inches outside the girl's tent. She had her head tipped forward into her hands. He could tell that she was having as much trouble sleeping as he was, and decided to sneak out to talk with her.

His stealthy escape from his tent allowed Mary time to put a considerable amount of distance between her and the camp. She was already on the other side of the road and three-quarters of the way to the trees. He was just now far enough from the tents to stop worrying about waking anyone else. She had long disappeared into the trees by the time he reached the road, but he knew exactly where she was headed. So he angled a little farther left in hopes of closing the gap. His calculations were right on, and he arrived at the grassy spot just moments after she had stretched out on the grass. As he approached her, she was a little startled. Seeing who it was, she quickly motioned for him to sit beside her.

Neither Mary nor Emit were aware that a female set of eyes were watching from just a few yards away. She had heard Mary leave the tent and was about to step out to follow her when Emit had emerged from the boy's tent. His total focus on following Mary had kept him from even noticing that he was being followed himself. Misty was too far away to hear what was being said. But she felt positive as to what was being discussed. After all, she had been the one that had told Emit just this evening to do this very thing. It appeared that he had decided to follow her advice. With these thoughts in her head and tears in her eyes, she decided that it was not proper for her to watch any longer. So she very quietly slipped back into the dense trees before making her way back to camp.

She was just steps away from her tent, when Ethan popped out of his. At first he seemed hesitant, but then he nodded and walked over to her.

They both spoke in whispers.

"You okay, Misty?"

"Yes. I drank too much water so had to go." She shrugged.

He smiled back, "Me too! See you in the morning."

Time passed before Ethan came hurrying back into camp. As he approached his tent, his movements became very deliberate so he would not wake anyone up. About 20 more minutes passed before Emit and Mary returned to camp. They shared a long embrace in the moonlight before he kissed her and they whispered goodnight to each other. Then they also quietly sought the comfort of their sleeping bags.

The next day brought breakfast, sunshine, and a fun-filled drive to the lake campgrounds where they spent the remaining days of their first annual camping trip. They were very happy days that temporarily obscured the intense dreams and emotional boundaries of these six childhood friends. A joyous drive home was the final act.

Once back home, each of them fell back into their daily routines and set about putting personal plans in action - plans that had been contemplated throughout their senior year. Their time was being consumed by the anticipation of starting this next phase of their lives. Since each was bound for a different college, there was no contact between the friends during the next week. This allowed for one of them to seek resolution of a compelling desire for a solitary road trip. Driven by an unforeseen cosmic power, an unscheduled quest began. It would start by returning to Cantor Basin Memorial Park.

Chapter 20

CRASH SEARCH

THE SAME BLUE SUV slowly rolled to a stop in the still, empty parking lot of Cantor Basin Memorial Park. Its lone occupant sat for several minutes after killing the engine. He was in luck. There were no other tourists here. So there would be time to really read the plaques, take notes and plan what to do next.

Ethan stared out the windshield as he thought of why he had come back. He couldn't understand why a dream and the associated visions had taken such a hold of him. Why couldn't he just let it go? He didn't understand why, but at this point he had totally given into the urge to find out more of what happened here in this valley. He chuckled to himself as he thought, 'Find out what?'

It was probably just a dream brought on by having been to the memorial. Reading the plaques during that first trip must be responsible for the dream. That has to be it. But those damn visions where so vivid. What could have possibly caused that? There must be something on those plaques that triggered them too, but what? That's why he was here. So why was he still sitting in the SUV?

The thud of closing the SUV's door echoed into the trees and amplified the feeling of being out here alone. As he approached the first plaque, a sudden eerie feeling crept over him. The first read of it provided no new answers. A quick look around brought his focus to another plaque that he didn't remember reading. He did recall seeing Maggie and Frank over by it. That was when he and Emit were goofing off before they ran into the trees. He stepped over and read it. Nothing jumped out at him here either. That left only the individual plaques around the circle. There was one for each passenger whose body was forever enshrined within the melted metal and plastic in the center of the circle. Each of those plaques bore just one name. No help there.

He wondered if he had just driven all the way here for nothing. Something had to be on the two large plaques near the entrance. He hurried back and read them once more. He was out of ideas and started back towards the car. Then it dawned on him that Maggie still had that brochure from the park ranger's hut at the entrance to the canyon. He never read it. Maybe that was where the clue he sought was hiding. That's it! But that was 30 minutes back down the road. His response was to say "Shit" out loud. He rolled his eyes and said it again, but this time drew out the S. "SSSSShit!"

That's when he remembered something he had read on the big plaque. There was mention of some guy that had a nickname of 'SS'. He rushed back to read the plaque again. Yes, there it was. His name was Samuel Stanford and he was the manager of the airfield where they had taken the bodies and plane parts from the crash site. He remembered passing a sign that said 'Airport'. Ethan realized that he really needed to talk to this old man. This could be the break he was looking for. His spirits lifted, and he now moved like a treasure hunter with a purpose.

As he drove back to the airfield, his mind was working through plausible reasons that he could offer as to his motivation for asking questions about the crash site. The final choice wasn't made until he saw the gated entrance to the airfield. He's a student and he'll just say he was doing a summer school research paper about the creation of the memorial.

To his complete dismay, the guard at the entrance told him that Samuel Stanford died a few years ago. But the guard suggested that he talk to Paul Strokes, who had worked for Sam and now was the new field manager. Ethan followed the guard's directions to the office building. Luckily, he had a yellow writing pad and pencil in the SUV to complete his cover story.

The secretary greeted him with a smile. "You must be the young man the gate called about. Don't worry son, Mister Strokes worked for Sam during that awful time. I'm sure he can tell you more than you'll need to write this school paper. You can go on in. He's expecting you."

Ethan felt obligated to knock at least once on the door before he heard a big, booming voice. "Come on in, young man." He was a strong-looking man with a full head of jet-black hair. He had a cigar in the corner of his mouth, but it wasn't lit. Seeing that Ethan was looking at the cigar, the man said, "I know what you're thinking son. I thought the same thing the first time I met Sam. He never smoked them either. Just chewed on them a few days and then threw them away." He pulled it out of his mouth and looked at it as he rolled it between his fingers. "Sam taught me a lot of things. Even this nasty damn habit!"

With that said, he put it down on the edge of his desk. "So, I understand you are doing some school paper about the crash in Cantor Basin. I have two kids in college so I know what you are going through. But I must say that I'm impressed that you drove all the way up here to do your research. Why?"

"Well, sir, I'm thinking about going for a journalism degree. I have to do an initial paper this summer for one of my first classes. It's kind of important that I make a good first impression, according to my parents."

"Your parents are right, you know. So where do you want to start?"

"I have plenty of information from the obvious sources. You know, the internet, news articles from back then, and I just came from the memorial park in the canyon. I made some notes from the plaques there, but it was just information that I basically already had. So what I'm looking for is information that only someone like you would have. I want to make my paper seem more personal than just stating cold facts that everyone knows. I would be very interested in anything that you could tell me like that. Anything whatsoever."

At first, Mr. Strokes shook his head like he was about to say 'No', then he snapped his fingers and smiled. "Young man, I think I do have something for you. There are three men that worked extensively on that crash site from beginning to end. They were the first ones on the ground there and the last three to leave. I'll bet they can help you put some realism in that paper you're writing."

Ethan smiled, "Great! Are they here?"

"No, but they are all only a 45-minute drive back down the road. And the really neat part is that they're kind of famous. I'm not sure how you feel about people that investigate paranormal stuff, but they must know what they are doing. They have a book out and I've even seen them on TV several times. Have you ever heard of a group called 'To Free Spirits'?"

Ethan immediately got excited. "You kidding me? My best friend and I read that book. We've seen them on TV also. But sir, they are not going to be interested in talking to me about a stupid school paper."

Paul smiled. "Well, son. You happen to know somebody that can get them to talk to you."

Ethan's face showed his confusion as he asked, "I do? Who?"

Paul reached for his phone. "Me, silly! I worked with them back then and we are still very good friends. Just a minute." He dialed and Ethan heard a voice answer.

"Vic, it's Paul Strokes. Oh, fine. Yes, they are all fine and still doing good in college. Thanks. Hey, I have a young man here that is doing a school paper on the Cantor Basin crash. He's driven all the way up here just to talk to Sam about it. Yeah, it was a real shame about him passing. He was my mentor and a very good friend, too. Anyway, I was wondering if you could talk to this young man and help him out with his paper. He wants to personalize it and make a really good first impression on his new college professors. Huh? Well I'll bet he could be there in about an hour. Great! Thanks!"

He hung up and wrote something down before he passed the paper to Ethan. "Here you go, son. This is the man's name, address you need to go to, and that is his cell number too. Just in case you get lost. He said just call him on that number. He's expecting you in about an hour, so I'd get going if I were you."

"Gee, I can't believe it, sir. I just don't know how to thank you enough, sir. Thank YOU!"

They stood and shook hands before Ethan darted out the door. He was still fastening his seat belt as he put the SUV in reverse. He couldn't believe he was on his way to talk to a man that he'd seen on TV. He wished his best friend was here. Frank would be freaking out about this, too. Ethan lost his smile as he realized that even Frank wouldn't understand why he was doing this.

Then he realized that he would have to tell Frank that he made this trip. How's he going to break it to him? Oh well, that was something he could work out later. Right now, he needed to decide what he was going to ask the man he was about meet. With so many things bouncing around in Ethan's head, the 45-minute drive seemed to have only taken minutes. He was almost in a daze as he walked up to Vic's front door and rang the bell. A few nervous moments later, the door was opened by an older lady with a very warm smile. "You must be the young man my husband is waiting for. Please come on in, son." She pointed to a door down the hall. "He's in his office right there. Just go on in young man."

Again, Ethan felt obligated to knock once before he opened the door. There was a man sitting behind a big desk and he stood to shake Ethan's hand. "Hello. I'm Victor Bells, but you can just call me Vic. Everyone else does."

"It is so nice to meet you, sir. I have to tell you what an honor it is to meet you. My best friend and I have both read your book. We've also seen you all on TV several times. I just can't believe I'm here talking to you."

Vic motioned for him to sit in one of the chairs in front of his desk. "Please, take a seat and tell me how I can help you."

"I'm afraid I'm not as prepared as I should be. I never thought I'd be here talking to someone as famous as you, sir."

"Forget all that hype about being famous. I'm just a guy like you. So, what do you want to know?"

"I'm just looking for information about that plane crash and everything that happened after it. I really don't know how to ask, or what to ask about. I just know that I need to personalize my paper. You know, not just restate stock information that anyone could get from newspaper articles, the internet or the memorial. I just need to know something that has not been reported before. Anything at all, sir."

Vic leaned back in his chair and put his hands behind his head. "So what made you decide to do a paper on a plane crash that happened 18 years ago?"

"I went camping last week with some friends. Of all the places we could go, we ended up going there. We all went to the memorial and it just hit me on the way home that I should do my paper on that plane crash. It was just an odd coincidence. That's all, sir."

"That's some coincidence, son. Now you are here and talking to me. I'd say that you are going to make one hell of a journalist, young man."

"Thank you, sir. I've always believed that things like this happen for a reason. It's like it was supposed to happen or something. This isn't the only odd thing that has happened to me lately." Ethan laughed a little. "But that's another story altogether sir."

Vic stared at Ethan for a few seconds before he sat up to lean on his desk. "Well as you know, I, or WE, are kind of interested in odd stories. So do tell."

"Ah, it's just some boring dream stuff. Well, that's not true. It's not really boring, but it is very weird. It's probably nothing, really."

Vic's keen senses immediately associated the mention of a dream with the proximity of the crash memorial. His instincts told him that this might be much more than a mere coincidence.

"So you had a strange dream while camping at the memorial park?"

Ethan lost all expression in his face and quickly objected. "I didn't say it was *my* dream!"

Vic had seen this trait many times before. Most people deny something controversial when they realize they have let it slip out. So Vic knew he needed to change the subject quickly, or his visitor would stop talking altogether. "Ah, don't worry about it. Everyone has strange dreams. They can be caused by all sorts of things. Usually you can trace a dream source to something right before you slept. Like a movie or a conversation, or a visit to a memorial park. It's how our brains work. I wouldn't worry about it, young man."

Ethan seemed nervous as he forced a smile. "I'm sorry, sir. I don't know what made me act like that." He briefly rubbed his right temple. "It's just been a long day. Sorry."

"I need to get something to drink. Would you like something son?"

"Sure. Anything would be fine. A soda of some type would be great."

Vic stood and moved to the door but stopped to look back at Ethan. "Feel free to look around my office." He pointed to the corner, "There are actually two photos of the crash site right there."

Once Vic closed the office door, he hurried to the kitchen and called Doc. "Hey, Doc! You need to go pick up Bob and get over to my house right now. There is a young man here who has had some disturbing dreams up at the memorial for the crash site. Hurry, man. He's acting nervous and I'm not sure I can hold him here. So hurry!" Then he poured two sodas and headed back to his office.

Vic assumed that Ethan would be checking out the photos of the crash site. However, he almost dropped both drinks when he saw what Ethan was standing in front of. It was Ed's item. The one Vic had chosen from the storage room that day. To his total amazement, Ethan was so focused on the item that he apparently hadn't heard the door open.

"So, I see you are admiring one of my most treasured gifts."

Hearing Vic's voice, Ethan was obviously startled and he attempted to hide his intense interest in the object by immediately stepping to the next item displayed on the wall.

"You have so many nice things in your office. It would be hard to pick just one to ask about."

Vic was even more curious than before. There was something about this young man, but he just couldn't put his finger on it. He handed him the soda and returned to his desk. He decided to play it safe and go off-topic until his partners arrived. He showed the boy some photos of several high profile athletes he had worked with over the past few years. Ethan gradually relaxed, although Vic noticed several times that he was trying to nonchalantly glance at Ed's gift.

Finally, the doorbell rang. Vic's wife called out, "I'll get it, honey!"

A few moments later, the office door swung open and in they stepped. Vic tried to make it seem unexpected by looking at his watch before saying, "I thought you two were going to meet Ben for coffee. What happened?"

Doc played along. "We were there, but his daughter called and said he was helping her with something at her house. So we thought we'd drop by and see if you wanted to do something."

Vic stood up and gestured towards Ethan. "Doc, Bob, this is Ethan. He's doing some research on the Cantor Basin crash for a college journalism class. Ethan, these are my partners, and they also worked up on the crash site with me. In fact, that's where we all met."

Ethan was all smiles as he stood and eagerly shook hands with the two men. "I just can't believe I'm meeting all three of you today. I've read your book and seen all of you on TV several times. It's a real honor to meet you."

Bob went into icebreaker mode. "Well, it won't be much of an honor after you get to know us better, son. Most people think we're crazy!" He then walked around Ethan and sat in a chair on his left.

Doc looked at Ethan and said, "Don't mind him, kid. He's the only one that people really think is crazy!" Then Doc sat in the chair to Ethan's right, and he motioned for him to sit back down. Vic added, "Might as well take a seat, son. When these two start talking, it usually takes a while for them to stop!" The three men all laughed and they were glad to see that Ethan was beginning to relax.

Doc said, "So, tell us about your paper and how can we help."

This question prompted Ethan to tell the same story he had told Vic. While Ethan was talking, Doc noticed him glance at Ed's gift on the wall more than once. Suddenly Doc interrupted him.

"I see that you keep looking at that thing there." He turned to Vic. "What is that thing, Vic?"

All three men knew exactly what it is, but Vic played along. "Oh, it was a gift from Ed."

Each man's attention was subtly focused on Ethan's face and

they each saw his expression immediately change as Ed's name was mentioned. The boy's eyes widened considerably and he couldn't resist openly turning to stare at it again. While Ethan's attention was on the item, intrigued glances ricocheted between each man. They each now knew that Ethan knew the name 'Ed'. But why did he know? And more importantly, HOW did he know?

Doc realized that the gloves must come off and they needed to ask some pointed questions of this boy. Even if it meant they could spook him into leaving. He leaned towards Ethan and spoke very softly. "What do you think that thing is on the shelf?"

Hearing the question, Ethan looked directly at Doc before he nervously asked, "What makes you think I know what it is?"

Bob's soothing voice said, "Son. We all know what that is. We are just curious if you do as well. No pressure, son. If you do, you do. If not, just say so. We would just like to know."

Ethan was now sitting on the edge of his seat as if he was ready to bolt for the door at any moment. "I, I, I think I really want to go now, please." He looked at Vic, "Please, sir. Can I go?"

Doc's voice was as non-threatening as he could make it. "Ethan. You are free to go any time you wish. But before you do, please hear me out. You have obviously experienced something rather phenomenal in that valley. It drove you to come this far. Think about it, son. Do you want to stop now?"

Ethan looked down at the floor. "This is just way too much for me to deal with. It's not what I wanted."

Vic immediately asked, "So what is it you wanted?"

Ethan's response shook the three men to their very souls. "I just wanted to find out a little more about the dream before I talked to Mary. I just don't want to sound like I'm crazy. Not to her."

Bob asked, "Why?"

Ethan hesitated and the men at first thought he was not going to answer, but he suddenly did. "Because I think I love her." Slowly the blank expression on his face gave way to an amazing smile. "No, I KNOW I love her!"

Bob asked, "Who's Mary?"

"She and I were born on the same day and grew up three blocks from each other. We've been friends all our lives. She was there on that camping trip too."

Vic asked, "Are both of you eighteen?"

"Yes, sir. But she was born one minute before I was." He chuckled before adding, "She always makes a big deal about being older than me."

Bob had both elbows on his knees and his face buried in the palms of his two hands. Doc glanced at Vic, before he asked, "Did she have a dream, too?"

Ethan swung around to look at Doc. "Well, I think she must have. She left her tent and ran off into the woods one night. She was crying and talking strange. I was really worried about her." Then, without any warning, Ethan stood up and said, "I really want to go now. Please. I just need to get out of here. I want to go home."

Doc motioned for the men to stay seated. He reached onto the desk and picked up one of Vic's business cards. "We understand, Ethan. But please take this with you. You call Vic here at this number any time, day or night. Okay, son?"

Ethan forced a smile as he nodded. "I will, sir. Thanks for talking to me." He opened the door and turned back to the men. "This whole thing has been weird from the start. But I somehow feel better now. Thanks!"

Doc waited until Ethan was passing through the door before he asked, "Son, what about your paper?" Since Ethan was just standing in the door and staring at them, Doc became very bold. "There really wasn't a paper. Was there, son?"

Ethan frozen, then finally mumbled, "Well, I, uh, I'm sorry. This was a bad idea. I'm sorry, sir." He turned and started walking but they all clearly heard him say to himself, "This is just too weird."

The three men sat there in a daze for a few moments until Bob mumbled, "Are you two thinking what I'm thinking?"

Vic said, "If we are, then we all think that was Ed."

Bob added, "Well if he is, I hope he gets to be with Martha."

Doc said, "You mean Mary."

The sound of Ethan's SUV starting up triggered a loud comment from Vic. "Shit! I didn't get his last name or where he's even from. Damn it!"

Bob jumped to his feet and ran to look out the window. "Crap! He's gone. We don't even have his license plate number.

Crap, Crap, CRAP!"

Ethan didn't even play the radio on the entire trip home. He kept thinking about all the revelations from Vic's office. So many things from the dream had been confirmed during that visit. He couldn't stop thinking about that object from the dream, and the fact that Vic even mentioned the name 'Ed'. When he heard Vic say the name, Ethan thought he was going to scream like a little girl. Wow, that was a very amazing moment! He just wished his best friend Frank could have been there to meet those three famous men. With this sudden thought of his best friend, his thoughts switched to wondering how he was going to bring this all up to Frank. How would he react?

The six-hour drive home seemed to only take one hour. At first he was still so excited that he didn't realize he was tired. He went to his room and flopped down on his bed to watch some TV, but was fast asleep in less than five minutes, fully clothed on top of the covers.

The sound of his bedroom door opening was quickly followed by the sound of Frank's voice. "Come on buddy, get up! I haven't seen or heard from you in two days, man. Let's go do something. Did you sleep in your clothes?"

Ethan's eyes were barely beginning to focus. "What time is it?"

"It's almost nine in the morning. Are you sick?"

Ethan still hadn't fully woken up. "Sick? No, I just got in late and must have fallen asleep the minute I hit the bed. It's a long drive, you know."

"Long drive? What drive? Where did you go?"

Ethan was still not totally awake, but he was awake enough to realize that he had just let his secret slip to Frank. His first impulse was to continue acting like he was not awake. "What drive? You know. The drive! Wait a minute." He tried to make his eyes look sleepy by only opening them halfway as he looked around the room. "Where am I?" He decided to escape to the bathroom and get his story straight before saying anything else to Frank.

After he splashed a lot of water on his face and flushed the toilet to complete the act, he emerged to find Frank sitting at his desk.

"So what did you do all day yesterday? Are you sure you

didn't go anywhere?"

Ethan walked over to his bed, looked at Frank and fell backwards onto it. "What's up with all the questions? Where would I have to go? Get real, man."

Frank stood up. He tossed a crumpled piece of paper and a business card onto Ethan's chest. "These fell out of your pocket on your way to the bathroom. You sure you didn't go visit Victor Bells yesterday?"

Ethan knew his secret was out now, so he sat up quickly. "Look, man. It's not what you think. Really!"

"Well I don't really know what to think. Apparently my best friend went to see a TV celebrity and didn't think to ask me to go. Did you really get to talk to Victor Bells? How? And more importantly, Why?"

"Yes, it was soooo cool! I met all three of them! It was just a fluke that I even ended up there. I noticed on the plaque that this man worked at the airfield. If I hadn't have gone to the airfield, I'd never have met them." Ethan didn't realize he had just given Frank another clue.

"The airfield? What airfield?" When Ethan didn't answer, Frank knew that he was holding something back. Then it hit him. Ethan had mentioned a plaque. "You went back to the crash memorial? Why?"

Ethan stood up and held his hands out as if he was trying to calm Frank down. "Look. I know what you're thinking. Please, can we just sit down and let me explain?"

Frank stood shaking his head as he stared at Ethan for a few moments before letting out a loud sigh and sitting down at the desk again. "What possessed you to go back up there?"

Ethan was very nervous. "Look, it all just happened. It wasn't even my idea."

Now Frank was very concerned. "Not your idea? I'm afraid to ask. Whose idea was it?"

Ethan almost seemed defiant about not answering. But in the end, he dropped his shoulders and confessed it all. "I know you're going to get mad, but just hear me out first. Please." He stared at Frank for a second then continued. "Misty said I'd never get past this if I didn't work through it. She said I needed to go back up there and see what I could find out."

Frank was out of his seat and on his feet again. "You told Misty about the dream? I can't believe you! We talked about this and you agreed it was best not to tell anyone about it. Are you nuts?"

Now Ethan was on his feet too. "Hey! I didn't tell her. Mary did!"

Hearing that, Frank was so stunned that he sat back down. "Let me guess. You told Mary?" Ethan eventually nodded. "Everyone is going to think you are absolutely crazy. I can't believe you told Mary. What were you thinking?"

Ethan slowly sat back down on the edge of the bed. "I didn't mean to say anything to her. It just kind of slipped out. When she mentioned having a bad dream, well, it just slipped out before I knew what I was saying."

Frank sat up totally straight. "Did you just say Mary had a dream, too?"

"Yes. Isn't that odd, man? That's when I just spit it out. See, it wasn't my fault!"

Frank's face reflected his total confusion at this new revelation. "Okay. So tell me about her dream."

"There isn't anything to really tell. She never said. It was that night that she ran off into the trees and we all went looking for her. Remember how she was shaking and crying? Man, I was really worried about her that night. It was after we got back home. She and I were talking one night. She mentioned it then and that is when I, well, told her."

"Ok, let's switch topics a minute. Tell me what you talked to Victor Bells and the others about."

Ethan sat on the edge of the bed and was obviously very excited. "You're going to love this man. He went to get us a soda and told me to look around his office. He had some pictures of the real crash area with parts of the plane still scattered all around. It was so bad looking. But get this. I saw that glass ball thing with whatever that is in the middle of it. He had it on a shelf in his office. It was right there. I know it is the one from the vision. It freaked me out to see it there. Then get this. Later he said that a guy named Ed gave it to him."

Frank's eyes widened, his mouth wide open as well. "You've got to be kidding me, right? He actually said 'Ed'?" Franks eyes were darting around but not at anything particular. "Now this is getting super strange! What did you do?"

"Well, they knew that I recognized the name and started asking me questions. It really freaked me out so I got out of there. My heart was pounding and I just needed to leave."

"You just stood up and left? What did they do?"

Ethan picked up Vic's business card and pointed it at Frank. "That's when they gave me this card and told me to call them any time, day or night. It was so odd how they were acting. It's like they know a lot more about this dream than we do. Weird, huh?"

"Oh please don't tell me you mentioned my name to them."

Ethan smirked with a little indignation. "Hey! You think I just tell everyone everything I know?"

Frank rolled his eyes. "How can you sit there with a straight face and say that to me? Dude, you're losing it BIG TIME!"

Ethan held his hands out, palms up. "Okay, okay, so I told somebody. Big deal."

Frank was back on his feet. "Dude! You told practically everyone. Don't you get it? Two of the three girls that were there know about it now. Do you really think they won't tell Maggie? And GOD knows who else the three of them are going to mention it to. THEY'RE GIRLS!"

"Stop worrying about it, man. I made Mary promise not to tell anyone. She's good!"

Again, Frank rolled his eyes before staring at Ethan. Eventually Ethan nodded and said, "I know, I know. So she told Misty. So what! We all tell Misty everything. You know as well as I do that Misty never spreads anything."

Frank paused a moment. "Well. You are right about that. Misty is very tight- lipped on most things. I just hope you're right man. Please don't tell me you're planning on going back to talk to the ghost guys again. Are you?"

Ethan had a serious look on his face as he responded. "No WAY! Those guys are scary as HELL in person. That whole thing with them just freaked me out to the MAX! I don't see that happening again. Here." He handed the crumpled paper and business card to Frank. "You take this. Keep it or throw it away. I don't want anything else to do with them. Too weird!"

Frank stood up and held out his hand. Ethan stood and took it. "Ethan. You're my best friend. You have to stop talking to people about this dream and stuff. Promise me, man. I MEAN IT! PROMISE ME! No more talking about it. Not to anyone. If the girls bring it up again, just tell them you've moved on and don't want to talk about it any more. Then drop it. They'll get the hint."

"Can I still talk to you about it?"

Frank smiled. "Of course you can. You're my best friend. Now let's stop talking about it. I'm getting a headache. Let's go do something and forget about this stuff."

The two friends spent the rest of the day running around with teammates they had played ball with in school. It was good for them to clear their minds and do guy things the rest of the day. However, that night Frank couldn't get to sleep for a long time. He just kept going over what Ethan had told him about Vic knowing the name 'Ed'. He always knew Ethan could get carried away at times, but this was different. Something else was going on here.

He jumped out of bed and looked at every letter on the business card. Then he smoothed out that crumpled piece of paper and looked at the address. It was then that he knew he had to go talk to Victor Bells.

Since Ethan was going out of town in the morning with his parents, this would be a perfect time to go do this. He finally managed to go to sleep, but he was up very early and on the road. On the trip there, he decided that he was just going to be straightforward with Vic. He smiled at the thought that he might get to also meet the others. He was concerned about everything Ethan had told him about what happened at Vic's house. The men would be able to tell if he was not being truthful so he might as well be honest, at least to a point.

As he walked up to the door, he felt very nervous. He had barely pushed the doorbell when a very friendly lady opened the door. "Excuse me ma'am. I'm Frank. I'm a friend of Ethan's. He saw your husband a few days ago. He gave him this card and said come see him whenever. I was wondering if I could see him please."

"I remember your friend from the other day too. Of course you can see my husband. I'm sure he'll be happy to talk to you." She showed him to Vic's office and opened the door. "Honey. This is Frank. He's a friend of the boy that was here the other day. Ethan was his name, I believe."

Vic stood and motioned for Frank to take a seat. "I'm very glad to meet you, Frank." Then he looked at his wife and winked with the eye that Frank couldn't see. She nodded and closed the door, then hurried down the hall and did what her husband had asked her to do, should Ethan or any of his friends show up.

"How can I help you, Frank?"

"Well, sir. I know Ethan came and talked to you the other day. I was just wondering if you'd talk to me about what Ethan told you. You see, sir, I know about the dream and visions." Then he pointed directly at Ed's gift on the wall. "And I know about you having that thing too. I even know that you mentioned a guy named 'Ed' to Ethan."

Vic smiled. "Wow. You are a rather direct young man, aren't you?"

Frank chuckled lightly and shook his head a little. "I'm sorry, sir. I guess that came out a little rude. I apologize. It's just that I'm worried about my friend Ethan. I hope you can understand."

"Of course I do. Your friend Ethan is working through some very confusing events. It's commendable that you took the time to drive all the way here out of concern for your friend. Very commendable indeed, young man. So, what do you want to know exactly?"

"I really don't know. Ethan has always been, well, crazy." He laughed nervously. "But this is just different. He's so consumed with this dream, not to mention the four visions." He was shaking his head while never losing eye contact with Vic. "I absolutely couldn't believe he went back to the memorial by himself, and then ended up here talking to you. Don't you think that's just flat strange?"

Vic ran a hand through his hair. "Before we get into this too deeply son, what do you say I get us something to drink? A soda sound good to you? Oh, and my wife made some cookies this morning that are absolutely to die for. Interested?" Seeing that he was, Vic stood. "I'll be right back. Just take a minute." He motioned around the room with one hand as he said, "Please. Make yourself at home. Look around at anything you want. Oh, by the way. I'm going to stop off at the bathroom first. You just drove in, right? If you want, there is one directly across the hall from this door. Again, make yourself at home, young man. Be right back."

With that said, he disappeared down the hall but left the door open so that Frank could see the bathroom across the hall. Vic was really just stalling for time until Doc and Bob could arrive. His wink to his wife was a signal to call them if any other kids showed up. Vic had snuck around the other side of the house to look out the front parlor window for his partners. Just as he felt he had waited long enough, their car flew around the corner. So he darted back around to the kitchen to grab the sodas and cookies before returning to his office.

Frank was standing in the corner of the office and looking at the two photos of the crash site. When he heard Vic return, he walked back to his chair and sat down. He and Vic were halfway through their first cookie when the doorbell rang. Frank heard Vic's wife walk past the office door on her way to answer it. A few seconds later, Doc and Bob stepped into the office.

Frank stood and smiled as he held out his hand towards the men. "I can't believe I'm getting to meet all three of you, too! This is so cool!"

Doc said, "What's up, Vic? I see you have another young man here."

"Doc. Bob. This is Frank. He's a friend of Ethan's. You remember him from a few days ago?"

Both men spoke at the same time. "Frank."

As they all sat down, Vic looked at his partners. "This young man has driven all the way here out of concern for his friend Ethan. That is as far as our conversation made it before these cookies called our name!"

Bob commented, "Consider yourself lucky, kid. In all the time I've known him, I've only seen him give away cookies twice."

Doc immediately added, "And it wasn't to us!" They all laughed before Vic added, "Well, they're damn good cookies, you know." Again they all laughed. Frank appeared relaxed as he finished his three cookies and sipped on the soda. Vic had finished his as well.

"Frank was just telling me he's worried that Ethan is obsessed with dreams and visions." He looked at Frank. "Isn't that where we were, son?"

"Yes, sir." Frank glanced at Doc and Bob. "Ethan has always

been somewhat high strung, so to speak. But he's worse since that camping trip and all this really spooky stuff that's happening. I'm just afraid he's kind of gone overboard. I think he's losing it totally. That's why I'm here. I was hoping you could help."

Doc took a deep breath. "Of course. We'll help any way we can. Do you mind if I ask you a few questions?"

"No. Sure! Ask me anything."

"Would you mind telling us as much as you can about the dream and visions? That seems the logical starting point." Doc looked at the other two men who immediately nodded in agreement.

Frank looked around at each of them. "I don't know."

Doc tried to reassure him. "Tell us whatever you can remember. Just start talking. Don't try to put it in any kind of order."

"Ok. The dream is in several parts, and doesn't make any sense, really." Frank closed his eyes, trying to remember. "The first part is about the crash. That's easy to understand though, because we had just gone to the memorial park that afternoon. But then there are these two people by a big fire. It's a guy and girl."

Bob interrupted. "What kind of big fire?"

"I don't really know. It's just a big fire. Sorry."

Doc nudged Frank back to the dream. "We can come back to that. Go on."

"Well, then there's something about this guy falling out of a helicopter. No, wait. He wasn't in the helicopter exactly. No, he was on something underneath it made out of wood. Kind of crazy, huh?"

Doc again sounded reassuring. "Nobody here will ever say something sounds crazy. Please. Go on."

"Well you might when I tell you the next part. It's about an old barn with a chimney."

Bob almost came out of his chair. "What kind of chimney? Can you describe it a little?"

"Well, it's not really attached to the barn. See, this is where it gets really nuts. I don't see what this could possibly have to do with the plane crash memorial."

Vic calmly asked, "Frank. If it's not attached to the barn, where is it?"

Frank answered so matter-of-factly that it caused the three men to glance around the room at each other. "It's inside the barn. Fell over on the ground right in the middle." He looked around at each man. "I told you this was really weird. But the really spooky thing is that there are all these civil war guys walking around in the trees up on top of a nearby hill. Told you it was spooky!" He shook his head a bit before continuing, "I even have to agree with Ethan that this part was very weird."

Since Frank had stopped talking, Vic asked, "Is that all of the dream?"

Frank scratched his ear for a moment. "Yeah. I think so."

Doc looked around at the guys. "Before you tell us about these visions, I'm just wondering why you called them visions."

"That's easy. They happened while walking around out in the woods after the dream. But I didn't call them visions. He did."

Doc eagerly asked, "Ethan called them visions?"

"Yes, sir." He shrugged and continued. "That's his thing. He can call them whatever he wants."

"So, tell us about them." Doc settled back into his chair.

"Well, first there is this guy and girl that start having sex in the woods by a creek."

Bob interrupted this time. "Now are these a different guy and girl?"

"No!" Frank looked up at the ceiling while slightly shaking one hand in the air. "They are the same two that were sitting by the big fire. You know how dreams jump around." Then he looked back at Doc. "I'm sorry, sir. I'm messing this all up. It's a lot to remember."

Doc spoke in a calming voice. "Frank. You're doing fine. Please continue."

"Anyway, they just disappear into thin air. On the walk back to camp there's this mist that formed. There are three men walking together." He looked back at Doc before he continued. "Now this part I remember, because it's kind of funny. There are two army guys and a lumberjack walking along. That guy and girl . . . " Frank paused to look at Bob. "The same two. They run up behind these guys and yell 'BOO'. But only two of them jump. It was like the third guy didn't hear it. Then those two turn and face the third guy like he did it. But he then points to the guy and

girl. Was kind of funny, that's why I can remember it so easy."
Frank was still looking at Doc but when Doc didn't laugh, Frank
started talking again.

"Ok, now we get to that ball of glass on your wall. The one
you told Ethan had belonged to some guy named 'Ed'. Anyway.
Those same three guys. You know the two army dudes and the
lumberjack? They're all dressed in civilian clothes and they're
in some kind of storage room. They keep picking up stuff and
looking at it but they usually just put it back down. It's like they
were looking for something in particular. In the end, each guy
picks something out and takes it."

Doc interrupted Frank. "You and Ethan have obviously talked
about this a lot. You've already mentioned the ball of glass, but
we were wondering if you'd mind looking at something else?"

"Sure. What?"

Vic rolled his desk chair to a cabinet and opened the two big
doors on top. He pulled out a small tray and put it on the desk
in front of Frank. There were ten items on it. Frank was already
looking at them when Doc said, "Just take your time, Frank. If
anything catches your attention, just say. No pressure, son. Just
anything at all."

"Did you guys show this stuff to Ethan? He didn't tell me
about this."

Vic said, "No. We just put it together in case Ethan came
back."

Vic had barely finished talking when Frank picked up a little
battery-powered robot. Doc asked, "Do you think that is one of
the other two items?"

"No. But my dad has one just like it from when he was a
kid. He never let me play with it." After he put the robot down,
he picked up an item that caused Bob to roll his eyes. "Hey,
this is one of the items." It was a shiny metal money clip with a
computer chip on the front of it. "I wonder how they attached
that chip to the metal."

Doc secretly glanced at the other two men while Frank was
still looking at the other items. "So do any of the other things
strike your fancy, Frank?"

"I'm afraid not, sir. Sorry."

Doc was more persistent this time. "Are you sure there isn't any other item on there from the vision?"

Frank shook his head 'NO', but then reached down and picked up a small pocketknife. "The third thing was a little knife like this one."

Doc asked, "You don't think that is the one? Why?"

Frank answered immediately and sounded very positive. "No. This one isn't broken. The third item was a little knife like this, but it's broken right here. And half the wooden handle was missing." Then suddenly Frank looked back at the open doors on the cabinet. "There it is!" He pointed to a lone knife on the shelf where the tray had been. "It must have fallen off."

Vic rolled over and retrieved it. Once he put it in Frank's hand, Frank said, "Hey. It says 'Ed' on what's left of the wooden handle."

Vic added, "It used to have his entire name on it. His name was Edward".

Frank started talking, "Ethan told me that you said that ball of glass was a prized gift from your friend 'Ed'." Frank's face lost all expression as he sat back in his chair. "That means you three are the guys in the vision. Aren't you? It was you that picked out these items." He leaned his head back and put his palms on his temples. "This whole thing just keeps getting weirder and weirder! There is no telling what Ethan will do when he finds this out. This could push him to do, well, there's no telling what it might make him do."

Doc softly said, "Frank. There is no reason to tell him if you don't want to."

Frank dropped his hands and sat up on the edge of the seat to look at Doc. "No. I don't have to tell him. But what about you guys? Are you going to tell him?"

"No. If you think about it, we didn't tell you either. You just figured it out by yourself."

"Well sir, I don't think I'm going to tell him then. I'm his best friend and all, but I don't see any reason to tell him this. Like you said, I figured it out. Maybe he won't."

Vic had a quizzical look on his face. "Frank. Earlier you said dreams. You used the plural form. So are there other dreams?"

"No sir. I was just not sure how to tell you there were different parts of the dream. But I did find out that somebody else evidently had a dream when we were camping."

Doc seemed eager to know, "Who?"

"Mary. Ethan let that slip yesterday at his house."

"Did he say what her dream was about?"

"No. I asked him the same thing. It must have been what sent her running off into the woods one night. It almost scared us all to death. Ethan went after her first. Then Maggie was yelling like a crazy woman at me and Emit to help find her. Ethan said it must have been that night."

Bob asked, "So do they like each other? Mary and Ethan, that is."

Frank laughed a little before answering. "Ethan has had a crush on Mary for a long time now."

Vic added, "When he was here, he said that he thought he loved her."

Frank looked shocked as he faced Vic. "What? He actually said those words? He said 'I love her'?"

Vic nodded 'Yes'.

Frank had a sudden urge to leave. He looked at his watch. "Wow. It's getting late and I have a long drive home." He stood up and the three men did the same. He held his hand out to Doc first, and then shook the other two men's hands also. "I really appreciate you taking the time to talk to me, but I need to hit the road. Nobody knows I'm here. I need to head back."

Doc said, "It was nice talking to you, Frank. I'm sure your friend Ethan will be okay, too. Just give it time. I'll bet Mary might just take his mind off all this other stuff."

"I hope so, sir. Thanks again."

The men watched from Vic's office window as Frank drove off. Bob said, "Well, at least we can find out who they all are now. Doc wrote down Frank's license number when we first got here."

Vic commented aloud, "That boy is a really good friend. He drove all the way here out of concern for his friend. Yep, a real good friend."

Doc nodded, "We all know how Ed wanted Martha more than anything else." The other two men nodded as Doc continued. "But he also said many times that he had always wanted that one good friend, a best friend."

Bob said, "Well, looks like he has one."

Chapter 21

LOVE GAMES

ETHAN'S DAY TRIP with his parents was proving to be nearly unbearable. Though he usually loved this trip with them, his mind was totally focused on Mary. His folks constantly said things twice to him before he finally looked at them and said, "I'm sorry. What?" This had happened so frequently that his mother eventually asked, "Are you okay, Ethan? You seem so distracted. This is your favorite trip but you aren't your usually witty self. What's on your mind, son?"

"I'm sorry, Mom. I'm just thinking about going off to college at the end of the summer. It's a big step for me." This wasn't really what he was thinking about at all. He couldn't get Mary off his mind. In fact, he was mentally rehearsing different ways to tell her that he loved her. But none of them seemed right to him so far. This had to be perfect. It had to be easy, yet sincere. There just had to be a way to casually get her alone in a beautiful spot. There he would bestow words upon her that were so eloquent she couldn't say no.

With that thought, he suddenly asked himself, 'No to what?' He looked down at his sweaty palms and wondered what he was so afraid of. His heart felt like it could jump out of his chest and outrun the car. Then it hit him. He was thinking about asking Mary to marry him! What? Maybe Frank was right and he had gone crazy. It only took a second before he shook it off with 'So what?'

He'd always liked her. But wait a minute - he was thinking about going from liking her to asking her to marry him. What happened to just asking her to go steady with him, be his girlfriend? Yeah, that made more sense. They needed to date steady first like normal people. He chuckled at that thought because even he didn't think it was normal to feel like this about her. But then again, why shouldn't he feel like this. They had known each other practically since birth. Lately, he had definitely noticed her being very touchy-feely with him, too. Wow, she had been putting her hands on him a lot lately. He smiled as he realized that she could already feel the same way about him.

Everything had changed since that camping trip. It had been a magical night with her in the trees when he was trying to calm her down. He always knew she was pretty. No, make that beautiful. And that night in the bright moonlight, she had been stunning! Yes, that was when he knew she had to be his. When he had put his arm around her, it had felt like destiny. Like it was meant to be. He had always thought that the cosmic crap that Misty talked about was just bull. But now he was beginning to think Misty could be right. How else could he explain the weird goings-on, and how they had brought him to this point in time? He couldn't. There was no rational explanation. So it must be fate, pure and simple. So why question it? He decided that tomorrow would be the day. The day he won her heart forever.

His mind had been on total overload the entire trip. It was late when they arrived back at home. He crashed on his bed and was out in seconds from sheer mental exhaustion.

The next morning arrived way too early. Ethan opened his eyes and realized there was too much light in his room for it to be early in the morning. A hurried glance at the clock confirmed that he had overslept. DAMN! Not today! Not the day he was going to win Mary over! He hopped out of bed and hit the floor running. A quick shower and fresh clothes preceded a mad dash to his car. Once inside and the car door closed, he called Mary's cell phone. No answer. He guessed she was probably at home so he would drive over there immediately and surprise her. This should be good.

The drive to Mary's house was made in record time and he practically flew to the front door. It seemed like an eternity before he heard anyone coming to answer it. Finally, there was the sound of the lock then it being opened.

"Hello, Ethan! I'll bet you are looking for Mary, but I'm afraid she spent the night with Misty. Sorry. Oh, and since I'm sure you're going over there, please take her phone charger and tell her to use it. We gave her the phone so we could check on her, and it works better if it's charged."

He took it and replied, "Yes, ma'am." Then he dashed back to his car. Another trip that he'd made many times before took less than half the time it usually did. He realized how lucky he was not to have been stopped for speeding. Maybe this was a sign that the cosmic alignment was in his favor after all!

Misty's dad answered the door and swung it wide open.

"Hello, Ethan. They're all upstairs."

"Thanks, sir!"

He tried not to appear too anxious to get up to Misty's room. He knocked once on her door and she immediately opened it.

"What did you forget now?" She saw him and looked shocked before poking her head out and looking down the hall. Then she looked back at him. "Ethan. I wasn't expecting you. What's wrong? You seem out of breath."

"Where's Mary?" He was smiling as his breathing began to slow.

"Mary? Well, you just missed her and Emit. They just left. I can't believe you didn't see them."

"She's gone? But your dad just said you all were upstairs."

"Come on, Ethan. You know my dad never knows where anyone is."

"You say she's with Emit? Why didn't you go with them? Where'd they go?"

"Well, I would have gone too, but I have to go somewhere with my mother in a few minutes. I'm not sure where they were going. But don't try calling her cell. It's dead again as usual. They were going to run by some store in the mall before going to her house to charge it."

They both heard footsteps coming up the stairs and they turned to see her father walking towards them.

"Hey, honey. Tell Mary that her mom called and gave somebody her phone charger to bring over here. They should be here any minute."

Ethan held up the charger. "Here."

Her dad smiled before he turned to leave. "Good. See, everything works out."

Misty was staring at her dad as he disappeared back down the stairs. "I totally love that man, but he doesn't have a clue."

"Do you know the name of this store? Or at least which mall?"

"Sorry, dude. You'll have to bloodhound it. Can't help you."

"Ok. Have fun with your mom. See ya later. Oh, but if you talk to Mary before I find her, will you tell her I'm looking for her. I really need to talk to her."

"You too? That's the same thing Emit said when he showed up this morning. What's up with you two? I know you both have always been in competition over her, but what's so special about today? Did the planets line up and nobody tell me?"

"Emit came over here to talk to her? He said that? What about?"

She sensed the tension in his voice. "Chill, dude. I'm sure you'll get to talk to her next."

"Okay. I better go find them."

She watched him go down the stairs. Once he was safely out of hearing range, she mumbled, "You do that. You find them and tell Emit I want to talk to him too." Then she closed her eyes for just a second before she slowly closed her bedroom door.

Ethan was sitting in his car and staring at Mary's phone charger in his front seat. Where could they have gone? He'll never find them. There were three different malls within 10 miles of here, and each one had at least 40 stores. It was hopeless. And she was with Emit! What if he beat him to the punch and asked Mary to go steady first? Surely not! She was supposed to be with him. Not Emit!

His cell phone rang and it startled him so much he hit his knee on the dash. A quick glance showed it was Maggie. "Hi, Maggie. What's up?"

"Well, Mary just told me that you have her phone charger and she wants me to get it for her. Where are you?"

"You're with Mary? Great! Where are you?"

"Slow down, speed boy! What's going on with you? Too much coffee?"

"Sorry, but I really need to talk to Mary. Can you put her on the phone?"

"Well no! She's already gone. What's up with you and Emit? He seemed all fired up to talk to her, just like you are. What's going on?"

"She's gone? Where? With Emit? When?"

Maggie started laughing. "Chill out, dude! You're going to pop an artery or something. I don't exactly know where, but I did hear Emit say something about a drive to the lake. Seemed kind of odd to me, but Mary was okay with it. So where can we meet so I can get her charger?"

There wasn't any response for a few seconds. "Ethan? You still there? Are you okay?"

His voice was quiet, as if he were depressed. "Yeah, still here. Why a drive to the lake?"

"Don't really know. I just heard something about being alone so they could talk uninterrupted. It must be very personal, I guess. Don't make me ask you again about that charger. She wants me to have it when we meet later at the mall. So cough it up, boy."

His voice sounded excited again. "You're meeting her at the mall? Great! Where?"

She shook her head. "Okay. I'm getting confused here. Are you asking me where I'm meeting her, or where to meet you? If it's her, then I'm going to track you down and kick you in the shin so I can grab that charger."

"Of course, it was where to meet you. You wouldn't really kick me would you?"

"Yes!"

"I'm at Misty's house. Pick a place."

"The coffee shop around the corner. Five minutes!" She hung up and talked to her phone as if it was Ethan. "You need to seriously take a chill pill, dude!"

When Maggie got to the coffee shop, she found Ethan sitting at the most secluded table in the place. He had one leg rapidly bouncing up and down. She couldn't believe her eyes. Was he drinking a cup of coffee? Oh my GOD! She walked up and stared at him as sternly as she could.

"What?"

"You have been talking 90 miles an hour and here you are drinking coffee? Are you crazy?" She rolled her eyes at him and then sat down. One hand darted towards Ethan. "Charger!"

He obviously didn't produce it fast enough so she kicked his leg under the table.

"Ouch! You kicked me!"

She flipped the fingers on her still outstretched hand. "CHARGER!"

"Not until you tell me where you are meeting her and when."

She started spelling, "C H A R G E R, now!"

When he didn't produce, she tilted her head a little and grinned. He immediately put the charger on the table. "Okay, okay! Now where and when are you meeting her?" When she didn't answer quickly enough, he asked, "Come on, Mags. Why are you doing this to me? I thought we were friends. Hey! I gave you the stupid charger."

She could tell he was not really joking around like he usually did. So she softened her posture before she spoke. "Ethan. Do you hear yourself? What's gotten into you? I'm just joking. She's going to call me from Emit's phone when they get back in town."

He displayed a fake smile. "Emit has a cell phone? Since when?"

She laughed. "I know! It was a shock to me too. After all those lectures how he'd never get one. Turns out he's had one for some time now but didn't carry it around. All this time he was hanging out with Misty and using her phone. Can you believe it? Men! I'll never understand you guys. Never!"

"I wonder how long they'll be out there?"

"I don't know, but it sounds like a while. She told me to go on and get my hair done because it might be this afternoon before they're done."

Ethan sat as close to the table as he could get. "Done? What do you mean done?"

She mocked him by sitting up close to the table too and then speaking slowly. "Well, whatever they are DOING, sounds like she wants to wait until they are DONE doing IT!" Even though she was just joking around, his depressed look made her wish she hadn't said it that way.

All he could muster was a grunt. "Huh."

"Ethan. Come on! Snap out of it. They are just talking about something they don't want anyone else to overhear. That's all."

He looked at her with sad, puppy-dog eyes. "They're just talking? You sure?"

"What else could it be? Sex?" She was laughing at first but then she lost her smile. "Oh my GOD! You think they're having sex? Really?"

He spoke slowly, "Do you think she would have sex with him?"

"NO! You can't be serious, Ethan. Look, they're just talking. Trust me. I'm not supposed to know, but I do." She saw his ears perk up on that comment. "No! Don't even ask me. I'm not telling you. It's not my place to say. I'm sure it's all going to come out soon. So we just have to wait until it's official. That means you too." He was her friend and she felt sorry for him. "I know you have a thing for Mary. But this is between them and you'll have to deal with it."

She had never seen him like this before but he was visibly angry as he stood up. "Oh, I'll deal with it. And him!" He walked off.

She finally caught up with him at his car. "Wait! Ethan, please wait!" She leaned up against his door so he couldn't open it. "It's not what you think. He's your friend and you're his. He would never hurt you. I can't believe you're acting like you would hurt him. Ethan. He's always been your friend and wanted you to be happy. When this comes out in the open, he'll want you to be happy for him. If you really are his friend, you will be."

He stood there looking down at the key in the door. He hadn't even turned it yet. He looked up at the sky and exhaled slowly.

He had one finger pushing on the key as he said, "You're right. He is my friend. Of course I'll be happy for him. He would be happy for me so it's only fair."

He turned to face her. She backed away from the car. He stepped sheepishly closer and gave her a big hug, which she returned tightly. She heard him very softly say, "I just thought, well, oh . . . it doesn't matter. I guess it wasn't really meant to be."

As he pulled back and began to open the car door, she asked, "What are you mumbling about? What doesn't matter?"

He finally seemed like his old self as he smiled at her. "It's going to be okay. Everything works out the way it's supposed to."

She watched as he sat down behind the wheel. "I'll call you when she calls me. Okay?"

Before he closed the door he said, "Sure. That'd be nice."

He didn't know where to go or what to do. He just needed to go somewhere and think alone. He drove to a spot on the river where he and Emit used to go to drink beer. It was the perfect spot to do this kind of thinking. He sat on the hood of his car and watched the water roll by him. He began to see the water as if it represented his life. It kept on moving. So would his life. He didn't have to know where it would take him, or what would happen along the way. Then he saw the riverbank as his friends. No matter where you went, they were always there to support you and help you find your way. It was obvious that nothing was more important than friendship, and that definitely included Emit.

He was so lost in his thoughts that he didn't hear his cell phone ring at first. He answered it just in time. "Hello?"

"Ethan. It's Maggie. Mary and I are going shopping. She said she'll call you later, but Emit wants to know where you are."

"Tell him I'm at the river."

"He said he's at the river. What? Ok! Ethan. Emit said he's on his way."

"Ok, I'll wait here. Bye."

It took Emit almost an hour to get there. He pulled up alongside Ethan's car and joined him on the hood. "Hey man. What you doing out here all alone? And no beer? Are you sick, man?" Emit was laughing but stopped as Ethan looked up at him.

"Emit, I need to tell you something."

"No, wait Ethan. I want to tell you my news first."

"Please, Emit. Just listen, okay?"

Emit saw that his friend was more serious than he had ever seen him before. "Sure, man. Sure."

"Thanks. I've been here for several hours, I guess. Just thinking and I've come to a conclusion." He turned towards

Emit and held out his hand for a shake. "We have been friends for our entire lives, and that means more to me than you will ever know."

"I hear you, bro. Same here."

"So I just want you to know that I'm happy for you. Really!"

Emit looked confused. "Thanks, but. Wait a minute. Okay, it was Maggie, wasn't it? I just had a feeling she knew. She told you, didn't she?"

"No man. She never said anything. Even if she had, what difference does it make? The important thing here is that two of my friends are happy and that makes me happy."

Emit still looked confused. "Uh, what do you mean two of your friends? Has somebody told her already? Who? Was it Maggie?"

Now Ethan looked confused. "What do you mean you haven't told her yet? What were you two talking about all this time at the lake?"

"At the lake? Oh, I guess you misunderstood. I was at the lake with Mary, not her."

"Well I know you were at the lake with Mary. Wait a minute. What do you mean you weren't there with her? Her who?"

"Misty!"

"Misty?"

"Yes, Misty. Mary convinced me to go tell Misty how I feel about her. It's just scary though. What if she doesn't like me? I respect Mary's point of view and all, but she's a girl. That's why I wanted to talk it over with you first and get a guy's opinion. You know, on how to go about telling her this mushy stuff. Mary makes it seem so simple, but I wanted to hear what you had to say. After all, like you said, we are friends!"

• • •

After Ethan had relaxed, the two friends talked for almost an hour. Ethan expressed his ideas about what to say and how to say it. Emit would suggest small alterations to customize the wording to his way of talking. Whatever he said to her had to sound like it came from him, or Misty might not believe him. In the end, both friends were in high spirits as they drove back to town.

Both were very anxious to see their special girl, but it was Ethan who called first. Mary's dad informed him that his wife and daughter had gone to his mother-in-law's house for the night. The dad was fairly certain they would be home tomorrow afternoon by 5:00. At first Ethan was depressed about this news, but he quickly realized this would give him a lot of free time to work on what he would say to Mary.

Emit waited until he saw the city lights before he called Misty.

"Hello? Emit?" She pulled the phone from her ear and looked at the number calling. "Whose phone are you borrowing now? Huh? This is *your* cell phone? Hey! I knew you'd break down and get one someday. It's about time! Huh? You've had it how long? Why would you keep it a secret all this time? So you could borrow mine? What? I just don't understand guys at all. You never make any sense. No, I don't have any plans for tonight. Why? Sure, I'm ready now. I'll sit on the porch until you get here. You're already outside? Okay! I'm on my way."

Emit watched as she bounced while she ran to the car. He had always been captivated by those little girl movements that made her ponytail flip from side to side. She was so cute and so very full of energy. The closer she came to the car, the more nervous he became. Part of him was trying to talk the rest of him out of saying anything to her at all. Yet, deep down inside, he knew it was time. He hoped and prayed that she would feel the same way about him.

She smiled as she got in. He turned up the music as they pulled out of the driveway. For the next 20 minutes, she told him all about Mary spending the night, and what had happened that morning with Ethan looking for her.

"So, where have you been?"

"I was down by the river."

She lost some of her smile. "The river? It must be your day for being around water. Huh?"

He glanced at her. "What? Why would you say that?"

"I heard you and Mary went to the lake today for a long time."

He glanced at her again. "Who told you that?"

"Sorry, I can't divulge my sources, buddy! So, where are we going?"

"I thought we'd go to that place where you go to think a lot. What did you call it?"

She now had a small look of concern. "It's called Tree Top Lane. Why are we going there?"

"I thought it'd be a good place to talk. Okay?"

"Talk? Didn't you spend several hours at the lake today talking to Mary?" She began pointing her finger at him as she asked, "What were you doing at the river?"

"Talking to Ethan."

She leaned back against the passenger door, a concerned look on her face now. "So you talked to Mary by the lake. Now you've talked to Ethan by the river and here we are going to Tree Top Lane to talk. What's going on, Emit?"

"We just need to talk. Isn't that okay? We are friends, aren't we?" They had arrived and he stopped right in the middle of an open area. It was about 50 feet higher than all the trees in the neighborhood below, and they were the only car there.

She sat up and twisted around straight in her seat before looking down at her feet. He saw that her mood had saddened. "What's wrong? You aren't smiling any more. Why?" He watched as she nervously rubbed her left eye. Was she crying? "Are you okay? What's wrong, Misty?"

She closed her eyes for a few seconds. "I think I know why we're here and what you want to talk about." He definitely heard her sniffle before she turned to face him. He now could see the tears in her eyes. "Don't worry Emit. You don't have to tell me. I've known this was coming ever since that camping trip."

"What are you talking about?"

"Look. I saw you and Mary down by the creek. I'm not proud of myself but I was curious what you were up to, so I followed you both. Now you've talked to her again, and then Ethan. Hey, I'm not stupid. You've always talked about her and we all know that Ethan has too. So let me guess. You and her are together now. I bet you went to break it to Ethan. That must have been rough, since you both are friends. You *are* still friends aren't you?"

Emit had his hands covering his eyes as he leaned back against the seat. "I knew this wasn't going to be easy."

"Emit. We can still be friends. Don't worry about it. Really!" She faked a smile as she tried to hide the fact that she was wiping tears from her eyes. But since he obviously saw the tissue she was wiping her eyes with, she said, "Yes I'm crying. I'm just, uh, well . . . I'm just happy for you both."

"But you don't understand. I don't want to be friends."

Hearing this, her face went totally pale and she froze from shock. After a few seconds, she spoke so very softly. "Not at all?"

Seeing her reaction and hearing her response, he rolled his eyes as he realized what he just said. "NO! Wait a minute! I mean YES! I don't want to be friends." He saw the total confusion in her eyes and he paused to take a breath. "I told them this wouldn't work. I should have just done it my way to start with." He unbuckled his seat belt so he could lean closer to her. He smiled as he slid one hand under hers. Then he gently covered it with his other hand.

"Misty. I don't want to JUST be friends anymore. I want you to be my girlfriend. I know you get mad at me sometimes, but I can change. I want to change. I want to be your boyfriend."

"But I saw you with her. And you were with her most of today too. I don't understand."

"I was talking to her about you. It's always been about you." Then he smirked as he added, "As much as you three girls talk, I was kind of hoping that they'd tell you so I wouldn't have to struggle through this. You know I'm not real good at talking about this sort of thing."

She dropped the tissue into her lap before reaching over to touch his face. She slid her hand along his cheek before letting it wrap underneath his chin. "Oh, I think you talk just fine. But maybe just a little too much." She started to lean forward to kiss him, but her seat belt stopped her advance with a jerk. As she looked down for the belt release, she felt one of his hands pull away. Then came the sound of metal clicking, and she immediately felt her freedom. This kiss led to another and another, until there were no words necessary. They both understood that the other had said 'yes'.

• • •

The next day was absolutely beautiful. The sun was shining, the sky was cloudless and the temperature was perfect. Frank was walking alone in the mall. His pace was quick because he knew exactly what he had come for, and which store had it. He was in and out of the store in less than 10 minutes, and headed back to his car.

Once he cleared the store entrance, he turned right and headed back towards his car. He couldn't help but wonder why girls took so long to shop. He came, bought and was already leaving. He had a cocky smirk on his face as his eyes noticed all the women who had probably been here for hours already. Two young women were just coming out of the store ahead of him. Neither one of them had bought a thing. No shopping bags in their hands. They were doing what he suspected—looking, not buying. As he passed that store's entrance, he glanced inside and saw Maggie. He didn't break stride as he altered course towards her. She was picking a shirt off a rack, looking at it and then putting it back. He started laughing because she too hadn't bought anything. She heard him laughing.

"Frank! What are you doing here?"

"Well! Unlike you, I've only been in the mall a few minutes and have what I came for already. I was leaving when I saw you. Need some help picking something out real quick so you can leave?"

She poked him with the shirt's hanger that she had just picked off the rack.

"And what exactly does that mean? You think you're a better shopper than me?"

"Well I must be, because I'm already leaving. You, on the other hand, are still trying to make up your mind what you want. Guess that does make me the better shopper!"

She displayed a blank face of contempt before she said, "It's not me that can't make up her mind. This is the third set of blouses that she's asked for. Even I don't take this long."

"Who's with you?"

"Mary. She's in the dressing room." She nodded towards the little rooms along one side of the store.

"Mary's here? That's odd. I thought she wasn't supposed to be back until 5:00 this afternoon."

"She and her mom came back early. She called and wanted me to come with her. So here I am playing fetch, and fetch and fetch and . . . ".

Frank interrupted her by holding out a hand, "I get it. I get it."

Before he could say anything else, they both heard Mary's voice and turned to look at her.

"Hi Frank! What do you think about my new blouse?" She looked at Maggie. "This is the one I want. Sorry, but you can stop looking now." She turned to her left and then right as she modeled it for them. "So what do you think, Maggie? Cute, huh?"

Maggie looked puzzled, "Yes it's cute but I don't remember giving you that one."

Mary shrieked like a little girl as she smiled and lifted her shoulders, posing for them. "You didn't. Somebody left it in the changing room. It was right there on the hook, so I tried it on and it FIT! What luck!" Then she turned to Frank again. "So do you want to hang out with us, now that I'm through shopping?"

"Sure. What do you want to do?"

Maggie immediately said, "I'm thirsty, so let's go to the food court."

After Mary paid for her new blouse, the three friends went for something to drink. Once they were seated at a table, Mary looked at Maggie. "I bet he doesn't know yet. You want to tell him, or can I?"

"Tell me what?"

Maggie motioned for Mary to tell him. "This is going to be a real shocker buddy. Emit and Misty are going steady!" Her face was almost beaming light towards him. Both eyes were sparkling and her beautiful smile gleamed.

"What? Since when?" He looked at Maggie. "When did this happen?"

Maggie was smiling, but again motioned for Mary to continue. "Emit asked her last night and she said 'yes'! Isn't that cool?"

Frank had that cocky smirk again. "Yes, and it's about time."

Both girls lost their smiles as they glanced at each other.

Maggie asked, "About time? Are you saying you've known that Emit liked her and didn't tell us?"

Frank's face took on a very guilty look before he mumbled "No."

The girls again glanced at each other, but this time it was Mary that spoke.

"If you didn't know he liked her, then . . . " She paused while she stared into his eyes as if she was trying to read his mind. Then she sat up straight and pointed an accusing finger at him. "You knew she liked him! How can that be? Even Maggie and I didn't know that."

Both Frank and Mary immediately noticed that Maggie's eyes had popped open before she looked away. The two of them now watched her. It was obvious that she didn't want to make eye contact. Mary now pointed an equally accusing finger at Maggie. "You knew too. Didn't you? And you didn't tell me!"

After a few intense moments, Maggie finally rolled her eyes and head before speaking. "Okay, okay! I admit it. I knew. But she made me promise not to tell anyone." She looked right at Mary before stressing, "ANYONE!"

Mary sat back and put one hand flat on her chest. "I just can't believe this. You're my best friend and you didn't tell me! Why not? It never stopped you before!" Realizing what she had just admitted in front of a guy, she sneakily cut her eyes at Frank for just a second. "It's no big deal. We're girls! We talk. So what?"

Frank stared at her with a blank face before he shook his head and sipped his soda. Maggie asked, "So how long have you known Misty liked Emit?"

"Oh, for quite a while now." He glanced towards Mary. "But I was asked not to tell anyone EITHER!"

Maggie was thinking out loud, "I wonder why she never told me that you knew?"

Mary quickly commented, "I'm still wondering why you didn't tell me!"

"So, now that you have your drinks, what are you two girls planning on doing the rest of the day?"

Mary again spoke. "Well I'm just waiting for Ethan to call me. My dad said Ethan was going to call me today. Look! My cell phone is all charged up. I wonder when he'll call?"

Frank took another sip. "At 5:00."

Mary looked at him and asked, "What makes you think that?"

"Because that's what time your dad said you'd be home." He noticed that Maggie had a questioning look on her face. "I talked to him before I came out here. I wanted him to come, but he said he was busy."

Mary asked, "Busy doing what?"

"I don't know. You should call him and find out. Then we'd

all know."

Maggie joined in. "Or we could go by his house and surprise him."

It's obvious that Mary liked the idea because she put her phone in her purse and stood up. "Sounds good, let's go!"

Once in the parking lot, Mary got Frank to ride with them in her car. He didn't talk at all during the ride to Ethan's house. It wasn't that he didn't try to talk, but the two girls were still carrying on about Emit and Misty being in LOVE. He decided not to try any more, since this was definitely not a conversation he wanted to join anyway.

At Ethan's house, Mary told them not to get out of the car. She wanted to call Ethan on her cell phone and ask him what he was doing. She pulled the phone out of her purse and pushed the button to turn it on, but nothing happened. She stared at her lifeless phone in the palm of her hand.

"I don't understand. I charged this all last night. There must be something wrong with the battery."

Maggie jokingly asked, "Are you sure you plugged it in?"

"Very funny girl! Of course I plugged it in. I did it right before we got out of the car at my grandma's house. I let it charge all night long."

Frank snickered. "I've been in your mom's car. That plug only has power when the car is on."

Mary looked totally lost as to what that meant. "Really?" Frank nodded 'YES'. Then she dropped her phone into her purse. "Hey! I have an idea for a prank. Let me use your phone, Frank." She was holding her hand back over the seat. "Come on. It will be funny. He'll think it's you calling."

Frank really didn't like this plan. But he caved to the pressure of two girls staring at him and handed over his phone.

"I'm not going to the mall with you, man. I told you that already. I'm busy."

"To busy to talk to me?" Mary started laughing into the phone.

"Mary! You're back early. Great! Hey, why are you on Frank's phone? I thought you were going to charge that phone of yours? Are you at the mall?"

"No, silly. We're in front of your house. Come on and go with us!"

"Who's we?"

"Me, Maggie and Frank. Hurry up!"

"Uh, all of you are out front? I'll be there in a second."

Ethan's feet only touched every third step on the stairs as he flew to the front door. He approached Mary's car on the driver side so he could talk directly to her. "I've been looking for you. Can we go somewhere and talk?" He nodded at Maggie and Frank before he leaned close to Mary's ear. "Alone."

She looked at him and said, "Why can't we all go to the lake. You and I can walk around there and talk." She looked over at Maggie. "It's going to be a very big full moon tonight. I think we should all go."

Ethan didn't know what to say and his hesitation allowed Maggie to comment. "Sounds good to me. I haven't been to the lake in a long time." She looked over her shoulder. "You in, Frank?"

Ethan couldn't believe his ears as Frank said, "Sure. Why not?" He dipped his head low enough to see Frank had an exaggerated smile on his face.

Mary was motioning for Ethan to back up so she could get out and he did. "I think we need to take your car so you can drive. Okay?"

Ethan couldn't believe they were ALL going to the lake. He wanted to talk to Mary alone. He was positive that Frank was only coming along to make sure he didn't talk about that stupid dream anymore. No, wait! He's mad because he wouldn't go to the mall with him earlier. Yep, that's it!

Frank held the back door open for Maggie to get in, then got in behind Ethan. The girls talked during the entire drive to the lake but the boys only nodded occasionally. Frank still presented his cocky smile at Ethan every time he looked in the rearview mirror. Finally they were there at the very spot where Ethan had envisioned being alone with Mary tonight. He parked his car by a huge rock that he and Mary used to sit on at night to listen to the water lapping on the shores of the lake. It was a scenic view during the day, and a very romantic one at night.

He left the music playing on low and hurried around to open Mary's door. Once she was out, they both strolled off as the sun was just beginning to go down.

"Frank. Why did Misty tell you that she liked Emit?"

"Well, actually it was an accident I think. I went for a run one night and saw her down at the park on a swing. When I got close enough to her, I saw she was crying. She wouldn't tell me why at first, but eventually she started crying really hard on my shoulder. She kept saying things like 'He doesn't even see me. I don't think he ever will'. Stuff like that. I asked who, and she barely whispered 'Emit'. So after she finally stopped crying, we talked a long time about it. Why?"

"Oh, no reason. I was just curious." She looked off into the trees, trying to see the other two. "What do you think they're talking about? Ethan sure has been acting strange lately."

"Who knows? Hey, you still have that game on your phone. Let's play it."

• • •

Ethan and Mary were walking side by side along a small cliff. They were closer to the tree line than the cliff's edge. It was over 50 feet down to the rocks and water below. From here, you could see the other side of the lake which was over four miles away.

Though Ethan had turned the music down, it was still clearly audible. Ethan had his thumbs stuck in the back pockets of his jeans. He walked slowly enough to stay right by Mary's side. She was gently swinging her arms in time with the music as she walked, taking slightly exaggerated steps. Occasionally she glanced over at him and smiled. He had seen her several times a week his entire life. But tonight, here by the lake, it was as if he was truly seeing her for the first time. The fact that her long hair was blonde was obscured by the failing sunlight. As he realized just how beautiful she was, the weight of his impending proposal began to make him very nervous.

"So Ethan, what did you want to talk about?"

"Well, I uh, well I wanted to, you know, talk about . . . " he hesitated for just a moment. "Us."

She was still walking as she stared out over the lake. "What about us?"

He stopped walking. She took another two steps before realizing that he had stopped, and then she stopped before looking back at him. They stood silent for a few seconds. Each clearly saw the other, thanks to the last rays of sunlight. The music from the car changed to a slow, emotion-filled song, as he stepped close to her.

"I wanted to find a smooth way to talk to you about something. I've spent all day thinking on it, but I can't remember a word of it now." He freed one thumb from his pocket and gently pushed her hair back to expose her face. A face that had been the highlight of every dream he'd had that week. "Mary. We've known each other practically since birth. We've played together from childhood through graduation, and have been good friends the entire time. I've always thought of you as special, and I think you know that. I know that there have been times when I made you mad, usually by accident. And I know that I've annoyed you to death on occasions. But I've always felt that you and I were, well, connected in some way." She started to say something but he quickly pressed two fingers softly against her lips. "Please. Let me get this out. I know I'm going to mess it up but you have to let me get this out before you sidetrack me. Okay?"

She acknowledged 'Yes' with a simple nod.

He let his hand fall to his side as he continued. "I know we all have given Misty a lot of grief over the years on her views of cosmic connections and fate. But you know? I think that she's on to something. Deep down inside, I always knew she was right. I'm not kidding when I say that I feel like we were intended to be together. I've always thought that. I just never knew how you felt. These last few weeks have brought us all into adulthood. We are out of high school and each of us bound for college. Two things have become very clear to me. First, I don't want to go to a different college from you. So I talked to my dad and we've already contacted your college. I've already been accepted."

She broke her silence. "And the second thing?"

He now took both of her hands in his and stepped closer to her. "The second thing is that I couldn't imagine another day without telling you how I felt. No matter what the outcome, I knew I just had to tell you. Mary, I love you. I've always loved you. I want to be with you and you alone. I don't know what is going to happen in college and I don't care. I just want to be with you. You are . . . ".

She had slipped one hand free and now pressed her fingers softly on his lips. "Shhh. My turn." It was obvious that his words had affected her deeply because her voice was breaking up as she spoke. "I've watched you since we were kids. I love all of our friends. Yes, I love both Frank and Emit too. But as brothers. I never understood why I always looked at you differently. Most times, I saw only you in the crowd and nobody else. It was always you. You were right there in front of me all my life, but I wasn't sure how you really felt about me. I wanted you to find me so badly. Oh, you always flirted with me just like Emit and Frank. But I never knew if you meant it. Now I know."

Though she paused for only a second or two, it seemed to be an eternity to him.

"Well? What do think, Mary?"

Since he was holding her hands again, she pulled them behind her back which wrapped his arms around her. With their lips just a breath away, she said, "Sometimes words just don't get the point across."

At first it was a passionate, yet gentle kiss. Then it morphed into a kiss filled with years of longing for each other. She released his hands to wrap her arms around him. He slid one hand up between her shoulder blades and pulled her in tight against him. His other hand gently cradled the back of her head. With pounding hearts and caressing tongues, Mary was proven right as to the shortcomings of words.

The kiss ended with her gently laying her head on his chest and closing her eyes. He slowly lowered his cheek until it rested on top of her head. Then he too closed his eyes to savor the warmth of her embrace. For several minutes, they enjoyed the feel of belonging in each other's arms. The soft music virtually danced on the cool breeze from the lake. Eventually they began to sway in a stationary lovers' dance. Moments of complete contentment passed slowly. Their eyes slowly opened to a dream becoming reality. Love blessed the moment even more by providing the enchanted light of a bright, full moon. Seeing this, she looked up into his eyes.

"Let's go sit on the rock. I know that is why you chose this spot, mister."

He glanced back at the car. "But they're in the back seat. They'll see us."

She pulled free, then took one of his hands to lead him to

their rock. "What are you afraid of? Do you really think they don't know what we're doing over here? She is my very best friend, and he is yours."

He submitted and followed her willingly. Once they had assumed comfortable positions side by side on the stone, they sat looking out over the moonlit water. Fingers were intertwined and her head found a perch on his shoulder.

"I'm so happy. I wanted us to go to the same college so bad. I can't believe you just up and changed to my college. It has to be fate, like Misty always said."

"All I know is that I totally loved holding you that night in the trees. It was killing me the way you were shaking, and your crying just broke my heart. You know, it really must have been fate. That dream of yours put you in the trees and that was the night I knew. And to think that if Maggie hadn't have insisted that we go camping in that valley, none of this would have happened. It has to be fate. Are you ever going to tell me what your dream was about?"

She squeezed his arm before she spoke. "Well mine was kinda weird and I'll tell you this." She reached up to pull his lips to hers. "You were in it."

Maggie and Frank were watching from the back seat of the car as if they were at a drive-in movie. Their view through the windshield was of a storybook ending. The big screen was painted with a picture of two lovers kissing on a rock. Moonlight washed over them both while illuminating the lake behind at the same time. He with his head tilted down and hers tilted upwards with one hand on his face. Frank noticed that Maggie was fighting to hold back tears.

"What's wrong?"

With her voice cracking, she said, "Mary told me once that she never thought Ethan really saw her. She wanted so badly for him to notice her, really notice her."

Frank reached around her shoulders, then pulled her towards him. His action allowed her to rest her head on him. She slightly twisted her hips so that she could rest one hand on his chest. Their eyes were glued to the scene in front of the car. After a few moments, Frank made a simple statement.

"Well. Looks like he found her!"

Chapter 22

A PROMISE FULFILLED

MAGGIE AND FRANK Continued to watch the two lovers sitting on the magical rock overlooking the lake. Ethan and Mary were enjoying their time together there on the stone. There were short periods of obviously playful pushing and pinching. This always ended in a slow, meaningful kiss. Then yet another playful lovers' wrestling match would erupt. Occasionally, an exaggerated yelp would hitchhike into the car on the gentle breeze and overpower the music inside.

These sounds from the rock were an affirmation of the love that was springing forth. Yet Maggie watched without even one muscle twitching. She was content being snuggled up beside a lifelong friend. One who had, just moments ago, showed such compassion while calming her emotions and drying her tearful eyes. He was always there for everyone when they needed somebody to confide in, no matter what secrets were shared, and he never betrayed their emotional secrecy. She needn't look up to know that he was busy watching her for any sign that she was under stress.

Frank was very happy that his friend's tears had stopped. He didn't need to see her face to know this. She was once again breathing slowly, and the small tremors of her shaking chest had long ended. He could finally relax because she was at peace. Only then did he dare to glance out at the two lovers on the rock. There, he witnessed his best friend experiencing a beautiful moment in heaven. Though his face held no expression, he was smiling on the inside.

With both of them fixed on the two lovers outside, Maggie began to speak.

"They look so in love. I'm so very happy for them both."

"Me too! He's wanted her for so long now."

"Well I never was sure what he wanted, but I definitely knew what she did."

"I know, and I really never understood that either. She was all he ever talked about when we were alone. But then when she was around, he seemed to mislead everyone on purpose by acting as if he was just kidding around. But I knew what was really in his heart. Listening to him speak about her all these years even affected me lately. I started to see her, well differently, and then it just all kind of changed when . . . " He stopped abruptly and she felt him pull away ever so slightly. She sneakily peeked up to find his face turned away and downward as if in deep thought.

A rush of embarrassment flashed through her as she realized that her friend was now the one having an emotional moment. She had appreciated his aid during hers, yet she had totally missed him slipping into one of his own.

"Frank, I'm so sorry." His response was to turn and look down into her eyes. Then his blank stare was gradually replaced with a questioning look.

"Sorry? For what?"

"It just dawned on me that you might have had thoughts of one day being with Mary, too. I know he's your best friend and that you're happy for him, but this has to be somewhat hard to watch."

Though he was still facing her, she saw the blankness return to his eyes as he processed what she had just said. Then his gaze showed that he had refocused on her face again. "You're very observant there, my friend Maggie." He turned to stare at the two on the rock. He tilted his head slightly backwards and exhaled slowly before grunting 'Huh'.

"I don't know why, but so many things have changed since that camping trip. Well, not really changed as much as became clearer. At least I thought so. It's odd, but I had never thought about her that way before. Somehow lately, I came to believe that she and I were supposed to be together." He smiled warmly at her as he added, "Dreams. You never really know how to interpret them, do you?" Then his expression became serious as he continued. "Even when they are so very clear, and seem so very real."

He paused to breathe softly before he mumbled, "That's life." Then he proudly said, "Well, they are my friends. They have found each other and I'm glad. Seems a dream brought them together. Looks like it all worked out!"

Her face immediately took on a questioning look. "Dream? Wait a minute. What dream?" She hesitated, then snapped her fingers loudly before pointing at him. "You know about Mary's dream?"

"Yes I know she had a dream. Why?"

"Well then how did her dream bring them together? I don't understand."

"Can't help you there, I wasn't told what the dream was. But I know about the dream Ethan told her about, and that those two dreams are not the same."

Maggie immediately closed her eyes and paused a few moments. "Wait a minute. Ethan told her about a dream? What was his dream about? And how do you know about Mary's dream?"

"Wow, slow down Mags! Why so serious all of a sudden?"

Maggie repeated her question. "How do you know about Mary's dream? I didn't think she told anyone else but me." Again, the loud snap of her fingers echoed through the car. "She told Misty and Misty told you, right?"

Frank shook his head slightly before he spoke. "No, Mary told me herself."

"She told you? I can't believe she told you! She made me promise not to tell anyone!"

Frank chuckled, and then smiled. "I can't believe you are so shocked. Don't you girls ALWAYS tell secrets that you swore to tell nobody else? Isn't that what girls do?"

She playfully hit him on the shoulder before she smiled. "You boys do the same thing, but not as much I guess." She sat there a moment, then looked at him. "I still don't get her telling you her dream. And since you know it, why would you say it brought them together?"

"Well, first of all, she didn't tell me what her dream was about. All she did say about it was that it wasn't about the same thing Ethan had mentioned to her. That's what she really wanted to talk about. The crazy dream Ethan had blabbed to her about. I had warned him that if he went around telling people about it, they'd think he was crazy. I was right!"

Maggie sat up and again became very serious. "Ethan had a dream? What about?"

Frank snickered. "Well, since he didn't tell ME not to tell anyone, I guess it's OK to tell you. Look, the highlights of the dream go like this.

"There was a plane crash, then a couple sitting by a fire of some sort. Then lots of stuff about some lumberjacks and army guys. Then something to do with Civil War soldiers and a ghost in a barn." He paused when he noticed her bewildered look. "See, this is just what I warned him about. Every time I hear this spoken out loud, it sounds crazy to me!" This time, he paused only a moment before he snapped his fingers. "Wait! You didn't know about this dream, did you?" She didn't respond quickly enough, and from her eyes, he knew the answer. "I can't believe the other two girls didn't tell you!" Again, he chuckled. "WOW. It never occurred to me that you didn't know about this crazy dream."

Maggie's face went blank before she turned to look at the rock. "So does he think that her dream was about the plane crash, too?"

"I know for a fact that he does. He told me so. We discussed what it could be about. We both agreed it had something to do with the plane crash memorial since she ran off into the woods crying that night. Once, he even mentioned something about them being linked by the dreams. Why?"

She looked back at Frank, concerned. "But he's wrong. That wasn't anything close to what she dreamt. That means this is all wrong. He's not supposed to be with her. This isn't what was supposed to happen!"

"Wow, Mags. What do you think was supposed to happen? Wait a minute. What was her dream about?"

"Mary was worried about going to college. She didn't want to be a cheerleader any more, but her mother was pushing her to try out for it anyway. Mary kept saying two things. One was, she wanted to live like a regular student and go to college like that. The other thing was that she really wished that Ethan was going to her college. But the dream only had half of it right. She said she saw Ethan switching to her school, but that she still ended up being a cheerleader because of her mom. That's why she was upset. I always thought she loved being a cheerleader, but she had been counting the days until high school was over. She said she felt locked into being popular there, and just had to ride it out. But she wanted college to be different. Since Ethan wasn't going to play sports anymore, she wanted them both to just be regular everyday students together." Then she glanced at the lovers again. "This is so wrong. I have to tell him before it's too late."

Frank was getting increasingly confused as well as concerned. "Wait a minute. Too late for what?"

She looked panicked, as her eyes were wide open and she was reaching for the door handle. "She's not the one. It isn't her!"

"Not the one? Not her? What are you . . . " Once again he stopped talking and this made her look back at him. His eyes were darting quickly from side to side then he started laughing softly. His laughing got louder and louder until he ultimately buried his face in both hands.

Though she hadn't lost her look of urgency to get to Ethan, she asked, "What are you laughing about? It isn't funny, Frank. There is more going on here than you think!"

He calmly said, "Yes there is, Maggie. Please. Just give me a minute. I want to tell you something, and then ask you something. Okay?"

She still was unsure and glanced out at the rock before blurting out, "Ok, but hurry up and get to the point!"

"Okay, okay. Maggie. I know this is going to come as a total shock to you, but it is the truth. I've always . . . " He closed his eyes and hung his head a moment. "Well, I've always been drawn to a friend of mine. She's funny and beautiful and sweet. I've always, ALWAYS wanted to be with her, but I never knew how to tell her. It just never seemed to be the right time. Or maybe I just told myself that because I was afraid she didn't feel the same about me. What if she was actually attracted to one of my other friends? I couldn't live with myself if I messed it up for them by getting in the middle of it."

She cut him off. "Frank. I understand where you're going but that isn't the case here. Trust me. There are things you just don't understand or know about. It's something bigger than, well, bigger than all of us. I know what I'm about to do is going to hurt at the moment. But it's the right thing to do in the long run."

He hadn't lost his smile. "Aren't you going to ask me who it was I wanted? Not even a little bit curious?"

"Okay, okay. Who was it?"

He leaned closer towards her. "You."

His response didn't hit her at first. She looked from him to the rock again before her back stiffened and she tilted her head to one side. She turned back to look at him as she sat back away from the door handle.

"Me?" her look of puzzlement gradually turned into a smile, only to fade to a stern look. "But you said you'd come to realize you wanted Mary. You said so just a few minutes ago. I heard you!"

His eyes were locked on hers. "No. That isn't what I said at all. I said that I had come to believe that I was *supposed* to be with her. I never said that I *wanted* to be with her. There is a very big difference, Maggie. It sounds confusing, I know. Hey, I've struggled with it these past few weeks too. But you are the only one that I've ever been interested in, or ever longed to be with."

She no longer wanted to get out of the car. Her eyes betrayed the fact that she was now sorting through a myriad of opposing feelings and assumed realities. Then her facial expression softened. "So you want to be with me? Why?"

"There isn't an easy answer to that. But I've felt this since we were children."

"This is all so confusing, Frank." She glanced yet again at the rock. "I don't know what to do, but I feel this is so very important."

"Yes it *is* important. You can't make the right decision without the right information, except in matters of the heart. If you feel like you want to be with someone, then that is the right decision, no matter how little information you have. But if you only feel like you should be with someone, well, then something is wrong. You should always follow your heart in these matters. You know, give your heart what it wants."

She took a deep breath. "You also said you wanted to ask me something. What?"

He now looked a little nervous. "Well. I'm going to go way out on a limb here. Did you have a dream while we were camping?" Her eyes popped wide open so he didn't need to wait for an answer. "I can tell that you did. It was about the plane crash, wasn't it?" Her mouth now fell open so he still didn't need an oral answer. "I'll bet that you also heard the name 'Ed'".

She blinked and almost fell over in the seat before she caught herself with a jerk. "But how? How can you possibly know that? I never told anyone that." She glanced down at the floor for a second then she looked at him once more.

"You said that the two of you talked about the dream. Were any other names ever mentioned? Besides the name Ed?"

"No, we just discussed that name several times."

She was looking at Frank but reaching backwards for the door handle again. "So I'm right. I need to get out there and stop this."

"No you don't, Maggie."

"Okay, Frank. Tell me this. Are you sure he didn't mention any other name?"

"Another name? Why?"

"Frank. I'm asking you a direct question. Did he mention another name or NOT?"

There was a very awkward pause before he answered. "No. I told you no already."

At first she dropped her hand from the door handle as she closed her eyes, but they reopened and her hand searched for the handle again. "That doesn't mean a thing. Two dreams, two people, no reason to think they would be identical. I'm sorry, Frank." She had both hands on the door handle as she bowed her head. "I have to do this. I'm sorry."

She lifted up so slowly on the handle that it was obvious she was still uncertain about what she was about to do.

Just as the door mechanism made the first little sound, Frank said, "But the two dreams were identical."

She froze in place then glanced over her shoulder at him. "How could the dreams have been identical if Ethan never mentioned another name?"

Frank rubbed one hand down from his forehead and let it fall from his chin. "Because I never told him that part of the dream. That's why."

She remained frozen for a few more seconds and stared at him. Then ever so slowly, she lowered the handle as she turned around to face him. "So it was your dream? Oh my GOD! You told Ethan. That's why you said he shouldn't be telling people. That's also why you used the word 'blabbed'. Isn't it?"

He smiled and shook his head. "I couldn't believe it when I found out he was telling it to EVERYONE!"

She smiled but paused. "So what about that other name?"

He hesitated on purpose before he answered. "It was a girl's name, and I think I'm looking at her."

She frowned big time as she said, "That's not it. It wasn't Maggie."

"No, it wasn't. It was Martha."

In that instant, there was a shared cosmic understanding. It would eventually fade into their dreams, but it was very clear to them at this very moment in time. They both experienced a flood of memories about a guy and girl falling in love in a forest. How they had fallen in love while watching men clean up after a gruesome catastrophe. How this newly-found love had cushioned the realization that they had died there. Of how they had made three new, good friends who had ultimately led them to a second chance at life.

Her lower lip quivered. "Ed?"

"Yes, baby. It's me. I promised you that I would never stop looking for you."

They fell forward into each other's arms as she whispered, "You found me."

A Special Thanks

I want to thank two people that read EVERY chapter as I was writing it and provided me with valuable feedback. They kept me focused and determined to complete the book.

Kenny Harasimo   —my brother
Becca Pearcy   —a good friend

I also want to thank these people who read various chapters and provided their own valuable feedback.

Karrah Harasimo Bleeker   —my beautiful daughter
Michael Bleeker   —my daughter's husband

I want each and every one of you to know how much I appreciated your help. You are what kept me going. It was a journey that I could not have made without all of you.

Lastly, I want to thank these two professionals:

Linda Ashton   —my editor
Patti Woods Rye   —my graphic designer

www.ingramcontent.com/pod-product-compliance
Lightning Source LLC
Chambersburg PA
CBHW020240120726
47904CB00001B/39